POSITION OF SUBMISSION

ALEX H. SINGH

Author Alex H. Singh

'A Dream is a glimpse of what you can have if you decide to walk down that path with no regrets...'

Alex H. Singh was born and raised in Toronto, Ontario. He is single and still lives in the city today as a successful USA Today Bestselling Author.

He spent 3 years in University (UFT) and took a variety of courses, including English Literature and English Media. He decided, however, that a career on another path would be best for him.

But it was writing that Alex has always been drawn, and he has been penning books in various genres since he was 18. He has since self-published 13 books and particularly enjoys horrors, thrillers, sci-fi & Fantasy. He is keen to see what his growing army of fans will think of his Fallen Kingdoms Chronicles Series, The Second Husband and Tapestry Series which are all set for release.

In his spare time, Alex is a big fan of taking short naps as it helps to rejuvenate him. He also exercises regularly and enjoys baking, making old favorites like cupcakes, cheesecakes and other sweet treats. As a self-confessed foodie, he enjoys trying out new and delicious foods with friends, from a variety of eateries around the City.

Alex' hopes for the future are to keep on writing books that people will enjoy reading and perhaps one day is able to do it full-time. He has already attained bestseller lists on a popular digital platform but would love to reach the Holy Grail of making the NYT List one day.

You can contact or follow Alex H. Singh, or simply see what he is writing next, at:

http://www.alexhsingh.com
https://www.bookbub.com/authors/alex-h-singh
https://www.facebook.com/AlexHSingh
https://www.facebook.com/USATAlexHSingh
http://twitter.com/USATAlexHSingh

All Rights Reserved.

Position of Submission

Edited by: Alex H Singh

Cover art by: Book Covers by Design

Formatting By: Purrfectly Haunting Formatting

ISBN: 978-1-989404-13-3

I dedicate this book to curiosities that allow people to explore their limits while finding themselves in a world full of wonder. Where pleasures and emotions become a storm from within and yourself.

Prologue

*H*is life has been an absolute whirlwind lately. Days and nights come and go and mash together in a blur; get up, coffee, train, theatre. Rehearse, socialize, dress up, play. It's exhilarating, it's exhausting, it's trying to find ways of keeping a show fresh through 8 repetitions weekly (having your mother show up with a bus full of rural Pennsylvanians is enough to keep you on edge and focused, thank you very much). In the meantime, some nights are on autopilot, but at least he's got Juniper by his side. Sweet, caring, actual pack of bubblegum Juniper who probably knows him better than anyone does, and who always respects his boundaries.

He's always been good at acting. Fast forward half a decade and he's on Broadway, for fucks' sake. And living with Caleb. They share a small 2-bedroom apartment not too far from the theatres, so it's convenient. That's really all it is. The two bedrooms are just another stage prop. Acting is what he knows. So he acts. And Juniper doesn't ask. And it's summertime, and his hair is getting long, he constantly wears his old hat backwards to keep the curls out of his eyes. He tries to keep up with the other shows in talks of a Broadway opening. He's heard of a new off-Broadway show that depicts life in New York City that he has been meaning to check out for a little while.

When he finally checks it out, he is blown away. This is not a traditional musical. It's jazz, it's Hip Hop, it's salsa, and it's incredible. He doesn't speak much Spanish (his high-school classes are deeply buried in his memory), so he knows that it's probably even better than he thinks it is. He is floored by the pure energy of the musical and the sheer talent of the actors. He finds himself, on more than one occasion, establishing contrasts between his own upbringing and what is being portrayed on stage in front of him. There is a truth, a realness to Heaven on Earth that tells him that it's not straying far from reality. He finds himself daydreaming about the ways in which his life could have been different if he'd only grown up in a city like New York, not in Middle of Nowhere, Pennsylvania. He wants to meet the cast. He knows, by virtue of being a theatre actor himself, that stage-dooring won't get him anywhere but on the fast track to not making an impression. It's something for fans, alright. But it's too artificial, and he doesn't want to meet the minds behind a show like that in a setting where all they do is sign autographs on autopilot and count the minutes until they can get back inside without hurting anyone's feelings. Plus, he's on their level, he's in the business, he's got contacts. He can probably make this happen in a way that'll be enjoyable for everyone (not that he could have predicted how his next Heaven on Earth encounter was going to unravel).

So he goes home when the show is over. Contrary to popular belief, he can get his way around the internet, at least enough to be able to learn as much as he can about the musical he's just seen and the man behind it. He reads about the purpose of Heaven on Earth being a desire to portray the diversity of New York City, and specifically the Washington Heaven area. He finds out that Sebastian Castillo, the composer behind the masterpiece, did grow up in that neighborhood, and wrote the musical as a tribute, a celebration, a representation of where he grew up. He starts reading up on him. What other shows he's written, what other projects he's been in.

Turns out this is his first project of that scale - he has never been on Broadway, even though it seems clear in Jake's mind that he could be headed there soon. The more he learns, the more he wants to meet him. It's not necessarily that he wants to work with him - he's probably out of his league anyway. But there is just this incredibly compelling energy radiating out of the man that would make anyone grateful to have the opportunity to spend time alongside him. Problem is, he isn't quite sure how to get there. He's not a writer, he's not a composer, he's not on Bastian's level. He's just an actor. Bastian probably doesn't need actors. He's probably got actors pooling at his feet for every role he creates. And, even if he did, Jake already has a stable role as the lead character in Autumn Spell, so it's not like he's looking for anyone to hire him anyways. So that's not on the table, there's got to be another way.

The next day, he comes to the theatre early (which, for anyone who knows him, is an extraordinary feat). He knows that Juniper will be there – he sometimes wonders whether she ever leaves the theatre at all. Sure enough, once he gets his keys, he heads to her dressing room and finds her in the middle of a yoga session, oblivious to the world with her headphones in. He sits down on her couch and waits for her to notice his presence. It's a few agonizing minutes before she opens her eyes and sees him diligently waiting for her.

"Jake? What are you doing here? Correct me if I'm wrong but I don't think I've ever seen you before, like, a half hour to places. It's 10 in the morning, Jake."

"I need to run an idea by you, it's probably a bit insane, but you can maybe help me. It's actually more of a project than an idea, but," he takes a deep breath and the words tumble out of his mouth before he can stop them. "I went to see Heaven on Earth last night, you know that show? It's about – growing up in the city and it was so brilliant, and the cast was so talented, and even though I didn't understand all of it, I just, I really want to–"

"Slow down, slow down. Where is this all coming from?" Juniper asks in earnest. She doesn't think she's ever seen Jake so flus-

3

tered, not even on opening night (and that was something). Something is definitely up with him. She stands up to go sit with him on her couch.

"I want to meet Bastian. The guy who wrote it. And he stars in it, he wrote it, he did, like, everything, and it's brilliant, Juniper, he's brilliant, I want to meet him. I could've stage-doored him but that just felt so, I don't know, such a fan thing to do? And no one likes stage-dooring anyways," Jake says with a chuckle. He's running his fingers through his curly hair, it's a nervous habit he's never managed to curb.

"Any idea how to accomplish that?"

"Juniper, if I had any idea I wouldn't be sitting in your dressing room at 10 in the morning on a one-show day, asking for advice," Jake pointed out.

"You have a point. Do we know anyone in the production? Where is the show playing, and what is it called again? I haven't actually heard of it, I don't know if I can help you."

"It's playing somewhere off 34th Street, it's not on Broadway. Not yet, anyway," he mentions. "Even though it's definitely got what it takes to be up here. Heaven on Earth. Sebastian Castillo."

As he's saying this, he can see Juniper's eyes divert and look at the door behind him. He turns around to see one of their understudies, Karla, poking her head through the door frame.

"Am I hearing this correctly? Jake's sweet tones disturbing the peace and quiet of the Lewinsky backstage, hours before show time?" she asks, leaning against the door frame. Jake in his hurry had completely forgotten to close the door behind him, or to keep his voice to a decent level.

"Apparently our national sweetheart's found a new musical of interest and he's dying to meet its creator. I've never seen him this excited before, so it must have been something," Juniper says with a glint in her eye. "You heard of Heaven on Earth before? I don't think I have."

"You're not serious?" Karla says in disbelief. "First off, how dare you not be aware of that show? It's probably going to move up here soon, it's a hit off-Broadway. Second, you never wondered why I'm only here a few days a week? I'm also an understudy for Bastian, apparently that's what I'm good for these days. Understudying my life away," she adds with a dramatic swoon.

Jake's blue eyes go wide. He had hoped that someone in the Autumn crew would be able to put him in touch with someone who knew someone who knew Bastian, but he had not expected it to happen this quickly or effortlessly. He's suddenly awfully nervous and isn't quite able to say why. He gulps. "You.. You know Bastian?" He immediately regrets the need that makes his voice quiver. He can't be obvious like that. Come on, Cole. You're playing a role outside your house, and that's okay, keep it up, you're going to be okay. Don't fuck it up. No one can know. Think of your career.

Karla laughs, easy. "Yeah, he's a really easy guy to be around. Isn't tomorrow your day off? I don't really know what he's planning but there's some type of filming in the works. He's trying to campaign to bring the show up here, so you could probably attend that with me," Karla offers. "I've got no idea what he's planning, though."

"If it's half as good as his musical, it'll be worth it," Jake hears himself blurt out.

The rest of the day goes in a blur. He goes out for lunch with Juniper and they walk around Times Square for a bit, but he can't quite focus on anything but the buzzing in his brain that hasn't left since Karla came in the dressing room earlier... Most people in the square are tourists, not musical theatre nerds, and it's not like they're world-famous, so they can walk peacefully before to head back to the theatre for that night's performance. He calms down. Comes back into his body, this role he's playing. He's okay. Anonymity is good. During the show, the crowd is nice; they clap when they have to clap, laugh when they've got to laugh. Time for the bows before he knows it, and he joins Juniper after changing back in his street clothes to go sign some Playbills. He catches Karla ready to leave as he comes back inside and they agree on meeting up the next day before to head to Bastian's video shoot. Jake goes home and to his surprise finds Caleb in the kitchen. He's got butterflies in his stomach that have nothing to do with the fact that he hasn't seen his boyfriend for a week because he was on vacation, somewhere upstate. He had forgotten that Caleb was coming back today.

Chapter One

*J*ake wakes up the next day at ease. He turns around to cuddle up to his boyfriend and linger in bed for a few more minutes. The sun is shining through the curtains and everything feels right until the events of the past two days come back rushing through his mind. His eyes snap open. Caleb is still asleep – he doesn't witness Jake's distress, which buys him some time to calm down. He's suddenly just as nervous as when he was coming home last night, so he decides to take a warm shower and let the water work the tension out of his shoulders. He takes extra time, leaves the conditioner longer than usual, washes his body twice. It's hot, it's summer, one can never be too clean anyway. He tells himself his careful routine has nothing to do with the day ahead of him. For all he knows, he's not even going to meet Bastian today, let alone talk to him. There are probably going to be dozens of people around, people that Bastian actually knows, and that therefore will be much more important than himself.

He gets dressed (nothing fancy, today is just another day into this life he's building for himself), grabs breakfast at the coffee shop near his apartment and meets up with Karla by the subway station so that they can make their way to see Bastian together. When they get there, Jake realizes that it's a much smaller setup than he initially thought. It's essentially no setup at all. Having seen the care with which everything in Heaven on Earth was orchestrated, he assumed that even a small campaign to get his show on Broadway would include Bastian going all out, with camera crews and makeup artists. He could not have been more wrong, so it's probably good that he didn't dress up in more than his battered hat and a t-shirt. He sees one of the main actresses in the show, someone holding a handheld video camera, and Bastian. Bastian. Bastian. His name keeps echoing in his mind like a mantra, and he's suddenly very aware of the tension in his muscles (it all came right back, despite his shower), and the way his hands became all clammy. Please, stay in character. Karla makes her way over to Bastian and he trails behind her, unsure of how to act now that he's here, hyperaware of his surroundings. He's got a role to play.

"Baz-Man, my man, always as bright as the sun shining in this beautiful sky! Tan resplandeciente como siempre," Karla exclaims. She's always so dramatic. Jake is terrified. And now they're speaking in tongues he doesn't understand. Is she talking about him?

"Sweet, sweet Karla. How are you today?" Bastian asks, energetic as ever. He steps back and unashamedly eyes Jake up and down for a quick second. Jake gulps. "And who is this beautiful specimen you brought here with you?"

"Ah, sí, casi me olvido. This is Jacob, he's in my other show, Autumn Spell. Nothing less than our main character. And he kills it every single night." Jake blushes deep red - he can feel his cheeks burn, and if she doesn't stop soon, it'll expand down his neck and no one wants that. At least he doesn't. And is that a double-entendre? Is he imagining this? What is going on?

Jake has lost the ability to form proper sentences. "Hi, um, yes. Jake Cole. Hi." This is not off to a great start, he is so awkward, oh my god, Bastian's never going to want to see him again if he thinks he's star struck. He extends a shaking hand and Bastian's stare is enough to have him combust on the spot. Or dig a hole into the ground. Or both. Maybe he's just going to disappear into the ground, and then combust, and no one will ever hear from him again, and it'll just be fine. It'll be a tragic story in the newspaper and everyone will cry. No, scratch that, that's a terrible scenario. Bastian grabs his hand and shakes it.

"I've got an idea," Bastian says thoughtfully, and a mischievous grin decorates his face. "Mi cielo, how about you go stand near that wall. Back to the wall, that column over there, hands too, don't move until I tell you so. I have a surprise for you." And who is Jake to refuse him? All logical thought evaporates from his brain and he doesn't have enough reason left to remind him that it's way too soon to space out. He does as he is told. Bastian said to go to the wall over there so he nods, and he turns around before anyone can look into his eyes. He knows how easy he is to read. A goddamn open book, that's what he is. He doesn't think of how he is much more spacey than he should be in a situation like this. Now is not the time to zone out, Jacob, his reason supplies, but he doesn't register. He looks back around once his back is solid against the wall. He can feel the rough material beneath his palms. He presses further back and Bastian is looking at him. And he is interested. Is that curiosity? He set something off and he knows it? That mischievous grin, again. Jake looks to the floor without being asked to. This is probably his most terrible performance as the straight version of himself. He isn't fooling anyone, but he doesn't have it in himself to worry. Not when Bastian has given him simple orders to follow.

Bastian talks to Karla for a quick minute, then gets his cameraman to stand by the other actress that Jake had noticed earlier, not quite catching her into the frame. He starts the video. And Bastian starts rapping. Jake can't focus on anything but his voice. Raspy is not the word - just, very... distinctive. Bastian has one of those voices you'd recognize from a mile away. Jake's intently watching as Bastian introduces himself, talks about his show, talks about kissing Gigi Cortez, and he's a bit thrown off at that part, and the rational parts of his mind come back from their momentary silence to remind him that Bastian isn't gay, right? And Jake is in a relationship. He shouldn't be thinking about this, but there is a magnetism to Bastian that he just can't ignore. Doesn't know how. And before he knows it, he's back in his body, ever so aware of how he is backed up against the column and Bastian sounds nervous, all of a sudden, and he's in front of him, singing so fast Jake can barely follow. It's not like he's got the attention capacity to take in much of what Bastian is saying anyways.

"You better tell the number one A list hottie right now that he's got to get off, cause he's never going to look like Jacob Cole!"

Jake's eyebrows shoot up his forehead and he smiles. He can't hold it in, but he's trying, because he doesn't know what reaction Bastian is looking for. Dropping to his knees is probably not what Bastian wants of him right now, so he stands. Bastian's looking at him. Everything is happening so quickly, his mind is blank but going a million miles an hour. Time doesn't stop. Bastian continues. "Woo! Damn, he's so cute, okay, I'm sorry but it's true," and he's looking at him like his life is in the balance, not Jake's, and that doesn't add up at all.

There's a nervousness that seems so out of character, but there's also a playfulness to his words, like Bastian is testing him. Is this a test? Jake has no idea, so he just smiles and he keeps looking at him and he hopes that his embarrassment isn't too obvious. He almost forgot for a second that there's a camera, and he's smack dab in the middle of the frame. He stands.

"Don't look in his eyes, you'll be taken in, you'll be breakin' into Autumn Spell,"

And all of a sudden, it hits him. His eyes are still on Bastian, he's still looking like a deer in the headlights, and the parts of his brain that he'd thought had melted away when Bastian first checked him out came back loud and rushing fast and knocking at all the doors, all the windows, banging. He stops listening to him, tries to keep his composure. But Bastian doesn't know. Bastian can't know. No one knows, not even Juniper, everyone thinks Caleb is his roommate for god's sake, and now this man he's known for a sum total of 10 minutes, at most, is flirting with him, and giving him orders, but he doesn't know, and he can't process that at all, this can't be happening. He's not ready. He can't do it. He needs to tell Karla, he needs to go back home, he needs to hide and never come out of his apartment again until he figures this out, what's happening to him? What if everyone knows, what if his cast mates know, his career is over. This can't be happening.

He looks up. The cameraman is putting his camera away, Bastian seems satisfied with how that went, Gigi is still on the wall doing nothing, and Karla is watching him with a concerned look. Jake's breath catches. She knows something is up, it's written all over her face. He looks at Bastian, they make brief eye-contact, but his fear must be showing because Bastian silently nods in response to Jake's pleading eyes and he can finally move. At least Bastian picked up on the way he reacts to orders. He doesn't know what he would have done if those orders weren't meant to be, and were just regular directions, he would have been stuck to the wall forever, or he would have had to disobey, on purpose, and that is a thought he never wants to have to ponder again. He mutters something about not feeling well, it's too hot, the sun is too bright, he's burning up, and Karla takes his hand as they make their way back to the train station. He's stuck in his head. Thoughts racing, a million miles a second, and before he knows it they're standing in front of his apartment and she hasn't let go of his hand this whole time.

"Do you need me to come up there? I'm not sure what's happening, but I don't have anything else to do today, I can stick around."

Jake needs a moment to remember how his throat works, he's got a voice somewhere in there.

"I.. I'm okay. I need to – I need to be alone. Sorry," he mutters. He turns around and rushes inside without looking back.

Chapter Two

*W*hen Jake enters his apartment, Caleb shines by his absence. He's probably at the theatre already. He won't be back until late at night, which buys Jake the rest of the day to process what happened earlier and figure out what to do next. He can't think. He goes to their bedroom, it's automatic, with the intention of curling up under the comforter, but he realizes his mistake the second he steps in. Going into the bed he shares with his.. boyfriend… every night just seems awfully wrong. He feels a tear roll down his cheek. He hadn't realized they were even on the verge of spilling. His breathing is labored. He backs out, Caleb's room undisturbed, and sees the unused bedroom across the hallway.

His bedroom. The stage prop. The one they didn't use once. People probably think he's some type of neat freak and that Caleb is the messy one, because they don't know the reason behind the room being so clean. Right? He rushes in, pulls the cover and it's impersonal, it's cold, it's unforgiving, and it's exactly what he needs right now. He needs to make sense of his thoughts so he creates a list in his head.

What he knows: Bastian. He knows Bastian. He knows that he can't possibly disobey orders. He knows that he's gay. He knows he lives with his boyfriend. He's an actor on Broadway and he doesn't have a show today. He knows he's got Juniper. He knows that he's not ready for the world to know. He likes organization. This is comforting. There is a truth to certainties that you just can't shake. Here are the things he knows to be true, and he can hold on to them the way infants hold their mother's fingers in their fist so tight they might die if they let go.

What he thinks he knows: Bastian has figured him out in less time than it takes to spell his name out to coffee baristas. There's no way that his interaction was a coincidence. It could have been if he was just directing a set, but he nodded, he nodded, for god's sake, because he'd noticed Jake all but glued to the wall. Which brings him back to the first list.

What he knows: Bastian knows.

What he can't process: being out. Not knowing who's got control. Someone knowing. And Bastian knows.

What he knows: Caleb can't know. Caleb can't know.

What he doesn't know: everything about Bastian.

For all he knows, he's been repeating for hours on end. He knows something else: he needs to get up, and back in Caleb's bedroom before the end of Caleb's show, and he needs to be asleep because if he doesn't fall asleep by the time Caleb slides under the covers behind him, it means that Caleb will talk to him and he can't have that. He's faintly aware of the hunger in his empty stomach, and the subtle pounding in his head, but he can't get himself to do anything about either. He gets up as soon as he's recovered enough brain function to remember how his limbs function. He gets out of bed and lets out a shiver, straightens out the comforter until all traces of him using his bed are gone. He breathes. It's not satisfying, he can't take a deep breath. There's a tightness around his chest that he just can't shake. But he breathes.

He goes back to Caleb's room and fires up his computer. He searches for pictures of Bastian, videos, interviews, articles, anything. He finds a few pictures where he seems close to other men, almost intimate – but he also seems to be like that with every- one. He replays his memory of Bastian greeting Karla earlier, how affectionate he was around her. And Gigi, too. It doesn't mean anything. He's obviously aware of the fact that he should be able to "tell" when other people are like him, at least that's what he's heard, but he's never able to tell which part is objective observation and what is nothing more than wishful thinking. And now he's just over thinking it all. He's not getting anywhere.

He looks at the clock on the wall: half past 10. Caleb will be home soon. Jake takes his clothes off, tosses them in the hamper – they unceremoniously end up hanging halfway out of it or directly on the cold floor. He's exhausted, his brain is still pounding, the tension in his body will not ease. He hasn't learned anything. He hates not knowing. He gets in bed, buries his head in his shoulders, and forces himself to relax his muscles one by one until he falls in a restless, dreamless slumber. He doesn't wake up when Caleb gets in bed with him.

When he does wake up, the grey morning light filters through the light curtains. He's uneasy and there's a quiver in his stomach that won't settle. Caleb's arms are wrapped around him and he could pretend the sweat covering his body is due to the humidity of the New York summer, to the heat radiating from the sleeping lump next to him, but he knows he would be lying. He shifts around and feels Caleb slowly rousing from whatever dream he was having. He's barely spoken with him since he came back, he should probably say something. The act he's putting on doesn't seem to be much about the outside world anymore.

"Hi, honey. It's early, you can sleep…" Jake whispers. He earns a grunt in response.

"Missed you," he mumbles under his breath. Tugs him closer. Jake gently untangles his arms so he can get out of bed. Drops a lighthearted kiss on Caleb's forehead, and that's an act he knows well, he's rehearsed it a million times over.

"Missed you too. I got to go for a run, and then it's off to the theatre, we have an early rehearsal today. I'll see you tonight?"

There's the first lie. He earns another grunt, resigned this time, and watches as Caleb turns around and goes straight back to sleep. He gathers some clothes, then his computer, and shuts the door behind him. He can't stand being home, and he's definitely not in the mood for a run, so he dresses himself up and walks directly to the theatre. The music from his iPod fills in the white noise in his head. He doesn't realize until he's standing in front of the stage door that theatre won't mean isolation like he so desperately wants. It means seeing the tech team, Juniper, Karla. Karla who saw him crawl out of his skin and back in yesterday. Karla who knew that something was up but didn't push, just made sure he got home safe. Karla who has probably talked to Juniper about this, because Jake likes silence but Juniper loves to talk, and Juniper knows him better than anyone. With the exception, maybe, of one other person, but that thought is too heavy to bear so he leaves it at the theatre door and walks in.

Jake mechanically grabs his key and makes it to his dressing room. He curls up on his couch and pulls the laptop from his bag. On autopilot, refusing to think of potential consequences, he goes back to gathering information on Bastian. He is so out of it, so engrossed in the words on his screen, that he doesn't notice Juniper coming in until she's peering over the top of the couch.

"Morning, my love." She speaks, soft, careful. She's testing the edges around Jake's body, feeling how sharp they are, figuring out how to get to him. Jake snaps out of his daze and his eyes go wide. He snaps the cover of his computer shut in a haste, as if it would make Juniper forget what she surely saw.

"...hi," he mutters, his voice smaller than ever.

"I talked to Karla yesterday. Do you want to talk?"

"No. Maybe? Yes? I don't know. I don't know what's going on," he whispers, panicky. Half of him wants him to get up and run, he's not ready, he doesn't even know what he would say, 'by the way Caleb and I are dating, we sleep in the same bed and we're a thing, we fuck every now and then?', and the other half is telling him that he can trust her, that if anyone has any chance of understanding, it's her. "I don't know what I want."

She makes her way around the couch and carefully picks up his computer from where it's balancing atop his knees. She lightly unfolds his tangled limbs and positions him so that he faces her when she sits down on the couch, their knees touching. She takes his hands and runs her thumbs across his knuckles. Butterfly touch. Feather-light. He releases the breath that had been stuck in his lungs since he left the set almost 24 hours prior. He looks up at her and it takes every ounce of will he can muster to look her in the eyes. He realizes that maybe he doesn't have to say anything, and he realizes that mostly he needs somebody who can read his distress without words. It's less scary when he doesn't have to put it into sentences. His thoughts can stay in the abstract for now, it's better this way.

"Oh, honey. You're okay. We're okay. I'm here." She moves so that she can kneel on the cushions and leans forward to take him in her arms.

To his surprise, a gut-wrenching sob escapes him, and all the tension in his muscles, in his body, in his mind, it all swirls inside of him like a hurricane and there is no way he can hold it in. Everything washes over him and he cries. It could be minutes, it could be hours. It could be days. He doesn't know. What he does know is that he's unhappy, he's not fulfilled, and this act he's been putting on is slowly eating away at everything good that's inside of him. So he cries, because he doesn't know what else to do, and because Juniper is with him, and because maybe she knows, and maybe that's not so terrible, because she's still here. She doesn't push him. She rubs his back, holds him tight, runs her hand through his curls, wipes the tears from his cheeks until he's all cried out. When he regains control of his breathing, however long after she sat down with him, she pulls back to look at him.

"It's okay not to know what you need. We can figure it out together."

"I think," he says, his voice shaky but much steadier than it's been in days, "I think I need to… talk this out." Relief washes through him after he lets the words out. The decision isn't on him anymore. It's out there, between them, and he's not holding on to its heavy weight anymore.

"Something happened yesterday, didn't it? Something shifted and something needs to change, is that it? Don't resent Karla – she only asked me if you'd gotten in touch with me, told me to be ready for the next time I'd see you. I connected the rest of the dots myself."

"I can't say that I know how to explain what's happened. Everything is so overwhelming right now, and if I make any decision, it's like I'm hitting dominoes and they're all starting an endless chain reaction, and that's," he takes a deep breath, "just terrifying." He stops for a minute to gather his flyaway thoughts. "I think you're right, even if I don't really know what happened yesterday, something shifted deep inside me, and something needs to happen."

The more he talks, the more he realizes that forcing himself to put his jumbled thoughts in coherent sentences is much more helpful than it is terrifying. Maybe all the over-thinking he's been doing wasn't in vain, but actually had a purpose, and everything flows much more freely now.

"When I met Bastian, yesterday, it's like a whole new world just opened up to me. I don't know how to describe it. It's like I felt new opportunities lay themselves in front of me, all at once, all unknown, but also, all… natural. Like I've found what I had been looking for but without even realizing I'd been looking for these things. I thought I was doing fine, and the weight of realizing I wasn't just completely crushed me. I could suddenly see how right things could be if I let them, and that made me see how wrong things are now, and I didn't know that before." He looks at Juniper, and she's intently listening, a strong and safe presence by his side. He takes a deep breath. "You know I've been living with Caleb for almost a year now. I don't think you'll be surprised, but… him and I have been much more than roommates. For a long time. But not for the right reasons, and that's what I realized yesterday. I think we're trying to prove something to ourselves, both of us. And then, yesterday, I met Bastian, and he saw me. Right away. He saw me for who I really am and it caught me off guard, and I completely freaked out." His breathing speeds up. "Oh God, what if I've completely ruined it?"

His thought process hadn't quite taken him this far since yesterday, because he would become paralyzed as soon as the thought of Caleb entered his brain. But now that he's allowed to think of himself as an entity, and not only a half of a whole, he can get past his immediate surroundings, and he can take a step back, and he can assess his reaction to the instant dynamic he felt forming with Bastian from the outside. And all he can see is a flustered mess who had to leave on the verge of a panic attack, and now Bastian probably thinks he's a coward, or an idiot, or just completely insane, or, or, or,

"Hey. Look at me. I'm losing you. Jake," Juniper says firmly. He looks at her, terror written all over his face, his eyes opened wide, trying to find anchor in the warm tones of her irises. "Breathe with me."

He does. It's hard, it's erratic, but he counts with her. Inhale, one. Two. Three. Four. Hold. Five. Six. Seven. Eight. Exhale, slowly, back down to zero. He closes his eyes. Repeats until he senses that his heartbeat has gone back to a normal speed. Maybe a bit above normal, but not nearly as under pressure. They breathe. They hear a soft knock on Jake's dressing room door. He opens his eyes, and Juniper is the anchor he needed. He's okay.

He gets back into his body, remembers how his muscles function, and goes to the door. One last breath to compose himself, he twists the knob and pulls.

His eyes fall on tan skin. Stubble. Flushed cheeks, a worried crease between his brows. Bastian is standing before him. Jake thinks he might pass out, unless someone catches him before he hits the floor, metaphorically or not.

Chapter Three

"What… What are you doing here?" Jake stammers out. He's too stunned to think. One and one don't always add up, it seems. His hand viciously grips the handle because that's the only thing that'll keep him upright.

"I just saw Karla on my way, here," Bastian says. His eyes look past Jake, in search for Juniper who is still sitting down on Jake's sofa. "She's looking for you, Juniper. You're Juniper, right? Nice to meet you." He flashes her a genuine grin and Jake steps off to let him in. Bastian extends his hand towards Juniper. "I'm Bastian. I work with Karla on Heaven on Earth."

That's a bit of an understatement. Juniper gets up and takes his hand.

"So I've heard. Nice meeting you too, Bastian. Do you know what Karla needs from me?" Juniper asks.

"Only that she wants to run some type of idea by you, maybe a choreography, I wouldn't know."

Bastian's flow is too posed, too calm, too careful. Jake is nervous. That's also an understatement. He's just had a full blown panic attack after basically coming out to his best friend and the very source of the entire mayhem is standing in his dressing room, making small talk as if everything was fine, but everything is so, so far from fine. His heartbeat picks up again.

"Alright. Jake, call if you need me? I'll go see what she wants," Juniper says carefully as she exits.

Jake shuts the door behind him. He can't tell whether that's the best or the worst action he could perform, under the current circumstances.

He doesn't ponder. Just goes back to his desk. He refuses to give Bastian the satisfaction of knowing just how much he's gotten under his skin, not until he knows that Bastian is as involved as he is - and he doubts that. He doesn't know what to do with his hands, with his arms, with his face, his body. He fumbles around, moves notebooks around. Settles for picking up the pieces of his costume and placing them on his chair. He tries to complete at least a round of deep breathing exercises inconspicuously. Just another actor thing, he tries to justify to himself. But Bastian's an actor too, he knows all about "actor things". He's not going to be fooled. Jake knows he's blushing. God, why does he have to be so damn reactive all the time?

When he can no longer justify focusing on his desk and ignoring Bastian, he braces himself on the back of his chair and looks up at Bastian's reflection in the mirror. He doesn't miss his own sight on the way and it's worse than he thought. His eyes are still bleary; he's got a deep blush on his face that extends in blotches down his neck, maybe lower. His eyes are wide and his hair is in quite a tousled state. He's not fooling anyone.

Bastian returns the stare. It's half caring, half amused. He's standing by the couch, resting a hip against the arm, one ankle crossed against the other, arms crossed against his chest. He exudes an air of subtle power and control. It's almost cocky. Not helping. At all. Jake feels so incredibly small under his stare, can all but feel himself shrink.

"You haven't answered," Jake states. His voice is steadier than he expected, but there's a very slight shaking to it. Bastian might have picked up on it, all depending on how attuned he is. Jake can't quite tell.

"I wanted to…" he searches for his words, which seems unusual for someone of his artistic caliber. It's a perfect contrast to the aura of confidence around him. "I think I have to apologize to you." So the easy powerful stance is at least partly an act. He looks down, untangles his limbs, attempts to ground himself.

Jake's not entirely sure what he should be responding, so he doesn't.

"I set you off. I… overstepped boundaries without meaning to and I think we should talk about it. If you want, of course," he added in a rush when he saw Jake's blank stare.

Jake doesn't have an answer for him, even if Bastian looks expectant, and he knows it's his turn to talk. But he doesn't know what Bastian wants from him. "Go on," he says, simply.

"You reacted to what I said in a way I didn't expect." Not a question – a statement. Between the lines, all that Jake hears is that he scared him. He totally ruined it. That's it, that's the end. He can feel the panic closing in around him and he's got nowhere to go because Bastian is right there, standing between him and the door. His distress must show because suddenly Bastian is talking again, backtracking. "No, no, it's alright, it's okay. You're fine. I should have been more careful about the way I talked to you. I wasn't thinking, I was all in acting mode. It's not an excuse, I can't be that careless. I didn't mean to set you off and all the vibes I'm getting from you right now are yelling that I did, big time, and that's not fair, and –"

"No one knows." Jake cuts him off. His audacity surprises him slightly. He definitely sounds more solid than he feels but there's an edge to his tone that betrays how terrified he feels at the implications. But the truth is out there, or at least a version of it, and he doesn't have much more of a choice but to keep talking because the cat's out of the bag and Bastian saw straight through his act in a fraction of a second. He's got nothing more to lose in this moment. He's looking at his shoes and the frayed carpet beneath his soles.

"I haven't… told anyone… who I really am. I'm not ready. I can't. Or I guess. Juniper knows. Since earlier today. But even Karla, I don't think, God, I hope not, because if she knows, probably everyone does, oh my god," he stutters out, rakes a hand through his locks. His thought are going too fast and he can't keep up. He looks up and sees Bastian's brows, slightly worried, and he's chewing on the inside of his cheek. And he's looking at him with purpose and again, twice in as many days, he feels like every cell in his body is on display for Bastian to read. "I don't know what I want and I don't know what you want from me and I don't know what happened yesterday, not really, I have a decent idea but I've never experienced something like that before." He can't stop talking now that he's started. "I don't know what you want from me, I'm terrified, everything is going so quickly and everything I thought I knew about myself turns out not to be true, exactly, and I'm not even sure I know myself anymore and how did you know???" he finally asks. The question came out solid, tangible, unplanned and unapologetic, his eyes locking with Bastian's. He puts the ball back in Bastian's court because he can't handle the way that Bastian is looking at him, hyper-focused.

"How did I know... what, exactly? You're going to have to be slightly more specific than that if we're going to have a conversation, honey." Pet name, a hint of confidence is back. It has a feeling of possessiveness to it, but maybe that's just wishful thinking. It doesn't feel wrong, Jake doesn't know if it's too early but he likes the effect Bastian has on him too much to care.

"That I'm... that I'm..." he suddenly realizes that he's never said that out loud, and it shouldn't be a big deal, but is seems like the biggest of deals and the heaviest of weights on his shoulders. He's feeling crushed by the looming pressure. "Gay?" He says, and it sounds more like a question, it's tentative, he doesn't want to scare Bastian away. He's trying out the word, how it feels on his tongue, in his mouth, how it works the muscles in his throat. And the pressure eases at once. It feels right. It's okay.

Bastian breathes out and holds his stare when Jake looks at him in search for any sign of discomfort, disgust, disapproval, but he finds none. "I didn't. Not outright, not really. I just saw you and decided to get you in my video and didn't realize until I looked back and saw that you were still glued to the wall that you were waiting for something, for me to do something. And I realized too late that I hadn't been careful, and so, I wanted to apologize in person because

I know I've upset you and I never in a million years meant to do that. Could we maybe go have dinner one day, as an apology? Will you forgive me?"

That's a side of Bastian that takes Jake by surprise – he's caring and there is no hint of overconfidence emanating from him anymore. He's sincere and honest and it doesn't feel like a trap. Just a dynamic that seems to flow so naturally in the space between them.

"I, uh, yeah. Yes, we can go have dinner, for sure." He's feeling calmer. "I… appreciate you coming by. I do." He's feeling as if a lot of his confusion has settled and maybe he'll be okay, maybe this will all be fine. Bastian's still here, after all. Jake closes his eyes for a quick second and takes a deep breath, holds it, releases. He feels his heartbeat slow and steady, more grounding than it's been in the past twenty-four hours. Has it only been a day? That feels slightly surreal.

He opens his eyes and Bastian has this crease between his eyebrows again – so expressive, always. He looks like he's got something to say but doesn't quite know how. Jake looks at the gears in his mind working and turning for a moment and witnesses the moment when he comes to whatever conclusion he's come to. It's Bastian's turn to take a deep inspiration and look up at him. Jake suddenly notices the height difference. Bastian had him feeling so small, he had felt so powerful in his stance, so in control, but right now he's nothing more than another musical theatre actor and Jake can almost experience this moment as an outsider, sees them facing each other, and he is much taller, much broader than him. He definitely feels that he is back in his own body, which is more than he could say since yesterday's scene.

The sound of Bastian's voice takes him out of his thoughts suddenly. "Do you want me to go?" he asks, hesitant.

"No." Role-reversal. There is no hesitation in Jake's voice this time. "At least… not right now? We haven't got anything until… what time is it, even? I've completely lost track of time"

Bastian looks at his watch. "Pushing on noon, right now."

"Today's a two-show day, so we've got nothing much to do

before, let's say, 2:30. You can stick around, if you want. I'm not sure that I'm very entertaining, though, and I haven't slept well, so…"

"I like it here. Different from the hustle of the 37. People are always gravitating around me, there, and I love it, I love the attention, but it's taking a toll. So."

He plops himself down on Jake's sofa and folds his legs underneath himself, sitting in the corner where Jake was earlier, which leaves Jake the choice to stand by his vanity, sit on that straight-back and uncomfortable chair, or sit in Juniper's spot. Role-reversal, right. He carefully sits down at a comfortable distance from Bastian. He's torn between wanting to close his eyes and maybe take a nap, or make small-talk, but he's terrible at that. He's the quiet type when he doesn't have to put on an act. It's the first time in a while where he doesn't have to pretend and god, it feels good. He tears his eyes off Bastian's body, wills the muscles in his shoulders to relax, tips his head against the back of the couch, folds his hands into his lap and closes his eyes. Exhales. Knocks his shoes off. They sit in a comfortable silence and he feels himself ready to doze off until he feels Bastian shift around and scoot ever so close to him. Suddenly he feels fingers in his hair just behind his ear, but it's cautious and soft. Not demanding, not crowding his space. It doesn't feel half as forward as it should. Feels like he's asking for permission, as if Jake was one to refuse him. He relaxes into the touch and Bastian tucks a stray curl behind his ear.

"Can I see the show? This afternoon, can I stay?" Bastian asks, shyly. Jake shoots him a side glance. He'd have thought Bastian much more assertive, especially after whatever interaction they had yesterday, he'd given him an order. But this is okay, too. And if he's honest, he kind of wants him there. He likes on stage performing, he's in his element when he does, and this will be a good reason not to perform on autopilot. He needs reasons. So he closes his eyes and inches into the touch, nods.

Chapter Four

*T*he show was good. Not the best show on his track record, but not the worst one either (there was one night, recently, when he'd embarrassingly forgotten an entire song and his cast mates couldn't stop laughing when they were supposed to be dramatically sobbing). He had felt drastically present in his body for the first time in a long while, and if he's honest, having to shove his pants down knowing that Bastian was looking at him made him incredibly conscious of his surroundings... and the fact that his ass was on display. Unequivocally more grounding than his mother bringing everyone they knew to the show, and that was a notable thrill, even if for entirely different reasons. This, however, was definitely a new feeling – he wasn't one for stage fright of self-consciousness, not usually. This is different, though. Everything is different now. Bastian is a game-changer of his own.

They follow through, there's no major incident. Good delivery from everyone, they have a great energy bouncing off of each other. Jake pushes the thought of Bastian watching from his consciousness as much as he can while keeping up the higher bar that his presence set for him. When it's time for bows, he doesn't know if Bastian had gotten down into the crowd or watched it all from the wings so he decides not to worry about him for another minute. He can do that. As he comes back up from his bow, he smiles to the audience one final time and walks offstage with the rest of the company. He chats with some of the guys because the nerves he'd tried to suppress came back rushing and he doesn't want to give Bastian that much power over him. Not yet, or at least, not here, not now. But he's also aware that he needs a tall glass of water and he needs to get to his dressing room for that, face the rest of the day. It's only mid-afternoon, even if he feels like this day has lasted longer than usual already.

He pushes the door open and his breath catches in his throat. He freezes. His eyes fall on Bastian sitting sideways on his couch, in such a manner that he has the doorframe in his line of vision rather than sitting with his back to it. He's got an arm slung across the back of the sofa and his back is resting against the armrest, easy.

"I like to think I make pretty good choices in general, but this is probably the greatest decision I've made in a while. That view was infinitely more interesting than the bodega we built out of the stage at the 37." The easy, cocky smile is back. He is definitely teasing him and enjoying every second of it. It makes Jake all warm and tingly inside while keeping him riveted in his spot, a hand on the doorknob.

If the sole sight of Bastian sitting on his couch, in his dressing room, like he fucking owned the goddamned place wasn't enough to stop him dead in his tracks, his words certainly would have held that power on their own. Jake feels a shiver make its way down his spine. He can pretend the blush on his face and the sweat forming at his hairline are due to the stage lights, right? No need to mention it's only getting intensified now. Stage lights. He tries to regain a bit of his standing and retorts, a few seconds too late for a proper dramatic effect but a reply nonetheless.

"You liked that, didn't you?" Not a question, a statement. It feels strange coming from him, he isn't usually this defiant. Bastian raises his brows, equivocally. Probably wasn't expecting him to be cheeky back at him, but what was the alternative?

"Someone's got an attitude today. Nerves?" Bastian asks, and that's not fair. Jake should be able to retort genuinely but part of him is okay with Bastian seeing straight through him. He drops his head and looks at his feet as he steps closer to the couch.

"I could probably use a massage," he drops. Didn't actually mean that as a request, mostly just a general bit of information about anyone who's on edge as much as Jake has been lately. Bastian rises from the sofa and makes his way towards Jake swiftly. He moves Jake around until he's sitting in the freshly vacated spot. Jake melts, goes pliant the second he feels Bastian's hands on his arms. Getting him to sit how he wants is nothing remotely close to a challenge. Bastian moves behind him and starts kneading at his shoulders. Jake can't remember the last time he had a massage and he makes a mental note to book appointments more regularly. Bastian is good at this. It's not fair. He has to stifle some deep moans rousing from his chest and barely catches himself in time when Bastian hits a good spot. Jake lets him ease all of his worries out of his system and all thoughts flee his mind as surely as do the knots in his muscles. He doesn't have enough rationality left in him this time to remind himself that it's too early to melt to this extent under Bastian's ministrations.

"As much as I love everything about spending time here and watching your incredibly tempting performance, I've really got to go to my own theatre now. They'll wonder where I've gone and I don't like answering questions. But I will take you out to dinner next Monday when we're both free again or my name's not Bastian Castillo. The only thing I need from you is a phone number. You can do that for me?" As if Jake was in a state to refuse him anything when he's got his hands on his back, his shoulders, up by his neck. He breathes in. Bastian slows down and comes to a full stop, steps back and gives Jake a quick minute to put himself back together. Presents him with a pen and a piece of paper because words are out of the question. Jake scribbles his number down and looks up as he gives the paper to Bastian, and Bastian is smiling ever so fondly at him. Their fingertips brush and a whole new spark rushes through him, all the way down to his toes. He smiles back and knows that his eyes light up as he does.

"I'll see you soon, mi cielo. In the meantime, keep killing it on that stage." He winks, the order is subtle but unmasked, and just like that, he's out the door.

He assumes that the crew and company sense that he needed some well-earned time alone. Maybe he's just lucky, but either way, the rest of the afternoon goes in a blink, uneventful. He undresses, gets in his bunk and naps through most of the gap between the shows. He wakes up just in time to gulf a bite down before getting back in his costume for the second performance that evening.

That first show and the following intermission seem to set the stage for the rest of the week. Bastian's words keep him focused on stage as much as his presence had done. He makes a point of relaxing before and after each performance, treating his body with care. He sleeps as much as he can while still keeping a healthy schedule, notices that his friendship with Juniper was probably stronger since the morning he opened up. Jake falls back into acting in his personal life, but around different people. Role-reversal. Whereas he can now be honest with Juniper, he has to start playing his boyfriend role with Caleb, which makes him realize two things.

Firstly, he learns that he has been acting that role out for a while and it probably isn't fair to him, but he doesn't know how to address it. Too much going on and too little certainty to offer a good explanation for the whirlwind in his head. Secondly, he notices that he's been rehearsing for long enough without even realizing how untruthful he is being (to himself and to Caleb) that keeping it up is a child's play – he knows the parts better than anything else at this point. There is a hint of guilt at the back of his mind telling him that he really should not be leading his boyfriend on, but he is also scared of change and there are so many implications coming with a break-up that he cannot process the idea, so he acts. He'll figure that problem out later.

8 shows a week. Bastian saw the first one. The remainder blurs together. He knocks them off in his head like switches. Each flick replaces a part of focus with equal parts excitation and anticipation. He doesn't know what to expect, per se, but he knows it'll be good. Bastian's good for him. To him. He wakes up on Sunday morning to

a text from an unknown number that simply reads "5 tomorrow, dress smart. We're taking over the city, and who knows? Maybe even the world."

Jake almost chokes when he reads the message for the first time. He needs to read twice (and three, and four times because really, Bastian?) to make sure that he's getting all the implications right and even that doesn't quite help. If anything, he's getting incredibly nervous with every word he reads over again. His final show of the week that day is quite the challenge because all the switches are flicked now and every ounce of relaxation he'd mustered has entirely been replaced by a fizzing electricity coursing through his veins. Autopilot has taken over so it goes by quickly. Before he knows it he's home and thanking every god he doesn't believe in for Caleb being out late that night because there is no way he can keep a straight face around him.

That night, he settles for a thorough shower that lasts until he runs out of hot water. Carefully washes every inch of skin with the soapy suds, conditions with extra care and then focuses on the feeling of countless drops of water hitting his body like a rhythm he can't quite follow but that keeps him afloat. He grabs the softest towel he can find and carefully dries himself off before tucking himself tightly under his blanket. He wills his mind to settle and conjures up the feeling of Bastian digging his palms and fingers into his sore muscles almost a week prior. His body instinctively relaxes and he falls into a deep, dreamless slumber.

He wakes up on Monday to a handwritten note from Caleb that he'll be out all day, that he'll see him at nighttime, that he loves him. He scrunches it up, files it under things he doesn't need to worry about, and starts getting ready for Bastian. He's got more hours than necessary so a jog through the city is necessary. He always looks healthier and feels better in his body after a good run, and he can use the extra endorphins. He cleans around the apartment, showers again and finds his best "smart wear", whatever the hell that's supposed to mean. Then it's a waiting game for the clock to show 5 and he's not sure how the nerves are going to hold up but there's nothing else he can do at that point.

Chapter Five

*J*ake fidgets. He is wearing a short-sleeved dress shirt, dark blue with a pattern of thin white lines all over. He's been told that navy brings out the blue in his eyes even more, and he's got a desire to please Bastian. It's summer in New York City, so anything more dressed up will have to wait. Bastian did mention "casual", though, so he hopes that this is alright. He's changed out of chinos and shorts a million times already but he's settled on a nice pair of dark tan dress shorts.

Casual. He kind of wishes that he'd probed Bastian a bit more regarding where they're going. He doesn't even know what they've got planned. Are they going to a museum, grabbing a picnic in Central Park? Going to a play, or out to a fancy dinner? He's never really been on a date before and he has not the slightest clue what to expect. He can feel his heartbeat accelerate on par with his thoughts. Anticipation is quickly coursing through his veins.

Jake is taken out of his reverie by the grandfather clock in his living room. It plays this age-old melody when the clock strikes 5 but he's barely ever home at that time, so it takes him by surprise. He'd given Bastian his address at some point during the previous week so if Bastian is late, it's probably a question of a few minutes. He's lived in New York City his whole life, Jake is sure that he can plan his travel times accurately. He forces himself to take a deep breath, everything will be just fine. He cracks his fingers and that's when he hears the buzzer. It's time to do this. His blood is crackling with nervousness by the time he reaches the intercom.

"Cole."

"I'm downstairs. Don't make me wait any longer, I've already been waiting a whole week to see you again. And that, Cole, is not fair at all," Bastian's expectant voice crackles through the receiver.

"On my way," Jake mutters. His words are already failing him. Great.

He makes his way down the staircase of his building and knows he's dressed appropriately when he sees Bastian in the lobby. He's casually leaning his hip into one of the chairs, not quite sitting but not completely standing either. Jake can't hold his smile in as he checks Bastian out – he's wearing black pants that could probably be a size smaller, but fit him nonetheless, and a nice-fitting navy shirt, sleeveless like Jake's but without the patterns. Jake stifles a chuckle but grins wide. Of course their shirts complement each other's. Bastian eyes him up and down, gaze lingering on the way that Jake's shirt tightens around his arms and chest, and Jake sees a hunger in his eyes. He gulps. It lasts only a second but it feels like a lifetime. He likes the appreciation he sees on Bastian's face.

"You sure clean up nicely. Not that I ever doubted, but I like what I'm seeing." Jake blushes at Bastian's words, looks to the floor. He's always had a hard time responding to compliments.

"Come on, we've got places to be!" With that, he pushes himself to stand and extends an arm towards the door so that Jake can lead the way.

"How are we getting there?" Jake asks, hoping to get some hints dropped in the answer.

"Train, sadly. I'm not trying to drive in the Capital of Mad Drivers. We're going normal-people way."

"And where are you taking me?" He's impatient. Doesn't like surprises, because he never reacts the right way and the last thing he wants to do is disappoint Bastian.

"No, no no no. You don't get to know that quite yet. Just follow me, yeah?" And Jake trusts him, so he stops asking questions and nods. There's an easy silence between them, not forced and not stressful. They ride the train for a while and Jake's not sure he's ever gone this far North before. He hasn't been in New York for that long, after all, so Bastian can't blame him.

When they get off the train, he needs to rely completely on Bastian for directions. He's in completely uncharted territory.

"I hope you don't mind walking too much, we've got a little ways to go."

"Walking is good. It relaxes me. I try to walk to the theatre as much as possible, when the weather allows." The conversation between them flows freely.

"Ever been to the waterfront before? Escape from the bustle and hustle from Manhattan?"

"Not really, actually. I haven't explored the city much. I'm not really a city guy, but if this is where I've got to live to get to be in the plays, then I'll bear. I generally just cycle to Central Park if I want some quiet."

"You're in for a treat, then. You're going to love this. I think. I hope." Small hint of nerves. Maybe Bastian is also affected by this and isn't as calm as he's letting on.

"Night of firsts, it seems," Jake blurts out, and he's not quite sure why he thinks relevant to mention this, here, now.

"Go on?" Bastian looks at him as they walk, intrigued.

"I've never really been on a… wait. We are on a date, right?" Doubt suddenly assails him and he really hopes he's got this right because the alternative is that he's just made a massive fool out of himself. Why does he always have to run his mouth and ruin everything?

"I like to think we are, yes. Unless you don't want it to be that? I want to get to know you."

"Oh god, okay. I thought maybe I'd…" he derails when he feels Bastian's knuckles brush against his. He feels the heat coming up from the sidewalk and his shirt feels tighter. His breath hitches and he's got a half a thought forming that wonders why he reacts to everything so damn easily, but mostly he just revels in the way his skin prickles where Bastian touched him. He looks up and sees intent focus sketched into every feature of Bastian's face, his dark eyes making him melt on the spot.

"You thought maybe you'd…?" Bastian etches him on.

It takes Jake a second to get back in his own head enough to process the question and find an answer.

"Maybe I'd gotten it all wrong. I got scared. For a minute. Wishful thinking gets the best of me."

Bastian cracks a fond smile at that. "You're so cute when you use your words," he says casually, and starts walking again. Jake blushes like he's 13 and a cute girl's just complimented him for the first time. He hadn't even noticed that they had stopped in their tracks.

Bastian takes the lead and Jake settles on following him. He pays attention to his movements, the way he walks, the way it always seems like a surplus of energy is powering Bastian and taints every behavior with giddiness, enthusiasm and a slight bounce to his step. He's in his element.

"Hold up a second –"

"Oh am I going too fast?" Bastian cuts him right off. "I just really like this neighborhood. Mi barrio."

"No, no, I'm fine, I – I was just about to ask what part of New York we were in. Is this the area in your musical? This is where you grew up?"

"It is, actually. Wait, you saw the play?"

Jake's eyes go wide. He hadn't realized that there hadn't been a chance to bring that up in conversation.

"I. Um. Yes. Just before Karla brought me to meet you, actually. That's part of why I wanted to meet you…" he hopes he doesn't come across as needy, now that the information is out there. Bastian doesn't want a date with a pathetic fan. Get it together, Cole.

"Oh? I hope I don't disappoint," he says with playful notes. Jake shoots him a look of disbelief.

"Oh my god, of course not. You couldn't if you wanted to." Jake mentally kicks himself as the words leave his mouth.

They make it to the waterfront soon afterwards and the closer they get, the bigger Jake's excitement grows. He feels simultaneously at peace and like it's time for Christmas vacations and that's an odd mix but it's highly enjoyable. He can get used to this. He lets his eyes drift shut and lets the slightly salted tones of the wind swirl around him, focuses on how it feels on his sensitized skin. He doesn't notice Bastian moving until he's facing him, inching just past what would otherwise be acceptable for friends who have known each other no more than a week and hung out once.

"Handsome, look at me." Soft voice but a discernable firmness. Bastian drops orders around like he was born to do nothing else. Jake opens his eyes and breathes in, takes in the view, the water, the marina, the boats. Bastian. Who slowly raises his hand and brushes his fingertips lightly against his cheek. Jake feels the touch in his entire body, the contact lighting him on fire as surely as the head of a match scraped against the matchbox. He blinks. Bastian's eyes are dark.

"You always been this reactive?" Bastian asks, marveling.

"It's hard not to blush when people point out how easily I blush," Jake replies and he tries his best to shoot a glance at Bastian but he knows it's not nearly as menacing as he wants it to be. He's using all his might not to drift.

"Hungry, beautiful? Hey, stay with me. I'd love to stay here and look at you until my eyes fall out but I'm kind of starving and I brought you here to eat, so how about we get on the move, huh?" It's cheeky but warm. Jake smiles.

"Let's do it," he says, determined. Bastian spins him around and he's now facing a restaurant he hadn't noticed at first. It's beautifully arranged right by the water, not hidden but definitely private. Dim lights on even though it's still light out, but Jake can tell that it'll only get more romantic as the night falls. His eyebrows inch up on his forehead and he turns to Bastian. "Wow. This place is beautiful. We're eating there?"

"Yes. I'm glad you think so. I absolutely love it here, even if I don't get to come down often, not anymore. It's a whole new feeling, at odds with Manhattan. Let's go get a spot on the terrace, or would you like something more private inside?"

Jake thinks about it for a second. He doesn't particularly enjoy making decisions himself. On one hand, he'd love to eat directly by the water with the nice breeze to keep them company. On the other, a table inside affords them some more cover away from prying eyes and feels more suited for conversation.

"Inside. Let's go inside." Might as well scream on the rooftop that he wants to be private and flirty while he's at it, Jake thinks to himself. Bastian looks like he's hesitating for a quick second and Jake wonders why until he extends his arm and plasters a brilliant smile on his face.

"Will you do me the honor of accompanying me inside, then, beautiful?" Jake breaks in a smile that can rival Bastian's in brightness and he takes his hand.

He knows it should feel rushed, but he knows that nothing has ever felt this natural before either. The energy flowing between him and Bastian ever since they met has been pulling them towards each other like a pair of magnets and he figures he's not the only one who feels it. And if he's not alone in that feeling, it means he isn't imagining it, and god, what a comforting thought.

They walk in hand in hand and find a nice, quiet area in the corner by the window. It's so perfect that it's almost eerie. The sun is still high in the sky but you can tell it'll be starting its descent soon. The rays filtering through the wide window are warm and golden, and when Bastian sits with his back to the water, it's almost like he's the source of light. It enlightens his features and there is something so deeply charismatic about him, but Jake can't quite pin it down. He revels in it instead and basks in the glow. They take a few minutes in comfortable silence to browse the menu and settle on some drinks to lighten the mood. Bastian settles for a Gin Tonic while Jake throws caution to the wind and orders a Cosmopolitan. He doesn't go out very often, so he treats himself when he does. Bastian chuckles at him in a playful way when the waiter leaves.

"Typical, huh? Or you're trying to impress me?" He teases.

"Hey! Nothing wrong with ordering alcohol that actually tastes good every once in a while. You don't get to judge me. I thought we were here to get to know each other. So there you have it." Jake says, a little on the defensive.

"Ah, honey, what am I going to do with you."

The drinks arrive and they order entrées. The conversation flows as freely as the liquors on their table and before they know it, it's dark outside and the view suddenly catches Jake by surprise and he needs a moment to take it all in. Through the window, he can see the moonlight coming high from the sky, reflected in the lazy waves of the bay. In the low light of their booth, he looks at Bastian unabashedly, with his short hair almost black, and his eyes dark enough to make anyone plummet at his feet. His inhibitions have disappeared, for the most part, washed away a little bit more every time he throws back a sip of his cocktails. He can feel the blush high on his cheeks from the alcohol and he can't stop running his fingertips through his curls. He wishes he could touch Bastian's hands, his neck, twist in his hair, but he doesn't have permission for that and he's not even sure that Bastian enjoys any of these things, so he keeps quiet and he keeps his eyes wandering between the view outside, Bastian's face, Bastian's hands, the beautiful lights in the room, Bastian's neck, his cocktail, Bastian's lips, until he hears him clear his throat. He snaps back to reality a second too late.

"Like what you see? Tell me, what else do you like?" Bastian's voice is very deep, a low growl now and the tide is quickly changing, that much Jake can tell.

He doesn't quite remember how to form words so he simply looks straight into Bastian's eyes. Bastian squeezes his hand to get him to focus. He is looking at him intently with inquisitive but soft eyes.

"Have you been with someone who keeps you on edge but also makes you feel comfortable?" Jake looks up at Bastian, awaiting his response and sensing the muscles in his body preparing to run for his own life if needed.

Bastian chuckles lightly. "I think so."

"Because that's how I feel when I see you, and this past week? Hah, this past week, knowing that I was spending time with you tonight..." He takes a sip of his liquid courage. "I almost didn't think I was going to survive, the suspense was torture and now that I'm here. With you. Right in front of me, and this view. This view. It's gorgeous but it's you, Bastian. You're you, you're a superstar and you brought me here... but there's something about you. Just being in your presence is calming, you make me feel as if my whole life has been in chaos up until now, and I'm breathing for the first time. And yet.. is it getting hot in here?" he starts sweating and feels as if he can't breathe properly, he needs air and he can't get any, his chest is tight and everything is too warm, and, and, and. He needs to leave. Now.

"Hey, beautiful. Can you do something for me? Can you breathe with me? Breathe in slowly. Deeply as you can. Hold it. Hold it. And let it go."

Jake is still wide-eyed but Bastian has asked him to do something so he tries his hardest and does his best. It takes him several repetitions to be able to get past something that was blocking his diaphragm high in its place, but after a few more tries, he manages to more or less sync his breathing to the slow and steady pace of Bastian's own.

"Stay here and breathe. I'll be right back. Breathe."

Jake doesn't want him to leave and wants to tell him to stay right there, but not at the cost of disobedience. He closes his eyes and focuses in getting back into his body. He feels oddly sober, all at once. He focuses of the feeling of the floor under his shoes, how he's touching the base of the table with his toes. He focuses on the air against his bare legs and the way the cushion feels under his thighs. He focuses on the feeling of his sweaty hands resting on his knees, the way his elbows are in contact with the sides of his body. He feels the back of the booth with his shoulders, forces his head slowly back until it hits the soft material. He breathes. Repeats until Bastian gets back. He's feeling slightly calmer and Bastian is still here, he didn't leave him, it's okay, he's okay, he didn't freak him out. It's okay.

When Bastian gets back, there's no hesitation in the way he extends his hand, not this time. The request is explicit and Jake grabs his hand, holds onto it as if his life depended on it, and Bastian pulls him into a hug, right here in the restaurant. Given, they're still in a darker corner and the place is almost empty because it's Monday night, but Jake still stiffens by reflex – he's never been physically affectionate with anyone in public (except for maybe Juniper but that doesn't really count). Bastian places a soothing hand at the back of his neck and Jake feels small but it feels good. Bastian whispers relaxing words directly into his ear and his other hand rests in the dip at the small of his back. He slowly lets some tension go. Jake tentatively rests his hands on Bastian's hips. Bastian pulls back slightly, and it's too early but they're in public, they can't just stay entwined forever, so it's okay. He gently but firmly places a hand on each side of his face and looks directly into his eyes.

"Are you feeling up for a walk, or do you want me to call a cab? I don't live far from here so we can do either. You let me know what feels best for you right now. Tell me what you need."

"Can we.. can we take a cab? I don't think I can walk right now." There aren't many things Jake hates more than asking for things, but it feels vital in this moment. And Bastian offered, so it's not like he had to demand, not exactly. This is a bit easier for him.

Bastian flips his phone on and phones a cab over by the docks, still holding Jake close to his own body. When he hangs up, he reluctantly parts and leads Jake outside. They both take a deep breath in the crisp seaside air. It's not cold, but it's definitely nowhere near as hot as it had been earlier that day. The drop at night can be felt much more sharply by the waterfront. With the adrenaline coming down in Jake's body and the exhaustion washing over him, he starts shivering. Bastian feels him shaking and runs the pad of his thumb across the side of Jake's finger where their hands are clasped together.

"You alright, beautiful?" There's a hint of concern in his voice.

"I'm sorry... I didn't mean to get all... panicky on you. I've just been really on edge lately, this past week has frankly been fucking insane, and there's so much I don't know and it just kind of rushed all over me at once, and, yeah, anyway, I'm sorry?"

A deep shiver runs through him as he finishes speaking and this time it's definitely more than just the chill. It's relief, it's an adjustment, it's jumping into the unknown without second guessing, and it's terrifying but it's good.

"Oh, honey. Please don't worry about that. I've been in your situation, I haven't forgotten. Shit's stressful. I got your back. Let's go. We've got this."

With this, the cab is pulling up and they cram in the back. Jake rests his head on Bastian's shoulder and they navigate the streets in silence, with the barest edge of salsa music playing through the speakers.

They get out and Bastian pays the driver. Jake makes a mental note of paying him back, or at least of getting him a gift to thank him. They go up a few flights of stairs and the easy exercise helps warming Jake up. Bastian fiddles with his keys and finally unlocks the door. Jake has butterflies. The panic seems to have fully subsided and he doesn't feel the alcohol in his veins, not after something like that.

"Mi casa. Welcome. This is where the magic happens." Jake blushes furiously at that. Bastian kicks his shoes off and lines them up by the door so Jake follows suit. Bastian turns to face him and extends both of his arms towards Jake so that he can take both hands in his. Jake complies without a hint of hesitation and Bastian walks backwards. They pass a kitchen and what seems like a living room, with bookshelves crammed with books, CDs, movies, and old vinyl records filling the room, and then Bastian leads him in a short hallway. He gets into the room in the far left corner.

His bedroom. Things are progressing so fast, but always within the realm of comfort, at least so far. Bastian closes the door behind Jake and rests a hand on his chest.

"Can you give me colors? When I ask, definitely, but if anything ever changes, I want you to let me know. I'm not doing anything without you agreeing to that. I don't know necessarily where this is going, but if we don't do this first, it's not going anywhere."

"I... I can do that. Green for good, yellow for careful but okay, red for stop?"

"You got it. How are you feeling right now?"

"I… green." This feels bold, especially after his emotions flying high all night, but this, right now, this is good.

Bastian removes the hand on his chest and places it next to his head, against the hardwood door. Repeats with his other hand. Jake can't escape. Well, he knows that physically, he could, and if he really wanted to he could just say so, but doing that is the very last thing on his mind. He gulps. His breathing picks up.

"How about now?"

"Green." No hesitation this time. "God."

"Something you want to say, honey?" Bastian moves his body closer. Jake is crowded against the door.

"No. No. I'm good. Please," he breathes out.

"Something you want from me?"

God, he's going to kill him with those questions. Staying silent would be so much easier. No thought process required in keeping quiet. So instead of saying something and making a fool of himself, he snakes a hand up between their bodies and uses a finger to tilt Bastian's chin up. His own head dips down and he finds Bastian's lips with his own. It's tentative at first, but they quickly gain traction. Bastian removes one of his hands from the door and moves it to Jake's hair, letting his fingers tighten and applying the barest pressure to his scalp. Jake gasps. His free hand moves to Bastian's hip and he pulls him closer, their bodies flush.

Bastian uses the break in the kiss that Jake provoked with his gasp to check in with him once more. Jake can't think in words so he just pulls Bastian's face to his again and tries to resume kissing him.

Bastian resists and that prompts Jake to open his eyes – he hadn't even realized he'd closed them shut. He looks at Bastian and his face is flushed, his eyes even darker than usual if that's even possible.

"I asked a question. I'm expecting an answer. Use your words, honey, or I'm stopping."

This is serious. Bastian has more self-control than Jake had originally anticipated but he likes that someone's got a head on his shoulders, because he doesn't. This also tells him that he wasn't wrong in trusting Bastian – he really does care about doing this the right way and won't let himself be carried away.

"Green," he whispers. "Please."

Bastian detaches himself and moves away from the door. Jake almost tumbles over without Bastian's presence to keep him upright. He looks equivocally at the bed.

"How's that look to you, huh?"

Jake licks his lips and moves. He doesn't think he can trust his legs right now, so he keeps a hand on the wall as he struts to the bed. He sits down on the edge as soon as he reaches it and awaits further instructions from Bastian.

"Move up. Get yourself in the middle of it, yeah? Lay down, head on the pillows." His voice is breathy and exquisitely deep by now. His gaze is ravenous.

Jake complies, pulls himself backwards before laying himself down. He has a brief moment of clarity for thinking that this is the softest bed he's ever tried and he never wants to move again. Not on his own volition, at least.

Bastian moves closer and kneels on the foot of the bed, by Jake's legs. He drops to his hands and crawls over top of him. Kisses him, and its insistent, it's not chaste. It's messy, Bastian licks his lips and Jake opens up, pliable. Bastian takes hold of one of his wrists and brings it over their heads, lowering his upper body in the process. Jake arches into the touch.

"Stay up there." He wouldn't dream of moving a single inch of his body.

Bastian uses that same hand to rest it on Jake's hip where the hem of his shirt is riding up above his shorts. Presses down lightly and Jake moans. Really hopes Bastian doesn't expect him to be quiet because the odds of that are incredibly slim. Probably nonexistent. Bastian pulls back, tugs at the hem of his button-down.

"Can I?"

"Yes, yes, go ahead." Breathy, a little shaky. Needy. He mutters filth under his breath.

Bastian sits up and Jake whimpers at the loss. He uses both his hands to undo the buttons on his shirt, starting at the very bottom. Feels reckless, almost dangerous. Jake is a mess, putty in Bastian's hands. Bastian's head dips down and he nuzzles as he reveals more

ALEX H. SINGH

and more pale skin with every button undone. He looks up at Jake
and makes eye contact as he dips his tongue in his navel. Jake thinks
he might combust right then and there, throws his head back against
the pillows. By the time Bastian reaches his chest, Jake is reduced to
a writhing mess on Bastian's bedspread and Bastian has to pull back
once more , this time to still his hips.

"Did I say you were allowed to move like that?"

Embarrassment floods Jake and he stops moving. Doesn't dare
breathe. Stays completely still.

"That look on your face is not an answer, beautiful."

"No. I mean. No. You didn't say I could move."

"So, don't. Easy."

Jake breathes in, because he might explode if he doesn't.

"Doing alright in there?"

Jake closes his eyes. This all feels so incredible, it's such a rush
and he's here for all of it, they're a good match and that's an understatement, but he also doesn't want to rush anything and regret later.
He knows he's not thinking straight. If he's honest, he's barely
thinking at all.

"Actually, Bastian?" He asks. Small, small voice.

"What's on your mind?"

"I... I want to take my time. I want us to take our time. I don't
want to rush this. Can we wait? I'm just, this is so good, all of it, all
of... you, but I've never really done anything like this before, and I
want to remember it."

"Of course. Of course, obviously. Whatever you want. You've
had a lot of emotions going through your brain, enough for a day,
haven't you?"

Jake knows this question is rhetorical, a statement more than
anything, but he nods anyways.

"Can I sleep here?" He asks, because he's not sure what to do
next, what to do in situations like these.

"Pues claro, of course you're staying. I'm not sending you off
anywhere at this time and in this state. I'm not heartless." With that,
he moves off Jake. "Do you need a minute to yourself?" So caring,
always.

42

"Maybe? I mostly, could I have water? Just tap water?" He doesn't feel like he necessarily deserves all of Bastian's kindness, not after ruining their date at the restaurant, and now this, but Bastian doesn't hesitate.

"Of course. I'll knock before I get back in. Take your time, handsome. Make yourself at home." With that, he gets up, straightens his shirt and leaves, closing the door behind himself.

Jake brings his hands to his face and rubs. He can't believe this is happening to him. He gets up and wants to get in bed, but he's worn his clothes out and about, rode transit, it's nowhere near clean enough for getting into bed, and not comfortable either. He sits on the edge of the bed. He doesn't know where Bastian keeps his pajamas, isn't sure he would even dare borrowing one, so he shrugs and finishes removing his shirt. He gets up, removes his shorts and socks, folds everything neatly by the bedside table and crawls under the covers. Pulls the sheets up to his chin – he's afraid that this might be too bold but he doesn't know what else to do. He wills himself to relax before Bastian comes back.

A few moments later, he hears the soft knock on the door. "Can I come in? I've got water for you."

"Yes. Yes, I'm okay," he asserts.

With that confirmed, Bastian pushes the door and a soft smiles sets on his lips when he sees Jake all tucked in. He sets the glass on the table and his eyes fall to the pile of clothes on the floor. He cocks an eyebrow. Looks at Jake with a playful smirk on his lips. Jake flushes a deep red and pulls the covers higher above his chin, suddenly very shy. His blue eyes are bright and wide.

"Is that how we're feeling?"

"I didn't know what else to do, I could, I can put them back on if you want, or maybe—"

Bastian cuts him off short. "I'm never going to say no to a cute guy like you shirtless in my bed. This is more than fine. Don't hide."

Jake lowers the sheets slightly but keeps his chest out of view. Bastian turns around and removes his own shirt and the wife beater he's wearing underneath it. "You good if I do the same?"

Jake can't quite believe he has to give his approval to such a request but does anyways. "Of course, if that's okay with you too."

Bastian proceeds to remove his pants and slides in behind Jake, under the thin summer sheets. He moves closer and rests his forehead at the back of Jake's neck. Inhales.

"It's not fair for you to be smelling this good. Not fair at all. I'm sleepy. Let's crash, shall we?"

With that, Bastian reaches over Jake to turn the bedside lamp off and lets his arm fall comfortably in the dip below Jake's ribs. He hums slightly. This is good.

"Bastian?" He murmurs.

"Hm?"

"Tomorrow, I…"

"Yes?"

"I want you to hurt me."

Chapter Six

*J*ake wakes up early the next morning and he feels positively sore in his arms and legs. Alcohol has always had this weird effect on him, regardless of how much he ate or hydrated himself before he went to bed. He always felt like he'd been run over by an 18-wheeler. He'd slept on his stomach, he has a hand under the pillow and it doesn't feel like his usual pillow, it's fluffier. It takes him a while to realize that his blanket isn't wrapped around him the way it usually is. It's lighter. It smells different. He opens his eyes and the door isn't in his line of vision like it's supposed to be and it takes a second for all the memories of the night before to flood back in, for him to remember where he is, and with whom. That's when he notices the arm thrown across the small of his back, just there, just holding, with as much intent as a sleeping body can provide.

He pushes himself up from the pillow for a second and looks on the other side of himself, his eyes falling on Bastian, still asleep, not quite close enough that their bodies touch, but not far by any means. He turns around under his light embrace to face him. He brings an arm up to Bastian's face, his fingertips grazing against the soft skin. Bastian stirs, scrunches his face up lightly, and he moves closer to benefit from the warmth radiating from Jake's skin. It seems automatic, he's not sure that Bastian is fully aware of his surroundings just yet. He wants to say something, but he's terrified of having morning breath, so he softly pulls himself out of under Bastian's arm and out of bed. He wouldn't know what to say anyways. He hears Bastian groan some while he makes his way to the bathroom as quietly as possible. He hadn't thought he'd stay overnight, so he doesn't have a toothbrush or fresh clothes. He opens the cabinet out of habit, not quite sure what he's looking for, and feels the relief in his shoulders when he spots the mouthwash. That'll do. He rinses quickly, then tries to tame his curls a little, gives up when he knows it's pointless. He looks at himself and takes a deep breath. Now that he's awake, he remembers what they did last night, and more importantly, the last thing he said before they both fell asleep. He gulps. Goes back to the bedroom, and he wouldn't defend in court that the shiver down his spine is due to the chilled air of the apartment.

When he enters, he sees that Bastian isn't asleep anymore. He's on his back, pushed up on one elbow, and he seems to relax a bit when he sees Jake.

"I was really hoping you hadn't left. I got worried maybe we'd gone too fast." Relief is thick on Bastian's tongue, that much Jake can discern. "Come back to bed?" Bastian asked, moving to the side to allow Jake to join him under the thin sheet.

Jake takes the open invitation and drops in Bastian's bed, tucks himself in close, breathes in the scent of Bastian's skin. He mumbles a faint "Good morning," and closes his eyes.

"I could get used to having my own human heater, even in this god awful summer weather. I really could. How are you feeling?" Bastian asks, and he's so caring, his arms are wrapped around Jake and this is good.

"I could stay here for a long, long time. I don't want to go back to real life." That's a lot of words for an answer, but he's comfortable, he's okay.

"Is there something you'd like to talk about? You said something, last night, and don't get me wrong, I'm interested. I do think it warrants a conversation first, though."

Jake holds his breath. He should have seen this coming, it was going too well, too fast. He's not afraid of the conversation, per se. He just knows it's going to be a hard one, however necessary it is. He wishes he could delay it, at least for a few hours, maybe forever. Maybe he could just never speak again.

"I don't really… know what to say?" He tries, tentative, straining his neck to look up at Bastian from his position on his chest.

"Can I ask questions, and you can answer them? I can walk you through, you don't have to say anything you don't want to, but that could work. What do you think, beautiful?"

Jake ponders that for a moment, and yeah, not having to hold the conversation on his own works for him. "Okay. I mean, yes. We can try that. What do you want to know?"

"Is there a particular reason you asked for what you did yesterday?" Bastian doesn't beat around the bush, dives right in. There's a thrill at the top of Jake's spine when he hears the question, but he wouldn't know where to start. Too broad, too narrow, too specific, not specific enough.

Jake is quiet for a moment, long enough that Bastian thinks he wasn't clear, and he's trying to come up with other ways of wording it, but then Jake opens his mouth, closes it a few times, pouts, like he's trying to find the right words. They don't come easily. His brows knit tight. He's better at reciting other people's words, that's what he does for a living. His own, not so much. Those generally stay just behind the concrete thought territory, abstract concepts, they don't get letters and words and acknowledgement.

"I haven't really thought about it much… It kind of just came out before I really knew what I was doing. I don't really want to think, most of the time. It's easier when I'm not calling the shots," and that much Bastian had figured, but he wouldn't embarrass Jake by pointing that out. He waits patiently for him to expand.

"What do you find appealing about it? About pain?"

"I don't… I think it has to do with control. I don't like being in control. I like not being in control. But the consequences are usually too… unpredictable, and I'm not good with uncertainty either."

Bastian isn't quite sure what Jake means, where this is going, but he softly encourages Jake to go on.

"I like that if we… decide to go rough… there will always be limits. I get to give up, in a way, and just shut down my brain, but I also get to contain the actual harm that could come my way." Once he gets going, it's a bit easier. Having to put things into words for other people to understand forces him to address his own feelings. "You know I haven't really come out to anyone before you," he adds. "I think that's related too." He's aware that the logical links are not clear, so he scrambles for more words. "I don't want to have to worry about calling the shots, and I don't have to, with you, it's natural and I trust you, and you know that much about me already, and you're still here."

"I don't have the slightest reason not to be here, right now," Bastian assures him. Jake sits up a bit, runs a hand through his hair.

"I can't come out because I'm terrified of what people might to do me. They could harm me, it could be serious, and I don't get to predict that, I don't get to control their reactions. But for some reason, with this, whatever this is, I know I can be vulnerable, I can be in that position, you'd never do something I don't want to do. I don't like over-thinking and I'm always over thinking, how I speak, how I dress, how I behave around everyone, all the time, and it's hard. Not having to make decisions or put on a mask around you, that's the opposite of hard and it's so easy for me to get lost in it." Everything is coming to him more freely, now. He looks into Bastian's eyes and sees interest, care, respect, and he knows he's safe here. "Not having to… worry… not having to make decisions, for once, that's really good. And the rush that comes with just, I don't know how else to say it, but surrendering? Then I can stop thinking and I can focus on the sensations. And the stronger, the better, because then I really don't have to focus on anything else, I can't focus on anything else, and that's what I want. And I know that I'm safe. And, I don't know, there's power in that? I can take power in giving myself away."

He's not sure that everything is logically sound, but it makes sense to him. He relaxes his shoulders, upper arms. Bastian replies and Jake almost forgot that he was supposed to walk him through it. Easier once he'd started.

"I can understand that. Definitely. I love it when you use your words. You want to say more for me? Let me in." And Bastian starts stroking his arm, and Jake can't disappoint him, not now, so he continues.

"I think, since there are boundaries here, this is good, and I don't have to worry about making decisions, for once. And that's really good. I know you won't do something that I can't handle. It's good not to have to worry about what's next. I can only do that on stage, usually. I can only put my own stuff aside when all my brain space is taken up by being someone else, but you're giving me that too, by letting me be someone else's, by letting me be… me. I just want to get out of my own head. I don't want to think. But I don't want to worry either. I don't know how it happened or why, I'm not sure that I understand exactly just what it is about you, but I get to be myself, here, and I'm not scared of your reactions. You… you figured me out right away and that isn't fortuitous. People can hurt me in real ways out there, but not up here. Not up here. I'm in control of giving away my control and that just feels powerful, and relieving at the same time? Does that make sense?"

"It does. I'm glad that I can be that for you. I'm not really trying to figure out why or how it happened, it just feels right, it felt right, so I went with it. So you don't want to be in control. And you get a rush from that. And you'd get a rush from letting me hurt you, because you know I won't go too far, or it won't have real consequences? Am I getting this right? God, I shouldn't be so affected by everything you just said, but you have no idea how good you sound."

Bastian is so much more concise and narrow than he is, and Jake feels like it makes much more sense coming out of his mouth, so he just nods. He really wants Bastian to kiss him, but he doesn't know what Bastian wants, so he doesn't say anything. Of course, Bastian is right. He looks down at his own hands in his lap, because that's the easiest thing to do right now. Maybe he doesn't have to speak ever again, that was so much, so many words, and now he feels a little overwhelmed, and a lot on display.

"Hey, beautiful, Jacob, look at me." And oh, that's something new, his full name, in this context. It shifts something inside him. He brings his eyes up to meet Bastian's, the most innocent mask on his face. "That wasn't easy. That was hard for you, wasn't it?" A statement, not a question. "I'm proud of you. You did well and I'm grateful that you trust me, and that you let me in like that." He sounds so sincere that it would never cross Jake's mind to cast doubt on Bastian's sentences, not now, maybe ever. He nods again, hums under his breath, lets out a sigh. He'd maybe go back to bed. "How about I make you breakfast, huh, gorgeous? How do you feel about that? I should reward you, you were brave. I got eggs and bacon and I want to spoil you. Can I do that?"

Bastian sounds almost giddy at the idea of taking care of Jake, so of course he can't help but grin and whisper a soft "yeah."

"Alright, let's get you some type of shirt, a sweater or something, the A/C is cranked out there, I don't want you to get cold. Oh, and, underwear? You don't have a change of clothes, do you? Let me grab you something real quick."

Jake shakes his head. With that, Bastian gets up and starts rummaging through his closet to find something that'll fit Jake. He mostly owns clothes three times his size, so it's not that hard a task. When he finds something he can see Jake wearing, he turns back, but doesn't hand it to him right away.

"Do you want to take a bath? Would that be good? I can run a hot bath and let you relax while I cook, and then you can join me and we can watch whatever's on TV on Monday mornings?"

"That sounds really good. Can I do that? Is that okay?"

"I wouldn't have offered if it wasn't. Come on now, come with me."

Bastian extends his arm, the one that's not still holding on to the sweater and the pair of plain black briefs, and leads Jake to the bathroom. They chat, easy, everything and anything while the bathtub fills up. Once it's ready and Jake's satisfied with the temperature, Bastian pulls out a few clean towels from a small cabinet and sets them by the bath. Jake watches him until Bastian turns back to face him, puts a single finger square in the middle of Jake's bare chest and pushes him back until his shoulder blades hit the cold wall behind him. He hisses at the sensations, not expecting the contrast in temperatures between the steamy air in the room and the cold tiles against his skin. Bastian catches Jake off guard, mid-hiss, and kisses him slowly, hoisting himself up on his toes to make himself a bit taller against Jake, pushing their bodies flush. The bath quickly gets relegated to the back of Jake's mind. He's got more important things to focus on, like the pressure of Bastian's taut body all along his own, the way his lips move against him, insisting, soft and hard at the same time, and he doesn't know how Bastian does that but he doesn't care as long as he doesn't stop.

"Don't do anything I wouldn't do, beautiful. I'll have breakfast ready for you when you get out."

Jake wants to shudder even though Bastian hasn't said anything remotely worthy of such a reaction, but it's all in the way he delivers it, how rough his voice is. Bastian turns around and Jake hears the soft click or the door when Bastian shuts it behind himself. He shakes his head, trying to regain his bearings. He spots Bastian's clothes by the towels and strips, lowering himself in the hot water. It's hot enough to burn until he's used to it, but it feels so good, always has.

His mind focuses on the pinpricks of the burning water on the most sensitive parts of his body, and somehow the thought of Caleb waddles its way through Jake's brain. He's really going to have to do something about him. About them. He doesn't think Caleb's going to be any type of surprised when Jake tells him they can't be together, that they're not working out, but that's another necessary conversation he doesn't want to have. He lets himself slide down in the tub and submerges his head in the heat. He lets out all the air in his lungs until they're burning, then comes back up and breathes in, deep, slow. Full. He finds shampoo and washes his hair, a bar of soap and cleans every crevice of his body, gets back under the water, it's a bit easier this time.

He decides that whatever this is, between him and Bastian, it's worth a shot, it's worth exploring. He's worth surrendering to. A certain serenity enters his pores when his brain thinks the words, and he's ready for whatever this ends up being.

He drains the bath and gives himself one last rinse under the shower head before he steps out and dries off. He takes his time toweling himself dry, lets the flush in his cheeks and on his chest settle some – he's always been like this around heat, his skin gets deeply flushed in blotches down his torso, for some reason. He's suddenly very aware of that fact. He pulls on the briefs and they hug his body tightly, then the hoodie, some theatre group design printed on the front, Bastian's name on the sleeve (of course), and heads back out.

He's assailed with the floating smell of brunch, potatoes and bacon and eggs, and it's the best thing he's woken up to in a long time. He makes his way to the kitchen and Bastian seems lost in his thoughts, doesn't hear him come back, so Jake throws caution to the wind and wraps his arms around Bastian's middle, rests his head on his bare shoulder and hides his face in Bastian's neck. He feels Bastian very briefly tense up in reflex before he relaxes in Jake's embrace, somehow managing to be the grounding force for the both of them as he's being hugged, pushing back against Jake's warm body. Jake takes advantage of the situation and runs his hands all over Bastian's bare chest, learning every curve, every dip.

Bastian carefully rests the spatula he'd been holding and turns around in Jake's arms, wrapping his own arms around his waist and resting his hands dangerously close to Jake's firm ass.

"Hey, gorgeous," Bastian speaks, locking eyes with Jake. "How was the bath?"

As means for an answer, Jake closes his eyes and smiles, humming softly. "Can you kiss me?" He whispers without opening his eyes, as if he was afraid that Bastian would somehow refuse him.

Bastian leans in and lets his breath ghost over Jake's lips for a hot second, just to gauge Jake's reaction to waiting. Jake holds his breath and he just waits. To hell with self-control, Bastian kisses him and Jake lets the air out. He parts his lips after a moment of hesitation and Bastian takes advantage of that, letting his tongue dart out and run across Jake's bottom lip. Jake tugs him closer and Bastian moves his hands lower in reaction before to capture Jake's lip between his teeth. He lets out a sound that's halfway between whining and moaning and it's all Bastian can do not to let his breakfast go up in flames.

He pulls off from Jake's face, not without tugging his lip with him for slightly longer than strictly necessary, and squeezes the soft flesh beneath his palms.

"If you still want that breakfast, I'm afraid I'm going to have to stop you here, beautiful."

He pushes Jake away from him softly so that he can go back to the diced potatoes. Not quite willing to part, Jake rests his hands on Bastian's shoulders and naturally starts massaging the muscles beneath his hands. He's pretty sure that if humans could melt, Bastian would be in the process of doing so, if the way he exhales low between his teeth is any indication. Not a hiss; more of a stifled moan, and Jake feels it trickle down his own spine.

Bastian takes a deep breath when Jake presses his lips at the base of his neck and noticeably stiffens.

"Jake." Firm.

"Hm?"

"Don't pretend like you don't know exactly what you're doing. Let me finish this, yeah? Go wait for me in the living room."

And yeah, he can probably do that. Doesn't want to, but Bastian's right, it's probably not the greatest time for him to be so forward. He scuffles to the living room and settles on his back on Bastian's couch, resting his head on a cushion and burrowing his hands in the front pocket of the sweater. He closes his eyes and waits, almost drifts out again by the time Bastian is done. He is so pliable, so comfortable, so cozy.

He cracks an eye open when he hears the sound of a plate settling on the coffee table and smiles when he sees Bastian crouching next to him, absent-mindedly playing with the string of the hoodie he gave him. He isn't sure what it is, but wearing Bastian's clothes makes him feel so intimately connected to him, and if the hunger in Bastian's eyes is any indication, he isn't immune to seeing Jake in his belongings either.

"Kiss me."

Jake turns his head fully to the side and brings his hand up to rest on Bastian's neck, arching on the couch in hopes to get closer to him. He doesn't think twice about parting his lips this time. Bastian's mouth against him, the insistence of his lips, the pressure – it's a promise of so much more to come and that is such a good thought it's almost too much. He moans low at the back of his throat before he can catch it. He feels Bastian's hand card between his curls, wrapping his fingers in his hair. Tugging, that perfect pressure. And then full-on pulling, and Jake's breath hitches, his heart probably misses a beat, perhaps a few. Bastian pulls his head back, tilts it, and he moves down ever so slowly to drag the tip of his tongue on Jake's jaw line. He bites on his earlobe and it's good enough that Jake wants to cry but it's probably too early, so he whispers Bastian's name softly instead, doesn't trust his full voice.

"What was that?" Bastian inquires, breath hot against his ear.

"Bastian. Please." Barely louder, if more desperate.

He can feel the heat up on his cheeks, insistent, and he's starting to think maybe wearing a hoodie wasn't the greatest idea, because if Bastian keeps it up he's going to need another shower and he just cleaned himself.

"We still have breakfast to eat though. I'm starving, what about you?" The contrast between the playfulness of his words and the edge of his voice are enough to make Jake squirm against the couch. "Come on, sit up for me."

He does, and Bastian plops down where Jake's head just was as he's pulling the coffee table closer to them both. He had a tray, both plates and two tall glasses of orange juice on it, and Jake salivates at the sight.

"You... prepared that for me?" And he might have forgotten what it was like to have someone caring for him, because Caleb? Caleb hasn't done anything of the sort in millennia.

"Well, I mean, clearly I'm benefiting too. But I don't usually put much more effort into breakfast than what it takes to get a bagel golden in the toaster and butter it up. So yeah, I think you can say I did," and Bastian throws a wink his way that throws his balance off.

"Thank you, Bastian. I appreciate it. I really do."

"You know what? I never used to be such a fan of my name. But I like the way it sounds with your voice. You should say it more often." That isn't quite a direction but it's something, and Jake will. He looks down. Blushes further, somehow.

From the corner of his eye, he sees Bastian grabbing a fork, sticking it through a potato and slowly bring it up to Jake's mouth. He opens up and lets Bastian feed him. Oh, and these are good.

"Hm. Bastian. What did you cook that with? This is delicious," he speaks.

"Family secret recipe. You don't get to know that just yet, sweetheart. Maybe later, depending how long you stick around. Will you stick around?"

"I'd be honored to."

He keeps eating in silence, lets Bastian feed him, and it's so domestic he almost hates it. He loves it a whole lot more than he hates it, though, so it's okay. It's more than okay. He could probably do this forever. Or maybe until he'd burst. He wouldn't put it past Bastian to try.

Bastian turns his TV on at some point and it's on a cartoon network. Bastian doesn't change it, he sits back half against the arm of the couch and Jake settles between his legs, his back cuddled up into Bastian, resting against Bastian's chest. He closes his eyes and focuses on the soft thump of Bastian's heartbeat that he hears when he tilts his head to the side. He feels Bastian's hands in his hair, stroking his jaw, tracing the tendons in his neck, ghosting down his chest with the fabric of the sweater between their skin. He could fall asleep again like this, if he didn't have this many butterflies coursing through his entire body.

Bastian does nothing more than that for a while, so Jake doesn't watch the TV, doesn't focus on anything but the feeling of Bastian's fingertips lightly grazing all the skin he can reach, constantly moving, never stopping their movement. Bastian's nails are short, too short to really mean anything, Jake doesn't feel them. He doesn't open his eyes until he feels a slight shift in the way Bastian touches him – it's less absent-minded, suddenly. He couldn't tell if there was a build-up to it, doesn't really mind either, but next thing he knows. Next thing he knows, Bastian's hand is resting above his heart, palm flat against the thick cotton of his sweater, but his fingers – his fingers haven't stopped moving, and two of them are swirling in tight circles around one of his nipples, and Jake can feel it harden under Bastian's touch. He stops breathing for a fraction of a second, and Bastian must have noticed how his chest stopped moving because he stops and presses his fingers around the bud, scissoring through the fabric but not moving. Not anymore.

"Too far? Too early?" Bastian whispers from somewhere behind him. Jake shakes his head. "Your words, I want to hear words. Use them."

"Bastian…" Jake closes his mouth, doesn't open his eyes.

"There something you want?" He's whispering but its deeper, maybe darker. Or maybe Jake's projecting. He doesn't want to care, doesn't want to think.

"You?"

"I like the sound of that," Bastian responds. "Come up here."

Jake would rather not move, but he figures he can kiss Bastian this way, and that, he wants. He wills his muscles to obey him as he brings himself up, facing Bastian now. Bastian, with his impossibly dark eyes, his perfectly tan skin, his soft hair. Jake breathes him in and Bastian pulls him in to kiss him slowly. Jake follows his lead, Bastian builds it up slowly. His hand is on Jake's jaw and he holds him there, the pads of his fingers gentle at first but getting harder by the second. Jake is resting flush against him, his arms on either side of Bastian, holding himself up just enough not to crush him. Soon enough Bastian is almost digging into Jake's jaw, his cheek, and Jake lets out a shaky breath, his brain zeroing on the sensations. He pants against Bastian's lips.

"What am I going to do with you, huh? You almost let me set this breakfast on fire, I shouldn't let you off the hook so easily."

He doesn't understand how Bastian can be so sweet and dangerous at the same time, he's probably got something to do with forbidden fruits, the promise of more to come, and Jake only wants to be under his control even more. He feels Bastian's free hand skimming down the side of his ribcage, up and down a few times repeated. The fingers in his jaw move to the back of his head, tangling in his curls, and he doesn't have a choice but to move his lips against Bastian's again. He shivers when he captures his bottom lip between his teeth and worries it. He shudders when Bastian's hand slides under the hem of his sweater. He feels a finger just past the waistband of his boxers, Bastian's boxers, and he's vaguely aware of the movement of his hips. Bastian uses the soft rotations of Jake's hips to slip his entire hand in Jake's underwear and he grabs. He digs his fingers in the muscle of Jake's ass and Jake can't stop the moan escaping his lips. Doesn't want to.

Something in the back of his mind tells him that he shouldn't be the one for Bastian to focus on, he should be the one to make Bastian feel good, not the opposite. He pushes himself up from his position against Bastian's chest and takes a deep breath before he starts moving with the intent of kneeling on the floor, but Bastian stops him, grips his hip, doesn't let him leave.

"Are we going anywhere?" Bastian asks, uncertain of what's happening in Jake's brain. Jake gulps. "Is this not good?"

Far from it – it's very good, it's so good, but he doesn't think he deserves any of it.

"Jacob, look at me." He does. "Use your words. Talk to me."

Deep breath. When he looks up again, Bastian's eyes are dark, dark pools, but his eyebrows are frowning in concern.

"I… you said…" He realizes that Bastian has never quite said anything about any kind of punishment for the breakfast thing, not specifically, but it was implied, wasn't it? He's on the hook, that he did say. "You said you wouldn't let me get away easily."

"Exactly. I don't want you to go anywhere just yet," and isn't that a sweet double-entendre.

"I want to make this good for you?" It shouldn't sound like a question, but it does. He tries again. "I want to be good for you."

"So be good and stop getting away from me."

That doesn't quite make much sense to him, but he complies.

Maybe it should – he knows about putting his own needs aside, he wants to please so desperately, – but Bastian shouldn't have to do this for him. He almost set the kitchen on fire, he shouldn't be the one getting off, and it all looks like this is where Bastian is headed.

"But... why?" He's trying to connect the dots and failing. Can't figure out why Bastian doesn't want him docile and kneeling for him.

"Why I want you here? Oh, honeybee. There are things I want to do to you that I definitely cannot do if you're not here."

And, well, that's more than enough for an answer. Sometimes, less is more. This is definitely sometime.

Chapter Seven

*B*astian's words echo on a loop in Jake's brain, and he can't decide which part of the sentence gets to him the most. " There are things I want to do to you that I definitely cannot do if you're not here. He wants to let Bastian do those things to him, whatever they are, he wants to please him. He'd be happy with letting Bastian do whatever he wanted with him, to him. He's not sure how that's going to go down, though, because right now he's the recipient of Bastian's ministrations, his focus and his intent and Jake doesn't get it but he wouldn't dream of voicing his concerns. He will comply to fit the scenario that Bastian has in mind, whatever it entails, because Jake refuses to believe he doesn't have one. He was born to follow other people's lead – playwrights, directors, choreographers – he was born to follow Bastian's.

He's brought back out of his swirling thoughts when Bastian cages his face between warm palms, making him look directly in his eyes. "Promise me you'll speak up if you need. I know it's easier for you to keep quiet, but I need you to say it out loud if I'm doing something wrong."

Jake nods.

"I want to hear you."

He takes a deep breath. "...okay. Okay. I will." He swallows hard.

"Thank you, beautiful." With that, Bastian pulls his head down and kisses him again, immediately sucking Jake's lower lip between his until he can bite down. Nibbles. Jake presses his face tighter against Bastian and feels his hands trail away from his cheeks to his shoulders, his ribs, his waist, never completely breaking contact until he reaches the hem of the hoodie that sits ruffled on his hips. Bastian's lips stop moving against his and he lets his jaw relax, letting Jake go briefly to tug at the fabric and slide it up his body.

"This has got to go, don't you think?" Bastian asks, not really expecting an answer as Jake pushes himself up just enough to create enough space to be stripped.

His heart flutters when he settles back down against Bastian's body, and they fit so well together. They hadn't quite gotten there the night before, Jake had stopped them before he even got his shirt off, but every pore of his skin that is in contact with Bastian's warm body is singing in harmony to the sky. He rolls his hips when Bastian's hands, back to resting on him, squeeze them tight. He exhales loudly through his parted lips. Bastian's hips swivel in response to meet him halfway and Jake knows that the look on his face is pure, unadulterated bliss.

Without being able to quite process how it happened, Jake finds himself pushed up from Bastian's torso, be it only for Bastian to have enough maneuvering to flip them around. Bastian is straddling him and holding his weight by pressing Jake's shoulders into the cushion of the couch. By instinct, Jake tilts his chin up and bares his throat for Bastian to exploit. He starts with teasingly light drags of the tip of his tongue from his earlobe to his collarbone, punctuated with the barest sharpness of his teeth grazing along the pulse points in his neck. Jake's hands rise to settle on Bastian's hips and his fingers are digging in, urging Bastian to press down on his lap, as much as physics will allow. Bastian is quiet, his breathing under control, and the only sounds that can be heard are the occasional pops when Bastian detaches his lips from Jake's skin. His pace is maddeningly slow and leaves Jake a whimpering, writhing mess, because Bastian doesn't press his hands hard enough, doesn't bite hard enough, doesn't suck bruises dark enough across his chest. Jake's brain is fizzing and keeps chanting more, more, more, and his skin demands harder, again, harder, but the words get stuck in his throat and all he can do is try to get Bastian to move and whisper a silent plea under his breath that he's not quite aware of letting out. For all he knows, this could last hours, days, weeks – he's lost track of time and the only thing he knows for sure is that he needs Bastian to move and he needs him to do so now.

Bastian pulls off and stills, the need evident under the self-control when he asks, "still alright up there?"

Jake catches himself in time to remember that Bastian won't take a nod for an answer, so he wills himself to open his eyes and lock gazes with him before he breathes out, "yes," and "please, Bastian." He shivers when he sees the fire in Bastian's black eyes in reaction to his name, and then Bastian is up, off of him, standing by the couch in less time than it takes Jake to blink in confusion.

"Don't move. I'll be right back," Bastian says with an ostentatious sweep of his eyes along the lines of Jake's body, a sly smile and the rise of an eyebrow punctuating the action when he gets to Jake's underwear, his boxers. Jake is suddenly highly aware of the need throbbing behind every beat of his heart and he isn't quite sure how he failed to notice just how much of an effect Bastian had on him. He feels incredibly small under Bastian's gaze, but before he can think twice about it, Bastian turns around as if the floor was made of dimes and walks out of his line of sight. He is painfully aware that despite the lack of physical restraints, he's not allowed to stretch, don't move, but the idea is all he can focus on. It's an insistent ringing in his ear, a moving dot behind his eyelid, an itch he can't scratch, he zeroes in on the visceral need to move and his complete inability to do so.

When Bastian comes back, Jake is in the middle of trying to breathe out every particle of air in his lungs just so that he can revel in the feeling of filling them back in. Anything to distract him from the need to move his muscles and the awareness that he can't. He looks at Bastian to find his extended hand ready to pull him up, so he considers it safe to reach out and take it. Bastian hauls him to his feet. His other hand is behind his back, Jake doesn't see what he went to get. He doesn't ask. Bastian puts an arm on the side of his neck, not pushing but absolutely not something that Jake can ignore, it is almost unbearably present, intimate, has the potential to be dangerous. Jake can feel his heartbeat pounding under Bastian's fingers where they press against his jugular and he almost goes dizzy at the sensation.

Bastian pushes. Jake staggers back, and he isn't sure whether he's supposed to stand his ground against Bastian or surrender, but Bastian keeps pushing, so he keeps walking backwards. His shoulders hit the cold wall first with a definite thud, and his head bangs suit. Bastian doesn't relent until the entirety of Jake's body is flush against the wall, as much as a human body could flatten itself and then some more. The only points of contact that he's got with Bastian's body are the solid presence of his fingers on his neck, his thumb ready to catch his air, and the way his forearm pins his shoulder against the wall. Don't move. He doesn't. Bastian doesn't let go of the pressure so Jake takes shallow breaths, he can still get air through but Bastian's hand was a promise that it was all but a guarantee that he would not be able to keep doing so.

Jake's abruptly brought back to a similar scene unfolding in his memory, although it's also unquestionably different — the day they met, the week prior, when Bastian asked him to stand against the column for his video. Jake couldn't unglue himself from the wall until Bastian nodded back at him, and a new rush of arousal shoots down his spine at the reminiscence, settles low in his stomach, strings all of his muscles out. He tries to swallow, encounters the hard presence of Bastian's hand that only serves to make that a task of its own.

He's taken out of his reverie by Bastian pressing himself flush against Jake, bodies lined up, and Bastian has to push up some to reach Jake's mouth with his. He stops a millimeter away from actually kissing him, and there is nothing for Jake to do but to whimper and melt in Bastian's hand. His knees give enough that the pressure on his throat tightens, Bastian is holding him up by the throat, finally kissing him when his fingers catch his breath. When Bastian pulls off and speaks up, it takes a moment for Jake to remember what words are and how to record their meaning properly.

"I'm going to blindfold you." No ceremony, no flowery – Bastian dives right in. "I'm going to hide your beautiful eyes, and I'm going to play with you, and maybe you'll think twice about jeopardizing my cooking next time around, what do you think?"

Jake feels like he should worry about the threat in Bastian's words that is barely hidden, but his brain sets on repeating "next time around, next time around" instead, because this means that Bastian is thinking long-term and that is delightful.

"I asked you a question, honey. I'm expecting an answer. Where did your words go?" Jake takes a shuddery breath, as much as he can under the restraint.

"Yes, please, Bastian," he tries.

His tongue feels dry, he could enunciate better, probably, lets it go. He'll worry about his enunciating when he regains the control that Bastian has taken over his body. He gets one last good look at the hunger in Bastian's eyes before Bastian finally takes his hand from behind him, lets the blindfold hang between their faces for a second, and takes his hand off of Jake's throat to effectively take his sense away. Jake breathes in sharply at the loss of pressure against his larynx. He's conscious of being putty in Bastian's hands and he wouldn't trade that feeling for the world. He's aware that Bastian knows exactly what he's doing to him and does it on purpose.

"I want you to breathe, now. Can you do that for me?" Jake hums. "Take a deep breath with me. Fill in your lungs completely. Hold the air in. Press your hands behind your back for me" Jake complies. Bastian's hands are running all over his face, tracing his cheekbones, his lips, his jaw. He moves down to his neck and very lightly runs his fingers over his pulse points, his tense tendons. He settles on his shoulders, thumbs swiping across his collarbones. "I want you to let it all go. I want you to forget everything that's on your mind. The only thing that I want you to focus on is what you're feeling. The only thing you have to worry about right now is how your body is feeling, and what I'm asking of you. I don't want you to move." Jake exhales and the tension that had accumulated that morning drips out of his muscles slowly, with every second spent breathing out. "Do you understand?"

Jake's head lowers of its own accord, he doesn't have to consciously drop his chin against his chest, this is the only logical step left to take. He breathes in and speaks up, a soft "yes, Bastian," for an answer. He focuses on Bastian's hands on his shoulders and doesn't think about stopping the shiver that runs down his spine when Bastian drags his hands lower down Jake's chest. He stops his descent momentarily to twist at Jake's nipples, rolling both of them between his thumbs and forefingers, and a deep moan forms low in Jake's chest to escape from his lips. Bastian takes a step back and drags his nails down Jake's torso until he reaches the waistband of his underwear. He hooks a finger on each side and Jake pushes his hips forward in response, just enough so that he's not completely pressed against the wall, looking to help Bastian undress him. Bastian nibbles against his skin again, and after what feels like an eternity, he finally, finally drags the fabric down Jake's legs. Jake hears the soft thud of Bastian's knees as they hit the floor in front of him and feels the light taps of Bastian's hands against his inner thighs, urging him to lift his feet so that he can discard the boxers completely then settle back and spread his legs wide. His skin lights up where Bastian presses his hands to keep his legs apart and Jake arches up, flexes the strong muscles in his thighs. Anticipation is making his blood boil, he's just waiting for Bastian to finally touch him, and he can't tell when that's going to happen, he can't do anything about it with his hands behind his back, and he knows his cock jumps at the thought.

"Well, hello there. Welcome to the party," Bastian teases with laughter tainting the hoarseness of his voice.

Jake lets out a shuddery breath and his brain is filled with please, Bastian, please, but he doesn't know if he's allowed to speak. He almost breaks when he feels the lightest touch of Bastian's fingertip down the side of his cock. He whimpers when Bastian reaches the base and wraps his fingers tightly around him, trapping him. He doesn't move, just grips, and Jake's brows knit tight. He can feel himself twitch in Bastian's hand, and the grip gets tighter — maybe he's filling out more — maybe it's a combination of both. He's shivering before long and it's clear, without Bastian having to express it out loud, that Jake does not have a say in what happens to him in this moment. Bastian hums and it's clear that he enjoys how aroused Jake is, how aroused he made him. Without releasing him, Bastian uses his free hand to flick at the tip of Jake's cock, tracing the slit with his fingertip, and a choked sob escapes Jake's lips. He doesn't notice that Bastian is picking up the precum that has started gathering until he moves up to smear it across his cheek, and he opens his mouth in surprise.

Once Bastian is fully standing again, he rearranges the position of his hand on Jake, tugs at him once, twice. Jake's arms tense and he rolls his hips to meet Bastian's hand out of reflex. Bastian stops moving right away.

"I thought I'd asked you to stay still, beautiful," Bastian speaks softly against his ear.

"Yes, Bastian."

"I want to give you what you want, handsome, but I can't do that if you don't follow my orders." Jake feels his skin erupt in goosebumps but he manages to keep his legs from giving way under him. "Will you stay still for me, now?" Bastian asks, dangerous. Jake nods. "That's right, you will. Maybe I'll have you stay quiet for me, too, unless I go too far for you. No more noises out of that beautiful mouth of yours. Think you can do that for me?"

It's a trap, Jake almost answers him out loud, he'd gotten used to speaking up when Bastian asked him. This shouldn't be too hard, though, quiet is good.

"Keep that up, you got it. You're doing great."

Bastian kisses him and there's nothing chaste about his kiss anymore. Bastian points his tongue, drags it all across Jake's mouth, probs in. Jake stays open and pliable, chases Bastian's tongue with his, presses his face to gain as much as he can. Bastian's hand starts moving against him again, insistent this time around. He's stroking, jerking with a purpose. There's a part in Jake's mind that gets a little bit scared that he's getting too close, too quickly, but he can't do anything to let Bastian know. His hands are behind his back, his legs are spread wide with Bastian's feet planted on the insides of his to keep him open, he can't roll his hips, he can't speak, and Bastian won't stop. Jake's face scrunches, he's moments away from his orgasm and he knows it, and his chest halts, he stops breathing, and —

Nothing. Bastian moves off of him so suddenly that Jake can't help but square his shoulders forward in shock, he's trembling, violent shivers rocking his body, his cock is swaying, useless between his legs. He's gasping while his brain tries to make sense of the lack of sensations and stimulation to his body, but he's not sure that anything is supposed to make sense at all.

The next thing he feels is a tiny drop of sweat coming down his ribs and just as fast as it'd left, Bastian's hand is back on his throat, pushing him relentlessly back into the wall where he'd been supposed to stay.

"Oh, I'm sorry, something you'd like to say? No? Didn't think so." Bastian truly, abruptly cuts off his air in the middle of an intake, for the first time it's not a threat anymore but a very real occurrence.

Jake's brain short-circuits, he might as well just die right there, maybe he will, he doesn't know, maybe it's okay, maybe – and Bastian releases. He gasps audibly and he knows Bastian can hear it, but he can't punish him for that noise, can he, when he's entirely responsible for it? His hand moves to cup his jaw and Jake leans in the touch as he tries to regain his thought process. Maybe he's lost it forever, for all he knows. Bastian kisses his jaw briefly before he moves down and sucks lightly at his neck. He knows better than to leave visible marks there for everyone to see.

The tip of his nose is soft against Jake's skin as he follows the lines of his neck until he reaches his shoulder, and without much more than the flick of his tongue as a warning, Bastian bites in. And he bites, let no one be mistaken, this one will show. Jake pushes into Bastian, he's arching, and he hopes that this won't count as disobeying because there is no way in which he can keep his body still under the assault.

The biting and sucking continues. Bastian is relentless, bordering on ruthless, Jake sent his head back to hit the wall with a thud a long time ago, his fingers are attempting to drill holes in his palms, and he might go insane from not being able to look at Bastian and the marks that he leaves on him, not being able to predict his next move. His brain is begging for Bastian to touch him again, to do something, and his resolve is faltering more with every new capillary breaking and blooming under Bastian's teeth. He doesn't notice right away that Bastian's creating a pattern on his chest, two steps down and one step up, the progression slow but definitely moving closer to Jake's erection. He doubts he's ever been this hard before, he's ready to bet that he's a violently dark shade of red, and he's stopped worrying about the precum dripping out of him a millennium back. Bastian is resolutely ignoring the throbbing need at the pit of Jake's stomach. His hands are running all over him, soothing the bites, toying with his nipples, pressing into his hips, sneaking between his body and the wall to pull his cheeks apart and grab handfuls of his ass. Jake can feel the wetness clinging to his blindfold and assumes he's probably let a few tears spill a while ago, but it's never bad, never something he doesn't want, so he doesn't speak up. Bastian doesn't ask, whether he'd noticed or not, and Jake is incredibly thankful for how much Bastian entrusts him.

He bites his lip when Bastian finally gets low enough on his torso to drop to his knees. The sound of his knees hitting the floor between Jake's shaking legs fills his brain and he never wants to let go of the sound. He can't help the anticipation, not anymore, even though he should know better, but Bastian is resting his cheek at the top of his thigh and he can feel the tiny pinpricks of his day-old beard catching on his skin. He moves a hand back around from where it was still kneading his ass and Jake expects a touch on his cock that never comes. Bastian starts playing with his balls, rolling them on his palm before he circles them and wraps his fingers tightly where they start, pulling ever so slightly on them, just enough that Jake's head drops and his lungs halt for a second at how over-whelmed the tug makes him feel. He doubts that he'll last long, whatever Bastian does to him next, his brain has been a second away from bursting for what feels like hours. Please, please, please, the mantra never passed his lips but never let Jake breathe. Bastian's fingers release his balls and he moves on to fondling, weighing them, and if he doesn't move on soon, Jake is positive that he will end up in a heap on the floor. The trembling in his thighs is getting almost obscene and he almost worries that Bastian will keep ignoring him and fail to catch him.

Every cell of his body thrumming with anticipation, Jake would have thought he was ready for the feeling of Bastian's warm mouth on his cock. He couldn't have been more wrong. Bastian, ever true to himself, gives him next to nothing to go by, but the way he points his tongue and runs it down the length of his erection feels like a blessing. Bastian rests his lips against the side of it before he speaks up.

"You've been so good, do you want to come, handsome?"

Jake tries to open his eyes to look at Bastian, momentarily forgetting that this is an action he can't be performing by virtue of the fabric over his eyes.

"It's okay, you can talk, I want you to answer me now," Bastian adds as his fingers come up to join his lips on the sensitive skin.

"Bastian, please," is all he can mutter out, his voice quivering.

"Ask for it." The steadiness of Bastian's voice is a perfect contrast to his in the air of the room.

"Please, Bastian... Please, can I come? I'm so close, I'm so close, please let me come," he begs, trying to keep his voice from cracking and forming into a sob.

For an answer, Bastian moves his head sideways, drags tongue and lips across Jake's flushed length and only stops when he positions his mouth at the tip. Jake thinks he might die if Bastian doesn't give him permission this very second.

"Fuck, yeah, go ahead, beautiful. Come for me, now." Bastian's swearing is the only indication that he's also starting to unravel at the seams, he's been so posed, so methodical so far, as far as Jake can tell, and before he can ponder the thought any longer, Bastian engulfs the tip of Jake's cock with his mouth, tugs his hand up the shaft until his fingers are flush with his lips and that's all he needs to burst in Bastian's mouth, one, two, three times, he loses count. His body shots forward as his orgasm washes over him and he almost topples over Bastian, folded in half that he is, with his knees giving way under him at last, and he doesn't have a choice but to take his hands off the wall to rest immediately on Bastian's shoulders if he doesn't want to fall over.

Bastian gives him time to recover while he holds his hips, helping Jake to stay upright through the waves that make his body buck and twitch several more times. It could be a second, it could be several minutes – Jake's brain is not registering, he is completely spent. After a while, Bastian pushes him up slowly so that he can get up from his position on the floor and take Jake into a warm embrace. He wraps Jake's arms around his own neck, then rubs soothing circles up and down his back before he moves to the base of his skull to detach the blindfold. Jake doesn't open his eyes right away, and Bastian covers his eyes with a hand to protect him from the blinding sun, helping him adjust to the change in brightness. He guides Jake's face into the crook of his own neck. Jake follows the guidance, breathing in the scent of Bastian's skin. He can feel another tear escaping his eyes, this one having the ability to follow a path down his cheek, and he feels his chest heave, barely manages to catch a cry before it escapes his lips. He feels Bastian's cradling hands around his skull pulling him up and away so that he can look at him.

Jake opens his eyes slowly, affected by the light shining through the windows despite Bastian trying to shield him, it's brighter than he was expecting, he squints, which has for result of letting another stray tear rolling down the soft skin of his cheek.

"Hey, hey hey. Are you alright? What's going on in there?" Bastian enquires, worry sketched into his features. He strokes Jake's face lightly, tracing his temples with his fingertips, smoothing his hair. "Jake, talk to me, sweetheart. Is everything okay?"

Jake needs to breathe in deep a few more times before he trusts his voice enough to speak. "I'm good, I... just need a minute. That... That. Was a lot. Thank you." He rests his forehead on Bastian's and keeps focusing on his breathing.

"Honeybee, you don't have to thank me. Come here. I enjoyed every bit of the way too. I just want to be what you need. Even when you almost set my kitchen on fire," he adds with a smirk and Jake blushes.

He's not sure that his face can get any redder, he doesn't need to look in the mirror to imagine what he must look like, sweaty, overwhelmed, dizzy and probably a proper amount of fucked out, but his heart flutters at Bastian's playful teasing. He hugs him tighter, and feels Bastian's arms settle around the small of his back, holding him tight and impossibly close. Bastian kisses him, he's putting all his care and love in it, that much Jake can tell, and he's content with just staying there forever if Bastian will let him. He just wants to not move, ever again if he can help it, and keep the comforting fog his mind is basking in for a long, long time. After a while, however, Bastian pulls back to look him in the eyes.

"See, I had a great time with you being blindfolded, but I really missed this, looking into your eyes. I think it might have been a crime to hide them from me for so long. I don't particularly want to go to jail, so I might have to think twice about doing that again, regardless of the divine reaction I got out of you with it," Bastian ponders out loud, as if this was perfectly normal small talk, dinner table chit chat. "Want to get back in bed, lovely? I know I do."

Jake hums in response, he's back in his wordless world and he's happy to stay in there for as long as he can. He lets Bastian take his hand and walk them both back to his bedroom, and Bastian takes a minute to rearrange the covers and pillows to make sure it's tidy and comfortable enough to tuck Jake in. He pats down his side of the mattress to invite Jake back in and wraps the blankets around him. The mattress is incredibly comfortable, absolutely perfect, and the sheets are so soft around his body — he couldn't dream of anything better, apart from maybe Bastian joining him under the covers.

"I'm going to go get you some water, alright? I'll be right back, gorgeous. Don't miss me too much." Jake hums, it's becoming a habit, and settles more comfortably, burying his face in Bastian's pillow and taking in its comforting scent. He can't decide whether he prefers this or the scent of Bastian's skin, when he hides his face in the crook of his neck and takes in the dip of his collarbone.

Bastian comes back to set the tall glass of cold water to the bedside table, and Jake cracks an eye open at the noise. The glass is already starting to sweat at the difference in temperature between the water and the air. Bastian slides in bed and cuddles right up behind Jake once he gets under the duvet. He throws a leg over Jake's hip and an arm over his ribcage, holding in his chest and pulling Jake close against him. The feeling of being so completely surrounded by Bastian makes Jake feel so at peace, everything is right in the world and he might be invincible if he manages to stay by Bastian's side a while longer. He thinks of the weight of Bastian's leg on his body, how tightly his arm is holding him. Bastian snakes an arm under his head, providing him with a makeshift pillow, and the way that he lays his head down on Bastian's upper arm allows Bastian to reach over and tangle his fingers in Jake's hair. Everything is just right, everything is soothing, and his breathing eventually slows down on par with his heartbeat – Jake falls asleep most naturally. The last legible thought that makes his way through his brain is about how he truly feels at home for the first time since he moved to New York.

Chapter Eight

*J*ake stirs awake a bit later that afternoon by soft music filling the open space of Bastian's bedroom. He's not entirely aware of what it is but it's soothing, it's relaxing, and he's cuddled up against Bastian – he wishes he would never have to move again. He tightens his arms around Bastian's body. He vaguely remembers falling asleep with Bastian holding him, he's not sure when they ended up facing each other, but he's not about to complain.

"Good morning, Jacob, if it isn't the loveliest girl in the place," Bastian sing-songs at him.

Jake feels his cheeks heat up and hides his face against Bastian's chest. He can get used to Bastian serenading him with his own songs when he wakes up. And maybe he can pretend that how Vee feels about Cleo is how Bastian feels about him, which makes Heaven on Earth that much better still. He feels Bastian's fingers through his hair and sighs happily into his skin.

"We have to get up, we've got shows to put on today, sadly." Jake groans at Bastian's words. "I know, mi cielo, I don't want to get up either."

Bastian brings his hand up to stroke through his hair and truly, it's probably a crime for them not to have weekends, per se. He's got a few questions running through his mind for Bastian — what time is it, what does mi cielo mean, do we really have to go, how long does it take to get to the theatres, what are we listening to, are we insane? — but he would rather stay quiet and listen to Bastian's heartbeat instead of asking them. Bastian stays immobile, save for his fingers on Jake's skull, for another while, Jake doesn't keep track of time. Eventually, Bastian's hands move to Jake's shoulders, tugging him up. Jake pushes himself up a bit from Bastian's torso, just enough to be able to look him in the eyes, his eyebrows raising in question.

"Why is your face so far from my face? I want to kiss you. I like doing that, a lot, and we didn't do enough of it this morning," Bastian speaks out, helping Jake to scramble up his body.

Jake pauses just before he lets his lips get in contact with Bastian's. "Is that a complaint? I was under the impression that you had a rather good time this morning, doing whatever you wanted with me. You could have kissed me more, you know," he replies with a tentatively teasing tone.

"Well, I was sort of preoccupied, this morning. Had other things on my mind. Doesn't mean I can't use your mouth for something better and make up for it now, though."

With that, he rests his hand on Jake's jaw, cradling his head, and pulls him in for a languid kiss. As new as kissing him feels, Jake also revels in how easy it is to be with Bastian. He feels the hand that Bastian still had on his shoulder trail down to brush his ribs and rest on his waist, their mouths never parting. Bastian softly rolls them over to the other side of the bed and settles atop Jake. He pulls back just enough to hold himself up on one arm and stroke the side of Jake's face with the other, the rest of their bodies lined up.

"Yeah, you know what, it might have to be a while before I blindfold you again. I'm not sure if all the fun I had was worth denying me the ability to look into your eyes. Sorry?"

A faint rose blush colors Jake's cheeks at that, he's never been known to take compliments well. Not that he doesn't love them, far from it – he just doesn't know what to say. He looks down, a smile lifting the corners of his lips as he mumbles a quiet "thank you." Almost immediately, Bastian's hand on his cheeks moves below his jaw and lifts his head back up, insisting on Jake to look right back at him again. Bastian dips his head again without breaking eye contact and Jake expects a kiss that doesn't come, not right away, and it's clear that Bastian likes to find out all the ways in which he can get a reaction out of Jake. Jake frowns before he tilts his head up, holding Bastian's gaze this time, and takes it upon himself to kiss Bastian, who chuckles at Jake taking the lead. Jake snakes his arms around Bastian's waist and holds onto his hips, pressing his fingertips into the soft flesh. It's Bastian's turn to groans against his mouth.

"Don't start something you can't finish, mi cielo," Bastian warns him – which only serves to encourage him.

"I wouldn't dare," Jake breathes out as he grabs on tighter.

"I thought you'd be more interested in taking it easy after this morning, no?" Bastian asks. And yeah, maybe he could, he doesn't think he's ready for another round right then and there, only a few hours later. But it's not really fair for Bastian if he doesn't even attempt to reciprocate, is it?

"I… don't want to make you feel left out," Jake confesses.

"You don't need to take care of me, Jake. I can do that on my own. We can just relax, that's okay."

"I want to do what you want too, you've just been doing everything for me this whole time. I want to take care of you, too," he explains, and kisses Bastian again.

He trails his hands down from Bastian's waist to run them over Bastian's underwear. Bastian pulls away a moment later, and he's not panting quite yet but his breathing is definitely not calm.

"Alright, alright, you don't sound like someone who wants to take it easy, now, do you?" Jake was far from being subtle but he still blushes in response at being called out.

"Well, what time is it? I know I took a bath this morning, but I'm sure I could handle showering again," he tries, hoping that the implication is clear as Bastian turns his head to look at the clock on the wall above Jake.

"It's just past two. I guess we would have time, yeah, that's a grand idea. I know I can definitely use a shower," Bastian replies and there's a glint in his eye that wasn't there before. "Come on, let's go. You can grab my ass all you want once we get the water running," he adds with a meaningful move of his head in the general direction of Jake's hands on him, effectively causing him to stop and blush furiously, once more.

Bastian gets up from his position on Jake's body and they head down together through the apartment to the bathroom.

Whereas Jake hadn't bothered putting clothes back on after their morning activities, Bastian for his part had never gotten his off, and that is something to which Jake wants to remedy in the briefest delays. He leans against the counter and watches as Bastian finds towels and sets them out, turns on the water, tests the temperature. He looks back at Jake once it's ready to go, playful smile on his lips.

"You just going to stand there and watch? And here I was under the impression that you wanted to, how'd you say, take care of me? Your words, not mine, honeybee," Bastian teases and beckons him closer. "Come on over, we don't want to waste water."

Jake follows and just when he reaches out to grab Bastian's hand, Bastian pulls on his arm and swiftly backs him up against the wall next to the shower. He can already feel the steam rising in the air. Not all of it is strictly due to the water. Bastian presses himself flush against Jake and looks intently at his neck as he trails a finger down the pulsing vein he finds there.

"Or at least… we don't want to waste too much of it."

Jake is melting, already, his knees not quite as strong as they should be. This wall thing that Bastian does is quickly becoming one of his favorite things and he can tell that it has the potential to become a problem for him. Or the opposite of one, depending on the point of view. He sucks in a sharp breath when Bastian's hand trails back up to cup his jaw.

"And so, I'm thinking, if we don't want to waste water, why am I still wearing clothes?" Bastian tilts his head down and kisses him, pushing himself up on his toes and teasingly swiveling his hips as he does so, all but slow-dancing with Jake, as much as that's possible with him absolutely pinned against the wall and somewhat unable to move. "Don't be scared, you can touch me, where did your assertiveness go?"

Jake groans against Bastian's mouth and Bastian responds by taking his hands, one by one, placing them at the small of his back enticingly. He wraps his own arms around Jake's neck and slowly peels him off from the wall to turn their bodies towards the shower. He doesn't stop kissing him, he doesn't need to ask a third time for Jake to finally take handfuls of his ass and he rolls his hips seductively in response to Jake's fingers digging in, pulling him up and close and flush through the fabric. Jake kneads for a second, getting the feel of it, somewhat dizzy at the fact that Bastian is letting – no, wants him to do this, and then he takes a hold of the waistband of Bastian's underwear and slides it down his legs as much as he can without having to let go of the kiss – Bastian can shrug them off the rest of the way. He's not entirely sure where to go next, what to do, but Bastian knows that he'd rather not be the one calling the shots so he takes care of that for him.

Jake watches as Bastian slides the shower door open and the steam engulfs him. His stare is ravenous when he asks Jake to follow him, and Jake wants nothing more than to do everything Bastian wants and asks of him. He shivers when he steps in and Bastian runs his hands up and down Jake's arms, contemplating.

"One day, mi cielo, I'm going to find out if you're strong enough to pick me up." Jake's brain hatches onto the one day. "You're strong enough for that, aren't you?" Bastian asks with a hand on his jaw.

"I might be? Maybe?" He replies.

"I'll find out eventually. In the meantime, I've got other ideas," he trails off and takes a last step or two into the shower, resting his back against the tiles and gently pulling Jake's head with him.

Jake follows and rests both hands on Bastian's hips, crowding him in, and he kisses him. Bastian reciprocates right away – if he's taken aback by Jake's audacity, he doesn't let it show. Jake puts everything he's got in the kiss, wants Bastian to know he means it, that he'd probably do anything Bastian asked him to do if it only made him feel good. Before long, he feels the fingers in his curls, dragging up and pulling, pulling, pulling, he's got no choice but to let go of Bastian's lips and follow his hand, effectively baring his throat. Bastian attacks instantly, he licks a stripe down his jaw and nibbles lightly at Jake's pulse points.

"How would you feel about getting on your knees for me, huh, honeybee?"

Jake moans at that, he couldn't keep that one in if he tried. He opens his eyes to get lost in the lust and desire he sees in Bastian's, and as graciously as he can make it, sinks down in front of Bastian.

"I like your hands, I want them on me, look at me, Jacob," Bastian directs him. He's still got a hand in his hair, he's stroking Jake's cheek with the other, tapping on the side of his jaw, open up .

Jake uses a hand to feel up as much of Bastian's body as he can, and with the other wraps slender fingers around Bastian's length. They lock eyes and without waiting any longer, Jake uses his tongue to tease at the tip of Bastian's cock. He feels the pressure on his scalp tighten almost instantly. Bastian rolls his hips slowly, leisurely, doesn't waste time. Jake can't blame him, he's probably been fizzing with arousal since the morning, so he doesn't want to tease any more than he has to. He wraps his lips around Bastian as he starts moving his hand up and down the shaft, he hollows his cheeks and swirls his tongue.

"You look too pretty like this for me, pretty eyes, you're good at this," Bastian speaks.

Jake relaxes his mouth as best he can and closes his eyes, it's easier with the water crashing around them. He lets Bastian take the lead, lets him hold his head where he wants it, lets him fuck into his hand and his mouth – he wants to be good for him, wants Bastian to take whatever he needs that Jake can give him. He bobs his head slowly, wants to make Bastian last.

"You feel so good, you like being good for me, don't you?" Jake hums in response and Bastian moans, his voice deep. "Your cheeks are all flushed for me, your mouth is so warm, is this what you had in mind? Is this what you wanted?"

Jake can't answer, not now, so he moves his wrist, twist on the upstroke, shows Bastian that yes, he wants this, he likes this, he doesn't have to think and this is good. The hand that he had roaming across Bastian's abs and his thighs comes back around and it's a feather-light touch at the sensitive skin of Bastian's balls before he fondles them, trying his best to give Bastian what he knows feels so good for him. If he's to judge by the whimpers coming out above him and the way that Bastian's movements become a bit rougher, a bit shorter, more erratic, he's doing alright.

"Jacob, come up here, please come up here," Bastian pleads. He moves off of him, confused, but doesn't question and doesn't stop his hands, follows the tugs of Bastian's hands at his shoulders. "Don't stop, and kiss me, look at me, I want my mouth on yours when I come," he pants.

Jake only needs a quick look into Bastian's eyes to see the undiluted want in his irises and he wants to get drunk on that look. He pulls him in right away and he tries kissing him, it's messy, he's breathing hard, unraveling, and Jake doesn't stop, doesn't slow, kisses Bastian as best he can while working his hand on him until Bastian's breath stops dead in its tracks and his shoulders hunch forward drastically, resting hard against Jake's chest, Bastian spills in his hand, on his thigh. He rests his head on Jake's shoulder and takes deep breaths for a while before he can function properly again.

"How did I get so lucky?" Bastian asks, he chuckles. Jake might easily be falling and he doesn't want to stop himself from doing so, not at all.

"I feel like I should be the one asking that," Jake replies.

He cocks an eyebrow up and without breaking eye contact with Bastian, brings his hand up to his mouth and licks his fingers clean before the shower takes it all away from him. Bastian looks at him, half highly interested and half in utter disbelief, he clearly wasn't expecting that. He whimpers a soft "oh, cielo," Jake revels in having the ability to make him melt, too, and Bastian's stare is back to ravenous in an instant. Bastian wastes no time in kissing him and stealing his own taste from Jake's mouth. He flips them around, takes the lead back – as if he'd ever really given it away – and pushes himself against Jake again. Jake wraps his arms around Bastian, holds him tight, holds him close until Bastian pulls off reluctantly.

"That's a lot of wasted water, let's get this shower going, we got to clean you up," he speaks and reaches for a bottle.

The rest of the afternoon is spent getting ready, they do both have a show that evening. They eat a quick something, get on the train, and Bastian wants to accompany him all the way to the Lewinsky until Jake reminds him that it might be better if they keep this, whatever they have, a bit on the down low for a little while.

The second he's on his own again, the thought of going back home to Caleb assails him. He can't keep this up, it's not fair, and he really doesn't want to be that guy – he'll break up with him as soon as he gets home, he needs to do this now or he never will, and he doesn't let himself second-guess. He goes straight to his dressing room, avoids small talk as much as he can, and goes through the show, auto-pilot. He turns all the switches in his brain off, off, off.

Next thing he knows for sure, he's unlocking the door of his apartment. He's barely noticed the commute home, he didn't stage door. The show went well, it wasn't his best, but it was alright. His brain was full of two things: the wonderful twenty four hours he'd just spent in Bastian's incredible company, which is saturated with more memories than anyone would need to get distracted, and the knowledge that his time with Caleb, as an item, as a couple, is coming to an end. He can see light filtering through the crack at the bottom of Caleb's bedroom door. He's home, and Jake can't possibly delay this any further. He takes his shoes off and takes a deep breath before crossing the apartment in a few long strides.

He pushes the door open to find Caleb talking on the phone, and everything in his tone of voice screams concern. He's facing away from the door – Jake clears his throat. The reaction that he gets from him turning around feels borrowed straight out of a Hollywood drama as he brings down the phone from his ear and his eyes widen in shock.

"He just walked in. Never mind. I'll call you later," he says in the device before he completely discards it. "Jake? Oh my god, where the fuck have you been? You've been gone... I don't even know how long! I came home and you weren't here, you never came home, did you even go to work? Why didn't you pick up your phone? I've been trying to call you since last night!" He speaks loudly at Jake – part relief, part stress, part boiling anger.

Jake expected that much, but it doesn't make him cringe any less. He could have been more considerate and let him know he wasn't coming home once Bastian decided to keep him over, but what would he even have said? Hey, sorry, went on a date, don't expect me home tonight? Or this morning, oh, I slept over at this other guy's place, he made me breakfast and we fucked before we went to work, of course not.

"I'm sorry. Caleb… we need to talk."

And just like that, his face falls, and all fight is gone from his body. It's eerie, it almost feels like he knows just what's about to come out of Jake's mouth. A soft "oh" falls from his lips as his shoulders slump.

"We… I can't keep doing this. This isn't news for you, we don't… what we had, we don't have it anymore, and it's been a while since it's been gone, you know that as much as I do. This isn't going anywhere, Caleb, what's the point of pretending?" Jake runs his hands through his hair nervously, ruffling his curls. "We're lying to everyone around us, they all think we're roommates, and I can't blame them – maybe that's what we should have been from the start. We're lying to each other, too, and I don't think it's fair for either of us to keep this up." The words tumble out of his mouth once he starts. "This isn't what I want. I'm sorry, I can't keep doing… whatever it is that we're doing. I can't do this," he adds, looking at the floor. He can't bear looking at Caleb's face right now and risk seeing the pain, the disappointment, the anger or the resignation he might have caused. He knows he deserves the guilt but he'll avoid it as much as he can.

"There… there isn't anything I can do, is there? I can't say I didn't see that coming, I'll be honest…" Caleb trails off.

"I'm sorry. I wish it wasn't like this, but it is, and no, I don't think anything can or should be done about this. I'll just… take the room everyone already thinks is mine until we can figure that out."

He's about to turn around and do just that when Caleb gets ahold of his arm, resulting in Jake looking his way and seeing his eyes well up just a bit under the frown on his features.

"Jacob... I did love you, you know. I don't know when that stopped being true, but it wasn't all pretend and I want you to know that."

With that, he tugs on his arm tentatively, yet firmly, and pulls Jake in towards him. He brings his hand to Jake's cheek and kisses him. Jake's brows furrow and he's not sure why he doesn't pull off right away, maybe he's too stunned − even though he does eventually, pushing Caleb away by his shoulders.

"I don't know where that came from. Sorry. One last time for the books, I guess. Just..." On that, Caleb pushes past Jake and leaves, the bedroom, the apartment, he's just gone, not without Jake seeing a silent sob shake his body.

By all standards, this probably went a lot better than Jake would have expected or anticipated, but he feels entirely inadequate, and not at home at all. He's stunned, he feels strangely empty, somewhat guilty, and it would have probably been easier to process if Caleb had been mad at him or upset at all. He could process a screaming match, he could defend himself but this, this silence, this resignation − this just doesn't make sense to him, he should have gotten some type of reaction, right? The fact that Caleb didn't even try to keep him sits uncomfortably with him. Shouldn't he have tried to prevent Jake from doing this to him? Shouldn't he have argued, tried to save it, say it was his fault and that he was going to change, for Jake, for them? Breakups were messy, and this felt like the opposite of messy. He turns around, looks around the room, their room, Caleb's room, he doesn't know what to do with himself. This doesn't feel right. And now, what? Where is he going to go, what's he going to do? He doesn't want to stay here, even though they've got the other room, the last thing he wants to do is to keep living with Caleb, be it only to keep from having to bounce from the theatre, to his boy− ex-boyfriend's, to Bastian's...

Bastian.

Yeah, he really doesn't want to explain that one to Caleb. He hadn't thought this through at all, had only thought of the second bedroom, the stage prop bedroom, and he wants nothing to do with it, but what is he supposed to do now? His entire life is in this apartment, everything he owns, and Caleb isn't gone forever that's for sure, he'll be back eventually and Jake doesn't want to be here for that but he's got nowhere to go.

He pulls out his phone, and sees that the battery is completely flat. Well, that explains why he didn't pick up Caleb's calls, at least. He scrambles and finds the charger, he's on autopilot, sits on the floor while he waits for the screen to light up. White noise all over his brain, everything is blank.

After what could have been days, months, years, the screen pops, bright white, and it starts buzzing, 1 missed call, 2 missed calls, 3, 4, 5. The voicemail icon pops up and he doesn't have it in himself to try and listen. He doesn't want the icon bugging him, so he calls his voicemail, white noise, composes his password, white noise, deletes them without a second thought, white noise. If it was something important, if it wasn't Caleb, they'll call him back. He'll take the risk.

He starts going through his contact list, thinks about going down to L to find Juniper, because she'll understand, she'll know what to do, and what other option has he got anyways? But another name jumps at him once he reaches hers and he presses it, refusing to think that maybe he shouldn't.

"Hello."

"It's over. I ended things with him."

"I… what? Jacob, is that you?"

"Yeah. Yes, Bastian, and I don't know what to do, I didn't think this through, didn't plan it – I broke up with Caleb, he's gone, I don't know where he is and I don't know what to do, I don't even know why I called you–" The white noise has made place to a storm he doesn't quite know how to contain.

"Hey. Hey, listen to me." Bastian's voice is grounding against the whirlwind that's just taken off in his brain. "Come over here. Grab a change of clothes for a couple days, get in a cab, or on the train, get over here. You're not spending the night at your apartment. I'm not leaving you alone with this. Come over here."

"Bastian, I can't, I can't accept this, you don't have to do this for me?" It's not really a question but it sounds both surprised and hopeful, especially after the tirade he's just blurted where every word tried to come in before the last one was done pronouncing. He knows he wants to go, but he really, really doesn't want to be a weight dragging Bastian back, especially since they've both got two shows to go through tomorrow.

"I'm not asking you whether you want to stay or come over. I'm not giving you that choice, not right now, not in this situation. I'm telling you. Listen to me. Pack something. And come here."

And, well, that's not something he can really argue. "You're not doing this out of pity, are you?" He asks, miserable, his voice small and barely above a whisper..

"No. I'd have wished for you to be here anyways, but now it's completely out of the question for you to spend the night anywhere but in my bed, so please, mi cielo. Get yourself here before I go and get you myself. Yeah?"

He pauses for a quick minute, just enough to make sense of his thoughts again. "Yeah... Bastian?"

"What is it, honey?"

"You keep calling me 'mi cielo'... what does that mean?"

"Oh, pretty eyes. It doesn't translate that well, it's much less endearing in English. It means 'my sky.' Because your eyes are the color of the sky, and that's all I can think about anytime I look at you. You have no idea. Not in the slightest."

Jake smiles at his phone – how can he not? And maybe he's always going to worry that Bastian is offering out of pity, but he's offered good arguments against that case, and he's been pretty clear on what he expected from Jake, so he murmurs a soft "okay" for Bastian.

They're both quiet for a moment before Bastian speaks up again. "Jacob? I'll send you a message with my address, okay? Will you call a cab? I don't want to wait longer than I have to."

Jake hums in response. "Okay. I'll see you soon," he utters, and a swarm of butterflies takes over the hurricane of thoughts he just experienced as fast as the storm had started.

When Jake gets to his apartment later that evening, Bastian immediately brings his bag to his room and proceeds to holding onto Jake tightly with the intent of never letting him go.

Chapter Nine

In some regards, it's not stranger than normal, the amount of thoughts swirling and crashing around Bastian's brain, breaking themselves up on the walls of his skull, as he pulls Jake in. He keeps him there. But in others, the content of the hurricane are slightly different.

He hopes it wasn't obvious, the shock and surprise he felt when he picked up Jake's phone call. He knows his thought process stuttered at his words, but he immediately (he hopes) decided that questions could wait, because if the distress he could hear was any indication, questioning would have only made it worse, so he pushed that back and focused on getting Jake safe and sound to his place.

Bastian spends the following half hour pacing his apartment. He's all the more thankful for their date of twenty-four hours prior for having given him an excuse to ensure that his space was to be spotless. All he has to do while he wait for Jake this time around is folding some clothes and putting the remains of his late dinner away. He's fidgety by the time he hears the knock on the door but doesn't waste a second when he strides across the floor.

Jake looks so disheveled, so haggard when Bastian opens the door that he immediately pulls him in. He takes the bag from his shoulder, drops it by the side of his bed and cradles Jake in his embrace as best he can. Jake wraps his arms around Bastian's neck, hides his face in the gap he creates between the crook of his own elbow and that of Bastian's warm skin, and he lets a single, shuddering, shattering sob escape him. Whether by instinct or by conscious will, he's not sure, Bastian weaves a hand up Jake's broad back and into the hair at the nape of his neck, his other arm snaking tightly around Jake's waist, holding him in close. He whispers sweet nothings against Jake's skin for a minute and strokes his hair, attempting to convey with his actions that Jake is fine, Bastian isn't mad, he's everything but, he just wants to be a grounding presence for Jake, whatever that entails and whatever that might mean.

"Cielo, let's get you into bed, yeah? There's a lot going on in here, isn't there?" Bastian asks, gently tapping his fingers against Jake's skull. Jake nodded in response.

Jake pulls off and the bloodshot eyes with which Bastian is met are enough to shatter his heart in a million pieces, but the hope and trust that he reads when Jake nods puts him back together just as instantly.

Bastian slowly backs out towards his bed, pulling Jake in with him, only parting to turn around and get his bed ready, dragging the covers aside to allow Jake in. He faces him again only to find that Jake hadn't moved, be it only to let his head drop in defeat, but he's not sobbing, so maybe this is going to be okay. Bastian reaches out and brings a hand to cup the side of Jake's face, silently encouraging him to look him in the eyes. The brightness of his irises amidst the tears that threaten to spill make Bastian's heart swell noticeably in his chest and he wants nothing more than to curse whomever brought his cielo this much heartache. He strokes his thumb across Jake's cheekbone, a frown forming between his brows.

"Can I kiss you?" He asks, and maybe it's odd, maybe he shouldn't request that when Jake is so clearly upset, but he can't think of a single other thing he could be doing to try and show Jake that he's not alone in this.

Jake replies by ducking his head and resting his forehead against Bastian's, breathing him in for a second or two before so let their lips graze. He hatches back onto Bastian right away, Bastian feels the tears that roll down Jake's cheeks on his own skin and wraps his arms around Jake's waist, again, maybe he's never going to have enough of this. He lets his hands roam across the soft expanse of Jake's lower back before he tugs at the hem, never quite breaking the kiss. Jake lifts his arms in response almost instantly, and it's all Bastian needs to drag the fabric up Jake's body. He's unhurried, doesn't have anything in mind but Jake's comfort, he hasn't forgotten that Jake seems the type who sleeps without a shirt on. He drapes the fabric across Jake's bag that's on the floor not far from them, cups Jake's face again with one hand as he rests the other on his hip, thumb on the warm skin, palm on the denim.

"Can I? Is this okay?" Bastian asks – the last thing he wants is for any of his actions to feel overwhelming, but jeans are not the most comfortable, especially not under covers.

A soft "please?" falls from Jake's lips and Bastian, caring as ever, gently unbuttons his jeans and slowly moves Jake around so that he can lay down. He toes his socks off, immediately rolls off and onto his stomach, in the middle of the bed, bringing his arms up under the pillow. "Bastian?" he inquires.

"What is it?"

"Can I… can you give me a massage? I need something to focus on… that's not what's in my brain. Please?" He sounds so hesitant, so adamant for asking, but of course Bastian can indulge – he wouldn't dream of not giving Jake what he needs in that moment.

"Of course. I like it when you use your words, you know that, beautiful. Give me just a second, yeah?"

He strips to Jake's level quickly, letting his clothes in a heap in the corner, but there's nothing awkward or inadequate, this feels intimate if anything –it's very, very good. He runs the pads of his fingers across Jake's shoulder blades before to settle, straddling him, his knees caging Jake's hips. He doesn't do much more than lightly running his hands across every bit of skin he can find, lingering on the freckles he finds – Jake is beautiful, absolutely stunning, Bastian isn't sure that he knows that about himself – before he drums lightly on the tense muscles atop his shoulders.

"Arms by your side, honey, if you want to relax. Pillow under your forehead so you can breathe, give me your arms," Bastian commands as he reaches to pull on Jake's biceps once he's arranged his head comfortably, to help reposition him. "Take a deep breath for me. Can you do that? Breathe in slowly, and when you let it out, focus on my hands on you. I don't want you to think of anything else, not tonight."

Bastian can already feel some tension escape from under Jake's skin when he lets the air out of his lungs. He lets himself melt into the mattress, and maybe he's not quite limbless yet but Bastian will make it a personal challenge to bring him just there. He kneads at the muscles in Jake's shoulders until he hears stifled moans, then moves on to his neck, his arms, his back, and his hands start hurting but he refuses to care because Jake is there, and he needs him, so he doesn't stop. He gets lost in his own thoughts eventually and it could have lasted a minute or an hour, but when he comes back to himself, Jake is absolutely pliant under him, his head lolling to the move-ments of his hands and he doesn't look to Bastian like a storm is still on the horizon. It's passed, for now; Bastian slows his movements and slowly bends down to press his body against Jake's and his lips to the back of his neck.

"Are you feeling better?" Bastian whispers. He gets a groan in response and that's more than enough. "Want to go to bed, gorgeous? Take it easy? I want you to stay relaxed. Can you do that for me?"

Jake is well enough out of it to take several seconds more than strictly warranted before he can get his mind around nodding. Bastian moves off of him and settles under the covers, bringing them around to cover Jake as well. To that, Jake turns his head to the side, resting on the edge of the pillow – he doesn't open his eyes but Bastian feels his arm extending, his hand reaching out to find his own, and he all but latches onto Jake, holding him as close as physics will allow, rests his lips on his forehead. They fall asleep like this,

Jake tucking himself into Bastian's presence and Bastian covering him as the most comforting of blankets.

Chapter Ten

*W*hen he wakes, Jake needs a moment to remember where he is. Who's with him. Why he's there. He feels fidgety, restless, almost instantly, and then everything hits him like a freight train and he opens his eyes in shock. He sees Bastian's face a few inches away from his, and while part of him wants to close his eyes and drift away in his embrace, he also feels a surge of guilt that he did this to Bastian, he should have told him about Caleb but he really didn't want to, and now Bastian's probably going to feel betrayed, or mad at him, or hurt, and Jake really can't handle that thought so he gently pulls himself out of under Bastian's limbs and goes to the bathroom before Bastian has a chance to wake up.

Bastian finds him an undetermined amount of time later, sitting on the bathroom floor, holding on to his knees tightly, and shivering – he hadn't bothered putting on a shirt or pants, and the tile floor is frankly freezing against his skin but he doesn't know that he deserves the feeling of Bastian's skin against his and the warmth of the blankets around them both. Jake looks up when the door opens, his gaze follows Bastian as he crouches down to kneel by his side. Bastian takes his hand.

"Do you have the habit of starting your day by sitting on cold tile for a while? Because I think we should have talked about it before I woke up wondering where you'd gone off to and if I had upset you…" Bastian trails off, but there isn't a hint of malice in his eyes when he makes eye contact with Jake.

Jake's not sure how Bastian could have upset him, he's been nothing short of wonderful to him. "You're not mad at me?"

"I've got no reason to be mad at you. Want to come back to bed now? I mean, nothing against the bathroom but I'd rather be comfortable and warm with you than cold and miserable down here. What do you think?" It's not really a question, Bastian takes his hand as he rises, pulls him upright and into a tight hug. "You're so cold, cielo, we can't have that," Bastian murmurs as he runs his hands all over the tight skin of Jake's back, soothing the shivers and the goosebumps as he does so.

He slowly walks him back towards the bedroom, Jake's reticence's melting away with every step. He sits back at Bastian's nudges and Bastian picks up the comforter from behind Jake to engulf him with it. He hooks a fingertip under Jake's chin so that he'll look up at him and scourges his eyes for any sign of discomfort when he dips down to press a kiss to his lips. Jake leans into it, Bastian is convincing. He wants to stop thinking.

"If I leave you here, am I going to find you again when I come back with coffee, or are you going to disappear on me?"

"I'll stay," Jake answers truthfully. It's not like he's got somewhere else to go anyways.

"Okay. I'm out of milk, so I'm going to go down to the corner store and I'll get you something from there. I don't want you to leave the apartment, alright?"

Yeah, alright. He'll readdress when it's time to go to the theatre, but for now, it's early, the matinee isn't until two, he's okay. He watches in a daze as Bastian dresses himself up and kisses him once more before he grabs his keys, his wallet, leaves, resigned.

Jake feels strangely empty when Bastian is gone. Was he that used to being around him already? If he had to rationalize, he'd say that it was really just so easy to let him in, to let him take over the white noise crowding his thoughts, let him take care of him. Maybe it was all happening way too fast, but he wouldn't have been able to stop it if he tried – that much he does know about himself.

He lets himself fall to the side, curled up with the blankets hugging him and he feels strangely comfortable, probably more than he's been in months of pretending and sleeping in Caleb's bed. This is good. Everything smells of Bastian, the pillows, the sheets, the room, the air, and so he focuses on that and tries his best to etch the feeling in his memory as best he can, knowing full well that you can't just conjure up scents but knowing that he will associate this one with this specific moment whenever he catches it. He feels small. He doesn't want to go to the theatre. I don't want you to leave the apartment, Bastian had said, and well. He doesn't want to either.

He hears it first, the soft clicking of the doorknob when the key is worked in, the soft padding of Bastian stepping onto the mat, the closing of the door behind him. He doesn't open his eyes. He smells it, then, the aroma of coffee filling in the room, the way that Bastian's skin has caught on the summer air. He breathes in. He feels it, next, when Bastian sits down on the edge of his bed, finds his hand and untangles it from the fabric of the comforter. Opens his fingers, Jake complies, he's pliant. The firm press of metal against his skin, he opens his eyes in surprise, looks down, and Bastian is holding a key to his palm, closes Jake's fingers over it, his own over them.

"Maybe we should talk about last night before long, but I have a feeling you won't be wanting to go to your apartment much in the upcoming days, so this one is for you. I want you to come here as much as you need. Even if we haven't planned it. Even if I don't expect you. Even if I'm still somewhere on Broadway when you're done and we can't make the trip together. Use this, okay, Jacob?"

It takes everything in Jake's being to tear his eyes from Bastian's hand on his. He raises his head from the pillows against which he'd fallen and cranes his neck to look at Bastian properly, pushing himself up on his elbow as he does so.

"Bastian, I don't know what to say... are you sure?" He asks, disbelief coloring his tone. He wants to accept it, God does he want to, but not if Bastian doesn't really mean it.

"Of course I am. I wouldn't offer if I wasn't. Will you keep coming home to me?"

"Okay. Yeah, I will, if you'll have me."

"Amazing!" Bastian exclaims, and happily reaches out to grab the coffee cups he's left on the bedside table.

Jake sits up, cross-legged with Bastian's blanket pooling around his hips, facing Bastian. He inhales the aroma and revels in the warmth emanating from the cup into the skin of his fingers, his palms. A soft smile paints itself on his face and he exhales slowly. He's not cold.

"Thank you, for this," he whispers. It's unclear whether he's referring to the key, the coffee, the offer, it could mean everything so he leaves it at that.

"You're welcome. I'm glad you're here, you know. This isn't just good for you, cielo, maybe one day you'll believe me." Jake takes a sip. "Will you tell me what happened last night?"

He gulps it down. "Uh... what do you want to know?"

"Who is 'him'?"

"Oh, um... Caleb. We dated... for a while. Everyone thinks we're roommates. We have a two-bedroom apartment, so people don't ask."

"I see. How long were you with him?"

"Uh, a couple months? It was around the same time we opened with Autumn Spell. It kind of just happened, but Bastian, I don't know why I didn't do it before, we shouldn't have been together this long. It wasn't bad, it just was... nothing?"

"Hey, it's okay. You did what felt right at the time it happened, you made the decisions that made sense then. I'm not judging that, honey. But you've grown, and you've changed, and decisions from a year ago might not be what you need now. And I can't blame you for that, can I?" Bastian rests his coffee back on the bedside table, picks Jake's out of his hands to offer it the same treatment, and grabs both of Jake's hands in his own. "You've changed and he's not what you need anymore and I won't have you be with someone who can only stifle your talent and your worth. I'm not having you stay with someone who can't give you what you need, handsome, now can I?"

He relocates both of Jake's wrists between one set of fingers and, with the hand that he has now freed, lightly grazes at Jake's neck. Jake feels a completely different shiver down his spine because the hidden meaning of that sentence is, well, not very well hidden. He lifts his chin by instinct. It might be counter-intuitive to offer yourself up like this but Jake doesn't care about other people's instincts, he only cares about his and how they react to Bastian's.

"I'd rather you have the ability to be authentic here rather than being held back with someone who can't give you this, cielo. Don't you agree?"

Jake swallows hard. He lets a shaky breath escape through his parted lips. He nods.

"Your words, honey. This early and you're already drifting, huh? What am I going to do with you?" Bastian teases and he's not helping at all. Jake breathes.

"I'm sorry. I agree. I don't know. I'm sorry I didn't tell you before, I should have." He doesn't know how he crossed paths with Bastian, how he was lucky enough to meet someone who had the ability to shut him down so efficiently and exquisitely.

"No apologies for last night. You're here now and that's what I care about. As for what I want to do… Maybe I can start with this," Bastian begins, and he moves himself around so that he's facing Jake, sitting on his haunches.

He kisses him and Jake flies away.

He's insistent, both of his hands now cradling Jake's head as he presses his lips against Jake's, holding him in place – not that Jake wouldn't be right there if he had a choice, but the drive with which Bastian kisses him, the way he takes control is enough to ease the worry in his mind, for now at least. He kisses him back, the movements of his jaw following Bastian's lead. He rests his hands on Bastian's knees in front of him.

When Bastian pulls off, it's both too soon and too late; too soon because Jake wishes he'd never stop, and too late because Bastian has weaved a web around him and it's holding Jake tightly in place. He couldn't escape now if he wanted. Bastian's fingers are around the back of his neck and his thumbs are grazing his jaw line, running over his pulse points. It's a thrill, always is. The only things on Jake's mind are how he so completely trusts Bastian and how he's now assailed with memories of a few days prior, when Bastian effectively teased him half to death before actually taking over his airways. He closes his eyes and tries to keep his breathing leveled. Tries not to be so obvious about it.

"Yeah, no. I'm not sending you to work today," Bastian says casually, "not when you've just broken up with your partner and probably haven't slept well... not when you're sitting here in my bed looking like you're ready to give up everything you've got if it means you can get my hands on your body," he adds. "That's what we have understudies for. Call yours, I'm calling Sami. We're staying home, today, and I don't want you to say no."

Jake considers for a moment – he's never called out, not once in months, regardless of the insomnia before the really big nights, regardless of stress, regardless of illness, and this shouldn't be a valid reason to but he wants nothing more than to agree with Bastian and stay right here where he doesn't have to pretend.

"But, Bastian... what am I going to say?" He blurts out.

"You had an emergency. Something came up. You can't go, but you'll be back tomorrow, you just can't make it today."

Bastian gets up and Jake is dazed at how much purpose he has in his movements. He wants to lay down and never move a muscle again if he can help it. Bastian finds both of their phones, hands Jake his, flips his own open and dials away. No, I can't go in, please, will you go, I'm fine, I promise, can you please? and he turns over when that's settled. Jake looks at him with wide eyes.

"They won't be mad at you," he reassures.

"I've never done this," Jake counters.

"Then they really can't be mad at you. Call him."

He scrambles to get to the contact, builds off of Bastian – hey,

I'm not well. No, I have to stay home, yes, I'll be okay, I haven't slept but I'll be okay, something came up. I'll be okay. He ends the call when he gets confirmation that Robert will cover for him. At least he doesn't have to call more than one of them. He looks at Bastian and the caring smile he gets is enough to lift all undue weight from his shoulders. He hadn't realized how tense he was.

Bastian extends his hand, grabs the phone back and settles it on the dresser to be forgotten for the time being. He gets back in front of Jake and runs the pad of his thumb across Jake's cheekbone, his jaw line, his bottom lip, Jake opens his mouth and Bastian settles between his teeth. Jake is hooked.

"So how'd you come across this? Tell me, how did you find out about this whole control thing? The pain and the breathing and the flying away?"

Jake's brows furrow, he's never really… thought about it actively, with words, apart from the other morning when Bastian asked him about it first. "I just went with it?"

"You reacted strongly enough that I had to nod to get you off the wall and you'd never questioned it?" Bastian asks, incredulous. "That… is pretty amazing," he finishes, making Jake blush.

"I remember once, I don't think he meant anything by it, Caleb had his hand on my wrist. We weren't doing anything, but he moved around and pressed my arm into the mattress, and all of a sudden I felt really… vulnerable? But I didn't trust him like this, not this much," and Bastian interrupts him by moving his hands to take Jake's hands and press them by his hips into his mattress, and, well. Bastian can't blame him for not finishing his sentence because now, every cell in his brain is focusing on Bastian's hands on him and the pressure, the pressure. It's a burning line straight through his spine.

When he'd met Bastian and he'd instantly been able to read him, it had sparked something inside him, it's like Bastian had found something he'd forgotten and shone the brightest stage light right on it, and he couldn't quite believe how he hadn't noticed or addressed it before. He'd never put that much thought into the process, but it was just like in between the moment he'd found himself pinned against the mattress and the moment he had met Bastian, the thought of being under someone else's control, being someone else's had worked its way into his brain, a small flame that had been hidden in the shadows, lurking, and suddenly it was enlightening every inch of the room and left nothing hidden.

"And the orders? The directions?" So many questions and he didn't have a pre-defined answer for them.

"I'm good at following them. I like to be good." This much was clear. "I know what's expected of me when I'm acting, where my limits are and what I should say. I like that someone's always watching and ready to step in to correct me, or reprimand me. Praise me. It's easy."

"Can I be your stage manager, then, mi cielo?" Bastian asks and yes, please. Jake nods as he looks up at Bastian, directly in his eyes, then down at his lips and back up. "I didn't hear that."

"Yes. Please?" So Bastian leans in and kisses him again, his weight bearing down on Jake's hands that are still in his grasp and he noticeably, visibly, physically melts against Bastian.

The part of his brain that's still thinking is wondering if Bastian really means what Jake thinks he means, but he won't ask because on one hand, speaking is the last thing he wants to be doing, and on the other he's terrified that it's too soon and that Bastian means that casually and he's not quite ready for that risk. Bastian pushes in, slowly, firmly, so he stops thinking and focuses on his lips and his hands and his wrists and, and, and. Bastian is pushing him back so he goes, and he was far enough down the bed that letting himself fall back won't mean hitting the headboard or having to relocate otherwise. So he goes. And before long, Bastian is pressing every-thing he's got down onto Jake and he's laying between his legs and Jake, if he had been honest, would not have thought the situation would lead here but to hell if he'd want anything else. He lets Bastian take hold of each of his wrists and hold them down slightly above his head, pressing down on them and that's all Jake can focus on until Bastian speaks up. His responses are a little bit slow. A little bit delayed.

"And this?"

He takes a ragged breath.

"Bastian, I don't know. Do whatever you want with me. Please?" Jake wraps his legs around Bastian, looking into his eyes as he does so. Presses him down, tightly against himself. Maybe if he's good enough Bastian's going to be mean to him, and that thought makes him want to sing.

"Can I leave marks on you then, honeybee? In places the audience won't see them. God, you'd look so hot with my bruises in your skin, I can already imagine it," Bastian adds, breathless while his eyes trail down Jake's naked torso. Jake shivers, again. "Can I?"

Jake wants to say yes, because the thought of having something from Bastian constantly with him, on him, is incredible. He'll be fine, as long as there's nothing on his chest where the skin shows when he unbuttons his shirt, he'll be okay. "Please?" he says, tentative. He tries again, wants Bastian to knows he wants it too, "will you bite me?"

Bastian groans and sinks his teeth in Jake's shoulder. Doesn't let go of his wrists and Jake can't move. It stings. It's good. It's so much, it's overwhelming, it's not enough, Jake wants more. He arches forward, presses into the bite, pushes his shoulder into Bastian's teeth. Bastian doesn't let go until several seconds after Jake's whimpers have become hissing, only let's go when Jake goes quiet, and then he sucks hard into the skin and the teeth are gone but Jake can practically feel the blood being rushed into the capillaries. Blooming. Bastian eases off, slowly. Lets his tongue dart around the overworked flesh in soothing little jabs.

"How was that, sweetheart?"

It takes him a while to come back to himself enough for him to be able to collect his words and arrange them in a coherent manner – all that his brain seems intent on providing is please, Bastian, fuck, Bastian, more and he's forgotten that he can use his mouth.

"What if I don't bite you again until you speak up?" Bastian teases.

"That's… mean," Jake breathes out through his teeth.

"Is it?" Bastian retorts playfully before he sinks down again, only a few centimeters below the first bite, which means that Jake hasn't quite had time to recover.

Bastian doesn't bite as long or as hard this time but definitely puts more effort into sucking a bruise into the skin, and one that'll last, too. Jake bruises ridiculously easily – that much he knows. Bastian peppers nips and bites and sucks bruises trailing down Jake's chest, far enough out that unbuttoning his shirt on stage won't reveal anything, until he reaches Jake's nipple. At that point he does nothing more than nibbling, invested in seeing how much he can get out of Jake like this. He removes one of his hands from its position on Jake's wrist but Jake doesn't move, let alone for the arching of his spine and the strumming of his nerves. Bastian's fingertips are trailing down his forearm and almost right away make way for the feeling of Bastian's fingernails scratching at his skin. He bucks in reflex when Bastian catches a sensitive area, his legs tightening around Bastian's waist.

Bastian's fingers graze at his throat, and he's still holding his other wrist down, still worrying his nipple, looking up at Jake as best he can from his position. He presses his fingers against Jake's lips, a silent request. Jake opens up and Bastian pushes in. Two fingers, hooked past his teeth, Jake laves his tongue all around them and moans when Bastian bites down on his nipple and clutches at his mouth. He sucks in a sharp breath through his nose and tries not to bite down on Bastian's knuckles, which results in him hooking the tip of his tongue just under the pads of Bastian's fingers, sucking them in until his teeth are resting just past the second knuckle.

Bastian pulls the hand that was still on one wrist down and says, "stay." Jake wouldn't dream of moving, he's sated, full of Bastian's teeth raw on his nerves and Bastian's fingers in his mouth and Bastian's bruises on his skin. His brain catches on the Bastian's. Jake can feel his eyes watering at how much he's feeling already, he keeps them closed to keep the tears in, keeps working his mouth around Bastian's fingers. Bastian's free hand is a ghost touch on his skin as he trails down, feather-light, stops to pinch down hard at the neglected nipple and he twists as his tongue resumes the teasing and Jake can't help but to tighten his thighs around Bastian's hips and grind up into him. "Impatient much, today, aren't we?" he hears in response to his movements, the air hot on the sensitive skin below Bastian's mouth. He whimpers around the intrusion in his mouth.

Bastian continues the intended descent of his hand on Jake's torso, down the side of his ribcage, over the fabric of the underwear he's still wearing, for some reason. He grips at his ass, slides a hand down his thigh and slips under the fabric when he brings it back up. Jake grinds, he can't help it, god, he hopes Bastian won't ask him to stop because he obviously will but he might die in the process. Bastian uses the movements of Jake's hips to his advantage so that he can get a better grip and Jake shudders when Bastian's fingers stroke against his perineum, circling him.

"Bastian, please," he pants.

Bastian moves down, runs his tongue in a thin stripe to Jake's navel. He removes his fingers from Jake's mouth. "What do you want, honeybee? Tell me," he requests.

Jake blushes, not sure that he can put words on what he wants, settles for a breathy "touch me," instead.

"I'm doing just that, patience." He'd never had much of that to start with.

Bastian sucks in one last bruise right under Jake's stomach and he pulls off, up. Pulls his hand out of Jake's underwear and he whimpers at the loss. "Turn over for me, come on," tap, tap on his hip.

Jake complies, unhooks his legs from around Bastian. Bastian looks down to him, smirks, brushes his hand tantalizingly against the sizeable bulge in his underwear and squeezes on his way to grab a hold of Jake's calf so that he can turn him over. Jake doesn't keep quiet. Bastian hooks his fingers in the waistband on both sides and pulls down without ceremony, wiggles the garment under Jake's knees, drops it to the floor and finally, finally, Jake's naked, elbows and knees digging into the mattress, arousal hot and heavy between his legs. Bastian settles behind him, parts Jake's legs further apart, holding him open with his knees pressing into his calves. He stays silent for long enough that Jake pushes himself up on one hand not knowing how to handle Bastian's rapt attention and he's met with a

Bastian who's biting his lip and palming at himself through his own boxers that he hasn't yet taken off, eyes hooded with need. Jake moans at the sight, can't quite believe the effect he's having on Bastian when he's doing nothing but reacting to his touches. He lets go of himself and rests both hands on Jake, massaging the muscles of his ass cheeks, kneading, spreading them apart and exposing Jake. Jake can feel his cock twitch, useless in the air and it has to be obvious from where Bastian is kneeling.

"You can handle spanking, can't you? You can do that, you'll be good for me?" Bastian asks, Jake would be dishonest to pretend that the tone of his voice doesn't hit him as hard as his words do. He arches his back. Bastian nudges, Jake's head drops back between his shoulders.

"Make me feel it," he mutters under his breath, cheeks burning at the shameless admission.

It's Bastian's turn not to reply for a few seconds too long.

"I want you to stay still and quiet while I get you ready for this. I know you can do that for me. But I don't want you to hold anything in when I hit you. I want to see how you react and I want to hear it. And I want to see how red I can make your ass before you're begging me to touch you properly."

Jake squares up, rests his forehead on his forearms, focuses on staying immobile. Bastian is kneading with purpose and Jake can only think of how he must look to him, eager and ready and aroused and he wants so much. Bastian's hands are warm against his skin, rubbing and soothing and massaging and Jake is good, Jake doesn't move, Jake waits for Bastian to decide that he's ready and that he can take it. Before long, he's fizzing, he feels alive and sensitized and warm all over, and.

Jake tenses in anticipation when he feels his hand rising off of his skin. Bastian sucks in a sharp breath – Jake follows his lead, does too. He hears it before he feels it, the clean sound of skin hitting skin and Bastian doesn't need to remind him to react because the switch goes off immediately and oh, wow. He drops to his shoulders and presses his face in the mattress, pushes back against Bastian's hand that is rubbing his skin, soothes the sting.

"I want you to count. I haven't decided when I'm going to stop but I want to hear your voice and I want to hear you count them. How many was that?"

"Hm, one, Bastian."

He hits again. Small whimper. "Two," he can feel his skin prickling. At "three," he feels the heat already, Bastian isn't giving it to him easy, going at the same side and kneading the other relentlessly still.

"Four" comes with a loud moan that he would have held in otherwise, but Bastian wants to hear him and works him to get what he wants. "Five, Bastian, oh, please." The intensity of Bastian's slaps is ramping up with every new one and he's on fire. He feels a single tear escape from the inner corner of his eye and run down to the bridge of his nose. He grabs his hips and feels the ripple down his spine when the soothing turns to the fierce bite of Bastian's fingernails in his flesh. He rests his hands by his knees, holding his calves.

Bastian switches it up, gets into a rhythm, "six, seven, eight, fuck," coming into quick successions and Jake almost misses the beat on "nine" because he got carried away thinking about the color of his flesh and how that must look to Bastian, because if the fiery red lines that erupt on his skin following fingernail drags are any indication, his ass is likely to be brighter than his face, and he knows how deep the blush must be on his cheeks and down his neck.

"What was that, sweetheart?" Bastian's voice is the wire that connects him to the ground to make sure he doesn't pop the fuse and he bucks into the empty air, he just wants Bastian to touch him again, and the fact that he doesn't know when he will, if he will is enough to draw a broken sob out of Jake. "N-nine," he gasps.

"Good boy, just a few more, you can take more, I know you can," and Jake replies with a litany of affirmations, "yes, Bastian, yes, please, more."

Bastian hits. Hard. If he didn't know better, he wouldn't be sure that the sound that echoes in the room came from his chest. "Ten," he's panting.

Bastian reverts back to his right cheek and oh, fuck, the fact that there was a delay for so long between the last hit and this one makes him want to sing to heavens, "eleven," "twelve" is back onto the left and he breaks. "Please, Bastian, please touch me, I need you, will you touch me?" he pleads.

"Should I?" he teases and of course he should, of course, but the thrill of maybe not getting what he needs is enough for Jake to bring his arms back around to wrap around his head. "Have you been good enough for me, pretty thing?"

"I have, Bastian, I have, please do something, anything–" and Bastian cuts him off with one more blow to his ass, maybe the strongest of all so far or maybe Jake's just really worked up, "oh, thirteen," automatic. Bastian, democratic, follows up on the other side for "fourteen" and Jake knows that he's definitely crying by now.

Bastian rests his hand on him, gentle now. He bends over Jake to press kisses to his spine, then moves a hand to wipe at the tears on his cheeks, which only makes Jake want to cry more. "Hey, you okay?" Bastian asks, checking in.

"Yes, I'm good, will you please touch me?" Jake croaks out.

"You've asked for that already. I'm touching you. What else do you want?" he continues, rubbing at Jake's temple, and Jake is too far gone to be embarrassed.

"Will you fuck me? Please? Use me?"

"You're so beautiful when you use your words, sweetheart. I'm not going to fuck you, not today, but I'll make it good, I promise. I got you," he says and he stretches above Jake, reaches out for the bedside table.

Drawer rattling, bottle cap opening, and the drag of Bastian's skin against the sensitive skin of his ass is enough to make him whimper. He reaches behind himself to touch Bastian's thigh, he needs so much more than he's getting and he feels so full, his heart, his brain. He retrieves his hand when Bastian draws back up and Jake automatically tries to follow him, not to break contact until Bastian sets a firm hand against the abused flesh and keeps him in place. Jake keens when he feels the lube on his skin, cold, so cold. But then Bastian is touching him, his fingers running up and down, warming up between the cheeks and no matter how

Jake moves against him he won't give him anything. He sobs again.

"Something you want, beautiful?"

"You," he replies before he can stop himself or try to explain. Bastian chuckles, affection all over the edges of the sound.

He pushes in, finally, finally, finally. Slowly, gently, one knuckle after the other until Jake is writhing under him when he pulls out and slides back in. Bastian takes his time feeling him out, brings in a second finger after what could honestly be years, Jake wouldn't know. He's rubbing his free hand all over the taut expanse of Jake's back. He scissors his index and middle finger as he keeps moving in and out, twists as he moves in him. Jake's mind goes blank when he hits his prostate, "right there, Bastian, do that again," swears under his breath and feels the sparks up his spine, firing up the nerves everywhere. He starts fucking himself on Bastian's fingers in earnest and Bastian groans at the sight, moves his hand from his back to his hip and grips tightly, likely bruising, keeps hitting the spot, Jake keeps grinding. Panting. Crying. He doesn't care. This is so, so good. He needs more.

"Will you come like this, sweet thing? I want you to come on my fingers. You'll be a good boy and do that for me, won't you?"

Bastian gets a high keen in response, and god, Jake doesn't know that he can, but he'll try, and Bastian's not teasing which is good, and he's got his fingers in his ass, the same ones that were in his mouth earlier, and he's got fingers digging in his hip, and he's got the fire of his skin where Bastian hit him, slapped him earlier, and he's got the image of Bastian looking at him like he'd eat him whole if he could and palming himself through his underwear from when Jake last opened his eyes.

"More, Bastian, please give me more, I need you, fuck, fuck," Jake chants with every thrust of his hips when he slams back on Bastian's fingers so that they'll keep hitting his prostate.

Bastian complies, lets go of Jake's hip to get more lube, and before long, he's got 3 fingers in Jake's ass dragging out and sliding back to the knuckle, hitting the spot every time and Jake is swearing and whimpering and moaning without a care in the world for who hears him and Bastian's left hand comes back down to smack him and oh, oh, he forgets how to breathe as he's coming, spilling on the sheets beneath him. Bastian works him through it, and Jake collapses when his brain fizzes out and he doesn't care that he's gross, that the bed is, he just needs to give his muscles a damn break.

Bastian eases out, wipes his hand on the edge of the sheets. Gives Jake a minute to recover and when Jake opens his eyes again, turns his head back to look, Bastian's underwear is pushed down his thighs and he's stroking himself with purpose, his hooded eyes are looking at Jake's marked body and the only thing left to do for Jake is melting further, he wouldn't have thought that even possible.

"Turn over," Bastian commands. The urgency isn't veiled at all, not at this point; all Jake wants is to follow his lead and be whatever Bastian needs him to be.

Jake uses all his might and the little bit of support with which Bastian provides him to get his legs back from on either side of Bastian and relocate, effectively rolling over to rest on his back in the middle of the bed. Bastian loses no time in discarding his own underwear completely after that and goes to straddle Jake's chest, caging in his shoulders, and he grabs one side of Jake's jaw to have him look up, directly into Bastian's eyes.

"You said you wanted me to use you, so I'm going to do just that. I think you've been good enough that you deserve a warning, so here's how it's going to go: I'm going to fuck your face, however I like, and you're going to take it because you're a good boy. You're my good boy, aren't you? Aren't you just my pretty thing, free to use however I want, because I can?" Jake nods frantically. "Snap your fingers for me, so I know you can?" Jake is confused at first but he listens and snaps for Bastian. "If you need anything, snap for me. Otherwise, I don't want to hear much as a peep out of you. Okay, handsome?"

Jake almost falls but he catches himself in time and nods, opens his mouth when Bastian touches his fingertips to his lower lip. He points his tongue and Bastian repeats his actions from earlier for just a minute, hooking his fingers behind his teeth. He never quite stops the strokes of his hands on his cock and Jake can see the precum at the tip when he looks. Before long, however, Bastian's fingers are out of Jake's mouth and he's rubbing his cockhead against Jake's lips. Jake looks at Bastian with wide blue eyes and licks at the tip, flicks up the slit without breaking eye contact. Bastian moans.

He takes the hand that had been on Jake's face and reaches up for the headboard, bracing himself up, then he lifts from where he'd been sitting on Jake's chest and eases into his waiting mouth. Jake closes his eyes by reflex, breathes in through his nose, keeps himself open for Bastian, brings his hands up to palm at Bastian's ass.

"Open your eyes. Look at me." He does.

Bastian fucks in his mouth, slowly at first, deep strides, but he is starting to lose his grasp on self-control and it's not long before his hips snap and Jake's eyes water at the assault, his brain shorting out at how Bastian really doesn't care about him other than for the pleasure he can take from his body, other than for what he can get out of using Jake. Jake's breathing is labored, his eyes welling up – will he ever stop crying? – he takes what he can get from between two thrusts but Bastian doesn't give him much time to get air in and that's also enough go get Jake's blood boiling. He works his tongue on Bastian as much as he can in his position and Bastian hisses, loses his rhythm some, Jake holds his gaze but he can see that Bastian's having trouble keeping his eyes open.

He pulls out suddenly and Jake whimpers at the loss.

"Stay right there, don't you dare move, I'm going to come and I'm going to do that all over you, fuck, fuck, what are you doing to me," followed with a string of curses and "keep your mouth open for me, good boy, I knew you'd be good at this," and he shoots. Some in his mouth – most of it on his chin, his cheek, all over his face, and Jake truly does feel used and claimed and so warm all over he could cry. (He does. It's good). He's panting, Bastian's trying to regain his breath, "you look so fucking good like this, you have no idea, you've got bruises all over your chest and your ass is on fire and your face is covered in come and, fuck, Jake, what are you doing to me?" he repeats. He taps his cock against Jake's chin a few times before he slides down his body and cleans his face off with his fingers, feeds him with it, kisses him through the mess. Bastian's still straddling him, he's got both hands cupping Jake's face and he's stealing his taste off of Jake's tongue with his own, he's peppering his entire face with kisses and making sure nothing's left on his skin. Going back to his mouth. Running his tongue against Jake's lips and Jake's teeth and Jake's tongue.

Jake wants to stay there forever.

Chapter Eleven

*I*t's more natural than what Jake would have expected, the rhythm he develops with Bastian. It's natural enough that, by the time a week goes by, he doesn't worry nearly as much that Bastian is just helping him out of pity. Natural enough that by the time their following Monday off rolls around, Jake finds himself awoken by the sound of a mug hitting the wood of the bedside table and the feeling of the mattress dipping under Bastian's weight.

Jake is on his stomach, arms under the pillow and his face tilted towards the soft sunlight hitting his features when Bastian straddles him and works his hands up to knead at his shoulders. Jake flexes and tightens his muscles as a substitute for stretching without really moving. He lets Bastian's clever fingers ease the knots from his body and doesn't attempt to quiet his moans whenever Bastian works the tightness out of him. He dozes off, too content and sated to bother trying to stay awake, until Bastian rests his hands on his waist and bends down over him to lay a kiss at the top of his spine.

"Good morning, honeybee. How are you feeling?" Bastian asks, casual.

Jake lets out whatever noise his throat will produce, a tired hum, and tilts his chin up towards the sun in an attempt to get Bastian's lips back on his skin.

"I'm not sure that I know that word, sleepyhead," he replies before he completely lays his weight on Jake, pressing his torso down against Jake's back and sliding his hands under Jake's stomach as best he can to squeeze at the soft skin.

Jake presses back against him when Bastian's nails catch. He's thinking of Bastian's weight on him, trapping him in place, and if that's not the greatest way to wake up, Jake doesn't know what else could ever be. He lets go of all his air and focuses on just being there.

Today is the first day he doesn't have anything to do. Nothing to pack, nothing to move, nothing to act. Nothing to prove. It's just him and Bastian and all of his belongings are finally here and he never has to go back to his old place, if he can help it. The past twelve days have been excruciatingly exhausting and he's never looked forward to a day off this much.

"Part of me really wants to keep you in my bed for as long as I can manage, but another part of me also really wants to take you on another date," Bastian voices out loud, digging his fingers into Jake's flesh and rolling his hips very slowly but very purposefully into the curve of Jake's ass. "What do you think, pretty thing? Will you go on a date with me?" Bastian asks before his teeth catch the soft skin of his earlobe and his tongue runs hot against the trapped skin. The contrast between his casual tone and the way he's playing with Jake's body – his hips, his fingers, his teeth, his tongue – is almost comical and Jake doesn't know how to assess the mood. Or rather, doesn't know how to focus enough of his brain cells to process Bastian's question when he has his teeth on his skin and he can feel the pressure of his hipbones against the muscles of his ass.

Jake keeps his eyes closed and stills his lungs for a moment, wanting to burn in his memory as much of what he's feeling as possibly achievable. Bastian drags his hands up from where he's trying to leave a bruised ache in the muscles of Jake's stomach, grasping and kneading and scratching up the sides of Jake's body. Over his ribcage. By his armpits. On the sensitive skin of the soft underside of his triceps, until he slides under the pillow to pin Jake's wrists down. The fact that he's still straddling Jake's middle means that he is completely flattened against him and Jake is helpless. The grinding of Bastian's hips evolves into a satisfying gyration. He forgets that Bastian had asked him a question.

"Who's got your tongue? I want to hear your voice, Jacob. Will you go on a date with me?"

Bastian's nose is drawing patterns across the small hairs at the nape of his neck and Jake senses a shiver rippling up his spine. He doesn't generally like hearing his full name, he'd left it half behind with everything else he'd shed when he departed from Rubin – but everything is different with Bastian, isn't it?

"Mhm, yes," he whispers. A date sounds like a brilliant idea. And he doesn't know anyone in Washington Heaven, so there isn't too much of a risk that he'll be recognized.

"Amazing!" Bastian exclaims, drawing back up and reaching out to grab the steamy mug on the bedside table, the original reason for Jake's awaking.

When he sits up, sipping on the coffee out of Jake's sight, his entire weight rests solely on the top part of Jake's thighs, where his body curves, where Bastian is caging him between his knees. With nothing more than the thin summer sheet acting as a barrier between them, Jake slowly swivels his own hips as much as he can from under Bastian, hoping to keep him in bed for a tad longer – they might not have been doing this for long, but Bastian wasn't known to Jake as somebody who would pass up an opportunity to ravish him. Maybe Bastian was a hell of a tease, but he'd never actually refused Jake's shy attempts to getting him worked up. So it doesn't cross Jake's mind that Bastian might this time around completely ignore him, especially not having felt him intently grind down on him not a minute prior.

"Oh, so you are awake, after all," Bastian teases. "Who would have thought?"

"Shut up, Bastian," Jake replies with a hint of laughter coloring his voice.

"And cheeky, too. Can't have that if you want me to be nice to you, now, can I?" Bastian replies. Jake turns his face into the pillow to hide from his blush at the accusation. Bastian always knows what to say. "Do you want me to be nice to you, Jacob?" His register is suddenly much lower. The threat that he won't be is not quite hidden by the honey in his tone.

Bastian drops a warmed hand to rest it on Jake's shoulder blade, then slowly drags his fingernails down the one side of Jake's back until he can palm and knead at the cheek of his ass. Jake pushes back into the touch. Bastian sees the flex when Jake tenses his arms and shoulders. Jake tries to drop his head as much as he can, which results in only his forehead resting on the pillow.

"You always get caught up in there, don't you? It really doesn't take much for you to forget how to speak." Not a question, this time.

"Bastian… shut up," he repeats, with much less conviction this time around.

He hears a sip of coffee. "Well, if that's what you really want…" he trails off. "Get dressed for me, handsome. We're going out."

With this, Bastian moves off of him, somehow not spilling the coffee, and lifts the sheet off of Jake to playfully slap his ass before he turns over and walks out of the room to leave Jake alone. Which is entirely enough of an incentive to get Jake out of bed – he hates being away from Bastian if he doesn't have to be. And Jake almost wants to hate how well Bastian already knows him. How easy it is for him to push Jake's buttons. And how affected Jake gets when Bastian does. He grunts in the pillow.

He gets up slowly, finds a pair of underwear and can't really say that he's surprised – he's not exactly hard by any means but he's definitely more aroused than he would have been for just waking up with the sun shining through the window. He smiles to himself, although he doesn't really want to give Bastian the satisfaction of knowing how easily Jake reacts to his attentions. He steals the sheet from the bed, wrapping his body with it as he stumbles through the room to follow Bastian, who is now leaning against the counter with his cup of coffee in his hands and a steaming matching mug on the surface next to him. The easy air of confidence that struck Jake when he first met Bastian, what feels like a lifetime removed from his reality, is magnetic. Jake will always be drawn to it. He looks at the floor and keeps walking over to him. Even though he's taller than Bastian, he makes himself a home in his arms and rests his face in the crook of his neck.

"Everything okay, beautiful?" Bastian asks, not able to see Jake's face to read it.

Bastian sets his mug down next to Jake's and wraps his arms properly around him. Almost instantly, Jake hums from just under Bastian's ear, and snakes his hands behind Bastian to hold him close. He can't grab onto anything, Bastian's lower back is pressed in tight against the counter, but unlike him he is stark naked – Jake can use that to his advantage. So he hums, holds him tightly and grinds into Bastian to rouse him, very lightly grazing his teeth against the taut skin of Bastian's neck.

"Oh, is that where we're at, now? I thought I'd said none of this before the date, and you don't seem like someone who's forgotten already," Bastian retaliates right away, craning his neck away from Jake's mouth to look at him.

Jake pulls back and looks into Bastian's eyes, searching for a sign that would tell him that maybe he's crossed a line – they haven't talked about this really, it's always just been Bastian going at him – but he doesn't find any. So he goes back down and grabs more skin, applies more pressure, runs his tongue around it and presses a thigh between Bastian's legs and moves his hips until Bastian's hands settle square on his shoulders to pull him back.

"What are you doing, huh?" Bastian's voice isn't as steady as he probably wants it.

Jake does his best impression of a completely innocent face. Bastian brings a hand to cup his face, thumb pressing into his jaw and fingers resting on his opposing cheek. It's just this much on the side of rough and Jake is satisfied, he smirks at Bastian. "Saying good morning?" Playful sparks in his eyes.

"Oh, no, you're not. You're getting yourself in trouble, that's what you're doing." He presses in. "Don't think I don't see right through you," Bastian says darkly.

He pushes off the counter to get his face closer to Jake's, always holding Jake's jaw tightly and just far away enough that their lips won't touch. Jake's hands settle on the bare cheeks of his ass and Bastian instantly retaliates by swerving them around and firmly pushing Jake hard against the fridge that was initially off to the side but now very, very solid against Jake's back. The sheet falls to the floor in the process. Jake's senses are overtaken by the cold of the refrigerator doors on his back, Bastian's fingers digging in his cheeks, the pure intent of Bastian's movements. He can't help but close his eyes and bring his hands to Bastian's wrist, not pulling but holding. He has to make a conscious effort to keep his knees from wobbling under his own weight. He gulps.

"Well, isn't this interesting," Bastian ponders out loud, rhetorical, which results in Jake opening his eyes despite his desperate frown and him being absolutely swept up by Bastian's rapt gaze, "do you have a thing for fridge doors, now?"

Jake opens up his mouth, tries to defend himself, but no words are coming to him. He keens.

"Definitely interesting. You're going to listen to me now. You're going to go and put some nice clothes on, and we're going to drink this coffee, and then we're going to go on a cute date so that I can court you. Understood?" Bastian commands as he crowds into Jake's space, simultaneously absolutely overwhelming and undeniably not enough so. "Answer me, Jacob," Bastian demands.

"Okay, okay, yes," he breathes out.

"Good."

Bastian lets go of his face and steps off, turning around and heading to the bathroom, leaving Jake resolutely behind. Jake intakes sharply, fills his lungs. He needs a moment to trust that his legs will support his weight before he can push himself off the cold door with a roll of his shoulders. He bends down to pick up the discarded sheet, takes the mug from the counter in hand, and beelines for the bedroom. Bastian said nice, so he picks out a button-down and some twill shorts. Wife beater. Socks. Bastian walks back in as he's sitting back up and reaching for the coffee – he needs so much of it if he wants to clear his brain at all. Which, honestly, he does, especially if Bastian is going to keep being an insufferable tease the entire time, which Jake would not put past him.

He watches intently as Bastian picks an outfit out for himself, drinking slowly. "Approve of what you're seeing?" Bastian throws cheekily as he's pulling his own shorts up. Jake shoots back a humorous glare, keeps sipping.

Once done, Bastian extends his hand to pull Jake up from where he's sitting on the side of the bed. He takes the mug from his hand and tugs him in close, brushes a hand briefly down the side of Jake's face before he moves to his neck so that he can pull Jake into a kiss. Jake's never going to get tired of the way Bastian holds him, a hand on his hip and one on his neck, his lips pressed hard against his own. He lets Bastian take over and scrunches himself down as much as he can, putty in Bastian's hands, parts his lips for the insistent exploration of Bastian's tongue. Bastian takes his time working with Jake's mouth. He nips and he licks, breathes Jake in, pushes in and draws back, plays with Jake's tongue until Jake's arrogance is long gone and he starts to drift.. Once Jake's breathing is slowed down so much that anything slower would be asphyxia, only then does Bastian suck his bottom lip into his mouth to bite. And he bites. The pressure is sharp, constant, inescapable. Perfect. Jake's breath stops dead in its tracks and he opens his eyes to look at Bastian. He breathes in fast when Bastian releases and he's thankful for the hand on his hip for grounding him because he otherwise would probably be long gone into a free fall.

Bastian presses his fingers in Jake's hip and Jake focuses on the anchoring fingertips digging into his flesh through the fabric of his clothes. He looks down by reflex, Bastian's lips, his neck, his shoulders. He follows the lines of his arm down until he's looking at his own body. Bastian shifts his thumb from where it was resting by Jake's ear and strokes until it's resting just at the edge of Jake's jaw. Jake leans into it, can feel his own heartbeat trapped beneath the skin and he feels the pulse quicken when he thinks about how easily Bastian could choke him, right then and there. He closes his eyes again and holds his breath when he presses his neck tighter into Bastian's waiting hand.

"We don't have time for this, sweetheart," Bastian utters slowly, "but I promise you that when we're back from our date, I'll choke you all you want." A pause, and Jake whimpers, a shudder of arousal running down his spine. "I'm reading this correctly, am I not?" Bastian asks, and Jake can't do anything but nod. "Okay, honey. I've got you. Come on, now," Bastian gently coaxes.

He lets go of Jake's hip but it was a tight enough grip that Jake still feels it, will feel it for at least a little while. Coffee mugs forgotten, Bastian leads him to the front door. Jake bends down, tries his best to tie his shoes even though he really can't focus, he can't stop thinking of the only time that Bastian has actually kept his breathing controlled, trapping his air for him, how absolutely effective it was in shutting him down. He stands back up and before he knows it –

The thud echoes in Jake's ears and he's vaguely aware of the fact that the back of his head has hit the wall with force. His fingers scramble up to grasp at Bastian's arm that is holding him by the throat, against the wall, Bastian slammed him bodily against the unforgiving surface, and he can't breathe, he wasn't expecting, Bastian had said, he can't –

And Bastian releases. Jake gasps in. His knees buckle when Bastian doesn't hold him. "Are you going to behave out there?" Bastian asks as he steps away, finding his shoes. Jake is trying to regain his thoughts and his breath, he's mesmerized by the way that Bastian's fingers are moving the laces, twisting and pulling and tying with ease. "Hm? Because if not, I'll have to punish you. I think you know that, don't you? You going to behave, lover?"

Jake is still panting, holding his throat. He nods.

"Words, Jacob. Answer me. Are you going to be good to me?"

Jake closes his eyes, drops his hands by his side. When he looks again, it's to stare at the floor. "Yes, Bastian."

"Good."

Jake doesn't move when Bastian puts on his own shoes. Doesn't move when Bastian opens the door, until Bastian takes him by the hand and leads him out. The weather is beautiful once they get outside – warm but not hot, not too humid either, and just the perfect summer breeze. They walk in comfortable silence, Jake trusts that Bastian knows where they are headed. He's in no hurry. He keeps holding Bastian's hand, keeps breathing in, and they keep walking.

"Oh!" Bastian exclaims, pulling Jake right out of his reverie. Jake looks at him, waiting for Bastian to expand. "Look here. Maybe we can stop by later, when we're coming back?" Bastian continues.

Jake wasn't paying attention to his surroundings in the slightest, and he is entirely dumbfounded when he sees Bastian standing in front of a storefront window.

"A… leather jacket store? Why do we need leather jackets? Bastian, it's ninety degrees out, we're in the middle of June," he points out.

"Well, no. Not quite. I mean, I'm sure we can find a few leather jackets in there, but we'll probably have a hell of a lot more luck if we're looking for corsets and ball gags. Or paddles. Handcuffs. Would you like handcuffs?" Bastian turns back around to look at him.

Jake's eyes go wide. "Bastian?" He asks.

"We can go shopping together! Find a couple things I can try on you. What do you think, honeybee?"

Bastian sounds far too giddy and casual for the scenarios that are developing in Jake's mind. He looks back at Jake when he fails to get an answer. He moves back from the window to Jake's side, his fingers now grazing at Jake's neck. A shiver down his spine. Bastian moves to whisper in his ear.

"I think I remember you asking me to hurt you…" Bastian says darkly, breath hot against his neck. "I'm sure we can find some things in here that'll do a much better job at that than my bare hands can."

Jake closes his eyes. He can feel the blush creeping on his cheeks. He'd blame it on the temperature, if anybody asked – as far as he's concerned, it's suddenly much warmer out than it was mere minutes prior. He tries to breathe out slowly and fails, he swallows before he whispers out a faint "Okay."

"Okay!" Bastian exclaims, as if that settled the score. He presses a quick kiss to Jake's cheek, takes hold of his hand again, and starts walking as if they hadn't just stopped. Jake almost stumbles but follows nonetheless.

Before long, they find themselves walking through a local market, hidden in some side streets. The atmosphere is calm, the market is almost empty, by virtue of it being an early Monday morning. Jake looks around, amazed at all the stands and the variety of products and produce offered. He lets go of Bastian's hand to explore around. Bread bakery on one side, locally-made jams on the other; quiche and soaps and hand creams, smoothies, and flowers. He tries some of the creams after the man behind the stand offers him to sample some of the fragrances, bends down to smell some flowers. After a few more minutes of taking it all in, he tries to locate Bastian, suddenly wondering where he's gone to – he doesn't see him, which sounds a bit improbable considering how calm the market is. He makes his way through until he walks by a pillar in the middle of the place. No trace of Bastian, he notices his breathing getting a bit irregular, he has no real idea of where he is in the neighborhood. He decides to get his phone to attempt calling him. He leans his shoulder against the structure.

Before he can press the call button, he feels a hand on his hip and whips his head around to be met with a ridiculously large and colorful bouquet and Bastian's voice, "Someone you're looking for?" before the flowers are lowered and he finds himself smiling and looking straight into Bastian's beaming face.

"You," he replies. "You left me alone!" Jake tries to reprimand.

"It was for a good cause, don't you think? I couldn't surprise you with flowers if you stayed glued to my side the entire time," and well, that's right, but that doesn't mean Jake didn't get slightly worried when he couldn't find him.

"Those are for me? They're beautiful. Bastian, you didn't have to."

"I know. I wanted to. And, besides…" Bastian crowds him against the pillar. "Maybe I'll take them away if you're not good enough. If you don't behave."

ALEX H. SINGH

Jake closes his eyes, takes a deep breath. He needs to figure out how Bastian keeps doing that, switches back and forth between the most light-hearted and casual of tones to using words that would be enough on their own to shut Jake down, let alone when they are uttered with the barest edge of a threat and with Bastian invading his space. He's overwhelmed with the scent from the flowers, the solidity of Bastian's body, by the feeling of his creeping hand and the fingers that Bastian uses to trace his lips, the pillar behind his back, and god damn it, he needs to keep himself in check because it's really not in his plans to get embarrassingly aroused in public. Bastian is making it harder than it needs to be for him to behave.

"Ready to go, sweet thing?"

Bastian steps off and grabs his hand again, pulling him along. Yeah, he's ready to try and get some sense back in his brain, and brunch will be an excellent way of doing just that. It's only a few more minutes of walking before Bastian opens up a door for Jake and he is assailed with the ever-incredible smell of brunch restaurants. A soft smile falls on his lips. He hasn't gone on a date with Bastian since the one night that ended in a panic attack, so he's determined to make today a good one.

They follow the waitress who sits them in a little cove, just a tad removed from most everyone else, and Bastian orders them both bottomless orange juice flutes. He sets the flowers on the booth by his side. Bastian takes no time to settle on what he wants and focuses on running his fingers across Jake's knuckles, skimming down the top of Jake's hand to his wrist, drawing patterns on the soft skin. Jake's aware of the fact that Bastian is looking at him intently. He asks his opinion on a few dishes and settles on a Farmer's Omelet. The waitress comes back with the orange juice and her notepad and Bastian orders for them both.

She leaves, Jake takes a sip, licks his upper lip clean. Looks at Bastian's eyes that are still glued to him. "What are you looking at?" He enquires.

"Oh, just your pretty lips, honeybee. Nothing much. Thinking of all the ways in which your mouth is talented. And all the ways I haven't tried to use it yet." Bastian's tone is so casual, absolutely in contrast to his words.

Jake almost chokes.

Bastian gets closer – they're in a two-person booth so he can just slide over – and he runs his fingers all along Jake's arm until he's back on his neck, he's always touching his neck and Jake will never tire. Bastian chuckles when Jake's breath goes erratic and he stills his lungs for a hot minute. He rests his fingers on Jake's pulse.

"I can't wait to feel how this…" Bastian presses in, "quickens when I use you. I want to feel your heart racing." He waits for a second before he keeps talking and Jake knows his heart skipped a beat. "You like that, don't you? You want me to use your body, huh, Jacob? And you'll let me, because you love pleasing me."

The blush on his cheeks must be so obvious, but he really doesn't have it in himself to care because the sole thought of Bastian not really caring about how much Jake is getting out of Bastian using him is warming his entire body up.

Bastian drops his hand and slides back to his original place in the booth.

"You know what?" He asks, and Jake opens his eyes to spur Bastian on. "I think it's a really good thing we came out for brunch. For you, at least." Jake raises an eyebrow, unsure where Bastian is going with this. "I'm not sure how comfortable it would have been for you to sit through an entire meal if we'd had a dinner date. Although," he adds, running his fingers through the condensation on his glass of juice, "that would also be a fun thing to test."

Jake is saved by the waitress coming back with their plates and he clears his throat, drinks some. His food is absolutely divine, Bastian likes this spot for a reason. Jake feels his heart grow full in his chest – he's here, with Bastian, on their day off and eating the greatest food he's had in a long time. Bastian looks like an angel to him, his dark eyes and his short hair and his tanned skin, the playful smile on his lips and the fact that he will not stop teasing. Maybe it seems illogical for Jake to allow Bastian to play with him, but to him, it makes perfect sense. It's the constant flood of scenarios with which Bastian casually assails him. It's in the way he can just lay back there and let Bastian set the rules. It's in how Bastian's presence is so very calming at the core and how his mind can perpetually be at ease around him, because he knows he can trust him. It's being able to be vulnerable with Bastian, for Bastian – that alone is more comforting than anything else. It's in knowing, deep down, that he loves all of this as much as Bastian does, and that Bastian wouldn't do anything he isn't into, and for that, it's knowing that he will always have extraordinary power over Bastian for the simple fact of allowing him to tease, allowing him to really get under his skin. Jake is temporarily surrendering to Bastian with the faith that he is being taken care of – and just that feeling alone is worth everything he cares about. And if you asked, he wouldn't want to give that up for anything.

He spends the rest of their brunch date letting Bastian hold his hand across the table, a comforting contrast to the playful little jabs at which Bastian was so good. He always takes stock of the feeling of Bastian's nails on his skin, how he holds his cutlery, how he moves when he speaks, how he plays around with the condensation droplets on his beverage glass. He looks at Bastian's eyes and his lips, the constant rise and fall of his chest and his steady breathing. He gets lost in Bastian's rhythm.

The anticipation returns the very second they step outside. The calm that Jake felt inside is almost instantly forgotten because he knows that their next stop is the shop they'd seen on their way, and he feels a little bit silly at the thought of going into a sex store with a bouquet of flowers. He knows that Bastian doesn't mind, Bastian likes when he's a bit silly around him, but still. Anticipation. Bastian leads him by the hand through the streets.

"Are you ready for this?" Bastian asks, almost skipping with energy.

"Uh, I don't know? Maybe not as much as you are?" Jake replies with a shy smile and a meaningful nod at Bastian's antics. "I don't really know what to expect."

"That's okay. We can work with that. I can walk you through, if you want." Bastian paused while Jake considered. "As much as I want you to use your words, honeybee, I want to see you explore with me by your side. This isn't either one of us shopping alone, it's us shopping together. Yeah?"

That settled some of the concerns in the part of Jake's brain that was a little stressed, a little overwhelmed. "Yeah, okay. I like that," he replied softly as he started walking with a bit of his rhythm back.

They walked the rest of the way in silence, Bastian fizzing with excitement by Jake's side and Jake trying his best to reign his thoughts in. He could feel his heart beating hard inside his chest, equal parts excitement and nervous agitation. He didn't have a bad gut feeling about this, quite the opposite – only, he definitely felt like this was a new step in… whatever this thing, with Bastian, was.

At that thought, however, he immediately became a little frantic. What did he have with Bastian? What if this didn't mean as much to Bastian as it did to him? What if, for Bastian, this was just something nice to pass the time, while he waited for somebody who could give him what he needed better than Jake could? The past few weeks had been incredible, as far as Jake was concerned, but it was exactly that, it was just a few weeks, what if he'd fallen further than he'd meant to and now he was reading too much into this? What if Bastian only wanted to have fun for a while and this was what this was about, just having fun? Jake didn't think he could invest so much of himself in something only meant to be informal. To him, this wasn't casually playing, they were going shopping for toys that Bastian would use on him and he really wouldn't be able to do so if this was meant as a short-term fling, an in-between thing. And god damn it, why did he always have to start panicking when he went on dates with Bastian? Was that a thing, now?

Jake doesn't notice that he's slowed down until Bastian is standing in front of him with a worried frown on his face. He lets go of Jake's hand to stroke a thumb across his cheekbones.

"Hey, hey, cielo, is everything okay? Talk to me, what's wrong? Jacob. Look at me."

He knows he must look a little haggard but he tries his best, opens his mouth but doesn't have the words, everything seems like too much to be uttered out loud.

Bastian looks around quickly and guides him to a bench he's just spotted, a little removed to the side of the street. "You know you can talk to me, honeybee, please tell me what's going on," Bastian pleads.

Bastian's holding his hand again and all that's going through Jake's mind is a litany of what are we, what are we, what are we?

"Are we together?" He blurts out. He doesn't really have it in himself to expand.

Bastian looks a little confused, "What do you mean, cielo?"

"I don't know, Bastian, we haven't talked about this, I've just been living at your place for a couple weeks and sleeping in your bed and I don't know where we stand, and I just realized that maybe we're not a thing, maybe I'm getting too deep in this, maybe I'm not, I'm not…" he trails off, shaking his head. He can't finish the sentence, even though the only word left to say is yours.

"Do you want us to be together?" Bastian asks with a hand on his neck, the flowers long forgotten on the bench behind him. Jake nods desperately. "We can be, mi cielo, I want us to be. I hadn't realized, I'm sorry – I didn't want to go too fast for you, I wanted to go at your pace, but I think I got just a little carried away, but I've got no interest in not pursuing this, Jacob. Is this about breakfast? Did I push too much?" And now Bastian sounds worried and it was never Jake's intention to worry him.

"No, yes, I don't… I just need to know that this is real, all of this, everything's been so good and it's better than I ever really thought being with someone could be, and it means so much to me but I can't do this if you're not serious too? I need to know that there's, I don't know, longevity? Because if not, if not, then I don't want to get hurt and I need to step back because oh my god, Bastian," he gulps, the weight of the realization hitting him square in the chest, "this means so much to me and you're everything I didn't know I needed and if it isn't the same for you then I need to keep myself from falling because I am, I really am, falling, please say something," he finishes in a whisper, looking down at the cement beneath their feet.

Bastian takes a minute to reply.

"Will you be my boyfriend? Will you please be mine?" Bastian asks, and the sincerity that Jake can hear in his words and read in his eyes is all he needs to be able to nod frantically at him. "Okay. Okay. I've got you, come here, sweet thing," Bastian says as he pulls him in a tight hug, as tight as it can be while sitting the way they are, cradling his head in the crook of his shoulder with both arms, a hand running through his curls.

Jake feels so much tension he didn't know he'd been harvesting and it all grounds itself in Bastian, his tension line to the earth to ensure he doesn't burst at the seams, Bastian, Bastian, Bastian. His Bastian. He tries taking a deep breath, it takes a few tries to get his lungs under control. Bastian is whispering sweet nothings in his ear, "you're okay, you're okay, I've got you, we're okay." When he feels steady enough to pull back, he gets lost in Bastian's searching gaze and it's only a few seconds before Bastian pulls him into a kiss, and Jake doesn't have it in himself to worry about the passersby because Bastian is holding him and he is soothing him and he is kissing him like his life depends on it, and he doesn't know that that's true for Bastian but he knows that his own so completely does.

When they pull back, Bastian smiles at him, his hand never stopping his soothing strokes against Jake's neck and his cheek. "Can I ask what brought this on, sweetheart? Was it the date?" He asks.

"No, no, the date was good, it was perfect, it's just…" he needs a moment to get his thoughts together. "The going shopping thing. It just feels really… intimate and important?" It's not really a question but he needs the reassurance that he isn't over thinking this. "I want to do this with you, I really do, but I didn't want it to feel bigger for me than it does for you and I didn't know if it was just going to be a game for you when it meant so much for me."

"Oh, cielo. No. This is an important step in this for me too, I'm sorry if I made it seem otherwise. I don't want to fuck this up, either, please trust me. You are just so, so precious and I would never forgive myself if I ruined anything with you. I've just been so caught up, you have no idea how enthralling you are, do you? What am I going to do with you?"

Jake blushes at that, he's not sure how to respond, not sure what Bastian sees in him.

"Can I still take you shopping, pretty thing?" Bastian asks with one last kiss to Jake's lips.

Jake nods. That was enough words for a lifetime.

Bastian gets up after a moment, strokes Jake's cheek one last time and extends his hand to pull him up from the bench.

Jake finds out that they were actually really close to the store by the time his mind got the best of him.

"Have you shopped here before?" Jake asks as they're about to go in.

Bastian's got a hand on the handle. "I have a few times, yeah. Why?"

"Nothing. Just wondering," he replies, too quickly to be genuine but he hopes that Bastian hasn't picked up on that fact.

Bastian lets go of the handle. "That didn't sound like a 'just wondering' question. Are you sure?"

"I just… I feel like I'm so inexperienced. And I don't want you to feel like I don't know what I'm doing, but realistically, I probably don't know what I'm doing?" He won't say that he's scared he won't measure up to Bastian's exes, but that thought is definitely eating away at him now.

"Well, that's what I'm here for. I want to figure you out at the same time you do. Regardless of what I've done in the past. I want to do this together and I'll be honored to answer your questions and show you the ropes and learn about what you're into and I want to be by your side when you figure that all out."

Jake takes a deep breath. Not trusting that Bastian is telling him the truth won't get him anywhere, so he tries to quiet his mind, or at least ignore the swirling thoughts in his brain and breathes out, "Okay. Let's do this."

Chapter Twelve

*B*astian opens the door and Jake is assailed with a swarm of butterflies. Or maybe they're actual birds. Butterflies don't begin to cover what Jake is feeling. Bastian holds the door open and silently invites him to enter first.

Jake takes two steps in and almost immediately stalls, overcome as he is at the sheer abundance of products in the store. And the obvious quality of it all. This is not a secondhand store in the slightest – the walls are covered from floor to ceiling with expensive-looking and expensive-smelling leather garments, most of them absolutely baffling to Jake. Bastian wasn't kidding. The floor is made of dark hardwood, the light fixtures are modern and very sleek, reflecting exquisitely on the displays on each wall. The store is narrow and elongated, with the vast majority of the items hung all around and beautifully organized. Bastian follows him in. When Jake stops in his tracks, he feels Bastian's hand on his lower back and the light pressure of a soft kiss to the back of his neck.

"Breathe, we are exploring together. I'm here. I only want you to have a good time and find something that you'd like, mi cielo. I can help if needed, but this is about you."

Bastian gives his waist a small squeeze before he continues his way inside, looking back with a seductive smirk on his face. He extends a hand for Jake to take and leads him to the nearest wall. He parks Jake in front of the wall and himself just behind, placing both hands on Jake's hipbones, squeezing, and setting his chin on Jake's shoulder. Jake revels in the comfort of feeling Bastian's warmth surrounding him and bares his neck when Bastian presses another soft kiss to his sensitive skin.

Everything in front of them more or less fits in the garment category, seems more appropriate for public outings and social events, and Jake doesn't quite see the appeal. It's a plethora of vests, jackets, shorts, corsets and pants, and it all looks fine and dandy but doesn't send a thrill down his spine. He tries to look down at Bastian to gauge his reaction, and Bastian does the same. They catch each other's eyes.

"No?" Bastian asks, not a hint of disappointment in his tone but pure wonder. Jake shakes his head, makes an uninterested face. "Just let me know if there's anything you'd like to see or try. Let's move on, pretty thing, there's an entire store's worth of stuff to look at. We can always come back up here if you want."

Jake moves on, Bastian trailing closely behind and never letting go of his body. They pass some mitts and face masks that look some-what intimidating to Jake, but then his eye catches. Bastian's words come back to him – I'm sure we can find some things in here that'll do a much better job at that than my bare hands can. His breath hitches for a moment before his feet take him further and he reaches out a hand to stroke lightly at the falls of a thick flogger. Part of him, the part that is keeping his breathing next to nonexistent, is absolutely intimidated and somewhat terrified at the heavy feeling of the leather on his palm when he picks up the falls. The part of him that has his brain both silent and going a thousand miles per hour, however, is wholly intrigued and wants nothing more than imagine Bastian holding that for him. Jake's vaguely aware of being greeted and Bastian politely declining the offer for assistance.

"That can pack a punch, you know. It can be a comforting thump or a sharp sting on your skin," Bastian informs him before dropping his voice to a stage whisper against his neck. "I'd love to have you bound to my bed and test your limits... and I can decide whether I want your moans to be pain or pleasure. I can decide whether you're begging me for more or for mercy."

Jake feels his own heartbeat accelerating in his chest. He isn't entirely certain of the reason behind Bastian's words affecting him so much, but hearing how much reverence Bastian had in his voice is a red-hot flash down his spine.

"Is that something you want, handsome? It is, isn't it?" Bastian asks, almost innocent if Jake didn't know better, if he hadn't been running his hands over Jake's quivering stomach.

Jake, eyes as big as galaxies, turns in Bastian's hands to look at him and nod. He hopes the plea makes it to his eyes.

"Okay, gorgeous. We can get one. How about we keep looking around for other stuff that gets your attention and then we can choose what specifically we'll bring home, what do you think?"

"Sounds good, yeah, okay," he croaks out.

Bastian kisses him softly before he nudges him over again, further down in the store. His gaze lingers on some paddles on their way to the next section – he wouldn't have thought that there would be such a variety. Wooden ones, hard plastic ones, leather things and metal devices, some with holes and some with studs and some with straps and Jake wants to try a ridiculous amount of them, be it only to sample how they feel on his body. He gets goosebumps. Bastian strokes his arm.

"You'd look so good in one of those," Bastian drops when Jake's eyes reach the gags. Bars and balls and rings.

"You think so?" Jake asks, sort of failing to see how he would but willing to try if it made Bastian happy.

"Mhm," Bastian replies. "Only thing, though, is that I'd have to get over how much I love asking you to use your words. Which is a shame, really. You're so pretty when you beg," he adds, teasingly. "I'm sure I can manage, though."

"You didn't seem to have an issue when my mouth was full of something else," Jake shoots back with a suggestive roll of his ass against Bastian who's still holding him by the hips and glued to his back. "It just won't be any pleasure for you when I make noises with this in my mouth, though," he adds, a cheeky smile painting his face.

From the corner of his eye, he sees Bastian who seems stuck halfway between delight and disbelief at Jake's audacity and, well, that only makes him want to keep teasing.

"Maybe I will have to keep you quiet later if you don't stop running your mouth," Bastian says and it sounds much more like a promise than a threat, so Jake has no intention of complying.

"Sure, Bastian."

If the smile that Jake sees on Bastian's face is any indication, he's enjoying this just as much as Jake is.

"Alright, alright. Take a look at those, tell me what you like," Bastian says when he detaches himself from Jake's body, gently slapping his butt as he lets Jake get closer to the panoply of restraints that are hanging before him.

Jake goes and he takes stock of all that is before him. He is, at first, taken aback by the sheer number of choices. Once his mind stops being astonished and can safely process information again, he starts assessing each item and each set according to how they'll feel on his body. Bastian won't only control him with verbal commands anymore – each belt, each cuff is a weapon in Bastian's arsenal to heighten Jake's arousal. His brain almost short-circuits completely when he thinks of Bastian restricting most of his movements. Almost in a trance, he gets closer, gets a feel for the materials. He sees some belts with holes along the entire length of it, ready to hold any part of his body hostage, and he likes that idea. A lot. Some classic metal cuffs – he's not sure that a set like that will allow him to fly away, too cold, too impersonal. Some sets are fabric only and he has no real interest. Padded cuffs, thick leather, soft lining on the inside – this is getting interesting. His eyes then focus on a set of what both seems like the most comfortable, based on how thick the cuff itself is, and the most sturdy – this will hold him. The cuffs are three inches large, the buckles almost intimidating, ring on the outside, already joined together by a clasp. He thinks of being tied to the headboard. Spread like a cross on the mattress with his wrists anchored down. With his hands behind his back, kneeling for

Bastian. Facing him. Even better – hands bound behind his back, on his knees, shoulder digging into the mattress, helpless and exposed before Bastian, and the sound of the sharp intake of air that he produces at that thought brings him right back down to earth.

Jake doesn't immediately realize what Bastian has in mind when he steals the cuffs from Jake's hands. Jake's in a bit of a daze, is a bit overcome, and it's not until Bastian lifts his wrist to move his arm behind his back and that he feels the cool leather against his skin that he realizes that Bastian is cuffing him. Right here. In the store.

He tries to look at Bastian from over his shoulders, can't quite get a look, but it doesn't matter because the next second, Bastian is yanking on the clasp that already holds the cuffs together, pulling his wrists down and back and tight and he has no choice but to follow the pull. He falls into Bastian's warm body, he's leaning against him, unable to move.

"This is something you want, lover? Want me to hold you down?" Bastian groans in his ear.

Jake bares his throat, tilts his head back to try to rest against Bastian, doesn't quite stifle the moan that takes shape low in his chest.

"You're not gagged yet, come on, answer me." he yanks Jake's wrists again, putting more pressure down on the clasp. "This something you want?"

He needs a second to arrange the words in his mind in a way that makes sense.

"Bastian, please," he whispers, almost a whine.

Bastian pulls harder. Jake shivers, raises his chin some more. "Told you I liked it when you beg. I'm going to make you do that more often, pretty thing." Jake keens quietly.

Bastian pushes him up, off of him, uncuffs him. He runs his hand up Jake's back and tugs at his hair, tightly tangling his fingers and applying tension just this side of painful.

"We aren't done shopping, pretty thing, I need you to focus. If you're good and if you behave while you're here, I promise to put the cuffs back on once we're home. Understood?" Jake makes a noise in agreement. "Okay, honey," Bastian concludes and turns him around to kiss him quickly.

Jake keeps his eyes closed for a hot minute after Bastian lets him go, trying to regain some clarity of thought. Bastian nudges him under the chin with one finger, causing Jake to open his eyes and look at him. He still feels a little hazed and he knows that his responses are a little delayed. He looks into Bastian's eyes and finds a balanced mix of adoration, interest and mischief in his dark irises.

"Yeah, we're definitely taking that home," Bastian says almost to himself. "What do you think of the glass case behind me, pretty eyes?" Bastian directs him with a slight nod of his head back towards that direction.

Jake's not sure how he hadn't noticed it before now, but if anyone asked, he'd had more than enough stock to take in from the second they walked in, so really he can't be held responsible for failing to take in a massive glass display in the middle of the store.

He approaches it – it seems like a higher-end display for items to be locked up like they are. And are those…

"Butt plugs?" He asks, a bit incredulous.

He hadn't been expecting those, focused as he'd been on impact items and restraints, but he guesses it makes sense for a store like this to also carry insertive toys. He looks back at Bastian with a question mark on his face.

"Ever worn one of those before?" Bastian asks him, curious and not teasing but interested and serious.

Jake gets closer before he replies. He could definitely see how much fun Bastian could have with them, be it only adding that to his earlier fantasy of kneeling, face first in the mattress with his wrists bound behind him – Bastian would get a show, and Jake would probably pay for it in very good ways if watching him entirely at his mercy got Bastian riled up enough.

He shakes his head, gaze glued to the glass case. "Haven't, no…" he trails a finger along the edge of the glass, looking at the different styles with interest.

They're all beautifully arranged in what looks like collections, various sizes and shapes, materials and purposes. Teardrop-shaped glass plugs that flare out at the rim; golden-plated plugs with gems on the end that are clearly mostly meant to look pretty; some mean, beady-looking stainless ones that get bigger with every bump and, lightly put, are frankly intimidating. Jake kind of wants to know how undeniably and inescapably full they would make him feel. There's a set that sets his insides alight – it's steel, and they have a blunter shape than the teardrops, which makes him shiver just thinking of how much he would feel it going in with little to no way of adjusting gradually. The stretch that Jake can imagine is enough to send a fiery signal down his spine. The stem is smaller but not insignificant, which makes him think that it's suitable for longer periods of time without discomfort while still being very aware of its presence. It looks heavy from where it is resting behind the surface and the handle, the handle, it's so delicate and beautifully designed, obviously meant for dexterity, which means that Bastian really can play.

He doesn't realize that he's stopped breathing until he feels Bastian's flat palm creeping up his back.

"Maybe I'll send you out to run errands with one of these in, this way it's easier for me to use you when you're back. You know, I'd miss you while you're gone, all the better to make sure you're stretched and ready for me the second you walk in the door because you've already been filled for a while," Bastian whispers in his ear. Jake can feel the heat and the blush creeping up his cheeks. His fingers grasp at the glass case tightly and he knows his knuckles are white even though he closed his eyes the second Bastian opened his mouth. "Or do you think they will enhance your performance?" Will, not would. "You'll have to make sure you don't flash your cast mates in the wings, though. I must admit that I had a pretty stellar view when I stayed backstage for your show. I think you'd really be able to channel the agony in the second act, I'd love hearing what this does to your performance…" Bastian suggests.

Maybe Jake dies a little inside, and he wishes he could feel offended that Bastian has even considered sending him on stage with a plug holding him open and ready but he also knows that the idea won't leave him until he does. He's starting to think that they really ought to get home soon or he won't be able to keep himself in check, and walking home mildly aroused is not in his plans in the slightest. And he knows that Bastian is fully aware of how much of a rouse he can get out of Jake, but that he is simply enjoying how desperate he can make Jake, especially when Jake can't do anything about it without giving himself away. He twists back so that he is facing Bastian again.

"Can you kiss me?" He asks. He doesn't want to wait until they're home, but he doesn't really know what he can and can't do considering their location.

"You never have to ask for that, handsome," Bastian replies before he tilts Jake's head towards his own for a quick kiss. "I think it's time we head home, huh? There's so many things I want to do to you and all of them are inappropriate to do in public. Hm. I'll get you some of those. And we can go get your cuffs and pick a nice flogger that you'll like, yeah?" Bastian inquires, pulling away from Jake and pulling his hand with him.

Bastian picks up the cuffs that he'd put back and Jake nods enthusiastically when he looks back at him. Jake watches as Bastian's free hand goes back to the wall to grab one of the belts to which he hadn't paid too much of a mind. Noticing Jake's gaze, Bastian throws him back a wink. Okay, okay – it looks very promising and the excitement is coursing high through Jake's body at the possibilities for the use of the belt. Bastian drapes it over his shoulder and hands Jake the set of handcuffs before guiding them to the floggers.

"So, tell me, what do you want out of these guys? They're all going to hit you differently, so I want to get what you think you'll enjoy most. How heavy do you want it to hit? How stingy do you want it to feel on your skin?" Bastian asks, and hm.

Jake can't really say that he's necessarily considered this before. "I think, I'd like something that hits hard. I want something that'll be heavy. And I don't want something that'll be too sharp... but you don't have to go all that easy on me. Is that something..."

Bastian turns back to focus on the wall and picks up something that isn't the thickest but not the slimmest either, both in terms of falls and in terms of their quantity. He weighs it in his hands for a second, seems satisfied at the feel of it, and hands it to Jake, handle first. Jake sets the cuffs in the crook of his elbow to pick up the flogger from Bastian's offering hands.

He tests its heaviness, how it feels in his hands – notices navy streaks and finds out that some of the falls aren't black. When Bastian sees him pick one up for closer inspection, he clears his throat.

"This one compliments your eyes," he confesses. "When you get really into what I'm doing to you, they get so much darker, and well. I'm not passing on the opportunity to beat you up with something that's made on measure for you."

That, to be quite honest, is an argument that Jake can't counter. He looks to the floor and he can feel the violent blush creeping up his cheeks and down his neck. He feels Bastian's hand on his cheek and looks up at him.

"What do you think, pretty eyes?" He asks, eyes lit up in hope.

"Yeah," he whispers. "Yes, Bastian, I want this one too," he tries again, not quite able to muster his full voice but still somewhere above a whisper.

"Alright. You stay here while I go get all our stuff, okay, hand-some?" Bastian proceeds to make him back up until his back is pressed against a wall that is devoid of stock. "I'll be right back. Wait for me."

Bastian steals the flogger and the cuffs from him and Jake gets lost in his thoughts. He's trying to think of what they're going to do once they get home, because now they've got enough toys for several scenarios and that's a thrill in itself, not knowing. He wants his hands behind his back but he also wants the pain, so maybe they can do both the restraints and the flogging but at different times, if he's good enough for Bastian. And he needs to ask what Bastian wants from him when he tells him to be good because he tried, he did, and Bastian seems pleased with him but he really doesn't actually know what Bastian expected of him.

By the time Bastian comes back in his line of sight, Jake is lost in thoughts of his body taking in the assault to which Bastian is sure to subject it. He picks up the bouquet from a thin bench by the door, he must had set it down when they walked in, then beelines for Jake.

Bastian's got this quiet, vibrating energy that passersby would fail to notice, but Jake is so entirely attuned to Bastian that there is no way it could have gone overlooked.

Jake doesn't register the rest of the walk home.

He does, however, register the soft click of Bastian shutting and locking the door behind him once both inside. He does notice Bastian setting the bag down carefully on the floor. He registers how he's never seen Bastian's eyes so alive but so dark. And he notices the way his body goes limp when Bastian hooks his hand under his jaw and pushes Jake bodily into the hardwood of the door behind him.

He notices his heartbeat picking up when Bastian's hand presses against his artery and compromises his air supply.

Bastian has his other hand trailing up Jake's thigh. Jake opens his eyes, hadn't noticed they were shut, to see Bastian intently watching his reaction when he palms at his fly to feel the slight bulge, feel him swell beneath his touch.

"You remember your safe words, pretty thing?" Bastian asks, his hand rubbing and pressing exquisitely at Jake through his dress shorts. Jake nods. "No, no, cielo. Give me words," he insists, the hand on his throat moving to hold his jaw, thumb stroking across his cheek.

"Colors," he whispers.

"That's right. I don't want you to speak up otherwise, unless you need to get my attention." Bastian strokes fingertips on his bottom lip, Jake opens up, docile. "Understood?"

Jake whines. Nods again. Tries to get Bastian's fingers in his mouth, points his tongue to taste the skin when he fails. His hands are flat on the door and Bastian didn't even have to ask but he wouldn't dare move.

"I want to hear every other sound you can make, though." Bastian's hand returns to his throat. "Every breath. Every whimper. Every moan."

Bastian presses tighter with every word. Jake feels lightheaded, and it's not because of the difficulty he's having at getting oxygen to his brain.

"You've been good, today, cielo. You've let me tease you all during brunch and you didn't protest. You've shown me what you like and you weren't shy about it. I want you to be good to me some more. I want you to take everything that I'm about to do to you, because you're a good boy, aren't you? I know you like pleasing me, I know that gets you going, so I'm going to ask you to do that for me again and focus on what I'm giving you."

Bastian finally closes in just as Jake manages to fill his lungs. Jake tries to swallow but it doesn't work, his throat is held tight, held closed, and Bastian's doing that to him because Jake likes it and he wants it and because he can, because Jake will always let him hold his life in the space between his thumb and his fingers.

He releases, almost too early, Jake could have taken more but he still slips a few inches down the door and he's panting.

"You look so exquisite when you're melting in my hands, cielo. I'll never get tired of the look on your face when I do..." Bastian stops his breathing again, "this to you."

Jake focuses on the stillness in his lungs. Bastian, with one hand, the one that was still feeling him filling out underneath the fabric, pops the button of his shorts open but doesn't move the process along. He then trails that hand up under Jake's shirt, and Jake is feeling the pressure now, his throat is working to get some air in and he can't gasp when Bastian pulls hard on one nipple, and there's a brief wave of faraway panic threatening to make itself known for a second before Bastian lets him breathe again. He takes a long, shaky breath in, opens his jaw once or twice, completely fills his lungs and Bastian's hands are still at his chest, except that now he's got both hands working on the buttons of Jake's shirt.

Jake watches him.

The second all buttons are open, Bastian pulls him off the wall with the panels, quickly sliding the shirt off Jake's shoulders and stripping him of his undershirt. Immediately once Jake's torso is free, Bastian spins him around and presses him back roughly against the wall, face first, so that he can gather Jake's wrists behind his back. Holding onto him with one hand, Bastian bends down to dig into the bag – Jake hears the ruffling.

"Don't you dare move," Bastian commands in his ear when he's standing again.

Jake won't. He keeps his wrists crossed behind himself and takes a deep breath while he can. He feels the soft leather against his skin when Bastian cuffs him. He hears himself moan but it's almost foreign, not really him. He tests his movements when both wrists are bound and he's stopped by the clasp between the cuffs with very little give – it's so definite, so concrete and present and inescapable. Almost too effective. He breathes out. He feels Bastian holding down the clasp between the cuffs and with his free hand, he's reaching around to finish unbuttoning and unzipping Jake's shorts so that he can strip him better, using the opportunity to palm at Jake through his underwear. Jake presses his face harder into the door when Bastian pushes both shorts and underwear off of his body at once.

Bastian's hand is back to hold down the clasp. Jake feels his arms being yanked behind him abruptly, and he has no choice but to follow Bastian's lead now. He looks behind himself to see Bastian grab the bag and push him towards his bedroom without much ceremony. Jake is thoroughly enjoying the rush and roughness of Bastian's movements. Bastian isn't trying to be careful with him, he's insistent and his movements are sharp and Jake wouldn't want him any less so. He stumbles in front of Bastian until they reach the bedroom.

"On your knees, on the bed, handsome," Bastian says darkly.

Jake complies, only to feel one of Bastian's hands holding onto his hip and the other pushing down on his shoulders until his face is in the mattress and he's bound, helpless and exposed for Bastian. He feels a shiver up his spine.

He feels Bastian stand just behind him, his knees brushing Jake's feet before he starts kneading at Jake's ass, warming him up, sensitizing his skin. He spanks him a few times for good measure, making Jake whimper each time, as if to make sure that Jake is in the mood enough for what's to come – but Jake has been anticipating this in various ways since they woke up and Bastian didn't let him have his way, so to say he's ready is an understatement – he is so much more than that. When the prickling of the blood flow rushing to warm his skin settles, he hears Bastian walk around to the side of the room that he can't see, and he is too limp and powerless to bother straining to look at what he's doing. He hears the plastic bag crinkling quietly and Bastian opening a bottle, which is already enough for him to tense and relax cyclically in anticipation.

"I think I'm just going to stick this in your body," Bastian says, rubbing the cold, slick weight of what must be the plug that they'd found at the store up and down from his balls to the small of his back, leaving Jake to keen quietly out of need, out of how much he wants to feel how truly full the plug will make him. He wants to beg, but Bastian asked to keep quiet, so it's all he can do to keep from breathing too hard. "I'm going to plug you and then I'm going to flog you until I've had enough and your skin is bright, and then maybe I'll fuck you. I haven't decided yet if you also get to come, so if I were you I'd make sure to keep still and quiet for me. Maybe I'll take pity of how hard and desperate you'll be." Jake can't hold his moans at that.

As he says that, Bastian applies pressure with the plug against his opening and Jake has a slight flash of worry that he isn't going to prep him at all, but Bastian doesn't push, he just holds the blunt steel against him while he uses his free hand to graze at his balls. Jake arches his back, clenches his hands – Bastian isn't giving him anything at all and Jake's incredibly reactive when he gets denied stimulation, everything is heightened because he is so focused on what his body is feeling and so lost in the anticipation. He knows Bastian can see him and he's probably having a blast at how easily he can string Jake along without actually doing much.

"Patience, honey. We can take our time, today, can't we?" Rhetorical, again. Bastian starts rubbing circles against him and drags a finger down the underside of Jake's length, making him jump in the process. Jake stops breathing to focus on the sensations. "Take a breath for me, Jacob," Bastian says almost immediately, poised as he wraps his fingers around Jake's cock that's hanging heavy between his legs and strokes him ever so slowly.

Bastian eventually sets the plug down by Jake's ankle and stops stroking him long enough for Jake to start wondering what he's doing, but there's nothing he can do to look at Bastian from his current position, with his wrists bound behind his back and his face pressed into the mattress.

Next thing he feels is Bastian's finger, this time, rubbing tight circles against him, slicking him up before pressing inside him. Bastian goes slowly but not agonizingly so; he draws back and pushes in a few times until he's settled to the knuckle. He stays still until Jake makes a small noise of pure need and then takes pity, says "Relax, honeybee, I got you," and starts curling and uncurling his finger inside Jake – Jake doesn't know if he's supposed to stay still but he can't realistically be expected to, so he clenches and pushes back against Bastian. He presses his face flat into the mattress to stifle himself out of habit, until Bastian realizes what he's doing and bends to grab him by the side of his throat, pressing most of his body against Jake's without taking his finger out of him.

"I said I didn't want words, but I want all your reactions, pretty thing. Had you forgotten already?"

That's a trick question, Jake will pay either way for forgetting or disobeying, he doesn't know what to answer – he isn't thinking clearly, it was just habit, just reflex, maybe Bastian will understand. He nods and feels a ribbon of shame course through his blood flow, whimpers in hopes that Bastian will have mercy. He hears Bastian tut behind him.

"Oh, we can't have that, can we?"

Jake feels the mattress dip, Bastian is on it, beside him in a way that he can have one hand ready to catch Jake's breath without having to stop fingering him. He pulls out entirely and Jake is breathing a bit too fast and Bastian comes back with two fingers and no mercy and Jake has no way of hiding because Bastian doesn't go slow this time, he pushes in at once and doesn't give Jake time to adjust to the stretch before he tightens the hand on his throat. Jake's brain goes blank, all that's left for him to feel are Bastian's fingers curling and driving into him and the burn in his lungs because he couldn't prepare. He can't get air in and he can't pull away without his hands to support him and he can't fall forward because he'll just choke himself worse and his thighs start trembling.

He pulls sharply at the restraints and Bastian lets go of his throat when he hears the clicking sounds of the metal clasps. Jake gasps and chokes back a sob, Bastian's hand lets him rest his cheek and his shoulder into the mattress again and it's rubbing soothing circles on his back.

"Don't forget again," Bastian says simply, and Jake shakes his head to say that no, he won't.

Bastian presses a light kiss to his shoulder before he turns it into a bite that's sharp enough for Jake to know it'll bruise. He starts scissoring his fingers and it's practical, really – Bastian's focus isn't to give him pleasure. Bastian's focus is to use him, and right now, that really just means prepping him for the plug that is still resting against his ankle. Bastian detaches his teeth from Jake's skin, soothes with his tongue before sucking hard on the skin, for good measure, before he pulls away to resume his initial position behind Jake. Bastian spreads his fingers to open him up a few more times and Jake arches into the touch, clenches on the emptiness when Bastian pulls out. He's stopped trying to quiet himself so he makes a desperate sound when Bastian rubs three slick fingers down the cleft of his ass. Jake feels the fullness and the stretch when Bastian presses in again, it feels so good, he's been waiting for this. He can feel himself twitch and Bastian must have seen it too because next, he's grazing at Jake's cock and rubbing tight circles, wet circles at Jake's slit.

"I think you're enjoying this a bit too much, cielo," Bastian says when he lets go. Jake can't be blamed, honestly. Bastian wipes his fingers on his ass cheek. "Yeah, you're having too much fun. How about we move this along, huh?" he adds, completely pulling out of Jake and drawing a soft cry out of his chest. He wipes that hand on Jake too.

Bastian pours lube directly on Jake, it's cold, clinical. Not about you, his brain supplies. He picks up the plug. Runs it down Jake's cleft again, gathering the wetness there.

"Take a deep breath and relax, Jacob." He does.

Bastian pushes the plug in slowly until he bottoms out. Fills him up. And oh, god, even though he's been prepared and fingered open, this is a lot, it's so much, it's heavy and it's blunt and Jake's full and he couldn't hold the noises in if he tried. He'd be begging, if he could.

"I love the way you're opening up for me, you're gorgeous like this. All helpless and eager and turned on. I've got so much more in store for you, pretty thing. I'm sure this feels good, but don't get ahead of yourself, okay? I'm just starting to have fun, here. Does this feel good, huh, Jacob?" Jake nods frantically, it does, he wants to answer Bastian but he can't, but it feels so good. "Will you keep this in so that you're good to go when I want to fuck you later? You'll stay open and ready for me, won't you?"

It's not like Jake could help what happens to him right then and there, but now he's thinking of Bastian's cock inside of him and that's not something that they've done, not yet, but Jake can't keep the image out of his head. He whines because he wants it and he wants it now. Bastian has a hand on his ass cheek, he's palming and kneading and digging his fingers in and hitting once or twice, and Jake can feel him pull and twist at the plug and his entire body shudders at the sensation. This might be perfect, if he ignores the throbbing need coiling in his stomach. He cries out when Bastian pulls the plug out completely, the breach is so much to handle because of the shape, he doesn't get used to it like he would if someone was fucking him because that's either in or out, doesn't hold his rim open. Bastian adds some lube, it's more than necessary and it's dripping down to his balls, and he inserts the plug again, in. Out. A few times. Jake is shivering and groaning and whimpering and moaning and everything is so good, he pushes back against Bastian every time. Bastian leaves it in when he's done teasing.

Bastian pulls him by the elbows, back in a sitting position, and Jake gets to have a look at himself. He sees his chest already flushed and heaving, he sees the drip of precum at the tip of his cock that is a far too violent shade of red for having been neglected. He blushes. And then he feels Bastian's arms around him. And the belt. And he tries to look back but Bastian is holding him in place and so is the leather band and he's tightening the strap just under his chest and right above his elbows, which means that he is even more restrained than he was. Bastian straps the belt tightly around him, very much so – Jake feels it when he breathes, his ribcage straining and unable to expand as much as Jake knows it can. He tries to move his arms at all. Fails. Okay.

Bastian hooks his fingers in the belt, pulls Jake towards him and Jake goes, his body limp. He thumps back against Bastian's chest. Immediately, Bastian's hands are on him, roaming across his broad chest, pulling hard at his nipples, Jake tries to arch to follow the touch but that doesn't really work either. He rests his head back on Bastian's shoulder, parts his lips. Bastian's mouth immediately attaches itself to his neck.

"Doing alright in there, handsome?" Bastian checks in, his breath tickling Jake's ear.

Jake nods and Bastian drags his fingers across Jake's lower lip, so he points his tongue and licks at the intrusion.

"Okay. I'm going to get the flogger, now. So keep your balance. I'm not going to have you count all the blows today. I just want you to focus on what it feels like. And I want you to speak up if it becomes too much. No other words out of your beautiful mouth," Bastian reiterates, pushing his fingers deeper past Jake's teeth before he lets go of him with a last twist at the sensitive flesh of his nipple. The slight twinge of pain has a low groan emanate from deep inside his chest.

Bastian pushes Jake off from leaning on him and makes sure that he's not going to topple over when he lets go of him. He unclasps the cuffs to get better access to Jake's back, but he leaves them on Jake's wrists. Jake takes a deep breath. He lets his arms go limp by his sides, wishes he could stretch the ache that is starting to build in his shoulders, but that worry flies from his mind almost instantly because next, next he's hearing Bastian take in a sharp breath and he feels the falls graze across the wide expanse of his shoulders, ever so lightly. He shivers and feels the goosebumps erupt on his skin, following the trail set in motion by Bastian. It's short-lived, and then the leather is gone.

Jake hears it through the air and tenses up but the blow doesn't come. The sound does, though, and it's loud and it's rich and just a bit scary – he looks back, a bit hazed, to see Bastian standing with a wicked grin and the falls in his hand. He does a few more snappy rotations, hitting his own hand for Jake's appreciation, just to get him fizzing with the anticipation. Jake drops his chin against his chest.

"Off your heels, handsome. Square up, you'll need all the balance you can get," Bastian orders with caution and for Jake to comply.

Bastian helps him move up from where he was sitting on his haunches, light taps on the inside of his thighs so that Jake will spread his legs and he's at the perfect height for Bastian. He runs his free hand across Jake's back, feeling the skin that isn't tender yet, scratches lightly from one shoulder to the other, just to see Jake's skin go warm and fiery where he drags his nails. Jake gets no contact for just long enough that he's wondering what plan Bastian has for him.

Bastian hits him. Not hard, by any means. Jake feels the rush of air by his neck and the hit on his shoulder blades. It's a thump more than it stings – the only word he can think of is comforting. He sighs when the falls hit again, tension getting knocked out of his body with every strap against his skin. Jake isn't sure how long it's been since Bastian got to do this, or how different this implement would be from what he's used in the past, but he gets back into a rhythm fairly promptly. He listens to Bastian's steady breathing. In, then out when he hits. Jake follows the rhythm for himself. He's pliant by the time Bastian gets acquainted with the flogger, each thump a constant occurrence, either on his shoulder blades or across the middle of his back where his spine curves. He knows that his skin is warming but it's nothing unbearable. He's in a haze. Everything is easy.

And then,

And then, everything isn't easy at all and Jake hears a violent whack and a shocked cry and he doesn't realize that it's from him because the sound escaped him before he could process that

Bastian had hit his ass and stunned him and his eyes are wide open and his mouth is gaping in shock and the wind's been absolutely knocked out of him by the sheer force of the blow.

He's gasping for air that isn't coming and then Bastian's hand is soothing the skin and he presses a kiss to the top of his spine. Jake lets a sob escape when lips become teeth and fingertips turn into fingernails and all he can do is press back into the touches because despite the pain blooming in his body, he wants so much more. He moans, a trembling but genuine sound.

"Your skin is so warm, cielo. So flushed already, you're beautiful. You're taking this very well, you know that? I like it. A lot." Jake is positively melting and his brain is shorting out at the contrast between the care in Bastian's words and the strength of his last blow, he's going to feel that sting for a long time. "Breathe, honey. Will you breathe with me?" Another kiss against his sensitized skin, Bastian's nose rubbing small circles against him. "I think you're ready for more, aren't you? I'm not going to take a break for a little while, now. I want to keep going at you and I want to see how much more you can take and just how hot and red your skin can get. You're too beautiful not to break, so I want to do just that." Jake is riveted to the slight trembling in Bastian's voice, as if he is as overcome as he, himself, is. Bastian grabs a handful of his cheek and he breathes to his ear, "You feel the heat radiating off your ass? Do you feel that? I can't wait to feel the rest of your skin engulf me with that warmth once I start fucking you, cielo, you'll feel so good for me," Bastian finishes as he takes hold of his earlobe to nibble.

Jake swallows hard through his panting. He tries to focus on his breathing that is all but regular. He's having a hard time not bucking his hips in the air, which is resulting in him rhythmically tensing and releasing the muscles in his thighs, and that only serves the purpose of being all the more aware of the stinging of his skin. He keens when Bastian lets go of his earlobe, when he moves back off of him and playfully slaps his ass as he does so. Jake is vaguely aware of a slight trembling in his body and he's not entirely sure whether it's just his heart working overtime or if he's legitimately shaking because of Bastian. He braces himself for the next impact of the falls against his reddened, abused skin.

It's not so intense when it comes, at least not after that one strike, but Bastian isn't playing – Jake thinks he's done playing – he is relentless. He doesn't give him time to breathe between the blows. He's constant, almost democratic, one side then the other, and Jake lets himself sway from side to side, working hard to keep his breathing steady as best he can. The pressure increases. The warmth of his skin turns to heat and he gets lost in Bastian's rhythm, in his gasps after almost every thump, and his staggered groans when Bastian starts going harder at him. He still can't move his arms much but he tries hard not to clench his hands, willing his body to relax under the hits and accept the onslaught, and Bastian won't stop and it hurts so good.

"Your posture, honey, you're doing so well, straighten your back for me," he hears, and it takes several more of Bastian's strikes for him to process the order.

His brain is basking in white noise. Bastian's hitting him, he's hitting him hard, and he's complimenting him, which would be enough on its own to get him to do next to anything if it means that Bastian is satisfied with him. Bastian likes seeing him like this, Bastian likes hurting him, that much is clear, so he gives himself up completely. It's as if Jake's body wasn't his. And maybe it isn't, maybe it's not just as if, maybe all of his thoughts and his pain and his heart really do belong to Bastian, and Jake almost thrashes against the bonds because he can't say any of it but he wants Bastian to know, he needs him to. The pain registers but it's far away, a purely physical problem while his mind revels in the trust that he has in Bastian, in the relinquishing of power into Bastian's capable hands. He doesn't know how long it lasts. He doesn't realize that he's let a tear fall, or two, or more, and he doesn't realize that the sobs are escaping his body with more and more regularity. If he focuses for a second, he can feel the pure strength that Bastian is now putting into his beating. He imagines it, a full body thing, and he can't really think past that image because it's such a good one that it completely takes over him. He's crying and he doesn't have a care in the world to stop.

The thumping has made place to stinging a while ago, the lines are blurred between not enough and too much and more. Jake can't think, isn't sure he could point at when or how pleasure became pain only for it to become pleasurable again – and how pleasurable it is really baffles him. Bastian ramps up the intensity steadily, keeps hitting, hitting, harder, and every time Jake thinks he can't take more he surprises himself. Bastian is grunting too, now; Jake thinks he might completely fuzz out and never come back to the realm of the living, and that. That is so completely fine by him if he can only stay in this moment forever. Trapped between the belt and the blows.

Jake feels Bastian's hand grazing across the welts on his back. He flinches out of reflex under the touch that he wasn't expecting, but leans back into it as soon as he regains control over his reactions.

"I could do this forever," Bastian half-whispers. Jake thinks he wasn't meant to hear it but he nods frantically anyway, god, please. "I know, I know." Bastian's hand is going down the side of Jake's ribcage, lighting an entirely different fire of its own, before he reaches down to cup Jake's ass. "Only thing is, I can't keep flogging you if I also want to fuck you." His tone is casual enough to kill Jake cold-blooded. His hand is reaching between his cheeks now to grasp at the handle of the plug that Jake had almost forgotten. Jake moans at the jolt of arousal through his body, hunches his shoulders forward, he is so on edge that the slightest movement inside his ass has him crying out for more. "And I really want to fuck you, you have no idea how much I want to do that," Bastian adds, his tone innocent as can be. "So this is what I'm going to do. Are you listening? I'm going to give you eight single strikes. Two on each thigh and two on each side of your pretty ass." A tug on the plug, Jake feels his forgotten cock jump in reaction. "And I want you to count them down for me. Out loud. So I would say, if you want to beg, now's the time to do it. You're allowed to talk, now, honeybee. Let me hear just how much you want me inside you."

Jake opens his mouth but he can't get a word out. He breathes hard and Bastian plays with the plug, twisting and pulling and shifting it inside him. Please, please, please, taking up all available space in his mind.

"I want you to beg me, handsome. I know you can."

A beat. "Please," he whispers.

"What's that, pretty thing?"

Jake's mind fidgets between all the things he wants to beg for – use me, fuck me, hit me, "Please hurt me," he blurts out.

Bastian doesn't bother replying right away. He pushes the plug forward, sticks a finger under the belt, pulls Jake back up, "Your posture," and then, "Ask for them. How many strikes, Jacob? Answer me."

Jake braces himself. "Eight, Bastian, please," he begs.

"Oh, you're such a good boy," Bastian says before he pounces.

The sting is so good Jake could sing to the sky. It burns, Bastian caught him where ass meets thigh.

He wants to be good, doesn't wait for Bastian to prompt him this time before "Seven" escapes his lips. If Jake thought that Bastian was going strong before (and he really did), it's nothing next to what he's doing now. Jake can hear Bastian's arm in the echo of the flogger. Two strikes on the same patch of skin has him so tense he feels the belt digging into his arms and he's violently shivering. He's surprised that he's still kneeling and holding his back upright, at least as much as he can.

"Breathe, cielo. Take a deep breath, we're almost done. How many now?"

He needs a second. Other side, it'll be okay. He wants the balance. He wants the pain. "S-six, Bastian," he speaks. He can't stop the sharp cry that escapes him and he feels the tears rolling down his dampened cheeks now. "Five, please, I want to feel it," so Bastian complies and it takes every ounce of restraint for him not to topple forward.

"Anything else you want, huh?"

He's too far gone to be embarrassed at the force of his need. "You," he pants and Bastian drags the falls so lightly against the welts on his back.

"That's not very specific, handsome. What do you want?" Bastian spurs him on.

"Fuck, Bastian," he gasps out, "will you fuck me, I want you to fuck me," he articulates between two sobs.

"I'm sure I can do that, you sound so good when you beg. Soon, mi cielo, tell me, how many more times am I flogging you?"

"Four, please hit me," and Bastian does, square across his ass and he breaks, he does, he falls forward, he's bent in two and he can't help yelping. Bastian yanks him back up so he sobs a broken "Three" and the tension leaves his body with the loud whack of the flogger, he can't stay upright, he can't. So close, he asks for "Two" when he can breathe again, it's the last area to be whipped and when Bastian strikes he flinches under the assault.

"Stay up, one more, beg for it," Bastian commands but his entire body hurts, it hurts, so much but Jake wants all of it, he always will.

"One," final, and he's so absolutely spent when Bastian strikes him with all his might that he barely notices folding himself over on the bed until his torso is flat along his thighs and there's a ringing in his ears, the pain, the pain, the pain, and Bastian's hands are on him and his lips are soothing but his skin is so raw that it just makes it worse, he's never felt so good. He feels a fleeting flash of worry that maybe he won't be able to sit tomorrow but that's okay because Bastian, Bastian did this to him and Bastian is so good to him and now Bastian will fuck him and that's too much to focus on to leave space for worry.

He barely registers when Bastian's hands leave his body to take his own clothes off. He's in his own world, reveling in having been good to Bastian and having taken everything Bastian wanted to give him without a second thought. He's basking. Everything is peaceful.

Jake feels the dip in the mattress when Bastian settles behind him. He feels Bastian's hands on his thighs and running up along the sides of his body. He feels the feather light touch of his lips on his skin, but everything is so raw that even that sends shooting sparks down his nerves. Bastian stills and breathes hard for a moment. Jake doesn't move.

"You're so beautiful, I can't get over it. You've been such a good boy for me, you're incredible. I wish you could see yourself right now, you have no idea how gorgeous your skin looks, do you?" Jake can't help but blush, hard, not that Bastian can see him. "How's your back? Think you can turn over for me? I want to see your face when I fuck you, can you handle that?"

Jake isn't sure, but he'll try, he'll try. He just, he needs a moment to come back to himself, and his body isn't cooperating right now. But Bastian is running out of patience, so before long, his hands turn insistent and he's got fingers in Jake's hair and fingers hooked under the belt that's holding Jake and he's pulling him up, Jake is thrown around until he's resting on his back and the sheets catch on his skin and he's all but hissing. He's whispering curses under his breath because Bastian wouldn't even have to touch him that he'd still be hurting him, be it only by virtue of forcing Jake's back to be in contact with the mattress. He can't move to escape Bastian, even if he wanted to, even if he wasn't bound to himself.

"Yeah, of course you can handle that, I didn't even need to ask, did I? That's how good you are," Bastian says, and Jake sees him stroke himself with one hand and reach down between Jake's legs with the other. "That's how good you are, you won't even complain about the pain if you're doing something for me, isn't that right?"

Bastian twists at the plug and Jake's lungs stall mid-intake. He holds Bastian's gaze, desperate, and his entire body tenses and bucks, his cock jumps, entirely obvious now. He's so hard through it all that it's almost comical. Bastian lets go of the plug so he whines, he needs the stimulation so much he thinks he might die without it.

"Well, good to know someone's having fun," Bastian teases as he bends down between Jake's legs.

Jake groans, the feeling of Bastian's tongue on his cock so real in his imagination he can practically feel it so he throws his head back and bucks towards Bastian but Bastian, he anticipated that, of course he did, and of course he's going to keep denying him. Jake thrashes as best he can against the belt and when he looks back down, Bastian's looking straight into his eyes and he laughs. Jake sobs, the hot breath ghosting over him too much to handle. He thinks Bastian might kill him and that'd be so much better than the torture to which he is subjected, he would embrace it fully.

Bastian pulls back without a single touch to Jake's straining cock. He sits back on his haunches and Jake watches as he reaches further down the bed and retrieves the unmistakable foil of a condom wrapper, which somehow makes everything so much more real, so much more concrete – and when in hell did Bastian even put that within reach, he's got no idea, but – Bastian's finally going to fuck him and that's enough to quiet the part of his mind that's trying to raise the concern of how much the skin of his back is going to hurt when Bastian starts pounding into him. So Jake watches, and Bastian rolls the condom down on himself, and he doesn't register the noises coming out of him when Bastian pours lube in his hand and starts slicking himself up. When he pulls at the plug and makes it shift inside him.

"Look at me, honeybee, I want you to keep your eyes open," Bastian says to ground him. "You get all caught up in your head but not today, gorgeous, I want you all here and focused. No retreating, you're not allowed. I still haven't decided whether you can come, so if I were you…" the playful tugs of Bastian's hand on the plug turn to a steady pull as he starts to take it out, and Jake really needs to relax his body because it's been in him for so long that it can't just be removed. "I'd listen," Bastian finishes when the head of the plug gets past Jake's rim.

Jake wouldn't be able to tell whether his whimpering comes from Bastian's words or his actions. It's most likely a mix of both, the thinly veiled threat in combination with feeling so empty. "Please," he mutters under his breath, holding Bastian's burning gaze.

Bastian leans down, holding himself up on one hand resting on Jake's chest, takes hold of one of his nipples when he starts rubbing the head of his cock against Jake's cleft. "Something you're trying to say, Jacob?"

Jake doesn't know what it is about Bastian using his full name that is so effective on him, but he can't possibly disregard any of Bastian's questions when he uses it. "I want you inside me, Bastian, please," he starts begging.

"Oh yeah? How much do you want that, huh? Tell me," he requests, applying pressure against Jake's rim, he's right there, right there.

"Fuck, Bastian, I can't take it anymore, will you please fuck me," Jake replies, requests really, his voice quivering with the need. The sobs are threatening to come back. They were never really far, maybe never left, trailed right behind Jake's need all along.

Jake almost blanks out when Bastian finally, finally presses in, finally he isn't teasing. His jaw drops open and his entire body is clenching and twitching, he wants to grab at Bastian's body, his arms, his shoulders, his neck, anything, but he can't, he's stuck, and Bastian is stretching him open so slowly he can barely keep his eyes open on Bastian's orders. He's throbbing, his brain swimming in arousal, he can feel his heartbeat in every inch of his body.

Jake wraps his legs around Bastian's waist when he bottoms out, because now that he's got him he's not about to let go. Bastian relocates his hands on Jake's body, one pressing down on his chest, fingers wrapped around the belt to hold himself up, and the other creeping up to curl around his throat. He's not choking him but he could, he really could, and Jake's lost in Bastian's eyes, the only thing keeping him from completely flying away. Bastian doesn't give Jake time to adjust. He starts slowly thrusting into him, and Jake is so on edge that every slide and drag of Bastian's cock pulls unashamed moans out of him.

When Bastian starts increasing his pace, the burn everywhere on his body merges into one – the skin of his back dragging against the mattress, Bastian pounding into him, how painfully hard he is, he doesn't know where one sensation ends and the other starts. And he's ramping up towards his orgasm maybe a bit too fast, but everything is so good, he doesn't want to know whether he can help it so he doesn't ask Bastian whether he can come.

It's not long before Bastian's hand on his throat becomes more than just a distant threat. Or at least, it doesn't feel like long, but Jake wouldn't know how to acknowledge time passing them by. He's more shocked at the fact that the room suddenly goes almost quiet without his sounds filling up the space – he doesn't have air for that, he can't moan, all he can hear are the slaps of Bastian's thighs against the back of his and Bastian's heavy breathing right above him. He notices a drop of sweat trailing down the side of Bastian's temple, he notices how red and full Bastian's lips are, he shivers at the undiluted need filling his irises. All of his senses are heightened, Jake feels everything too much but he can't focus on anything for more than a fraction of second – there's the blood pulsing hard under Bastian's hand as it tries to reach his brain, Bastian's knuckles digging into his sternum and shifting slightly every time Bastian moves, there's his cock, hot and heavy and hard and leaking all over his own stomach, and there's Bastian who's now all but pounding into him as best he can from his position, and he can't breathe, his lungs are stuck and unmoving and his mouth is gaping, trying to get air in until Bastian lets go of him and he's left gasping for his own breath.

Bastian removes his hand from Jake's throat just enough to relocate it to his jaw and roughly pulls it open to thrust two fingers into Jake's mouth.

"I want you to beg me, Jacob, come on, tell me what you want," Bastian pants and Jake moans.

"Ugh, fuck, keep fucking me, please can I come? I might come if you don't stop, please don't stop, I'm so close, everything hurts so good, Bastian, can I?" he pleads as soon as Bastian's fingers leave his mouth.

"No. Not now, you can't come yet, handsome, you better not come without my permission," Bastian replies with a snap of his hips punctuating his every word.

Bastian relocates, he lets go of the belt and the loss of pressure almost knocks the air out of Jake's lungs the way Bastian hitting him would have. He grabs the back of Jake's thighs for leverage, and if Jake thought Bastian was pounding before it was nothing next to how he's fucking him now. He hits Jake's prostate and Jake really can't keep from throwing his head back at that, he can feel his own cock twitching and jumping on his stomach every time Bastian fucks into him just right and his moans reach new heights – he gives himself up to Bastian with abandon, sounds laced with murmured pleas.

"Look up here, cielo, stay here with me, you like when I fuck you like this, you like when I pleasure myself with your body and deny you, don't you?"

Jake hears his own sob more than he feels it wrenched from his body, and his orgasm is so close but Bastian said no, he said he can't and he will explode, he's going to die, he can't survive this, there's no way, he opens his eyes to look at Bastian and feels the tears fall down to his temples.

"Oh fuck, honeybee, you're so hot like this, all flushed and needy and open for me, do you want to come?" Bastian asks, as if that was even a question.

"Please, Bastian, please let me, please may I come?" Jake babbles.

Bastian slows the rolls of his hips, lets go of Jake's legs to slap a blow to his ass before he bends down over Jake and grasps at the buckle of the belt. Jake keens at the loss of intensity, he doesn't want Bastian to stop, but now the buckle is unfastened and Bastian's pulling at the belt, opening it. Jake's not sure he remembers how to move his arms.

"Touch yourself for me," Bastian commands as he thrusts slowly but so deeply inside Jake, making him buck in the process, and that can't be right, can it? Jake's brain is short-circuiting, how is he not supposed to come if Bastian's fucking him so hard and he's going to jerk himself, he doesn't think he can hold it in. "I'm really close, so you're allowed to come if you can before I do, so I suggest you do that and do it now, or your window's passed."

Bastian pulls out of him in one drag and Jake whimpers, his brain supplies no, come back, no, fuck me, but then Bastian is grabbing his thigh and removing the condom and he's stroking at himself with purpose and Jake's mesmerized, Jake's empty and Bastian isn't fucking him and his hand is cold and numb and his entire body is shivering, there's so much pressure but then Bastian's coming in thick ropes all over him, draping his stomach and his hand and his own cock and Jake hasn't come but his orgasm is right there, and this entire image before him is so hot, his back is in pain and his ass is burning, and,

And it hits him like a freight train, he spills, all over his hand, over his stomach, all the way up to his chest and he can't breathe, he can't think, he's stunned but he couldn't stop, could he, with Bastian telling him he could come and telling him to touch himself and then releasing all over him, Jake couldn't possibly halt it but now Bastian's going to be disappointed and he might cry, for real this time.

Bastian picks up Jake's hand and looks at it just long enough for Jake to feel himself withering under his attentions. He brings it close to his mouth, licks his fingers while looking at him. Jake shivers, doesn't know how to read Bastian, doesn't know how to react.

"I should be displeased and upset with you for disobeying me, but…" Bastian's tongue darts out to clear Jake's palm. "You taste and look so damn sweet covered in this hot mess. I'm sure you won't mind making it up to me, because I have a punishment in mind, handsome," he finishes as he brings a hand to push Jake's leg back up against his torso and slaps hard at his exposed ass.

Jake yelps in surprise, he's e's very sensitive and everything kind of really hurts now – he doesn't mind, doesn't care much, but he's aware. Bastian doesn't seem too disappointed in him, he doesn't seem upset, mostly surprised and entirely mischievous already. Jake knows that he should take stock of Bastian's threat, he's in a daze and he doesn't know if he can move at all, so he lets Bastian run his hands on his abused flesh, up and down his thighs, his sides, his arms. He doesn't think of the drying come on his stomach until Bastian speaks up again, "I'm going to get up and get a warm wash-cloth for you, okay, cielo?"

Jake tries to nod but he doubts his muscles got the memo, he tries his best but it's not enough. Bastian lifts his hand to his face and presses a kiss to his palm. My boyfriend, his mind supplies, and a whole new rush of endorphins engulfs him. He's vaguely aware of Bastian leaving the safety of his bed. He's back almost instantly, as far as Jake can tell. Jake has closed his eyes but he feels Bastian, ever so carefully, cleaning up the mess on his chest and over his stomach, a perfect contrast to his earlier ruthlessness and exactly what Jake needs now. He feels the light peppered kisses that Bastian leaves on him and if he's not careful, he's going to fall right asleep.

"Let's get you some water and a bit of food, and then we can stay in bed all you want."

Jake hums. Bastian doesn't leave the bed, so Jake assumes he must've gotten everything when he got up for the washcloth. He doesn't over think, opens his mouth when Bastian has him drink water, stay hydrated, complies when Bastian asks him to take a bite. He rolls over into Bastian's arms, curls up, feels Bastian's hands soothing the sensitive skin of his back (bruises, he thinks, he hopes), and then he's scooped up in Bastian's embrace and breathing in the scent of his skin.

Bastian is murmuring sweet nothings at him. Jake feels a few tears escape his eyes, he's in no distress and pain is distant, but he's just got the shit beaten out of him so it's only fair that crying is part of coming down from it.

"I'd love to run you a bath handsome, but this will have to wait until later. I don't want you to move too much, and I know you would do anything for me in this state, we can't have you nearly drowning. But later, okay?"

It sounds like a brilliant idea. Right now, though, all he wants is Bastian, and he's got Bastian. So it'll wait. And he just needs to be with Bastian, no thoughts, just warm skin surrounding him and keeping him safe.

Okay.

Okay.

Jake isn't sure why he's still awake when he hears it, rationally should be rightfully asleep, but.

He feels Bastian's hand carding through his hair, his lips pressing soft kisses to his head.

He hears Bastian whisper a shushed "I love you," and he hopes he's not half-dreaming, he hopes he's not imagining his voice. Bastian probably thought his boy was all tucked safely and off to visit Morpheus.

That is the last thing on Jake's mind before he falls into oblivion. Being Bastian's boy, and Bastian loving him.

Chapter Thirteen

*J*ake wakes up from his nap late afternoon, maybe early evening, to Bastian reading on their bed next to him, drawing patterns across Jake's scalp absentmindedly. When he tries to move, to roll closer to Bastian, the muscles everywhere in his body scream in protest and he's reminded very swiftly of the reason he was taking a nap in the first place. He can't help the groan that escapes his lips.

"Welcome back, pretty thing," Bastian greets him. "How are you feeling?"

Bastian's hand moves from his curls to his shoulder blades, grazing his fingers over the marks that Jake's skin is bound to show.

"Like I've been hit by several trucks?" He tries, making Bastian chuckle.

"How does taking a bath sound, then? We can go clean you up and relax, yeah?"

Jake looks up at Bastian from his position on the pillows and nods. Bastian slides a hand under Jake's torso, helps him up so that he can sit on his heels in front of him. Bastian reaches to cradle Jake's neck with his hand, pulls him closer into a kiss, and Jake rests a hand on Bastian's thigh for support. He lets Bastian kiss him, pliant in his hands. Fleetingly wonders whether he's really heard Bastian murmur to him as he was falling asleep or if his mind was playing tricks. He doesn't have it in himself to ask, so he doesn't, just lets Bastian take however many of his kisses away. Bastian's mouth and his hands make themselves more insistent for just a second before he pulls Jake away, Jake keeps his eyes closed just a moment longer while he breathes out.

"Dale, cielo. Let's get you cozy and warm. Let me take care of you," Bastian demands.

Jake follows his lead to the bathroom, stands in the doorway while Bastian gets everything ready, large towels by the bath. He runs warm water, makes sure it'll be hot enough to be comforting but maybe not as hot as Jake generally would go, which is probably a good thing. Jake isn't sure that he can take the prickly, barely tolerable heat he usually prefers for his baths and showers. Bastian adds almond oil to the water and the comforting scent envelops them. He stands up and reaches out for Jake's hand when there's nothing left to do but wait for the bath to fill up. He pulls him in close and kisses him again while they wait.

Bastian cups Jake's face with both hands. "You're beautiful, you know that?" He asks, looking deep into both eyes, stroking Jake's temple and obviously enjoying the blush creeping up Jake's cheeks.

Bath ready, Bastian settles in, pulls Jake in front of him. Jake stifles a hiss when the warm water comes in contact with his thighs, so sensitive, he sits down and needs minutes to get used to the water on his skin. He's curled onto himself between Bastian's legs. Bastian traps water and oil in his cupped hands, lets it cascade down Jake's back. The burn, it hurts but is heavenly.

Jake feels Bastian's hands slide under his arms and past his ribcage, pulling him back against him. He hums and turns his mind off. He focuses on the exquisite warmth of Bastian's torso against his back, the steamy air around them, Bastian's hands roaming free across every inch of his chest. He has his head resting in the crook of Bastian's shoulder, so he feels kisses on his hair and nibbles on his earlobe every now and then. This might be the best day off he's had in a really, really long time.

"You know what else was really good, sweetheart?" Bastian inquires after the quiet has enveloped them for long minutes.

Jake hums questioningly, intrigued, uninterested in forming words for his own.

"I had a hunch, since the day we met, that you were going to blow all of my expectations... but I wasn't expecting you to do it so soon. You're a lot stronger than you know, cielo. You're learning yourself and how your body reacts to different sensations, but you're so in touch with yourself about it. And you can take... god, you can already take a lot more than I expected, especially for somebody who hadn't quite been beat up the way I did earlier," Bastian praised.

He's rocking Jake in his arms, gently but enough for the skin of his chest to catch onto Jake's welts and send sparks through his entire body. He's got a hand holding Jake's under the water and one creeping up the side of his neck. Jake stops breathing, and he's not entirely sure that it's conscious, it's just what Bastian does to him.

"You have no idea how proud of you all that makes me, and how happy I am that I get to learn about your body and your mind at the same time you do. With you. You didn't have to give me all your trust without second guesses the way you did, but you did, and really – you have no idea how hot that is," Bastian concludes with kisses down Jake's neck and squeezes of his hands.

Jake starts breathing again even though Bastian's hand doesn't go away. He leans into the touch and breathes slowly enough that anything slower would mean not breathing at all. He's happy to stay right there for however long Bastian will want him to. Or at least until the water's cold. Bastian is holding him and resting his face in the space between Jake's neck and his shoulder. He's sated and content to just spend time together, quietly, until he hears Bastian's stomach rumble from behind him and realizes that maybe he's a tad hungry too – they haven't really had any more than a bite or two since the morning, and then Jake slept off the overstimulation, the excess, the satiation. Bastian really does shut him down, but right now, food sounds like an absolutely divine idea. He just can't bring himself to actually do anything about it.

As if he'd been reading his thoughts, Bastian lets go of Jake's hand where he was holding it underwater and slides it up his arm until he's gently pushing at his shoulder, a silent encouragement for Jake to sit up. He feels Bastian's hand run down across the welts on his skin once more, causing him to shudder and push back into the slight burn, before he speaks up.

"Let's get food, gorgeous. We can make a quick, easy dinner and watch a movie? Would you like that?"

Jake hums, leans forward. He wraps his arms around his knees, giving Bastian enough space to get up from behind him so that he can help him out. He takes the towel that Bastian hands him, carefully wraps it around himself, and Bastian kisses him as soon as he's pat himself dry. Jake feels Bastian's hands cupping his face and bringing their foreheads together. Jake would give up all other sights if he could just look into Bastian's eyes forever. He bends down this time, taking over the languid kiss that they exchange next, and feels Bastian smile against his mouth when Jake wraps his arms around his waist.

"Turn around, cielo. Let me take care of your skin, will you?" Bastian speaks up when they part.

Jake nods and turns his back to Bastian, facing himself in the mirror above the sink. His hair is all tousled, curls made worse in the steamy air; his eyes are bright and his cheeks are flushed red. Bastian's hands roam his chest, as if he's never going to get enough of Jake. He peppers quick kisses across the abused flesh of his shoulders and Jake catches his eyes in the reflection, not quite mischievous but cheeky nonetheless. He raises an eyebrow at Jake through the mirror and bites down gently on his shoulder at the same time as he pinches both of his nipples between his fingers. Jake breathes out and his lips part, his eyebrows furrow – he isn't quite sure what to do, whether he should press back against Bastian or into his hands, or try to protect himself somehow. Bastian makes the choice easy by letting go of his shoulders and his chest to reach around Jake's body, opening the cabinet and pulling out a clear bottle, red cap and colorless solution.

"This'll make you feel better, handsome. And the faster you

heal, the earlier I can start playing with you again," Bastian explains as he removes the bottle cap.

Jake watches as Bastian grabs a face towel from the counter and pours a small amount of the unscented solution on it. He drops his chin down on his chest when Bastian presses the cloth against his back, the coldness a stark contrast to his heated skin. He breathes in deep, Bastian works his way across his shoulders, down the back of his ribcage, and down to his ass cheeks after removing the towel that Jake had wrapped around himself. It's an odd feeling; his skin feels tighter, but it did soothe the dull ache of his abused flesh. Bastian's lips replace the cloth; Jake sighs and reaches for Bastian's hands on his hips. He's turned around and he follows the lead, and before long the bottle is forgotten on the counter and Bastian's lips are against his own, his tongue making itself a home in his mouth, his fingertips grasping at his body as if he was scared of Jake running away from him. As if. Bastian could play him just like he would an instrument he'd invented himself and Jake would let him.

Bastian pulls away too soon. "Stay here, cielo. I don't want you to get cold," he explains vaguely before he slips out of the steamy air of the bathroom.

Jake's eyes follow him to the door and the glint of the mirror behind him catches his eye. He stalks back, twists his body. He wants to see. He wants to look at the marks that Bastian gave him because he hasn't quite gotten to see that just yet. He can't see it all, but he can see how his skin is still flushed in certain places, how it's starting to make way to deeper marks that look like they might last longer, scattered across his shoulder blades. He tries his best to contort, see the purple streaks Bastian mentioned, but he doesn't quite manage. He's got a hand on his shoulder, though, trying to pull himself further so that he can catch a better glimpse, and a trembling shiver runs up his spine when the position forces his fingers to dig deeper into the skin and muscle, a mute pain echoing through him.

He's mesmerized when the door opens and Bastian is back, thick hoodie in hand. The same one he'd picked for Jake the first time he'd slept over. He doesn't know why he's suddenly feeling nervous, or guilty, it's not unlike when he was a child and his mom found him reach into the cupboards for hidden chocolate bars and he'd get a light scolding for it. He feels like he's found something he wasn't meant to find, went looking for some forbidden treasure and found himself with it. Without a word, he lets go of his own shoulder and looks to the floor at Bastian's feet. Bastian's feet who are moving closer to him, Jake closes his eyes until the sliding sound of the drawer opening and closing fills the quiet and Bastian is pressing a hard plastic shell into his hand.

"You'll see better with this, gorgeous," he hears Bastian say, simply.

A handheld mirror is resting in his palm and Bastian lifts his arm up, aiming to help Jake look at the reflection of his back through it, and God. His eyes go wide, he doesn't register the soft "Bastian" that falls off of his lips.

Bastian lets him look until he's had enough, which, he must admit, takes a long time. He can't help it. He can't tear his eyes off the bruised skin. Not when Bastian sets the sweater down on the counter. Not even when he crowds him against the counter, and again, not when he starts nuzzling at Jake's neck and landing soft bites wherever he can reach. He only stops getting lost in the marks when he sees Bastian's hands rising in the reflection until his fingers graze some welts and he scratches lightly, causing his breath to catch in its tracks. He knows he lets out a soft moan, as much out of pain as it is out of pleasure. Maybe more so.

"Hmm. So what do you think?"

Jake looks away from the mirrors and down to Bastian's face to meet expectant eyes staring intently. He nods, a hushed "thank you" breathed out, and it's probably not the answer that Bastian expects from him but it's all he can think, so in a way, he did answer Bastian.

"I can't wait to see how else your body reacts. This won't last very long, we'll see them for a couple of days at best, depending on how fast you heal. The witch hazel will help," Bastian explains with a movement of his chin towards the solution he'd settled on the counter. "Do you know that your skin flushes really easily? It was already bright pink, pushing on a beautiful red flush and I was still only warming up."

Jake feels a shiver down his back when he thinks back to the first few impacts of Bastian's flogger against him. Bastian's hands move to the back of his thighs and he scratches up, digging deep enough for Jake to push himself off the counter at the pull, and that was clearly his plan because next, Bastian is grabbing his ass cheeks, and he's grabbing hard. Jake whimpers quietly.

Bastian is whispering against his ear when he speaks up again. "Can I test it some more? Will you let me use paddles and crops and my hands until I know how they make you react?" Tip of Bastian's tongue against his neck, teeth lightly in his earlobe, Jake tenses at the thought and closes his eyes. "I'll beat you up until you're my own personal palette of colors and I know you'll be enjoying it because of how hard you'll be for me."

Jake kisses Bastian this time, doesn't wait for him. He doesn't have the words to explain how he feels so he tries to show him instead, that yes, he'll let him, and yes, he'll enjoy it. Mid-kiss, he's brought back to himself falling asleep after his flogging, and to how he thinks he's heard Bastian say he loved him, but he really doesn't actually know. He slows down, not entirely on purpose. He breathes, rests his forehead against Bastian.

"What's on your mind, sweetheart?" Bastian asks after a moment, after he's pulled back and likely noticed the crease between Jake's brows. He watches as Jake opens his mouth to speak but his words are caught in his throat.

Bastian brings a hand to his face, stroking his cheekbone with his thumb.

"You know you can talk to me, honeybee, what is it?"

"This morning, you..." Jake takes a deep breath, grounds himself. Tries to. "I heard you say something before I fell asleep."

He looks up into Bastian's eyes, tries to read him.

"Can you say it again? Please?"

"I don't think you were supposed to hear anything, pretty eyes," Bastian teases, with the result of Jake blushing and looking away. "What did you hear?"

Jake whines, that's not how this was supposed to go, he's the one who asked first, how is he the one on the up end of a question now? That isn't fair at all. He huffs.

His blush darkens, he feels it extending down his neck now, and Bastian's still holding his face, playing with his hair. Waiting. Smiling.

Bastian strains his head up towards Jake, pressing a chaste kiss against his lips in encouragement.

"I'm in no hurry, cielo. I want to hear you say what you think I said. Take your time, that's okay," he comforts him.

Jake is starting to come back to reality, and he's starting to get a bit chilly, a bit cold standing naked in the bathroom. He shivers slightly, and Bastian notices, wordlessly unfolds the sweater and coaxes Jake into pulling it on.

"You said you loved me?" He mumbles when he's emerging from the fabric. "But maybe it was just in my head. Or a dream. I don't know," he finishes, questioning.

"Would that have been a good dream, at least?" Bastian smirks.

Jake's definitely embarrassed now, because in all of that Bastian hasn't said a single thing that confirmed that he even spoke up at all. And he's making a fool out of himself if it was just wishful thinking. He doesn't know how to read Bastian's face, but his heartbeat is picking up now, he can feel it in the vein in his neck where Bastian is touching him, which means Bastian can feel it too. He nods.

"And if I were to say that to you now and mean it, would that be okay?"

Jake's brows furrow out of how much he wants to hear that again and he frantically nods.

"Well, I do. Love you, I mean. You're beautiful and perfect and let me have my way with you, and now your body is all marked up with me." Bastian drags his free hand up under the sweater and down Jake's back, fingernails digging across the tender flesh and the welts on his skin, making Jake shiver. "And I love it. And I love you and I want to keep doing this for a very, very long time," Bastian concludes with a chaste kiss on his lips. "Now put this on and we can go get comfortable and snuggle up on the couch," he says after a moment, handing Jake a pair of clean underwear.

By the time they've eaten an actual meal and are settled on the couch, Jake is entirely satisfied to be cuddled up against Bastian and to let him pick whichever movie he wants to watch. He tries to find a comfortable position – his knees are stiff from kneeling for so long, his wrists are tense from the bondage. He rolls them, frowning from focusing on the feeling, the ache in his muscles.

"Everything alright, honeybee?"

Bastian must've noticed him testing his body.

"Yeah, yeah, I'm…" he trails off, just remembering how it felt to have the cuffs and the belt and to be kneeling for Bastian and he couldn't keep the blush and the smile from spreading on his face. "Just stiff from earlier, is all," he finishes.

He doesn't need to be thinking of the specifics of what they did earlier, honestly. He doesn't. He doesn't know that he's ready to play again, only a few hours later, but it'll be all he can think of if he doesn't stop himself.

"Did you have a good time?" Bastian inquires, pulling Jake against his chest on the couch and playing with his hair.

Jake groans quietly. "Yeah. I did." He twists around to be able to look at Bastian. "Thank you."

If anything, he enjoys the strain in his limbs and his joints. It's a good way of remembering that this is all so real, that it is happening and that it works so well for both of them.

"And what did you like, earlier today? I want to hear your thoughts," Bastian coaxes.

"Oh, um." His mind is flipping through all they've done in rapid successions and he can't help but to squirm in Bastian's lap. There goes not thinking about it. He bites his lip, almost scared of the vulnerable position in which he will put himself with the admission, but he knows Bastian and trusts him to be responsible with the information. "Being… completely at your mercy. I liked not having a say in what you were going to do to me."

Bastian scratches at his scalp now, fingers turning insistent. He's not unaffected by Jake's words.

"And why is that?"

"I don't know… I think, because in a way you force me to push myself. I like seeing what I'm able to do for you." Bastian is quiet, Jake can tell that he wants him to expand. "I want to be able to give you this. I want you to be proud of me," he confesses. "I want to take what you'll give me because you think I can, even if I don't. Think I can, I mean."

"Is there anything I did to you that you didn't think you'd be able to take?" Bastian asks, and he's a bit breathless, that much Jake can hear.

"At the end, the countdown," he answers truthfully.

"The single strikes?" Bastian confirms that they're talking about the same thing. Jake nods.

"I didn't think... it was really hard. I didn't think I would last. But I wanted to," he says as he pushes himself up to look at Bastian, "I wanted to because you wanted me to and I didn't want you to be disappointed, and I did get through it and... it made me really hard." He blushes violently at the admission. "I was proud when I got through and I wanted you to be proud of me too."

He doesn't register that he's dropped his gaze down do his hands, twisting in his lap, until Bastian drags a finger under his chin to lift his face up.

"I am proud of you," Bastian says simply while he pulls Jake's face towards his own to kiss him.

He's got a hand cradling his jaw and the other on his thigh, easy of access since Jake is still sitting between his legs. Jake leans forward, taking balance on Bastian's chest, twisting his body to mold itself against Bastian's torso. He parts his lips when he feels Bastian's tongue grazing at his bottom lip and meets him with his own. He wants to ask for something but he doesn't know if he's allowed, doesn't want it to be too much but the idea can't leave his brain and he's all tense just thinking of it. He breaks the kiss, lightly panting, and rests his forehead on Bastian's. He whispers his name.

"What is it, cielo?" Bastian replies.

"Can I... can I ask for something?" Jake pleads without looking up.

Bastian strokes his cheekbone with his thumb. "You always can, sweet thing."

Jake breathes in. Once, twice. "I just don't want it to be too much to ask for," he tries.

"Just say it and we can talk about it if it is," he's reassured.

Deep breath again, but Bastian doesn't rush him. "I want," he attempts to start, but it sounds too selfish of a formulation. "Can you use the plug on me again?" Jake whispers, embarrassment creeping up his spine. His heart flutters. He liked the feeling maybe a bit too much.

Bastian tilts his head up again and presses a chaste peck on Jake's lips. "That is never too much to ask for, Jacob," Bastian replies. Jake looks and sees a hint of hunger in Bastian's eyes, behind the delight. He kisses him. "Besides, I still do have to punish you for not following my orders, and plugging you could be a very good start for doing that, don't you think?"

Jake bites his lips, this probably doesn't fare good for him but if he gets to be plugged while Bastian punishes him, maybe everything will be worth it.

"There's something I haven't told you," Bastian says after a moment of silence where nothing but their breaths could be heard. He must see the question painted on Jake's face because he continues without missing a beat. "I actually bought you two different sizes earlier." Jake gulps. "I used the smaller one on you this morning, but I'm not done playing with you, so there's also one that's noticeably bigger than that. I haven't decided which one you should be getting now, if I decide to keep you plugged for the evening…"

That is quite a terrifying prospect, Jake realizes. He remembers how it felt inside his ass earlier and he remembers how big it was and if he's honest, he's not sure that he can take much more than that, or at least, not when he's still so sensitive from earlier. He has to blink a few times.

Chapter Fourteen

This is how, a half hour later, Bastian is resting his back against the arm of the couch. He's got Jake sitting before him, between his legs, with his head resting on his chest. He's got a knee drawn up against the back of the couch and a foot tucked in just under Jake's calf. And he's got a hand up Jake's sweater (his sweater, really), drawing teasingly light patterns on his abs, scattering light pinches here and there, and regularly staggering upwards to play with Jake's nipples, keeping them sensitized and standing to attention.

And he's got the movie on. (The Little Mermaid, out of all movies).

And he's got the plug worked snugly inside Jake's ass.

Jake's wondering whether this was a good idea at all. Let no one be fooled – he realizes that he is entirely responsible for his predicament, because he's fairly certain that they would have snuggled comfortably and relaxed and watched the film together. He's fairly certain that Bastian was going to keep him calm and sated from their morning scene. But he had to open his mouth and ask for something and now he can tell that he got himself in trouble, because he knows that this can't be Bastian's endgame.

He could deal, if it was, but he still technically has to pay for disobeying Bastian's orders and coming without permission, technically, and he doubts that simply having to sit through some nipple teasing and having the plug in is all that Bastian has in mind for it. (Thank god Bastian let him have the smaller one. That he knows he can handle... technically.) Only thing is, he doesn't know what else is coming his way. That's the slightly unnerving part.

He's trying to focus on the movie. But Bastian is purposely pretending to be unaffected, cold, detached through it all; he isn't holding Jake's hand or playing with his hair, he isn't whispering lowly into his ear. It's as if nothing is out of the ordinary, except that Jake is acutely aware of the bulge in his underwear that is traitorous of his interest in the proceedings and he knows Bastian knows, too. The alternative is impossible, Bastian knows what he's doing and he's constantly so perceptive. Jake can't fool him, couldn't even if he wasn't so aroused. He's trying not to squirm, because that makes the plug move inside him and he really doesn't need the extra stimulation, but. Staying still is a challenge of its own when Bastian's perfect, clever hands are running all over his torso with no further purpose than to keep his skin alive and reactive, his blood pumping, his heart skipping beats.

"My, my, you're so fidgety tonight. Why don't you relax and sit still, handsome?" Bastian says after, after, god knows how long since the movie started. Almost painful tug at his nipple, Jake wills his chest not to heave forward and mute the pain. "Plus, this can't be all that comfortable on your back, can it? Doesn't your skin hurt more every time you squirm?"

Jake groans. He's not quite as pliant as he generally is with Bastian. He's a little bit too much on edge for that and Bastian isn't giving his brain anything to focus on, so he's just. He's just. "Shut up, Bastian," he mumbles under his breath, not exactly confident in his desire to talk back at Bastian. He finally arches into Bastian's hand because he's still pulling and pinching and Jake's will isn't herculean, not right now. Bastian pulls farther away until Jake's can't arch any more, and then some. Jake whimpers.

"Oh and snarky, too. It'll be easier for you if you just trust me, you know," Bastian explains. "Do you trust me?"

"Yes, but Bastian," he tries, but is cut off by Bastian's free hand brushing against the front of his boxers, unashamedly palming him. He whimpers and pushes up into Bastian's fingers, every muscle in his body working to hold him up.

"But what, cielo?"

He doesn't know where that sentence was leading in the first place. Or if he did, he forgot when Bastian touched him through the fabric. He takes a deep breath – it's a lot more shuddery than he wishes it would be – and breathes out a murmured "Please" when he exhales.

He rolls his hips into the touch. He can't help it, nor can he halt the tremors running up his spine.

"Something you want?" Bastian mouths at his ear.

"You know what I want," Jake grits through his teeth. He might be running thin on patience.

"Mmm, I think I do, but it's more fun when I make you say it." Then Bastian is quiet for a second before he breaks into song, "I want more," he sings for Jake. "Or actually, I should have made you sing that, you're a better singer than me and it fits your situation much better. I mean, I'm getting what I want. You aren't."

Jake needs a minute to shake off the dazed lust in his brain before he can take in that Ariel is now singing Part of Your World. Bastian has let go of his nipple, finally, but he's still pressing maddeningly lightly at the front of his boxers which are becoming more tented by the second. He also has a finger dragging the bottom hem of his underwear up Jake's thigh and he really can't blame him for not following what's happening on screen, let alone which song is playing. The contact of Bastian's finger on his skin is lighting him on fire, it's electrifying.

"I think it's time that these should go," Bastian announces sharply as he hooks his hands in the band at Jake's waist, nudging at him so that he'll lift his hips and allow Bastian to undress him.

Jake doesn't have enough rational thinking capacity to quite understand how Bastian's hands slid under him, grabbing at his cheeks briefly before shifting the plug, dragging his fingers against the handle just enough to make it move inside Jake, but he feels his cock unashamedly jump at the stimulation. The way the plug shifts inside him sends sparks in his entire body. It's a good thing he's still trapped in his boxers , for now at least, because his reaction is entirely less noticeable this way. He holds the position, his hips elevated, for as long as he can until his thighs start quivering. Bastian waits just this side of too long before he slips the garment down Jake's thighs and Jake kicks it off, springing himself free.

"Aren't you having just a little too much fun here?" Bastian teases, skirting a furtive finger up the side of Jake's erection, his arousal fully on display now. He can even see a small bead of wetness clinging at the slit of his cock, and he feels like he should maybe be embarrassed at how turned on he is after next to no proper stimulation.

Jake shakes his head, he wants to say that no, this is excruciating and Bastian has barely even started teasing him, that he knows, but his body is betraying him. He wants to hate it, the teasing, wants to hate Bastian for being so good at playing with him and jumping with both feet onto all of his buttons, but he knows that he wouldn't trade this for the world. He is guilty of loving everything that Bastian makes him do. And there's nothing he can do about it. The thought of using his own hands to relieve some of the tension from being mindlessly teased doesn't even cross his mind, it's not like Bastian would actually let him touch himself. Bastian shifts behind him, he's leaning down to reach the floor. Jake turns his head just in time to see Bastian picking up a bottle of lube – Jake remembers him bringing it to the couch after he'd prepped him and worked the plug into him, not an hour earlier. He should maybe have seen this coming. He watches as Bastian pours lube into his own hand. The movie is still playing in the background but Jake hopes Bastian doesn't expect him to pay it any mind.

When Bastian wraps his fingers – his slick fingers – around him, Jake's mind goes blank for a hot second while his body arches against Bastian, and a broken moan falls from his lips.

The moment of quiet bliss is over almost instantly, though,

because Bastian's hand starts moving right away, and he is working wonders on him. It's just the perfect amount of pressure, a languid speed. Bastian plays around for a while, seeing what reactions he can get out of Jake, depending on whether he's just stroking his length, or running his fingers around the head of Jake's cock, across the slit at the top, or even just playing with the sweet spot just under the head where Jake is so sensitive. It feels so good. Jake revels in the sensations that Bastian is giving him. He tries not to get too aroused too soon, but he feels himself growing harder and fuller in Bastian's hand, and he slowly starts rolling his hips alluringly to push into Bastian's grip, slowly fucking into the warm space created between his thumb and the rest of his hand. He hears a soft moan fall from his mouth eventually, and somehow that seems to bring him back to reality. His thoughts come rushing back at that, because god does this feel good, it really does but Jake doesn't know, he doesn't –

"Are you edging me? Am I allowed to come?" Jake blurts out between two strokes of Bastian's fingers, his hips still rocking.

"Knowing helps you, doesn't it, pretty thing? I absolutely am. And no, you aren't allowed. Of course not," Bastian replies, eliciting a sound that is equally a whimper and a sob from Jake's throat. "Shh, shh, you're okay. Don't get so tense, now. We're just playing. And the more tense you are, the least fun this is going to be for you. But I'm not stopping just yet, so it's your choice whether you'll make this easy on yourself or not, honeybee."

Well, that is… that's easier said than done. Jake doesn't think he could relax if he tried. Bastian slows his hand until it's resting at the base of Jake's cock, he extends his fingers lower to graze ever so lightly at the sensitive skin of his balls. Jake's breath is picking up, and his heartbeat, too, and he's not sure he can handle what Bastian's doing to him, he's not sure at all. He's never actually been denied while he was also being played with. He's been edged, by Bastian, a few times, he's been asked to wait, but there was always the knowledge that he'd eventually be worked up to an orgasm. Or if he wasn't allowed, he at least wasn't being teased – just distracted. Ignored. But not tonight, not tonight, and he is definitely breathing too fast now. He hears his heartbeat in his ears, pounding. Bastian lets go of him and he doesn't know whether that's a good or a bad thing. He whimpers and he doesn't know whether it's from the loss or out of relief.

Bastian shifts behind him, just enough that he can tilt Jake's face towards his own and look into his eyes. He strokes Jake's cheek with his clean hand, cups his face briefly before he rests it on his sternum, over his lungs.

"Cielo, stay with me here. Can you breathe with me? Can you focus on that?" Jake's gaze drops and he tries to follow the rhythm of Bastian's chest when it moves against him. He tries. He's a bit better. "I know this isn't easy on you, I know it's difficult. I need you to try and steady your breathing for me, now."

Bastian is quiet and still for a while after that and okay, okay. He can do this. He wills his lungs to take it easy, no need to freak out, he's in no actual danger. Bastian's here. He'll take care of him.

"That's good, keep that up. You're doing so good, Jacob, you're taking your punishment and you're doing great, but I don't want you in distress. The fact that you're letting me do this is a lot, I know that, but you're here and I know you can do it for me. You can, can't you?"

Jake closes his eyes. Breathes. He nods. He feels lighter already. Bastian wouldn't make him do anything he can't handle.

"Can you give me a color? Tell me how you're feeling," Bastian requests after a minute.

He thinks he might have said yellow, if he'd been asked a moment or two ago, but. He takes a deep breath in. "Green," he whispers – he doesn't trust his voice enough to speak any louder.

"That's my good boy. You're doing very good. Just trust me and lean back, will you?"

It takes another deep breath or two for Jake to make sure that his breathing is back to normal and steady enough that he can trust it, and by then, he's got Bastian biting gently at the shell of his ear, softly humming along to the film. Jake may be breathing properly, he is starting to feel a bit too hazy to notice what else is happening, because Bastian's pace is quickening and he's starting to respond to the touch again, trembling slightly and grinding his hips up to meet

Bastian's every stroke. The hand that held his neck is dragging across to the front of his throat and two fingers are extended to touch Jake's lips that he immediately parts. He darts his tongue just past his teeth, just far enough that he reaches the pads of Bastian's fingers, and he moans both because of the fingers in his mouth and the ones stroking him into pure bliss.

"I'm not asking for much, only your voice," Bastian whispers darkly, breath hot on his neck.

And then he removes his fingers from Jake's mouth, but before Jake can voice his protest, Bastian is holding him by the throat, tightly, squeezing, and stops Jake's breathing, mid-intake. Jake's eyes snap open.

A part of him thinks that maybe he should react to that, maybe he should feel something like fear, or at the very least stress, but the only logical step left to do is collapsing back into Bastian and waiting it out. He feels the way his heart is trying to pump blood up to his brain but Bastian is interfering, he feels how strong Bastian's fingers can be, and he feels the tightness in his lungs when they expect oxygen but they aren't getting it. He focuses on that.

Bastian releases his grip after only a short while, and Jake gasps in, it's a reflex, it's instinctive. At the back of his mind, somewhere, Jake is glad that he isn't testing his ability to stay conscious, that he isn't pushing Jake to his limits. To make up for the lack of warning, maybe. He bares his throat, bucks his hips, that he can't help. He wants so much more. His entire body feels sensitized and he's writhing on top of Bastian, and he knows he won't be allowed to come regardless of how much he begs, he knows that, but it's not like he can stop the pleas falling freely from his lips.

"You're so hot when you beg," Bastian tells him, approval coating his every word. "Don't think that's going to change my mind, though, cielo. Don't work yourself up too much, now," he continues while he increases the speed of his hand, the contrast between his words and his actions maddening.

Bastian's got Jake all ready to melt for him, between the hand stimulating his cock – maybe a bit too fast for someone who will not be allowed to come, but he doesn't want to think about the fact that he will be denied – and the fingers in his mouth and the being made unable to breathe, and he has no clue how he is supposed to keep from being worked up because Bastian is doing everything he likes and arousal is coursing high through his bloodstream. He can almost feel his release, just out of his reach.

"I know, I know, but Bastian, please, please," he can't help but to beg, even though he knows he won't get anything for it, he needs to ask. He needs to give that decision up.

Please turn into wordless whimpers and moans, and for a minute, all that can be heard are the desperate noises coming from Jake's mouth and the relentless, slick sounds of Bastian working him up, Bastian who has fingers still grazing at Jake's neck or toying with his nipples and whose hand feels so fucking good when it's pleasuring him. Jake feels his body tighten, he's close, he's so close. It's right there, entirely within reach if only he was allowed. And when he's trembling violently at the fact that he needs to hold his orgasm in, when he doesn't know how much longer he can keep from coming, Bastian stops his movements on his cock and he stops his breathing again, oh, oh. Jake wants to moan or beg or do anything, really, but his mouth isn't his and the words get stuck where Bastian's fingers catch them, they never make it to his parted lips. He doesn't count the seconds, he hopes that Bastian is, because he can't think of time, not right now. He distantly feels Bastian's fingers toying at the slit of his cock and collecting the wetness that has gathered there, and then he's seeing black dots and his mouth gapes further open in a useless attempt to refill his lungs. He's only good at making quiet, strangled noises, and arching and rolling his hips up into the empty air with his cock bobbing, useless in the space between his thighs.

Bastian releases and Jake gasps loudly when he inhales again. He can practically hear the rush of blood to his brain when Bastian's fingers aren't in the way anymore. He's panting. Hard. And he's dizzy. And needy, oh god, he needs so bad. There's a twitch in his body, almost a spasm, when Bastian grips his cock again. His brain fills with what he knows he won't be granted, he knows he won't be made to come but he can't not think about coming, he can't. He can't tell whether the few words to which he has access – please, Bastian, fuck, god I'm so close, please let me come, please will you let me come, I need to, please – he can't tell if they're in his mind or if he's speaking them out loud.

"Shh, no, honeybee. You know you can't." He must've been intelligible, then. "Just let me do this, this isn't about you, just take it like the good boy you are, I know you can. Shh, it's okay, lover. You're okay. Just let me have some fun with your body."

Jake bucks, he can't keep still and he's all but thrashing in Bastian's arms, "Okay, okay, Bastian," Bastian who's working him up and who won't stop, but he has to, soon, if he doesn't want Jake to come, because his orgasm is right there and it has been too close for too long. Bastian shoves two fingers back in his mouth again, rough, deeper this time and pressing hard on his tongue. Jake hears the broken moans coming from his chest, feels himself throb in Bastian's hand, feels the rush of blood and need pooling deep inside him, feels the sweat trickling down his sensitive back and the plug shifting and pleasuring him every time he moves. He feels like he's getting harder but didn't know that was even possible. Bastian's rhythm is increasing, he's jerking Jake off so fast and relentlessly and Jake might die.

And then Bastian, again, completely removes both of his hands, emptiness in his mouth and around him. A wretched sob escapes Jake. This is too much, it's so hard, he's so hard. He cracks an eye open to see his erection standing flushed and proud between his legs, a deep shade of red from being teased so much, and twitching almost rhythmically. He sees the glint of the lube in the low light and the precum that has started to drip from him. He doesn't notice the tears that spill from his eyes until Bastian touches his face to swipe them off. He doesn't know when he started crying, but he also doubts that it matters much. He's tense. And his body loves the tension and as much as he wants to hate how desperate Bastian makes him, he knows he'd let him do this every day if he wanted to.

"Such a good boy for me, aren't you? You're doing so well, Jacob." He can't lie – he loves the praise and encouragement and he is willing to do a lot of things if it means that Bastian is proud of him.

"Bastian, please, please let me come," he begs, not entirely conscious of making the decision to speak up. He doesn't really mean it, he just gets lost in knowing just how much he isn't in control.

"No, honey, you can't do that. Don't worry about coming," Bastian reiterates, and Jake might explode, because how is he supposed not to worry about it?

That's when he notices, he feels Bastian moving behind him, tiny ruts of his hips, and even though there's fabric between them, Jake can feel Bastian's own hard length pressing into the small of his back. Jake's not sure how he hasn't felt before now how Bastian was gently grinding into him too, because every press of his erection against the bruised skin of his back makes it erupt in sparks of soreness, not exactly painful but entirely noticeable.

Bastian's free hand dips into Jake's sweater, why is he still wearing a sweater, but before he can ponder the matter further, Bastian is tugging and pinching hard at his nipple, and it hurts so he arches into the touch, his other hand is back on his cock, his desperate and aching cock, and he sobs once more. Bastian rolls the hardened bud between his fingers as he starts edging Jake again, and he isn't gentle, but before he can think much of it, Bastian releases the tug and the pinch at his chest. With final strokes of his hand, Bastian pulls back, he pushes Jake off from him, and nudges. Jake looks back at him in question and he's not sure that he's ever going to be able to breathe normally again because he only knows panting, now.

"Down, boy. On your knees. On the floor."

He complies, but he's confused. Until Bastian gets up, too, and pushes his underwear down to his thighs, just enough to take himself in hand right in front of him. Jake's eyes flutter. His face is hot, he can feel the blush extending all the way down his chest.

"Hands behind your back, handsome, open your mouth."

Jake doesn't know if it's because of how on edge and hazy he is or if it's just how he always is, but there's something captivating about the imperative orders that Bastian is giving him. The thought of not listening doesn't cross his mind. He kneels next to the sofa, wrists crossed behind his back, looks up at Bastian with pleading eyes. He parts his lips and moves closer to take Bastian into his mouth but he's stopped by a hand weaving its way into his hair before he can taste Bastian. He moans.

"No, cielo. You only get to watch today. You'd have too much fun if I let you suck me off."

Jake blushes brighter than he's sure his face already was at the accusation. Bastian is right, of course he is, he wants so much to be good to him that having the chance to give him head would be self-ish, not selfless, and Bastian caught that. He huffs softly, a slight frown between his brows forming, but he can't pout with his mouth wide open like it is.

Bastian starts jerking himself off, then, and he's right there and Jake can't touch him, but he moans nonetheless at the sight. His brain is overcome by the fact that Bastian is so aroused just from teasing him and edging him and reducing Jake to a writhing and squirming and desperate mess in his lap. He's this hard because of Jake's reactions to what he was doing to him, and despite his desperation and despite his frustration and the ache between his legs, Jake feels pride surge in his chest that he can provide Bastian with this much pleasure.

"Please, Bastian," he speaks up after a moment of just looking at Bastian's hand moving on himself, mesmerized, and listening to the distinct sounds of skin sliding against skin, eyes drawn to the fluids gathering at the tip of Bastian's cock.

"What do you want, pretty eyes? What are you begging for now?" Bastian asks, voice low and breathless.

Jake realizes that he isn't entirely certain what it is that he wants to ask for. "Please just use me," he decides on and looks up into Bastian's eyes.

"Oh, that's what I'm doing, don't you worry," Bastian replies. "Off with your shirt, honeybee, I don't want to get it dirty if you can't keep still," he commands.

Jake scrambles to remove Bastian's sweater from his body, a

quick flash of embarrassment going straight between his legs at Bastian hinting that he wouldn't be able to catch all of his release, and god he hadn't realized how hot it was getting in there. He locks his wrists back behind his back without Bastian having to tell him.

"Good boy, you're so eager and willing for me, even when you're getting nothing out of it. How did I get so lucky? Don't move, cielo," Bastian breathes out. When Jake looks up again, his eyes are hooded with need and his irises look even darker than usual. "Don't move," he repeats.

Jake had thought that, with him kneeling and keeping his mouth open for Bastian, he'd actually get to give Bastian some pleasure, or at least that Bastian would indulge him and come on his tongue. He hadn't thought that Bastian would really only keep him there as something to be looked at and not touched, but here he is, with Bastian's orgasm washing over him while he's still standing a few inches from Jake's face, forcing him to shut his eyes closed. And it means that, by the time Bastian's hand stops moving on himself, Jake's got some of Bastian's load on his cheeks, on his chin. Some of it landed on his lips and in his mouth. And some spilled on his chest. He's dripping and he's stunned, he wasn't expecting that, his breathing is a little fast and his heart is beating overtime, but without moving his hands he tries to clean himself up as much as he can with his tongue.

"You're very pretty, you know," Bastian breathes while he drags a finger through some of the mess he's just made on Jake's face to feed it into his eager and open mouth.

Jake snaps his eyes open just in time to see Bastian tuck himself back in his boxers and turn around in direction of their bedroom. He leaves Jake hard and panting and claimed on the living room floor.

"Are you coming, pretty thing?" Bastian asks from afar, and Jake gulps, because he still hasn't, and he still needs so much. "To the bedroom," he adds when Jake fails to reply. Oh.

Jake doesn't feel in control of his movements. Part of him is too stunned to think at all, so he doesn't really register the gap between Bastian asking him to follow and his body actually moving. He doesn't react much when Bastian meets him in the doorway and puts a towel into his hands, when he tangles his fingers in the hair at the back of Jake's head to tilt his head down, when he presses a kiss to his forehead. He complies, automatic, when Bastian tells him to go and take a shower and clean himself up and take out the plug so that he can get in bed with him.

That, that his brain latches on, being in bed with Bastian. It takes up most of the free space in his mind. So much so that before he knows it, he's stepping out into the steamed up air, patting himself dry so that he can get back into Bastian's room and his bed and his arms. His mind is slowed down and even though, distantly, he knows that he's still aroused and kind of worked up, he's floating on some type of quiet cloud and it's filling all the right parts of his brain.

When he walks into the room, Bastian's got a tall glass of water waiting for him, and he's set up the pillows to make some sort of fort around Jake's side — two where his head will rest and one on the opposite edge, so that however he lies, he's huddled in close with softness on one side and Bastian on the other. He melts a little at the sight and strides in to take the water from Bastian's hands, drinking most of it in one go while Bastian takes the towel off of him and pulls the sheets back to invite him in. He crawls over Bastian and into the spot he's prepared for him, curls up on his side and into Bastian's body, throws an arm around him. He needs the closeness, knowing he's cared for, both emotionally and physically. He doesn't generally get this intimate with Bastian, he's often just being held but he doesn't usually hold Bastian himself. Tonight, though, every-thing feels like a bit more. More personal. More risky, almost — boundaries are being tested. So he hides his face in Bastian's chest, inhales the scent of his skin that he is starting to code as home, his home, and he lets his fingers draw patterns on Bastian's warm skin.

"That was mean," he whispers, his voice so small that Bastian squeezes where his hands landed on Jake's body.

"Hm? What was, cielo? Do you want to expand?" Bastian replies, curving the ball his way and softly grazing at his back.

"You left me alone," Jake replies without much more insight.

"Alone and dirtied and worked up." Jake stops himself at that, even though there's another that his mind supplied for him. He doesn't mention that he felt a bit humiliated, now that he thinks about it. Not in a bad way. He just was.

"Well, you were being punished, after all. Got to make sure you learn your lesson and that won't happen if I reward your disobedience, pretty thing." Jake looks up when Bastian strokes his hair. "Plus, just because you aren't getting what you need doesn't mean I don't get to have fun," Bastian adds equivocally.

Jake squirms a little at that. He hadn't quite realized just how much Bastian would get out of being mean to him and it's stirring something inside. "You had a lot of fun," Jake says although it's presented more as a query, a way of getting maybe a little bit further inside Bastian's head.

Bastian hums. "Of course, I did. I wanted you to know just how turned on you make me when you're all desperate because of me. And what better way to do that than to come all over your pretty face without letting you get your fair share of it? I think you should be thankful you got to see that at all. I even fed you some because I know how much you love it when I use your mouth," he continued.

"And then you left, once you got what you wanted." Jake isn't distraught, not exactly, and he doesn't want Bastian to think that he is so he holds his gaze. He sees a flicker of wonder, some dark interest in Bastian's mind.

"I did." A pause. Jake squirms, Bastian watches. He's interested. "I wanted to give you time to collect yourself and think about what you'd done, lover. And then you could make the decision to follow me yourself, to come and figure out what you need and what you want from me. How did that make you feel, handsome?"

Jake frowns slightly in concentration. "I... I felt embarrassed, but it felt good, in a way. It wasn't, it wasn't shame. It caught me off guard, but... if you did it again... I think it would be good." He looks down.

"Which part, handsome? The ignoring your needs, or leaving you alone? Or the using you just because you love it when I'm selfish?"

Jake's blushing, he knows, he can't help it when he's giving Bastian all the ways he can play with him. All the ways Jake will let him play with him. "The using me. Was that your plan all along?" Jake asks, looking up again. "To make me realize that I enjoy not getting what I want at all? That, that I liked feeling... humiliated?" He finishes quietly. "Can you do that again?" Jake whispers, and Bastian smiles so sweetly before he pulls him up to kiss.

"Of course I can, mi cielo," Bastian speaks softly when they break apart. "Thank you for telling me. I want you to keep being open about what you want and what you like, okay? I want to give all of it to you. That you feel comfortable enough to be vulnerable with me... I like it. A lot. It's kind of hot."

When that falls from Bastian's lips, Jake's reminded that he's still just a little uncomfortable, just a little on edge still, but he tries to keep himself from squirming as much as he can, he doesn't think Bastian is there to bring him all the way up to the point of breakage again. He doesn't think he can handle it again, so he just holds him tighter and rests his lips against Bastian's heart. The orgasm can wait. Everything else can wait. He's with Bastian, and Bastian thinks he's interesting and not weird and he's into it, and. Everything is good.

And that's how, the next day when he walks into the theatre, he needs to stop by Juniper's dressing room and borrow some of her makeup, because despite the bath and the care, there are decidedly still red blotches on his ass and he can't really go on stage like that.

Chapter Fifteen

"*D*espués de usted," he says, opening the door for Jake.

He wanted to get into the habit of taking Jake out, on Mondays. They maybe hadn't been together quite long enough to call it a habit, but Bastian would do his best for them to be headed there. He'd already started, with the brunch the week prior, and now dinner. He'd also gotten in the habit of picking him up at the Lewinsky, every night after their shows – the schedules worked perfectly. Heaven was longer, but it almost always started earlier, so it ended just in time for him to change back into his street clothes and walk to Jake's theatre for the end of Autumn Spell. It was regular enough every night that he didn't need to explain who he was and why he should be let in anymore, everyone on the other side of the artist door either knew him as the Heaven guy or had seen him with Jake often enough not to think it weird.

Tonight, though, Bastian is taking him out for dinner. Nothing too fancy, he's taking him to a small and cozy local joint where he's been going since he was a child. He's confident that Jake will like it, he loves being the one to take him to new places. Make him try new things.

"Bastian, what is this place?" Jake asks once he's stepped in, turning to Bastian with wonder etched in his features.

"One of my favorite spots around here. You'll love it," he replies, pressing a hand on Jake's hip to encourage him forward. "Better than Applebee's, cielo. My little cielito."

"Hey! I'm taller than you," Jake half-heartedly tries to protest, but Bastian can tell that part of him loves it when he gives him pet names. He can't help the hints of possessiveness that color his speech whenever Jake's the subject. "And stronger," he adds when Bastian shoots him a quirky, one-eyebrow look.

"I have ways of dealing with both of those things, I thought you knew that."

They get interrupted by a waiter before Jake has time to retort anything, and it's sublime, Bastian gets a kick out of seeing Jake fidget because of him. He gets the greeter to give them a little booth off to the side under warm, reddish-pink lighting. The whole place has a soft glow to it in which Jake seems to be reveling, it's quiet and cozy and just romantic enough without being cheesy.

"Height and strength don't mean so much when you're kneeling and handcuffed, do they?" Bastian says brightly the second the greeter is out of earshot, without missing a beat, just to see the half-hearted glare that Jake gives him.

"Why do you always do this?" Jake replies, and Bastian smiles because the dimple at the corner of Jake's mouth betrays him.

"Well, it's just too easy to fluster you. I really don't think I can be blamed for teasing you," Bastian says, lighthearted as if he'd been commenting on the new puppy on the block he'd met on his morning walk. Puppies will always be deserving of attention, but Jake is more so.

And right now, Jake especially is so, because Bastian's got an idea that's likely to get Jake very worked up, in a very good way, but he's got to get him distracted and unsuspecting first for maximum effect.

He doesn't open his own menu, he's been around for long enough, often enough to know exactly what he's going to get, which opens up a world of opportunities to focus on Jake.

"This is your trust test, honeybee," Bastian announces when Jake opens his menu, causing him to look at him confusedly. "I need to know you're trustworthy, you know? Make me proud, show me I've got a good reason to keep you around." Jake huffs, he'll always take a challenge, Bastian loves him for it. "You may be good in bed, you're cute and you can sing, sure. But I got to make sure you also have a good taste in food, don't you think?"

"What, Bastian! It's not fair, I've never been here before!" Jake says, slightly indignant, but straightening his back nonetheless. Little clues that he's down.

"It's part of the fun, of course," Bastian reassures him.

He's staring intently at the features of Jake's face when he looks down – he's scanning the choices with purpose. Bastian smirks when Jake makes little confused frowns, but he doesn't speak up about what throws him off so Bastian doesn't offer explanations. Jake should know he can just ask. He can't help it for so long, however, and he's soon reaching to take one of Jake's hand in his and pointing at a few items on the menu.

"Okay. Okay. God, I really don't know," Jake says, and he's squirming beautifully in his seat. "Will you order for me?" He asks, looking up at Bastian with a light blush spreading down his neck. He always blushes so ridiculously easily, it's Bastian's favorite.

"It'll be hard for you to pass this test if you don't even give me options, don't you think?" Bastian replies with a playful smirk.

Jake huffs quietly, barely audible over the ambient music. "I'm hesitating between two, there are too many things I could get, they all look good. What do you think of either the, um, stuffed plantain ball, with the pasta and the shrimp, or something simpler like that scampi chicken?" Jake looked up at him, evidently scanning Bastian's face for approval.

"Hmm, yeah, cielito, those both sound like decent ideas. I guess I can make you pass this test, yeah, even if you needed a little bit of encouragement."

Bastian gently squeezes Jake's hand that he's still holding, grazes the pads of his fingers on Jake's wrist.

From the corner of his eye, Bastian sees a waiter coming towards them with glasses of water, wading through the restaurant.

"You know what else I think you should get?" Bastian asks, but before Jake can question him further, they're interrupted.

"Hello there, I'll be your waiter for the evening," he introduces himself. "Would you like to start with anything to drink at all?"

"Could we get a bottle of what you think is best paired with what we'll order?" Bastian says, retrieving his hands and automatically flipping his menu to the wine page.

"That can absolutely be arranged. I take it you gentlemen have had time to decide what you will be eating tonight?" The waiter asks, drawing a notepad from his apron.

"We have, thank you. Could we please get a plate of your crab meat in creole sauce dish for me, and a seafood and penne-stuffed plantain for him?"

"Crab and plantain, definitely. Both come with white or yellow rice, as well as salad with shrimp or seafood vinaigrette – what would you prefer?"

"I'll have yellow rice and the seafood vinaigrette," Bastian replies and adds, "what about you, Jacob?"

Jake clears his throat. "Oh, um, yellow rice sounds good, I'll have the shrimp vinaigrette, please."

"Noted. For the wine, I would recommend a light Albariño, directly from southern Spain; the dry taste is exquisite to balance the seafood, it is a favorite of our chef and patrons." Bastian smiles at the waiter and confirms that they will go with that pick.

By the time he's gone with the menus, Jake has reached out to tangle his fingers with Bastian's again. He brings Jake's fingers to his mouth and kisses his fingertips. Nibbles softly on them before he drops their hands back to the tabletop.

"Oh, yeah, what were you going to say? Before the waiter interrupted. You wanted me to get what?" Jake asks. He's got no clue what he's getting himself into.

"Hm, it's not much. It's something I think you should get for me. Well, for us, I guess. It'll be good for you too. But I'd like to know you got it to please me," Bastian explains, just to get to see the little frown of confusion painting itself at Jake's brow bone.

Jake uses this moment to take his hand back, grab his glass. Take a sip of water. "Okay... I can probably do that, what is it?"

Jake is talkative today, at least more than usual. Bastian likes it. He doesn't seem to have picked up on the mischief in Bastian's eye. He likes that too.

"I think it's something that'll be pleasurable. You'll enjoy it. And I'll have more ways of getting reactions out of you," Bastian says, purposefully not looking at Jake but at the way his fingers catch the droplets forming on the outside of his own water. Jake is quiet. "And it'll suit you very well. It'll require some temporary... adjustments. I'll have to be a little bit nicer to you for a while. So we'll both have to show restraint, I'll have to be gentle with you. But I probably won't be able to keep my hands off of you."

He finally looks up to see that Jake has stopped moving, he just looks thoroughly perplexed, and he's holding his water in midair.

"Piercings." A beat. Deepening of Jake's frown, he's tilting his head imperceptibly to the side, he's clearly unsure where Bastian is going with this. "Nipple piercings. Both of them."

Jake licks his lips. His eyes go wide, he seems to have forgotten that he was about to drink. He licks his lips and Bastian has maybe too much fun seeing how much Jake can blush even under the pink hues of the lighting above their heads. Maybe. Clean thump of glass against wood, Jake drops his hands to his thighs and squirms, Bastian smiles – he is just so beautiful when he's all flustered, he doesn't know if there's anything he enjoys more than a squirmy Jake. He can't tell whether it's from excitement, maybe a bit of anticipation for the pain, perhaps it's the fact that Bastian dropped that bombshell on him in such a public space. It's probably a bit scary for an idea if Jake hadn't considered it prior.

Jake quickly glances around. It's clear to Bastian that the gears are working a million miles a minute in his brain. He clears his throat. "You, um. You think I should do that?" He asks, lowering his voice to a stage whisper. It's clear that Jake is trying to meet his eye, but can't quite muster the resolve to hold his gaze.

"Uh, yeah. Don't you think that could be fun? You'd constantly be so sensitive for me," Bastian replies with a face that he knows can only be read as a clear fuck, yeah.

"Where did that… idea come from?" Jake inquires, mostly curious – which means it's not a no, and that makes Bastian want to be both nicer and meaner to his sweet, little, innocent boyfriend.

"You know, the first time I pressed you face first into a wall. It would have been even more effective. I'm almost sad I haven't been able to be all that mean to your nipples yet. They deserve some attention." Bastian pauses, looks around for the waiter, reflex, "and now I kind of just want to go back home already so that I can do just that."

"But we just got here," Jake protests softly, his full voice not quite back yet.

"Well, yeah. I'm aware. But you know what, it's okay, because now I still can have you be all on edge and anticipating for what I've got in mind for when I get you back in my bed,"

"I'm starting to think this is your goal," Jake replies. "To get me all worked up in public. You did it last week at brunch… you're doing it now," Jake reasons out loud.

"You can't blame me, seriously, cielo. Not when you're always reacting so much to everything I say. And you love it, or you'd ask me to stop, but instead you just sit there and take it and blush." Bastian raises an eyebrow, looks at Jake intently to make his point in case, and Jake somehow does manage to blush deeper when he looks down. "Teasing a cute boy into being all worked up and whimpering is so good, Jacob, so good. Who wouldn't want to be the reason you can't string two words together, when you look good enough to eat when you can't speak?"

The waiter chooses this moment to reappear, setting two glasses of wine on the table. "Gentlemen, your bottle of Albariño," he announces.

He pours a small amount of the pale liquid into Bastian's glass, who picks it up, twirls once or twice before he brings it close to his lips to take the zesty smell in and taste its crisp flavor.

"Is this to your satisfaction?" He asks.

Bastian locks gazes with Jake; corners of his mouth curling ever so slightly into a smirk as he replies. "Very much so, thank you."

His eyes never leave Jake's. And Jake can't avert his gaze, the waiter being focused on them both. So he blushes instead. Bastian doesn't stop looking at him, he doesn't move – he wants to see Jake squirm and falter, so he stares until the waiter gets the cue and leaves them be.

"So what do you think? Will you get them done for me, pretty boy?" Bastian says, faux-casual tone that he hopes doesn't betray the eagerness that is starting to animate him.

Jake takes a deep breath and closes his eyes, drops his hands into his lap, and looks down. He nods, shyly – it's almost imperceptible, but it's there, and it sends a thrill down Bastian's spine when he imagines just how delightful Jake will look when the barbells go through his sensitive flesh.

"Your words, I want to hear you," he says, trying not to think of the low pitch on which his voice has taken. How raw and raspy he suddenly sounds.

"Okay, yeah," Jake breathes out. "I can… I can get my nipples pierced for you," he says, looking back into Bastian's eyes to emphasize the last words. Bastian smiles. Jake's pupils are wide.

It takes everything in him not to request their meals to go as soon as they get them – he's here to treat Jake, he reminds himself forcefully. But he's hungry for something that the restaurant can't quite afford him, so the bill can't come soon enough.

By the time he manages to get Jake back home, his patience is wearing thin, his movements are rough. Bordering on aggressive. There is no finesse, he doesn't want to be careful; his mouth is on Jake's as soon as the door is shut closed behind Jake's back, he can't keep his teeth off of Jake's pulse points. His feverishness is all directed at Jake, though – he wants to take him apart in all the ways of which he can think. He wants to bite him and bruise him and hurt him and completely make him come undone. He wants Jake so dazed with sensation and pleasure that he forgets how to speak.

So he flattens his hands on Jake's shirt, smoothing the fabric before he moves his mouth up Jake's neck. He makes his fingers insistent when he sinks his teeth in the sensitive skin. He rolls his thumbs around Jake's nipples just to feel him shiver, then pinches as much as he can through the clothing. Jake is already moaning in the warm air, hands clutching at Bastian's sides.

"You have no idea how badly I want to see you wearing clamps, cielo," he whispers, breath warm against Jake's ear. "How badly I want to see you writhing in pleasure when you imagine how you will feel once your nipples are pierced, my mouth finding them and teasing you until you can't handle it," he adds, taking the shell of Jake's ear between his teeth.

"Then do it," Jake pants, so low Bastian isn't certain of what he said. He backs him up slowly, until Jake's back is against the wall and he's caged between Bastian and the wooden surface.

When his head hits the wall, Jake lets out a small puff of air. He's already feeling a bit slowed down, for cause of Bastian breathing those dark promises into his ear.

"Say that again, Jacob, I want to hear that again," Bastian asks.

"Then do it, Bastian, do it, please." His mind repeats that, please, please, please. There's no rush like having Bastian's attention focused on him, all of it, and having Bastian lost in his own world of shattering Jake and stitching him back together – nothing is equivalent.

Bastian doesn't reply, not with words. But he presses Jake tightly against the wall, he pinches and tugs harder, he bites deeper and Jake is thankful for the wall behind his back. He can feel his knees losing their steadiness and his body relaxing under Bastian's touches.

Before Jake can feel like he's had enough, Bastian pulls away, grabbing fistfuls of Jake's shirt to drag him towards his bed.

"Strip."

The command comes, harsh and unforgiving – Bastian isn't playing. He's looking straight into his eyes, his gaze is hard. He has a finger holding Jake's chin and Jake, Jake is having trouble breathing properly. He needs a moment to will his trembling fingers steady enough to get his buttons opened.

Bastian doesn't let go until all the buttons are undone and Jake has started shrugging his shirt off from his shoulders. At that point he turns around, goes for the dresser. A little box sits atop it; Bastian reaches for it. Peers into the contents, wordless, long enough that Jake is down to his underwear by the time Bastian speaks up again.

"So, this isn't supposed to cause you a great amount of pain. But I do want to test your sensitivity, and this will do a good job of showing me just that." He turns around to face Jake's now naked form standing still for him. "See? Sweet little alligator clamps. I'm being nice," Bastian adds, to make Jake gulp at what mean implies. "Hands behind your back, handsome," he requests as he dangles the chain holding the clamps as he walks back towards him.

Jake takes a deep breath, not quite sure what to expect but a wave of delighted anticipation spreading through his body none-theless. He wraps the fingers of one hand around the opposite wrist and clenches. He watches as Bastian takes a clamp in each hand, tensing the chain, Jake's muscles mirroring that tension. He prepares for the pinch but it doesn't come, not right away.

"Open up, cielo," Bastian orders as he's raising the chain to Jake's face.

Albeit confused, Jake parts his lips, relaxes his jaw ever so slightly, just enough for Bastian to set the chain between his teeth. It isn't comfortable but he bites down, staggers back a little when Bastian pushes it further in, wrapping his fingers around the back of Jake's skull. Holding him in place. Bastian kisses him, the makeshift gag stretching his lips a little, making him a bit awkward but still eager enough to kiss back as best he can. It's sloppy, with the metal digging into both cheeks, but Bastian has always liked him a little overwhelmed, a little disheveled. He thinks distantly that maybe he should feel a little out of place, being naked while Bastian is still fully dressed. He maybe should care about that but he really doesn't. It makes him feel a little vulnerable, a little on display, and he likes it. A lot. So he keeps kissing back as much as he can in his predica-ment, and he rests his hands on Bastian's hips to hold onto, half out of wanting to feel Bastian's body under his palms and half out of needing an anchor not to fall.

Bastian eventually stops kissing him, but not before Jake feels breathless and lightheaded. He applies more pressure on the chain, pushes the extremities further at the back of Jake's head so that Jake doesn't have a choice but to walk backwards until his knees hit the bed. His lips are straining under the pressure that Bastian is applying when he pushes the clamps further, the chain is pressing deep into his cheeks. He lets go of it once Jake is resting beneath him, just this side of tense, but eager nonetheless. Bastian doesn't move the clamps when he stops holding them; he only frees his hands so that he can relocate to Jake's chest and start warming up.

"Don't close your eyes, pretty thing. I want you to look at me," Bastian demands when he settles atop Jake, straddling his hips, sitting at the bottom of his abdomen.

Jake tries to control the shiver that rushes down his spine when Bastian runs his fingers across the wide expanse of his chest. It's not entirely the feeling alone; it's the fact that Jake is very aware of Bastian's end goal – the clamps, tonight, sure, but the piercings soon, too – but also the fact that he is unable to move, at Bastian's mercy, and stark naked while Bastian is still completely dressed. He isn't sure why, but. Maybe that's a thing. And when Bastian sits on his hips, he can't pretend or ignore the fact that he is absolutely interested in the proceedings, despite the fact that neither he nor Bastian have acknowledged his arousal, surprisingly. Bastian doesn't usually pass an opportunity to comment on the fact that Jake reacts very easily and so obviously to what Bastian does to him. Bastian works him up so much, constantly, that being aroused around him is becoming second nature – he's proving all the behaviorists right, he's responding automatically to Bastian's words or his hands on him, regardless of where they are. He locks eyes with Bastian, bites down on the metal links between his teeth, and can't help but rotating his hips, just slightly, when Bastian finally takes hold of both of his nipples between deft fingers. He can't help the moan that escapes his parted lips when the fabric of Bastian's jeans drags against the sensitive skin of his erection – it's not the most comfortable of feelings, but it is something, and right now Jake will take any stimulation he can get.

Bastian lets go of the pinch when he feels Jake's attempt at gaining friction, raises an eyebrow at him as if to ask if he really did feel Jake grinding under him.

"What was that, darling?"

Jake huffs and Bastian presses the heels of his hands down into Jake's shoulders.

"I think you should stay still if you want me to keep being nice to you, nothing keeps me from taking out another set. And…" Bastian pauses, slowly and very purposefully rolling his own hips down into Jake's, grinding hard onto his very obvious erection to make Jake groan. "We'll get to that later, don't you worry. Just relax," Bastian says as he bends down to press a kiss to Jake's lips.

He keeps kissing him after that, and Jake isn't tempted to do anything that might get Bastian's lips away from his, so he wills his body to stay still as much as he can, considering the circumstances. The fingers have resumed their teasing, and Bastian won't still his hips, so it's harder than it should be to keep from straining into the touches. But he focuses on kissing back, focuses on how Bastian's teeth are never too far from biting into the pink skin of his lower lip. If he focuses on that, he can try not to respond to the stimulation on the rest of his body; and keeping himself under control to please Bastian is a weapon-grade way of arousing him further. He hopes that he won't be leaking all over Bastian's clothes, but really, all bets are off. Jake feels hot all over.

Before long, however, Bastian's mouth wanders. He plants kisses along his jaw, making him throw his head back to expose his throat. He feels his Adam's apple move when he gulps, he feels his vocal chords vibrate when the teeth in his neck make him groan in reaction. He can feel Bastian's hunger; he isn't hiding that. And when the digits on his nipples leave to make space for Bastian's tongue, he feels the ripples of pleasure down his spine, the way his blood pulses all the way down to his toes. And when Bastian tugs back at the chain, to take it out of his mouth so that he can use the clamps for their designed purpose, Jake can't help but open his eyes again and look at him, be it only to see the undiluted need in Bastian's eyes. He falters under the intensity.

Bastian sits back up, rests the clamps on Jake's chest; and

judging by the intensity of the blush that he can see on his own skin, and if the warmth he can feel all the way up his neck and to his cheeks is any indication, his face must be matching. Bastian uses both hands to roll Jake's nipples between thumb and forefinger, getting them both standing hard, at attention, before he takes hold of the handle of the clamps. He doesn't stop grinding down on Jake. When he lets the rubber-covered teeth bite into the flesh, Jake keens. And when Bastian tightens the minute wheel at the other end of them, Jake's jaw drops open and a small "Oh" falls from his lips.

The pressure is exquisite. It's relentless; both similar and incredibly different to what he is used to with Bastian's fingers and his teeth. It doesn't move, doesn't relax, doesn't become less intense because unlike Bastian, the clamps don't let go after a few seconds. Jake frowns, the new sensations taking a while getting used to. He takes in a deep breath, only long enough to be able to keep making increasingly desperate noises of which he is barely aware, and somehow the fact that the clamps move with him makes his brain want to short-circuit.

And then Bastian pulls on the chain, and despite the fact that Jake is trying his damnedest to stay still, he really cannot keep from surging forward, arching into the pull. He breaks into a mantra of pleases, his brain is full enough with the sensations that although he can hear Bastian say something to him, he really cannot make sense of the syllables. He would not have expected such small devices to have this much of an effect on him. He tries his best to focus back on Bastian's eyes, but it proves a task much harder than expected, and he doesn't quite succeed. Bastian lets go, and Jake falls back on the mattress. He reaches up, and the hand that was pulling on the clamps is now touching Jake's cheek, the pad of his thumb across Jake's bottom lip.

"I was right, you look so fucking good like this, cielo. All sensitive for me. Can you give me a color, gorgeous? How are you doing in there?" Bastian asks.

It takes a second for Jake to stop panting and heavy-breathing long enough to gather his words and stutter, "I'm, I'm okay, Bastian, green. I'm okay, please?" but when he does, Bastian bends down to kiss him and whispers a soft "good boy" against his heated skin. Jake shivers.

Bastian continues kissing and biting him, except this time, he doesn't keep to his mouth and neck. He trails down, spends a lot of time putting bruises into Jake's shoulders, sucking with his teeth fixed in Jake's skin. When he reaches Jake's chest, he pulls back just enough to make eye contact with Jake, and he lets his tongue dart out to lick at the exposed tip of Jake's nipples above the clamps. Jake's eyes roll back, his head hits the pillow – he doesn't have a care in the world for who hears him groaning and moaning because it's so much stimulation, so much sensation, the clamps are tight enough to hurt but Bastian is also pleasuring him, so he doesn't know whether to arch into Bastian's mouth or shudder away from it. It's dizzying. He feels like his entire body is on fire, electrified, and Bastian hasn't even touched him properly yet. Jake is intoxicated with the tightness in his muscles, the tension, the stabs of pain on his chest and the soreness where Bastian's teeth leave deep marks in his body, he can feel the blood rushing and just how hard his cock is every time Bastian shifts above him.

Bastian moves down and relocates between Jake's legs, not without one last roll of his hips to make Jake's breath hitch in his throat. He replaces the tip of his tongue on Jake's sensitive nipples with his thumbs, which is enough to make Jake cry out in reaction, and he feels himself twitch now that he isn't trapped under Bastian. He feels Bastian's lips back on his skin, trailing nips down his torso.

"You've been so good for me, Jacob," Bastian starts, interrupting himself with kisses to Jake's skin as he moves further down. "Watching you... give yourself to me, it's so..." he continues, stopping every other word to continue his descent and leaves a few more bruises along Jake's stomach. He doesn't finish his sentence because his mouth wraps so beautifully around the head of Jake's cock, so warm and inviting and it feels so good – there's no way in which Jake can stop himself from pushing into it, not now. So he does.

He lets Bastian's name fall from his lips, he tightens the death grip that he has on his wrist under himself, clenches his empty hand around a fistful of the soft sheets beneath him. Bastian lets go of his thumbs on his nipples, moves a hand to hold onto the chain – and just that shift is enough to get Jake straining again. He reaches up with his free hand to Jake's gasping mouth, touches his parted lips with his fingertips. Jake rolls his tongue around the intrusion and Bastian pops off.

"That's good, handsome, you're doing so good, don't stop," Bastian tells him.

Jake isn't sure whether Bastian is aware of just how much he loves his hands – anywhere on him, yes, but it's that much better when he shoves his fingers into his mouth – or if he puts his fingers at Jake's mouth out of it being a thing for himself too, but. He isn't sure he could stop muffling himself by sucking on Bastian's fingers if asked to. So hopefully Bastian is just as into it as he is, because he really doesn't want to have to stop. He increases the efforts of his tongue around the pads of Bastian's fingers just as Bastian dives down on him, he isn't aware of biting down until Bastian tries to remove his fingers. When that doesn't work, he pulls on the chain to get Jake to gasp and free him, and Jake chokes back a sob at the pain shooting from the focal points on his chest and at the emptiness in his mouth. He's getting close, what with Bastian working relentlessly to suck him off, and the clamps holding both his nipples hostage, and Bastian having given him his fingers to taste.

The next thing he feels has his eyes popping open in surprise despite the fact that his entire body feels like it is being pleasured by Bastian. He feels the wet tips of Bastian's fingers that were just in his mouth, he feels them just resting at his entrance, and sliding back and forth to graze at his perineum. He's too far gone to voice his concerns, but he manages to lift his head just enough to see Bastian's face – and his stretched lips – tilted up towards him. He pops off.

"Don't worry, cielo, I'm not going to finger you dry. But I couldn't pass up an opportunity to get yourself wet, come on, now," Bastian explains, and if his goal was to get Jake embarrassed and blushing and groaning, it worked. "Do you want to come, handsome? I think you do, I can taste you," Bastian's fingers still moving against him, the chain still tensed just enough to get Jake dizzy. He nods, bites down into his own lip. "Tell me, then. You know to use your words, tell me what you want."

He's still working on that, he is, voicing out loud what he wants Bastian to do to him. "Please, Bastian, can I?" He asks, bordering on being too far in his own head to speak at all.

"Can you what, Jacob?" Bastian retorts, because he can, because he loves flustering Jake.

"Can I come, Bastian, please will you make me come?" He replies, and he has to drop his head back down at the admission, at the force of his need. When he feels Bastian's tongue back on his cock, and his fingers that still haven't stopped moving, he clenches his eyes shut tight and breaks into a series of pleas for Bastian to give him what he needs.

"Are you sure you want to come now?" Bastian asks next, and he doesn't know who in his right mind would answer no to that. "Because I haven't even started fingering you, and that's definitely part of my plan for tonight," Bastian says as if reading his mind, fingers driving insistent and pushing just this much inside that Jake can feel himself clench at the minimal intrusion. "Are you sure you don't want to come on my fingers, cielo?"

"I don't know, Bastian, I'm close, I'm there, don't make me choose," he pleads, his brain swimming in arousal.

"Well, if you don't know..." Bastian trails off, and with a final kiss at the head of Jake's cock, moves off to the side of the bed to retrieve their bottle of lube. Jake groans, his cock twitches and he bucks uselessly in the air.

Jake watches as Bastian pours some on his fingers, plural, and his entire body shudders at the thought of Bastian barely prepping him with one finger before he's pushing two inside him. He's not putting that past him. Bastian likes to push him. So when Bastian settles back between his legs, he pushes Jake's knees out, spreads him until there's a bit of tension in his thighs, too, from the position – as if he wasn't tense enough already, as if he needed more of that. Bastian grazes his fingers down Jake's cleft for the anticipation factor, and doesn't give Jake the slightest of chances because next thing he knows, he is steadily pushing inside him with the two fingers that he's got covered in lube. As if he'd been reading his thoughts.

"Oh, oh god, Bastian, please." His eyes roll back out of reflex.

He doesn't need to be prompted to beg, this time. Especially not when Bastian, fully settled in, barely letting Jake time to adjust to the stretch, dives back down onto his cock and reaches back up to tug mercilessly at the chain joining his abused nipples. Jake's body doesn't know what touch to follow, everything is divine – he tries arching into the pull, he tries thrusting up into Bastian's mouth, he tries pushing back against the fingers inside him, but all three cannot be done at once. He is a squirming mess on Bastian's bed and pleasure is overriding the tension everywhere in his body. He finds a rhythm with his hips, down and up again, every single move-ment stimulating him to breaking point, Bastian's mouth and fingers so good at bringing him to the brink and the clamps so tightly closed down on his nipples that he is in pain, but it hurts so good he can't picture it any other way. He can't think clearly.

"Bastian, oh fuck, please, please fuck me," he mutters, not really mindful of his words or of what he's asking. He just wants Bastian so bad that being fucked seems like the only step left for him to rightfully lose his mind. "Bastian, I'm so close, please let me come, make me come or fuck me," he asks.

Bastian doesn't pull off of him, he doesn't reply; he keeps thrust-ing, keeps bobbing his head and sucking, keeps pulling on the chain, until Jake doesn't have it in himself to even moan. He strains against the sheets, arches off the mattress, and he comes, wordless, buried inside Bastian's mouth, his entire body clenching to a rhythm that Bastian has designed for him. He bucks violently, it's a powerful orgasm, and he's almost shying away from Bastian's mouth because of how sensitive he is and how many times he has felt himself pulse in it.

When his back hits the bed again, and he's panting, eyes shut, breathing hard, and his body is still thrumming but not pulsing, only then does Bastian relent the stimulations that he was imposing on Jake.

"I – please don't stop, please," he requests when his body is spent, when Bastian is pulling off and out of him.

"Oh, what was that, sweetheart?" Bastian said, stopping his movements, maybe to make sure he'd heard Jake right – Jake has never asked to keep being stimulated after an orgasm.

"I still, I… I still want you to fuck me, please," he begs, causing Bastian to thrust his fingers back into Jake with a curious, albeit satisfied hum, which has Jake crying out. "I don't want to feel empty yet, you make me feel so full, please fuck me?" Jake phrases, regaining some of the working parts of his brain.

"Then let me take these off, and you can bet your sweet ass I will grant that request, you're so good for me, you're doing so well," Bastian replies as he uses his free hand to carefully remove the clamps from Jake's nipples.

Jake whimpers, he feels sore all over, and he isn't sure that his nipples will ever feel normal again, but he is so dazed and content, even though he is still somewhat desperate for Bastian to ravish him. He thinks of Bastian using him to get off, with little concern for how sensitive he is going to be (or rather, with all the concern but doing it because of how over-sensitive Jake will be), and it's almost enough to get him moaning again. Bastian thrusts his fingers in a few more times, testing the waters and getting Jake writhing on his bed again, before he pulls out completely with little taps of his fingers against Jake's hip, a silent direction to turn over.

When Jake does, he feels the mattress shift as Bastian steps off of it – presumably to undress, he's still wearing clothes and if Jake knows him at all, there's no way that could be comfortable with how turned on Bastian has to be. Bastian has never been one to hide how hard he gets just from taking care of Jake, or being mean to him. And Jake really can't complain, because the way Bastian gets when the entirety of his focus is on someone… that is not a feeling he can explain, there are no words for how that feels, the unwavering intensity of Bastian's energy that has no other outlet than the body that he is touching. When he looks to the side, Bastian is grabbing a wrapper from the bedside table to hold it between his teeth as he undoes the button of his jeans. Jake doesn't hold his moan in at the sight, because Bastian's arousal is clear in every cell of his body, every message of his body language, and as spent as Jake feels, and as much as he knows he can't get hard again this soon, he feels a thrill down his spine. He wants Bastian so much, he's got a hunger that is just this side of alarming per its intensity.

"You have no idea how ready I am for this, Jacob, no idea. I was thinking that I'd ask you to blow me, or maybe I wouldn't ask and just fuck your mouth anyway, but this is so much better. So much better. You're so desperate for me to fuck you, you don't even care that you already came, is that right?" Bastian asks, and Jake hopes it's rhetorical because the only reaction he can give is to hide his blush against the mattress and arch his back to make himself more alluring to Bastian, to put himself that much more on display and show just how eager he is to be fucked. "You're going to be so sensitive, but that's what you want, isn't it? You want me to make you feel it, don't you?" Jake nods, shifts in anticipation when he feels Bastian's weight dipping into the mattress between his legs. He is completely exposed. He loves every second of it. "How much more prep do you want, darling? I'm so ready for you, tell me what you need."

Jake feels a shudder run up his spine when a finger runs along his cleft, followed almost immediately by the much bigger, much blunter head of Bastian's cock. His breath catches. "Just, Bastian, just fuck me, please, I want you, I'm ready," he stutters, not able to form full sentences. He never will match how Bastian runs his mouth when they have sex. He pushes his ass back against Bastian to urge him forward.

So Bastian does, he uses both hands to knead at Jake's ass cheeks and make him tilt his hips further, rock back against Bastian. He feels him line himself up and push, slowly but steadily, and Jake's eyes roll back, his body responds automatically, he's not sure when Bastian lubed himself up but it feels so fucking good even though it hurts a little, the stretch, the fullness. An obscene moan passes his lips and he's lost in his ecstasy. He can't help but to clench tightly around Bastian, he feels so big without proper preparation and in Jake's spent state. He rocks back against Bastian when he finally bottoms out, he knows he can take it, Bastian has topped him often enough before to know he can take him without problem, he just, he just. He just needs to will his ass to relax and let him in so that the stretch and the pain become pleasure.

"Fuck, Jacob, you feel so fucking good, you're so good, god you're so tight for me," Bastian groans when he finally gets into a rhythm.

Bastian's moans and his words punctuate every push of his hips and every slap of skin against Jake's ass. Jake feels his fingers dig deep into the skin of his hips, it's rough, everything is, but he doesn't want it any other way. There isn't quite anything like giving himself up fully for Bastian, letting him use his body for his pleasure, so even though it hurts, even though his body feels like a string that's been pulled too tight for too long, and even though Bastian's picking up his pace before Jake is ready for it, even though he somehow can't manage to get used to the fullness like he usually does, through all of it he's still begging for more, harder, rougher, come on, Bastian, fuck me, use me. He's stopped caring whether his mind is translating his thoughts into words long ago, and he's just focusing on every shard of sensation rippling through his body every time Bastian moves.

"How do you want it, handsome, what do you want? Use your words, fuck, tell me what you want, you're so good and you're so hot like this," Bastian breathes out, heaving slightly.

"More, I want more, please, can you, can you please give me more?" Jake replies, mindless.

To that, he feels one hand leave his skin, not before he pressed his nails in, and reaching to grab a fistful of Jake's hair. Never stopping his hips. Bastian groans, yanks Jake's head back in a way that makes his entire body shift, and it changes the angle at which Bastian is penetrating him.

"Like this? Is this what you want, handsome, more like this, huh?" Bastian says, voice low and dark, and absolutely breathless.

Jake pushes himself back on all fours, on his hands rather than his elbows, to better be able to fuck himself on Bastian and push back against the hand in his hair. His movements are erratic, it's not getting easier but he's lost in the sensations regardless. With him being higher up, his back straighter, and Bastian half bent over him, Bastian is directly stimulating his prostate now. He feels weirdly detached from the physicality of his body; his head is still swimming in arousal, he can't stop moaning with every push and drag of Bastian's cock inside him, and he can feel himself twitch every time Bastian is stimulating him just right, but there's also a twinge of pain from the overstimulation, and Jake can feel himself leaking all over. His mind doesn't know where to go, what to focus on, and he's thinking that he might just lose it altogether. He's panting and moaning and groaning in time with Bastian's thrusts. And somehow, this still doesn't feel like enough, he still feels like he can take more, even though he can barely take it as is, he still needs more, bigger, fuller. Greedily, he rocks back roughly against Bastian, he's trying to grind his way into feeling, feeling – he doesn't have words, just knows that he wants so much it eclipses everything.

He goes silent when Bastian's hand, the one that is still on his hip, treads down to the swell of his ass, and the thumb runs up and down his cleft, just barely catching on the rim. Bastian's hand doesn't stop there, however; it dips back across to his hip and reaches down to take a hold of Jake's cock, which can't be more than half hard, so that results in a string of expletives falling freely from Jake's lips and his body violently shuddering in Bastian's embrace. Bastian lets his hand fall from Jake's hair, and Jake feels his torso lay flush against his back. He can hear Bastian's little, desperate groans in his ear, the type that are generally too low pitched for him to hear. And the hand that Bastian just freed wraps itself around Jake's throat. It stays there, unmoving for a while, feeling the vibrations of his vocal chords, before he decides that it's time to keep Jake from breathing – all the while stroking his cock, jerking him hard and fast. His brain fizzes out, and he honestly doesn't know how much longer his body can take the assault, even though he knows how much pleasure he's getting out of Bastian like this. But he's being fucked, he's being jerked off but he can't get hard, not right now, and Bastian is choking him and his ass won't stop hurting even though it's nothing that he usually can't take, and everything about him is oversensitive, it's so much.

He gasps in, or tries to, but he can't, so he does the next best thing he can think of and just starts actively riding Bastian, because now that his hands are both very busy, the focus is less on pounding into Jake and, well, he can't have that. He can feel his heart trying to work overtime, it's pounding insistently under Bastian's fingers but the blood isn't getting past, nor is the air. His mouth falls open further and he's vaguely aware of making the occasional strangulated sound but Bastian hasn't yet let go. Something about today feels more possessive than usual, but Jake really needs to breathe now, he is falling forward and he can feel the pressure everywhere in his chest, on his neck. His elbows buckle when Bastian releases his death grip, at last, and all the blood rushes to Jake's head at once.

He manages to coax a broken "Bastian" out of his throat once he has enough air for that, prompting Bastian to reply with a hum to spur him on. At this point, Jake has only one intelligible thought left for himself – "Use me," he replies, his voice rough. Teeth are sinking in his shoulder in response.

Both of Bastian's hands leave his body momentarily, they are back just long enough to push Jake forward into the mattress, so that his full body is collapsed against the sheets. He doesn't have the strength to resist. And the next second they're back on him, one hand holds his hip tightly in place and the other, the other Jake feels in the form of slick fingers up the cleft of his ass. His brain can't connect those dots, and it's as if all muscle mass has left him, so he lets him do with his body as he pleases. He has a transient thought for every movement of Bastian's shifting his own body up and down the bed, creating friction against his raw, half-erect cock for how it is tightly trapped between the bed and his abdomen. He doesn't feel the tear that escapes one eye from the hyper stimulation.

When he feels it, at first, he isn't quite sure that his body is relaying the stimuli properly. But surely, Bastian keeps pushing, he keeps stretching, and the movements of his hips have almost come to a stall, because, oh, fuck, Jake doesn't know how and can't think of how but Bastian is definitely pushing in a finger inside him, too, next to the girth of his cock to which Jake is still trying to adapt. He can't process that, the only words his brain can produce amidst the short-circuiting and the white noise are holy fuck and Jesus fucking Christ does he feel full, does he feel absolutely stretched out, and well, he can't say that Bastian hasn't found an absolutely overwhelming way of granting his request to be used for Bastian's pleasure. Jake isn't at all sure that it's something he can actually handle, though, at least not after he has already come tonight, and as much as he's trying to accommodate Bastian's cock and the however many fingers he's shoved up him besides it, it might be too much for him. But he wants to be good, he wants it, but it hurts and he isn't really able to shut his mind off and convince it that it's pleasurable. He cries out when Bastian slams back into him and makes the sheets shift down the underside of his cock, he shudders, and when Bastian just stays in, deep and big and inescapable after a few testing thrusts, when Jake hears in his breathless voice whisper an echoing "holy shit, Jacob, fuck," he can't help but to reply with a small "Bastian, Bastian, I, ah, yellow," because even with the praise and the possessiveness it really just hurts and Jake wants to be good but he can't right now, not like this, not if he can't even look at Bastian, so he lets out a pained sob, because he is in real pain now and he can't make his brain code is as the good kind of pain.

He feels a bit ashamed, in a distant part of his brain, that he can't take what Bastian is giving him but as much as he wants to, every square inch of his body is sore and tender and too much, too much. Bastian pulls back a bit, he's still inside him but he's pulling his fingers out, at least, because his cock Jake thinks he can still handle, it's just the extra stretch pushed him all the way to the point of breakage and he can feel a tear or two rolling down his cheek.

"Hey, hey, cielo, talk to me, do you need to stop?" Bastian's voice is laced with concern, which makes Jake feel better, in some twisted form of logic.

"Yes, no, Bastian, ah. Can you, can I turn around, please, I need to see you, I need you," Jake says unsteadily, twisting under what feels like a hundred-pound weight on top of his body.

"Of course, of course, come here," Bastian replies, already carefully sliding out of Jake so that he can manipulate his body around.

Once he's flipped Jake on his back, a tangle of limbs and exhausted body parts, Bastian settles back against him. He's got his hands roaming across Jake's arms and his chest, to the tiny sore spots of his nipples, to the side of his neck, and then Bastian is kissing him. He's kissing him, and Jake is kissing back, and he feels Bastian's fingers wiping a tear and his lips kissing what he can only assume are tear tracks on his cheek with soothing "Shh, shh, it's okay, you're so good, thank you for telling me," spoken against his skin like a new layer of protection. Bastian doesn't stop kissing every inch of his torso and soothing him with his hands running all over Jake.

When he can get a word in, when his brain is not trying to send alarm signals, he breathes out, "Will you come inside me, please, I need you," and Bastian's mouth is driven insistent all over his skin. "Don't jerk me, I can't, please don't touch me but please don't stop fucking me, Bastian, please," he requests, because that is okay, he will be okay. He will be fine, just fine, if he only gets to tip Bastian over to climax too.

As he is saying that, Jake reaches with both hands to grab onto Bastian's hips and urge him to penetrate him again. He hooks his legs around Bastian's thighs as best he can, to meet him halfway, encourage him to move and let him know that he's fine for this, that he doesn't want to stop everything, he really doesn't – it's just that, with not being able to look at him when he was facing the mattress, not being able to read him, and with all the extra stimulation to his entire body, it all became too impersonal, it maybe went too far on the whole being used thing. He needs to know that Bastian does care about him, about Jake, for more than just some hole to be fucked, even though he did request for him to just use him – he's fucking his boyfriend, he's fucking Jake, and that's an important distinction to him. Being used, per se, that is still fine, that's still true – and as long as Jake gets to look into Bastian's eyes as he does, and touch him, and kiss him, Bastian can do as he pleases with his body. So he breathes out with a deep moan as soon as Bastian gets back inside of him, with Jake's hands on his hips and Jake's legs locked behind him, and one of Bastian's hands is immediately cradling his face – that's very good.

He lets out a few words when Bastian finds his rhythm again, "ah, Bastian, yes, yes, oh fuck," punctuated by the noises coming out of Bastian too. "I want to feel you, Bastian, I've been good, I've been good for you, will you please come inside me, can I feel it?" He encourages.

With that, Bastian lays himself down on top of Jake so that he can press kisses to Jake's neck, to his jaw, to his ear. He slows down a bit, moving with less desperation, a bit less unbridled roughness. "Shhh, cielo, of course I'll come inside of you. You're my good boy, and you deserve this, you've done so well and I'm so proud," he whispers in Jake's ear. "You've been so good for me, handsome, can you be good just a little bit longer, huh? Can you do that for me?" Bastian asks, checking in while he's comforting and reassuring Jake.

Not quite wanting to form words, mostly focusing on making Bastian feel good, he hums to let him know that yes, he can and he will keep being Bastian's good boy. Bastian drops to his elbows, one on each side of Jake's head, in a way that he can weave all of his fingers in Jake's hair and tighten just enough for Jake to feel it. He is rocking gently against his body, his chest rubbing against the highly sensitive and reactive skin of Jake's nipples with every movement, Jake letting out small huffs of air every time his breath catches. With Bastian's hands in his hair, holding his head tilted back just this much, and his mouth moving up and down Jake's neck from the crook of his shoulder to the sensitive spot behind his ear, Jake's trying to make it as good as possible for Bastian in return. He's moving his hips in rhythm, he's dragging his nails up and down Bastian's back, and he's clenching around Bastian with every new thrust.

"Your body feels so good, Jacob, the way you're reacting, you feel so good, you're so tight around me, I'm close, you're getting me so close," Bastian continues, voice dark in Jake's ear. "I'm ready, lovely, can I come, do you want me to? Ugh, you're amazing, you feel so good, I'm going to come, can I do that?" Bastian adds, the stutter of his hips becoming a bit more pronounced, less calculated, less controlled.

"Please, Bastian, please, I want you to, please come," Jake stutters. He redoubles his efforts, increases the movements of his hips to stimulate Bastian better, to make sure that he can give him the best orgasm.

"Fuck, oh fuck, Jacob, ugh," Bastian says, his hips bucking just a few more times before he comes with his teeth in Jake's shoulder to muffle himself. Jake feels the warmth spilling inside him, he is so sensitive and so fucking worked up that he feels the last few twitches of Bastian's cock that is buried to the hilt in his ass, and he wishes he could give Bastian more but everything in his body is screaming too much and he really needs a break from, from, from any and all stimulation if he doesn't want to lose his fucking mind.

"Oh god, Bastian, thank you, I'm sorry, I'm–" he cuts himself, pushes against Bastian's hips with all the strength he's got left in his muscles and hopes that it's enough, that Bastian will get the message, that he will hopefully regain enough of his executive functions to pull out of Jake, gently so.

Jake vaguely thinks that Bastian must have kept himself from coming until he asked Jake, or something of the sort, because the release really was immediate to Jake's answer. And the way he asked, the very fact that he asked, it made Jake all warm inside and gave him the push he needed to keep doing what Bastian needed out if him. Bastian asked him permission to have an orgasm, he asked for Jake's okay to come inside him and Jake didn't really know what kind of power that entailed until he had it, and while that power is not something that he needs the way Bastian does, he can see the appeal. He won't go out and seek to have that rush, but in that moment, it felt right, it felt natural, it felt –

Caring. It felt caring. Bastian was letting Jake know that he was still in control of whether things were too much for him. He was letting him decide what he could and couldn't handle, he was letting him know that his feelings, his headspace, his body, as much as he wants and needs to give them up completely to Bastian, at the end of the day, were still unequivocally his and that he wasn't just there to passively receive whatever Bastian felt like throwing at him. He let him say, one last time, explicitly, that he was fine, he was okay and he really did want Bastian to release while buried deep inside him. So the next tear that falls from his eye, this time, is not out of reflex to physical pain, it's not from a gut reaction to humiliation or psychological distress. It's from gratitude, it's to thank Bastian; it's from knowing just how truly safe he is in Bastian's arms, it's for having found him.

"Hey, hey, cielo, are you okay? I know this was a lot, but you were so brave, you let me fuck you even after you came, you let me play with your nipples until they hurt, and you let me over stimulate you and you did so good, you're so fucking good, handsome. I love it when you let me hurt you, you have no idea how much I love it when you completely let go for me, shh, it's okay, come here, pretty thing," Bastian comforts him.

It's probably to expect, Bastian has no way of knowing that this isn't why Jake is crying freely now, but Jake isn't one to try to shut him up when Bastian is comforting him like this, when he's complimenting him and telling him everything that Jake is doing right. Bastian now has his arms wrapped around him, he's pulling Jake in close to hold him tight against his own body, and he must have pulled out while Jake was having his epiphany. But Jake is being kissed all over, he's getting his tears wiped off his face, he's got Bastian's soothing hands all over his body and in his hair and on his damp cheeks, so the truth can wait, he decides. He'll wait until he can move again before he makes any decision. Everything can wait another little while. For now, he's completely happy being silent, in Bastian's arms, and letting his tears fall freely to help with letting out everything he's feeling, because he's always feeling so much when he gets like this.

And when Jake gets like this, Bastian knows – or at least, he's figured out, since they've been together – that the best thing he can do is to physically be there for Jake, to let him know that he's available emotionally, too. So while he knows that they'll have to shower, so that he can examine all of Jake and ensure that no injuries need tended to from how he pushed his body, all that can wait until they

have had some time to get reacquainted with each other, to reestab-
lish their trust and intimacy.

He's pressing small kisses to Jake's jaw, rubbing small circles with
the tip of his nose. He's lying to the side, body against Jake's all the
way from his shoulder to his toes. Jake has wrapped an arm loosely
around his shoulders and weaved his fingers gently in between
Bastian's.

When his breathing slows down, once the tears have stopped
flowing and Bastian feels Jake's grip on him loosen, he untangles his
hand from Jake's to cup his face. "I'm sorry handsome, but we have
to get you up and washed before you go to dream land," he
explains, grazing Jake's cheek with the tips of his fingers.

He gets a small, indignant puff of air in response, a sad pout on
Jake's lips and a frown between his eyebrows. He pushes himself off
of Jake, pulls him into a sitting position and presses a nice, languid
kiss to Jake's lips, and maybe that one really just is because he can't
keep his face off of Jake's (and really, he can't be blamed for that).
Jake's responses to the kiss, while positive and telling Bastian that his
lips are welcome, are delayed – nothing is immediate. When Bastian
pulls his face off of his boyfriend's, he can see that Jake is in no state
to make any decision on his own, not right now. He looks properly
fucked out, which he probably is, and is leaning heavily into Bastian's touch anywhere their skin are making contact. He helps Jake to
his feet and, without letting his hands go and without giving Jake an
opportunity to complain, leads him to the shower. Jake's movements
are slow, but he isn't wincing, his face stays relaxed and while he
keeps his eyes open as he's walking, he closes them and wraps
himself around Bastian for support as soon as the water is warming
up. Bastian can't help but smile at the fact that despite everything
that he does to him, or perhaps because of those very things, Jake
still has no hesitation to hatch on him for support and comfort. He's
still worried, that's a given, that he might have gone too far tonight
and that Jake pushed himself too far just to please Bastian or not
worry him, he's a bit scared that he might have lost the control he
generally keeps in check when he's topping or domming Jake and
that as a result, Jake might suffer, but he tries his best to read the

situation objectively. Maybe Jake is crying, maybe that is to be expected, but he's still here, he's still following Bastian's lead, and doesn't seem to only be doing so because there is no other soul on which to attach his own.

Carefully, with warm water and a set of towels at the ready, within reach for them when they're done, Bastian maneuvers Jake's body so that he is standing directly under the stream. Jake immediately lifts his face up to meet the water and Bastian closes in behind him, as much out of wanting to make sure that Jake is steady enough to stand in the tub and out of a desire to be as close to him as possible, because he can, and because he wants to. He runs his hands over Jake's torso, his hips and his ribcage, down his arms. He presses his lips to Jake's shoulders. He takes up a sponge, finds the most soothing soap that they have (because he maybe is some type of soap snob and has several scents at the ready at all times), lathers it and starts slowly cleaning the entirety of Jake's body. He's careful at the most sensitive places – no need to get Jake worked up if he doesn't take stock of the bite marks, the bruising areas, his nipples. By the time he's done, Jake is facing him again, he's resting his hands on Bastian's hips, and he moves to rest his forehead in the crook of Bastian's neck. Bastian kisses the parts of Jake's head that he can reach, and while he's generally not a fan of standing in the running water, he can't bring himself to deny this to Jake. So he stays, no one will die from a few extra minutes of a shower.

"Everything okay in there, cielo?" Bastian asks after a minute, or two, or more, breaking the comfortable silence that had established itself around them. Jake nods almost imperceptibly against his shoulder, moves to wrap his arms around the small of Bastian's back. "We don't need to talk about this right now, that's okay, but I want you to know I'm very proud of you. I'm so happy with what we did, even if I may have pushed you too far. But thank you for telling me when I did. I always want to know that, okay. Thank you for trusting me with… everything," he concludes, pulling Jake as close as he can.

Before long, the shower is turned off, their bodies dry, and Bastian has taken care of settling Jake comfortably in their bed. He's got Jake on his side, hugging a pillow tightly against his chest, knees drawn up. Slow, steady breathing – this is good. So Bastian settles behind him, close, running his hand ever so gently down the side of Jake's ribcage, to the dip at his hip, soothing rubs down his thigh. His lips never leave the expanse of skin between Jake's shoulder blades, he covers every inch, every knob of his spine, every freckle he can make out in the low light. It's the least he can do, to build him up. When Jake pushes back against his touches, Bastian slips his arm under the pillow and pulls him close against his chest, draws his legs just under Jake's to have as much of their skin touching as possible. He can't stay like this forever, he gets sweaty, they both do, but for it'll have to do because he can't think of not touching Jake's body with as much of his own as physically possible.

The evening is replaying in Bastian's mind as Jake is drifting off to, Bastian hopes, a land of comforting dreams. He wants Jake to know that he's safe in his arms, he always will be, even (or especially) when Bastian is poking at all his boundaries, stretching them, pushing them, finding where they can be modified and how Jake can grow with him; and doing that, well, he's bound to go too far and break a few of them, if only it means that they'll come back stronger. He knows Jake most likely only needs to feel that sense of safety across all layers of his consciousness; not only when he's awake, not only when they're playing, but through all aspects of their lives, with each other and in moments apart, and most especially in his slumber. But even knowing this, even knowing that it might be necessary to hurt Jake to heal him, despite knowing that it will happen, that Jake will break sometimes and that's okay as long as Bastian is here to stitch him back together… he can't help feeling like maybe he should have waited, or been more careful, he could have reined in his hunger. But he didn't because he wanted to see how far, how much Jake could be pushed.

He can't decide how to read Jake coming down, or even before then, when he urged him to continue past safe wording, although he only did keep going because Jake asked him to, but what if he did out of concern for Bastian, what if? What if he didn't want to disappoint Bastian, what if he forced himself, his body, to push through the pain just because he didn't want Bastian to think of him as less, or not good enough, or, or, or. Jake does have a tendency to cry, that wasn't a first, but he generally only does so while things are happening to him, not once everything is over — and now, there is a chance that Bastian might have read the signals wrong. Sure, they'll talk it out, he knows they will, but. He doesn't like the little swarm of worry that takes flight at the pit of his stomach.

He falls asleep clutching Jake's body, his forehead against the nape of Jake's neck, breathing in the soft scent of his curls and of his skin.

By the time they wake, Jake has turned over to be facing Bastian, he's entwined their fingers, laced them tightly together. So before any word is spoken, Bastian pushes Jake on his back, he takes all the time with which the world presents him with his lips on Jake's own, on his jaw, on his neck, on his chest; a plead, a silent thank you and vibrant apology that he hopes is transferring with all the electrons that leave the confines of his body to go refill Jake's energy.

Chapter Sixteen

"Oh my god, Bastian, you scared me," Jake gasps, a hand on his heart, shaking his head.

Bastian is standing at his vanity across from the door, hips resting on the counter, arms crossed; Jake is entering his dressing room, in costume, just walking offstage from the matinee. Doesn't matter how often Bastian surprises him, his show always being done just in time for him to undress and rush to the Lewinsky for the Autumn finale; doesn't matter how often Jake walks into a dressing room that isn't actually empty, he still jolts every time. His body still erupts in goosebumps every time he lays eyes on Bastian, too, that hasn't changed, regardless of how hot he is from the stage lights and the dancing.

"I want to see them," Bastian says as a form of greetings as he takes strides across the small room and closes the door behind Jake.

"What?"

"The bruises, your bruises, please take your shirt off," he requests, his hands busying themselves with Jake's buttons.

There's this thing they've been doing, Jake isn't sure how or when it started exactly, can't pinpoint a moment. But Jake more often than not is covered to varying degrees in bite marks, bruises either black and blue or deep shades of violet and crimson, to the point where he's had to get makeup specifically for his chest, for the scenes he spends with his shirt ripped open on stage. But for some reason, it had been a few days, his bruised chest had gone mostly back to normal with only faded remnants of Bastian's teeth here and there, too faint to really be worthy of notice. So last night, this morning, Bastian had taken great care of remedying the situation and had spent forever, forever sucking bruises and biting to break veins under Jake's skin, making sure Jake was bleeding into his own skin the way a drop of ink expands on blotting paper and becomes one with the fiber. But it's been a few days, and Bastian has this restless energy of a man who hasn't been eating in days and is presented with a buffet and he can't get Jake's shirt open fast enough to soak in the sight.

"Hold on, Bastian, wait – let me get a wipe, you won't see anything right now," Jake explains when Bastian's brows furrow because he knows the stains should be darker on Jake.

He untangles himself from Bastian's hungry hands, uses the opportunity to finish unbuttoning his shirt and hangs it on the nearest chair. He pulls a makeup wipe from a small box on his vanity and methodically starts revealing the concealed colors with which Bastian had so expertly painted him. From the corner of his eye, he sees Bastian creep in behind him until he's caging Jake in, hands on his hip bones, chin on his shoulder, the mirror in front of them both. Jake can hear how Bastian's breathing is already a bit ragged, a bit heavy; and with every bruise that he uncovers, he can feel Bastian's hunger radiating off of him in waves until he's done and he's got Bastian's teeth fixed in his shoulder. Bastian drags his hands up Jake's torso, his short nails digging fiery lines up his abs; Jake marks so easily. He'd never quite realized just how easily he did until Bastian made a point of never letting his body go unscathed.

"Oh, I'm going to bruise you," Bastian half-whispers and half-sings to Jake, and it could be silly but the intensity between them takes precedence over any humor.

"Oh, you're going to be my bruise," Jake replies automatically in the same hushed tone, pressing back into Bastian's embrace.

Jake watches as Bastian's hands drift all over his body, he watches how one creeps up to his chest, his collarbones, wraps delicately around his throat; how the other one trails down to rest over the zipper of his trousers and cups him through the fabric, pressing softly, assessing. Jake needs to take a breath and will his body not to surrender to Bastian's touches, not here, not now. Getting hard at the theatre is hardly on his to-do list for the day. But when he opens his mouth to speak, he can hear the breathlessness in his own voice.

"Bastian, come on, not here, let me take my makeup off and we can go home? Why are you so eager?"

"You have no idea, do you? How I can't stop thinking about the marks I've left on you when I leave you to parade around and show your body off to a thousand people who have no clue what you're hiding? I almost missed a cue today because I couldn't stop thinking about this," Bastian says as he squeezes Jake with both of his hands, resulting in Jake automatically bucking his hips into Bastian's grip on him and relaxing instantly because of the threat to his airways.

"You made me come, what... six hours ago," Jake replies with a quick glance at the clock. He's not sure what point he's trying to make with that comment. His heartbeat is picking up, that much he can feel, getting more insistent under Bastian's grip.

"Not my fault you woke up hard, gorgeous, I couldn't let you come to work with morning wood, could I? You can't blame me," Bastian retorts, fingers playing along the seam of Jake's pants.

Jake's eyes drift to the side, where he can see the dressing room door behind them. It's closed, but Bastian didn't lock it. People never come in without knocking, without asking, but they could. Jake forces his body off of Bastian's, away from his touches, turns around swiftly to get lost in Bastian's dark eyes. He wants to drown in the hunger and arousal he finds undiluted in his irises. He drops to his knees, never breaking eye contact. His hands instinctively rise to Bastian's belt; he expertly undoes it. Bastian cradles his head with both hands, one finding its way to hold Jake's jaw while the other tangles in his curls. Jake takes his time, draws out how slowly he unbuttons Bastian's pants and brings down the zipper. He pushes the jeans down, makes a show of running the tip of his tongue over the fabric of Bastian's underwear, over the clear outline of Bastian's growing erection. At that, Bastian groans under his breath, mutters something to the effect of Jake being a tease, and backs him up until Jake's back is flat against the drawers of his vanity and he's got no way of escaping if he tried. Jake doesn't stop his teasing at that, however; he drags his fingertips along the hard lines, he nuzzles the base of Bastian's cock, he wants to rile him up, he wants Bastian to be impatient. So he doesn't reach in past the band, he doesn't pull Bastian's boxers down to his thighs, he only keeps palming and pressing and running fingers and tongue over the thin fabric, he mocks taking the tip of Bastian's cock in his mouth by closing his lips as best he can around the head that he can easily see and tasting the dampening spot that darkens the cotton where Bastian is starting to drip from arousal.

"Is your throat sore from all of that angelic singing? Or are you just wanting to get in trouble, huh? What are you trying to get?" Bastian asks, fingers tightening their grip in Jake's hair.

"Not sore," Jake replies, but before he can expand on how he just really likes seeing Bastian react to his touches, he's cut off by Bastian's voice retorting "Not yet" and "Get to work, handsome."

He can hear the rasp in Bastian's voice, and to say he doesn't get aroused by his insistence and quiet confidence, despite the fact that Bastian gave him bruises before he made him come earlier... that would be a lie. He can feel himself twitch, he can feel how his pants are getting tighter. But this isn't about him, he wants to make Bastian feel good regardless of what he might get out of it, so he hooks fingers from both hands under the band of Bastian's underwear and tugs down to free him. He hears Bastian exhale at last when his fingers make contact with the warm skin. He looks back up into Bastian's eyes when he takes hold of his cock and lines himself up. He licks, a light tease to taste the clear fluids accumulating at the slit, and Bastian moans at the sensations. They hold each other's gaze until Jake finally, finally is done playing and engulfs the warm weight of Bastian's erect cock with his mouth, wrapping his lips tightly around the shaft, sucking to hollow his cheeks and pull Bastian farther in, and Bastian throws his head back when he hits the softness at the back of Jake's throat. Jake wraps his fingers around the base of Bastian's cock for what won't make it past his lips, he brings a hand between Bastian's thighs to graze at the sensitive skin just behind his balls. He has a fluttering thought for the fact that they could get caught; anyone could come in and they'd find him shirtless, covered in bruises, disheveled and blushing and hard and his boyfriend's cock in his mouth. They'd find Bastian with his pants down around his thighs, hardly dignified, ass bare, holding Jake's head in place with both hands and thrusting his cock in and out of his mouth, fucking his face. Jake moans around Bastian at the thought, he can't help it. It'd be incriminating, he'd probably be ashamed or at the very least humiliated to be found in this position, so very clearly at another man's mercy, and yet he can't help but feeling the heat, the need, coiling tightly at the bottom of his stomach. He flutters his tongue against the underside of Bastian's cock as much as he can, he twists his hand slightly with every movement of Bastian's hips, and he keeps his throat as open as he can for when Bastian accidentally pushes in a bit farther than genuinely comfortable.

"You're so beautiful on your knees, did you know that?" Bastian says, breathless, when he looks back down to Jake, petting his hair with the hand that's not holding his jaw.

With that, Jake starts bobbing up and down, never letting his tongue go still, making every effort to keep a constant pressure with his cheeks and his lips around Bastian, trying his best to keep his throat relaxed, focusing all the attention he has left on the hands that are still working at the base of Bastian's cock and between his legs. He's still shifting and twisting lightly, fondling and pulling Bastian's balls. There aren't many things he loves more than seeing and tasting, in this case, how much pleasure he can provide Bastian. He doesn't care much about any discomfort when he knows how much Bastian loves him like this, either. It feels fucking amazing.

He knows Bastian isn't going to last long, because he had already denied himself in the morning to focus on Jake's erection when they woke, and had to wait until his hard cock had softened before he could really dress himself for the day. He's already twitching, he's already making a mess of Jake's face. Jake doesn't tease – he isn't that reckless anyways. He works relentlessly to keep the pressure even with his sucking, he stimulates the sensitive skin of Bastian's balls and ventures a finger just behind them to touch his perineum and draw circles at his rim, until Bastian's breathing gets a little irregular and no amount of breath control classes can come in handy in a situation like this. He never stops the movements of his tongue, flattened under Bastian's hot and heavy length, doesn't stop either when Bastian starts praising him.

"Just like that, handsome, you're doing so good, don't stop, you know what I like. You know how much I like fucking your face, don't you?" Bastian asks rhetorically when he starts bucking his hips faster and rougher and effectively fucking him.

Jake moans, echoing Bastian's compliments, and that gets him some more encouragements to not slow down, to keep going.

"Do you want to make me come, cielo? Or do you want self-control, huh? The longer we do this, the more you can risk getting found out, did you think about that?"

Jake's eyes are starting to water under Bastian's movements, and he tries saying that yes, he's making Bastian come, he wants to be good, and yes, he's aware that anyone could come in at any time, but all he can do is a restrictive nod because it's not like Bastian is about to pull out to let him talk. He pumps his hand around Bastian, using all the saliva he's producing that's slicking him up.

"Tongue out, pretty thing, I'm going to come on it, keep your mouth open, I'm close," Bastian commands.

Jake doesn't really have a choice, a hand tight in his hair pulling him back. Bastian lets go of his jaw, bats his hand away so that his own can take hold of himself. Obedient before him, Jake looks up and relocates his hands to Bastian's bare ass. He opens as wide as he can, tongue flat and sticking out as much as it can for Bastian to only rest the head of his cock on it while he starts jacking himself off, quickly, sure of how to move on himself. The sight is glorious, Bastian with his eyes closed and head tilted up a bit, his shirt rolled up a tad, a hand holding Jake tightly in place and the other one moving on his cock. Jake grabs tightly on Bastian's ass and he feels it clench in time with the stutters of his breath. But before he can actually push Bastian over the edge, he moves back and widens his eyes in shock, because he's just heard a soft knock on his door. His unlocked door. One that anybody could decide to open without notice, not that they would, but they could, and –

"One second, please," Bastian says at that time – so Jake didn't dream the knock – his voice somehow as posed and calmed as ever. He grips the back of Jake's head with his free hand and positions him right back where he'd been, so that the head of his cock is resting perfectly on Jake's tongue, ready to release in his willing and open mouth. "We'll come in a second, hold on," he finishes, throwing a wink Jake's way and effectively letting his orgasm wash over him as he's saying that.

He lets go of the back of Jake's head once he's done, pulls out and slides his hand under Jake's jaw to press it closed, the silent command to swallow barely hidden – as if Jake wasn't going to in the first place. So Jake does, feeling his Adam's apple bob up and down under Bastian's hand, and Bastian whispers an awed "Good boy."

Bastian tucks himself back in, he sees Jake's street t-shirt on the back of his couch and throws it his way before he strides towards the door without a look back Jake's way to make sure he's dressed and standing.

"Oh! Hey Bastian, good to see you!" Karla's breezy voice chimes in. "We were just thinking of going out with the cast, we wanted to invite Jake. Want to join us for dinner somewhere around?" She asks, without missing a beat, without commenting on the blush on Bastian's face or the awkwardness in Jake's stance as he's hurrying to smooth down his shirt.

"Would have loved to, I haven't met everyone here yet. But I can't, I'm stealing your main character for the rest of the evening," Bastian replies. Throwing a glance at Jake, he immediately keeps going, "Pretty thing, gather up your stuff and find me when you're ready to head out!"

Bastian walks out with Karla at that, and Jake, taken aback, hears something to the effect of just because Bastian has declined the dinner invitation doesn't mean he can't still meet the cast members he hasn't yet before they leave the theatre. And the look he throws Jake just before he leaves, that look brings Jake right back to the night, a few days prior, when Bastian had gone down on him, fingered him, made him come and then fucked him, because it's the same awfully caring gaze, it's the same amount of adoration in his irises that Bastian had for Jake the morning after that scene. Jake had fallen asleep crying from how close to bursting his heart was, but Bastian had thought that he'd pushed him too far, so they'd talked it out, the next morning.

Jake had been awoken with Bastian's lips pressed to his jaw, his neck, his chest, down his torso. To his arms and to his hands. To his lips.

He'd been greeted with a quiet "Good morning, my love," more chaste kisses. When he'd refused to open his eyes to press Bastian closer to himself and burrow his face in his shoulder, the phrase had been followed with a careful "How do you feel? Did you sleep well?"

Jake had taken a few seconds to get reacquainted with his limbs. He'd dug his fingertips into Bastian's back as best he could with his sleepy weakness. "I slept... well, I don't remember falling asleep. Is it morning already?" He had asked without expecting an answer, but opened his eyes to find Bastian looking up at him from his chest and nodding. "I feel good, I think," he had continued, but he'd found a dull ache in his lower body and a tightness in his thighs as soon as he'd tried to rearrange himself to better accommodate Bastian. "I feel... sore. My legs hurt," he'd frowned.

One of Bastian's hands had immediately trekked down to his thigh, trying as best it could to soothe the ache away. "That's probably to be expected. I have to admit, I was pretty impressed to see how accommodating your body was for me last night. I wasn't expecting you to give me so much," Bastian had told him.

"I was surprised too. It wasn't too much, the physical part I mean, you've fucked me plenty of times before. I just..." he'd taken a breath then, trying to find words that would convey everything he'd felt before, during, after his safe-wording. "It was just a lot to process," he'd said.

When Bastian hadn't replied to that, Jake looked down to see both pride and a trace of apprehension.

"I think, if you wanted to try again, you probably could push me again and, um, add more when you fuck me." He'd felt a rush of blood through his body, his face and his torso were coloring in pink. "But even if I wanted to be good for you, last night, I wasn't able to," he'd added, looking away, a faint and unwelcome feeling of shame creeping in. He'd wanted to take what Bastian wanted to give him, he did, he wanted to make him proud, but. But.

Bastian's face had relaxed somewhere along that answer. "What made you speak up, cielo?" He'd asked, bringing his hand to stroke the lines of Jake's jaw. "Something I did was too much and I know you well enough to know you wouldn't have spoken until you'd been trying to push through it, so I want to know what it was. Can you tell me?" Bastian had inquired.

He'd kissed him again, patient as ever, and Jake could tell he really was trying to make sure the same wouldn't happen again. He just had to calm his brain down, convince himself that nothing bad would happen from being honest, nothing terrible would happen because he had spoken up, and Bastian wasn't going to be disappointed. He'd tried to twist away, too on display, with Bastian laying on his chest like that and looking straight into his eyes, but the muscles in his thighs had complained with a sharp pain reverberating through his lower back. Bastian had felt it, however, and he'd lifted himself off for Jake to roll on his side; it would be easier to talk with Bastian's arm around his waist than it was with his irises burning through Jake's soul.

"It was just so intimate, for me. I think, yeah, it's that it felt really intimate and important to give my body with so much… abandon, I guess," he had breathed. "But the way we were, it also made me… it made you feel foreign and that didn't… work for me. Not in that moment. I couldn't – I couldn't tell if you were… using me for me or just, just fucking whoever was at your disposal… but if you're taking me like this and pushing my body to its limits, I need to know that you aren't just doing it for your own enjoyment, you're doing it for us, you're doing it because it's you and me, and not some other, better, more willing guy out there," he'd finished with a hint of trembling in his voice.

Jake had turned around then, facing Bastian again.

"Did I hurt you? Was it painful, is that why you cried?" Bastian had inquired, bringing a hand up to Jake's temple.

"It wasn't… painful per se. It hurt, it did, but – I know it could have felt good, maybe with more prep, maybe when I wasn't already so over stimulated. That's why I want to try again," he'd finished in a hushed whisper, dropping his gaze.

"I was trying to grant your request of fucking you and using you. I did it wrong, or too fast, or too intensely," Bastian had tried to explain, but Jake had cut him short by shaking his head.

"It's not that, it wasn't wrong, it was – I want to know, I need to know, when you're pushing me like that, that it's you and you're using me, because I'll let you, because I –" he'd taken a deep breath. "Because I love you and I trust you. And as long as I know that you're doing it because it's us, and because I'm yours and because you care, then.., please do keep pushing and using me."

"Okay, cielo. Thank you for trusting me with this. And thank you for letting me in," Bastian had said, thinking it might be the end of that conversation.

"Wait, you asked about why I cried. It wasn't because you hurt me, it wasn't because it was too much. Well, I guess in a way it was. But after everything, after I spoke up and asked you to still keep going even though I was uncomfortable, as long as we changed positions, I kept going because I wanted to be good for you. But it hit me, when you asked to know if you could come inside me, that… even if I give you all of me, and even though I do want you to take what you need from me, you still checked in one last time to make sure I was okay and to let me know that I was – still – in control of what was happening to me. And I guess I wasn't expecting that, I guess I thought giving myself to you meant giving that right up and I hadn't realized that… that wasn't true. That even though I'd given you all the green lights, even though I'd asked you to keep going and to please come inside me, you still let me decide that I was in a space to accept or refuse that and… I don't know. It meant more than I'd expected. So yeah, the physical side of it was a lot to handle and maybe too much, but that isn't what made me cry, it was really just... gratitude. For how cared for you made me feel in that moment," Jake had finished.

Bastian had kissed him then, a hand on his jaw, pushing his body against Jake.

Jake is abruptly brought back to the present moment when a door somewhere in the hallway slams shut, the noise followed by a cheery "See y'all on Tuesday, have fun tonight!" and shakes his head to try to jumble some sense back into his brain. He quickly scans the room to see if he should bring anything home other than his keys and wallet, and decides that whatever Bastian has in mind doesn't require him to bring his backpack home for the night – so he leaves it behind, turns the lights off and locks the door behind himself to start venturing to find Bastian.

He follows the post-show bustle to the common room, where he finds most of his own cast, and Bastian, social butterfly that he is, holding a few simultaneous conversations. He goes to him, to let him know that he's ready whenever Bastian is.

"Oh, there you are!" Bastian exclaims when Jake approaches. "You'll have to excuse us, I've promised that I was making him dinner tonight and I still have to hit the store for last minute ingredients. But if I'm around next time y'all go out, I'll be sure to join!"

With that, they head out of the theatre and start walking for the train. Bastian's going on about his show, his cast, Karla, drinks and dinner parties. Jake's only half-listening.

"Everything alright, handsome? You're distracted," Bastian says suddenly as they're going down the station stairs.

"What? Oh. Yeah, I– I'm fine." In a considerable state of distraction, he pulls out his pass, gets on the platform.

Bastian replies with a soft "Okay, handsome," and spends the ride with a hand on Jake's thigh, drawing patterns on the denim.

Jake's lost in his thoughts. He goes through the motions, automatically, of standing up right before 181st, of letting Bastian exit first, but he grabs his hand when they hit street level again and stops Bastian.

"What do you see in me? What did you see the first day we met that made you want to get to know me? Why do you... love me?" Jake blurts out to a stunned Bastian who, despite the surprise, brings a hand to Jake's neck to soothe the tension away with his fingertips.

It's been most of a week since Jake had safe worded, since Bastian started being more gentle than usual both during and outside of their scenes, and well. That's gotten Jake wondering. Little specks of worry coursing through his bloodstream and gathering momentum every time they got pumped through his heart. Little flecks of insecurity here and there that have made Jake a little more distant even though he craved nothing but proximity. As far as he's concerned, he's just some guy Bastian picked up one day, he's just Jake, he's not the most handsome or the most willing or the most vocal, he gets too caught up in his own head for that. He doesn't have the highest pain tolerance or the best bruise colors or, or, or. So as much as he's dreading any type of conversation like the one he's just brought up, he knows somewhere deep down that it's a necessary one because he really does fail to see what Bastian sees, to look at himself like Bastian looks at him, and that's affecting him more than he cares to admit.

"Hey, hey, Jacob, look at me," Bastian says, turning around. "Where did this come from?" He asks, and even though Jake knows it's rhetorical, he can't help but shy away from Bastian's eyes on him. "Let's get you home and I'll tell you every single thing I love about you. Because this isn't a conversation I want to have at the top of an escalator and you deserve all of my attention for it. In the meantime, though, I can already tell you that you caught my attention the second I met you. You are more than I ever dared hoping for. I can already tell you that I never expected this but what I felt when I met you has only been getting more intense. And I don't want you to stress about the fact that I'm asking you to wait until we're home, because the only reason I'm making you wait is so that I can spend the rest of the day wooing free of any outside distraction, and in the comfort and intimacy of our place, because I always want you all to myself and I can't have that here," Bastian concludes, with a sweeping gaze to the busy street around them.

So Jake does his best to shut down the parts of his brain that are still worried, and by the time Bastian has him sitting comfortably on their couch, he's just happy to have the rest of the day to be together. And Bastian, being Bastian, sits down next to Jake and starts babbling on about how he doesn't actually even know where to start because there are so many, so many things he loves about Jake.

"You could… start from the start. Why did you even ask me out? Why do you keep me around? I mean, I know you love me, you said so often enough, but… why?"

Bastian chuckled at that. "I think you would probably have more reason to be worried if I hadn't asked you out right after we met. I mean, being real. You showed up with Karla for my call to get Heaven on Broadway, and I don't know anything but your name and just how clear your eyes are, and I ask you to stay on the wall so that I can use you in the verse and you… stay there. I had to nod to tell you that you could get off of there, and seriously… I would have been insane not to want to know more about you after that. You're so good that you took orders that weren't even meant to be that kind of orders, from a stranger you knew nothing about, and just waited until you were allowed to move again? Anyone with a hint of aware-ness would have known you were special with that. I knew you were something else the second you complied like it was the most natural thing in the world. You can't blame me for wanting to push that button again when I know you're so good you're even going to follow orders in public."

Jake feels his cheeks blush at the praise. "I don't know what it was about that day… I just know that there's no way I could have not listened to you. I know there's no way I could have disre-garded your orders even if I had wanted to. But I didn't. It all just felt… so natural. I didn't have to think about it twice."

When he looks up to meet Bastian's eyes, he finds him staring with a fond smile, and all the kindness and pride in the world.

"And I'm ridiculously glad, every passing day, that you were there, and that everything just happened the way it did. I have to ask though… you left really early after that. Was everything okay? I know I came by the next day, and we talked, but we didn't really know each other."

Bastian is expectant, now.

"I think I just got really freaked out that you saw right through me so... effortlessly. Something changed that day and meeting you was some sort of catalyst that made me realize that the life I was living wasn't mine, and that I didn't really want it to be my life. And you showed me some glimpse into what it could be, but I'd been so set in my ways for so long that I really didn't know what to do with that information. It was... unsettling at best. I was terrified." Bastian takes his hand. "And I didn't know that you also felt it, I didn't know if you'd actually caught on to anything or if I'd made everything awkward, or ruined everything, and I didn't really have a way of knowing what I even felt, so it was destabilizing at best." Jake looks down to the way Bastian's fingers are running along his knuckles, how he is entwining them with his own. "But I'm glad you came by to see me the next day. I'm really glad you did. And I don't want to think about where I would be right now if you hadn't, not only the part where we aren't together, but... you just came into my life and suddenly everything made sense and you had all the answers I didn't know I was looking for. All the answers I didn't know I needed. So thanks for that. Sorry if I left abruptly."

"I'm really glad I came by too, but cielo, you have nothing to apologize for. It was a big day for you," Bastian comforts him, making Jake realize he'd never thought about how it must have felt to be in Bastian's shoes, that day, past finding some boy who'd drop everything because he told him to.

"How did you... what happened when I left? What made you decide that you had to come and see me?"

"Your reaction, I know it was mostly instinctive for you, but I think it was still telling. I think it was recognizable if you knew what to look for, you had some tell-tale reactions that my brain coded as being submissive at best – you never asked questions, you just went and did as asked, you had a hard time holding eye contact. I hadn't realized that it wasn't really something you had discovered about yourself, though, which makes me really happy because I get to see you learn so much about yourself, how you navigate and use that side of yourself. I love seeing how in tune you are with it and how you're learning about what you like and don't like with time. But back to the day we met, I know it destabilized you that you caught my attention and that there was something between us, but I do want to say that I didn't have a way of knowing if you'd be into me at all, past hoping you would be. But I was definitely into you. You were on my mind the rest of the day, I barely got anything done with the video we shot. I barely slept that night because I was trying to figure out a way of getting in the Lewinsky without it being my theatre. I knew I had to see you again to figure out if I was just wishful thinking, just imagining that you'd been following the orders I gave you, I had no way of knowing if I wasn't just projecting. I needed to know you were real because I wasn't entirely sure you were."

"Did, um. Did Karla let you in then?" Jake asks, wondering how Bastian had indeed gotten in.

Bastian nods. "She did. I think, correct me if I'm wrong, that she was with you when you left the set? I don't think she realized that you got into your head because of me, or I'm not sure that she would have let me see you before a show."

"I just told her it was the sun, that I was having some bad reaction to the heat… I wasn't sure she believed me. I'm still not sure she did but I guess it doesn't really matter now, she let you in and… here we are."

"And I'll never be able to thank her properly for that." Bastian takes that moment to get closer to Jake, bring a hand to his jaw and kiss him gently. "You know what else I love about you?" He asks. Jake shakes his head. "I love that you've trusted me so much since the day we met. You let me in and you allowed me to open your world and that'll always be invaluable to me. I can't wait to see where this all takes us. I love how responsive you are to me. You have no qualms about offering every but of you, every muscle, every inch of skin. I love that you allow yourself to be so vulnerable and so resilient with me, and that you are so honest about what you want and what you need from me."

Bastian kisses him again at that, and Jake kisses back with everything he has. He can feel Bastian's words resonating within him; he really did want to offer him every cell of his body, he did want to be vulnerable with him, and he couldn't not respond to Bastian's words and his actions if he wanted to help it. He wants to see just how much more Bastian will allow him to learn about himself, and he wants him to be the one to bring those changes on for Jake. He wants to grow into his wants and needs and instincts for Bastian – he wants to submit to him, so fully, so completely, and without a second thought, because Bastian is so perfect for him. He wants to make him proud. He wants to make him happy, and content, and sated. And he never wants to disappoint him, because he feels he might die if he does.

After a while, Jake can't say how long, but – after a while, Bastian pulls back, he stands up and extends a hand for Jake so that he can pull him up from the couch too. He leads Jake to their bedroom, always making contact with their hands or their lips, feeling each other up in one way or another. Bastian presses Jake against the door frame, bodies lined up, and starts pulling at the hem of Jake's shirt. Out of habit, Jake brings his arms up, lets Bastian strip him of his shirt. Bastian takes a minute, again, to run his fingertips over the plethora of bruise on Jake's chest, his shoulders, his stomach. He attaches his mouth to Jake's skin again and adds some new crimson and purple stains on Jake's chest. Jake lets him, he'd be lying if he said he didn't like Bastian's attentions. Even if he wasn't into the sensations or the looks of it, he'd still would be mad not to want to witness Bastian's own reactions to a bruise-covered Jake. Having Bastian's entire focus at any time is already enough to make Jake feel lucky; having Bastian speechless when he takes his shirt off? That's something else entirely.

By the time Jake's belt is undone, his own hands have started wandering and undressing Bastian. By the time they reach the bed, they're both stark naked, and Jake is already half hard, partly because he never really came down from the arousal he felt when he had Bastian's cock in his mouth, in his dressing room. Bastian pushes him down on the bed and climbs atop him so that he can keep kissing him, just another minute, or two, or ten because he can. Jake presses his body into Bastian, pulls their hips flush. They stay like that for god knows how long, taking each other in as if they don't spend the majority of every day together but rather, like starved souls who haven't encountered each other in centuries. Jake doesn't know if it's because they are still relatively new to each other, if it'll fade or when, but he doesn't want to think about a world where they aren't so starved for each other, so he kisses back. He is no superhuman, he can't help but grind his hips up into the dip between Bastian's hip and his thigh, and he knows it isn't dignified to get friction like this but Bastian's skin is so warm, and he is kissing him breathless and he's just given him more bruises so really, Jake cannot be given a guilty verdict.

When Bastian feels Jake move against him, he reciprocates for just a second, before he leaves Jake's mouth in favor of his neck, for the sensitive skin and tendons he finds there. He draws a line from Jake's ear to his collarbone with his tongue, he holds himself up with only one arm so that he can use a free hand to play with Jake's nipple, tugging and twisting and pinching until Jake is a breathless, moaning mess under his fingers and his mouth. He continues his descent, only leaving Jake's nipple alone once he's in a good position to relocate his hand and wrap his fingers around Jake's cock. Jake opens his eyes, drags his head up to look down at Bastian, for the sole purpose of being able to see him, looking so good and so smug with a grin on his face, holding his erection so that he can ever so slowly stick his tongue out and, never breaking eye contact with him, lick a broad stripe on the underside of his cock. Jake can barely keep his eyes open with that and has to hold his breath, but he knows Bastian likes it when he tries, so he just melts into the touches and lets all the air out of his lungs when he starts rotating his hips. He moves to get stimulation from Bastian's hand, and Bastian lets him, which is somewhat unexpected – he usually restrains Jake's movements one way or another, whether it be with their belts or by pushing Jake's hips flush against the mattress or by simply ordering him to keep still for him, which he obviously obeys. But there's something different about today, and Jake can't pinpoint it.

So he moves his hips, fucks the warm space that Bastian is creating with his hand, whispers expletives when Bastian's tongue plays on his skin and swears out loud when Bastian engulfs the tip of his cock in his perfect mouth, because although he got sucked off in the morning, he will never get tired of the way Bastian's mouth feels on him. He throws his head back when Bastian hollows his cheeks. But that, like kissing, like biting, doesn't last. Jake, indignant, raises himself on one elbow, almost spits "Bastian, no, what the fuck, why'd you stop," but stops at thinking it instead. Because Bastian is climbing up his body again.

Except that this time, he's relocating himself to straddle Jake, whose hands automatically land on his firm thighs. So it doesn't make sense to Jake when Bastian, instead of bending down to kiss him, leans to the side to get lube, because he's essentially just made his perfectly fine access to Jake much, much harder by choosing to sit on his stomach.

Except that this time, when Bastian pours lube on his fingers, lays down to have his head in the crook of Jake's neck, when he reaches behind himself, he isn't reaching for Jake's cock and a weirdly angled hand job. He isn't contorting to reach past Jake's balls to penetrate him. He's not reaching that far at all but he lets out a moan against the heat of Jake's skin. Which makes no sense, until, until.

Oh. Oh. Fuck.

Bastian is decidedly, absolutely, unequivocally… fingering himself. Open. While straddling Jake. Who, despite already thinking he was perfectly hard enough a minute prior, now can feel himself twitch and he can feel the rush of blood through his body, pooling at the pits of his stomach, and unmistakably making his cock fuller and that much harder, despite the confusion in his brain as to what's happening and why and how they got there. His body doesn't care about that, this body only knows that this is insanely arousing and it's responding accordingly. And Bastian, now, too, is starting to rock his hips, he's grinding on Jake, still without a word save for his breathy moans. He's rocking back and forth on his fingers, his cock getting a bit of stimulation on Jake's abs this way, and Jake's own erection getting some pleasure every time Bastian's ass drags against it. His breath is hot against Jake's neck, his moans desperate in his ear, so Jake grips harder on Bastian's thighs and he starts the swivel of his hips to encourage Bastian to move.

"You're going to fuck me," Bastian tells him. Not a maybe, not a question. He's not here for a conversation. This is a certainty, an order, a promise. "You're going to fuck me and you're going to be so good, and if you're good enough I'm going to let you come inside me," he pants. He pulls back from Jake's neck, rests his free hand at the base of his throat. "But I need to get myself ready first, cielo, because I haven't done this in a while and you, my love, were blessed with something much better than the men I've been with before," Bastian says.

With that, he arches his back to get a better angle. He throws his head back, tightens his grip on Jake's throat to keep his balance. Jake's breath hitches even though Bastian's not pressing hard enough for that. He contorts to get a better angle, his chest heaving when he breathes, his hips moving him back against his fingers. Jake's brain is… maybe not functioning anymore, it's swimming in arousal and he doesn't know what to do with himself. He starts running his hands all over Bastian's body, he so rarely gets to do so, and his thumbs are soon drawn to Bastian's nipples. He draws light circles over them, testing the waters, but Bastian moans. He takes that as a good sign, as an approval to keep going. He flicks his thumbs over the hardening buds, he brings his index fingers into the mix and rolls the sensitive flesh between his fingertips. Bastian's hand tightens on his throat in response.

When Jake can tear his eyes from Bastian's face and his neck, from looking at how his nipples are reacting to the stimulation, he checks out the rest of his body; the way the muscles in his thighs are tensing and clenching around his waist in time with the back-and-forth movement of his hips; the way both his shoulders are working, one to bring his right arm far enough back to penetrate himself, the other supporting his weight with the hand he's got on Jake's throat; the way his abs are subtly doing their part of the work, too, and. Jake almost feels guilty for looking, because of how insanely intimate this feels, but when he lets his eyes stray down to the dark patch of groomed hair between his legs, he sees Bastian's cock, surprisingly hard considering that he just came in Jake's dressing room not two hours ago. And he sees a clear string of fluid connecting the tip of Bastian's cock to a slick pool that is starting to form on his stomach. He moans loudly and swears under his breath at the sight, at how arousing this whole moment is, at how hot Bastian is looking when he's writhing with abandon atop him.

Before Jake can ponder the matters of his own arousal further, however, Bastian finally pulls his fingers out. He lets go of Jake's throat and twists around to grab their bottle of lube. When he pours some on his fingers, this time, it's not to stretch himself more open. He wraps his fingers around Jake's cock, and the slick contact makes Jake's eyes roll back – he's been hard to some extent since Bastian got him on his knees, has been wanting more since Bastian got between his legs, so it comes as a relief.

"Stay still, handsome, I haven't done this in a long time," Bastian says as he moves his hand up and down, getting the entirety of Jake's cock wet enough to be fucked with it.

When the head of his cock is pushed against Bastian's rim, he has a fleeting thought of worry, out of habit, because he isn't wearing a condom, before he remembers that they've just got test results back – they're fine. They haven't fucked since, though, apart from having given each other hand jobs and blowjobs, so the weight of what they're about to do hits Jake square in the chest. He's not only about to fuck Bastian for the first time, which he'd never even thought would happen let alone as a fantasy; he's about to fuck him without any kind of barrier, skin on skin, he's going to feel the heat of his body directly on himself, and he can feel himself twitch in Bastian's hand at the thought. Bastian lines himself up, and starts pushing himself down on Jake. When the head of Jake's cock breaches the ring of muscle, Bastian moans, a quiet "Oh, fuck, and he lifts himself back up. He repeats the movement a few times, sinking further down each time, and when he lets go of him, Jake starts thrusting up. Lightly at first, but he gains momentum, and he's so turned on.

Bastian turns back around to look at him. He wipes his slick hand on the sheets – they can wash them later – and rests both hands on Jake's chest. He's calling the shots, like he usually is, and despite the fact that he's fucking himself on Jake, he's still definitely in control. Jake grabs on to his knees, he's meeting Bastian halfway every time Bastian rises and sinks back on his cock, until his head drops and he's seated all the way and pressing his ass hard on Jake's hips. "Oh fuck, Christ, cielo, you feel so good," he moans, grinding his hips but not moving up anymore, he's just taking stock of how Jake feels inside him, and Jake is trying to compute just how tight and hot and fucking wonderful Bastian feels around him. He thinks he might pass out from the bliss he is feeling.

"Can I touch you, please, Bastian, can I?" Jake asks. He wants something to do with his hands and this only seems logical, he wants to make Bastian feel so good, he wants to give him so much pleasure.

In lieu of an answer, Bastian drags both hands from Jake's chest to his neck. "Only if I can choke you," he replies, and Jake immediately bares his throat. Bastian clenches his fingers.

His entire body instantly feels distant, secondary only to the pressure on his airways, to the way Bastian's fingers tighten on his skin, to the way he can't breathe out, can't breathe in. He tries, by reflex, he always will, even if only to be reminded that he cannot. Specifically to be reminded that he cannot. More than not being able to answer to his lungs' pleas for oxygen, he wants to feel that he is completely and unequivocally Bastian's; he is trusting him with his life, with his blood and his brain and his heart, so every reflexive attempt to get air to his system is a powerful reminder of that.

Bastian lets go when Jake's mouth drops open and he makes a strangled sound without really meaning to. Jake gasps in, refills, and feels Bastian bending down to bring their faces together. Instead of kissing him, however, he ducks to the side and takes Jake's earlobe into his mouth, bites down gently. "If you want my hands on your throat, handsome, you'd better pay attention," he whispers, dark and menacing. Jake shivers, he's abruptly reminded that the reason he was being choked in the first place is because it was contingent to him being allowed to wrap his hands around Bastian's cock. "I'm not doing this for you," Bastian says with a light squeeze to give Jake a taste. "I'm doing this because I can, because I want to, and I'll only do it if you're a good boy for me, because I know how much you love it."

"I'll be good, I can be good, I promise, Bastian, please," he begs, his fingers digging into Bastian's inner thighs and inching ever higher.

"Go on, then," Bastian says, and he starts grinding again to get stimulation from Jake's cock, buried deep inside him, as he pulls back from his ear.

When Jake does, he takes a hand to Bastian's balls and fondles them, takes the other to wrap softly around the warm weight of Bastian's erection. It's not as slick as could be, but all the fluids that are spilling out of Bastian are helping with that. He draws tight circles with his thumb at the head of Bastian's cock, collecting the wetness there and spreading it around. When he starts properly jerking him, Bastian resumes taking his breath from Jake. Jake's doing his best, this time, not to forget that the only way for him to get choked today is by pleasuring Bastian; so as much as breath play does to him (and it does so much to him), he forces himself not to fly away so quickly, to keep moving his hips to meet Bastian's with every thrust, to keep his hands twisting and pumping. Focusing on that helps him not think of the pressure in his chest when his lungs start complaining, it allows him not to think of how hot and red is face is getting, he doesn't wonder if or when his lips start becoming faint shades of blue.

"Keep that up, cielo, you're doing so good," Bastian breathes, and he starts riding him more actively.

He doesn't ever let Jake quite recover from the bouts of choking – whereas the first two squeezes of Bastian's hands lasted a while, and he had time to prep in between, he doesn't continue with that pattern. Instead, he's stopping him breathing shortly, never enough to get him to the point where he wonders how much more he can take, but it's relentless, he barely gets time to empty his lungs and refill them. It's a superficial supply of air, and it takes a lot of focus, it's probably more intense than any other configuration of breath play they've done in the past, and Jake can't even focus on how it affects him and how he should react because through all of it, he still has to stay in his body, he can't fly away, he has to keep fucking Bastian and jerking him and make him feel good. There's very little space left in his skull that isn't used by how good it feels to be fucking Bastian (and he feels so fucking tight and hot around his cock), his instinct to let his brain shut down and the active work to not surrender to that very instinct. There's maybe no space left at all.

"You're being so good, you're perfect," Bastian tells him between two bouts of choking. He keeps a hand on Jake's throat – without pressure, just resting – and brings one to stroke his cheek, his temple, his jaw. "Do you like this, by the way, huh? Do you like fucking me?" Bastian asks, phrases punctuated by the sounds of their skin when he slams back down onto Jake. "Tell me," he requests when Jake visibly fails to find his voice.

"Yes, Bastian, I do," Jake pants with the first semblant of a full breath that he's had in a bit. His voice is rough, lower pitched than usual, probably both due to the strain on his throat and the arousal and adrenaline coursing through his veins.

"Do you want to come, handsome?" Bastian says, weaving his fingers through Jake's curls and pulling his head back to bare his throat even more.

Jake's brows furrow, he does, he does. He hadn't thought that far but now that Bastian has planted the idea into his mind, it's maybe all he can focus on. He locks gazes with Bastian, and he nods, because he's just a bit too desperate for more words.

"Then get on top and make me come first, pretty thing," Bastian orders him, while he rises and gets himself off of Jake. "You got to earn it, show me you deserve it," he says.

When Bastian attempts to move off of him, Jake grabs his shoulder and his thigh and flips him on his back, invigorated with drive and strength that were absent a second prior. He's determined, he wants this as much as Bastian does. There's a flicker of surprise on Bastian's face that is near instantly replaced by something closest to hunger, tinted with pride for his boy. Maybe a hint of challenge as well, to bank on Jake's energy.

Jake gets a hold of himself to get lined up with Bastian's entrance, his breath is taken away as soon as the tip of his cock breaches him, doesn't resume until he's seated and Bastian's moan makes it to his ears. He's holding himself up with Bastian's leg, he has a death grip on his calf, and he's soon panting. He reaches with his free hand between their bodies and hopes to god that Bastian won't stop him touching and stimulating, because Jake needs to come, he's realizing that he's been so close for probably a while now, so he needs Bastian to come and do so now. The slaps of his thighs against Bastian's ass, Bastian's moans that are punctuating them, the heat and pressure around his cock, it's all so good and so much and spurring him on that much closer to his release, but he hasn't earned that yet. He redoubles his efforts, he wants to make Bastian fall apart under him.

"Oh, fuck, Jacob, just like that, good boy," he moans. He's breathless and Jake wants more of that. "Make me come, I know you want to, I know you can, you're so good, come on, come on, don't stop, keep fucking me, don't stop," Bastian pleads, and Jake isn't sure what part is an order and what part is begging but he doesn't know if it really matters at this point.

Everything is so hot, he might lose his mind, he doesn't know if he's ever been this turned on and this motivated before. Time has stopped around them and nothing matters other than their abandon and pleasure, other than their breathlessness and ecstasy.

"Please Bastian, oh, please," he gasps, working the hand he's got wrapped around Bastian's cock that much faster, that much better, the way he would to make himself cum.

When he feels it, at first, his mind almost blanks out – but Bastian is straining off the bed, he's clenching rhythmically around Jake's cock in his ass, he has his head thrown back and his neck is all protruding veins and tendons and his hands are scrambling to find Jake's body. His mouth is open but no sound is coming of it, strings of cum are painting his own belly white, getting over Jake's fingers that haven't stopped yet their frantic movement; his cock is pulsing in Jake's hand time with the spasms if the muscles around him, and that's all Jake needs to be sent right over the edge and join Bastian in his bliss. He comes, wordless, head dropping to his chest and he has to hold himself up if he doesn't want to crash right on top of Bastian. His whole body feels electrified, so powerful and so spent simultaneously, he keeps the movement of his hips going, keeps fucking Bastian to make his own orgasm last, it's erratic and sloppy but so good, and the wet feeling of his own release, inside Bastian, around him, the sensations are making his brain short-circuit.

Without thinking twice, almost automatically, he starts lapping at Bastian's chest; he'd dropped low enough, close enough to his skin that it's really a no brainer for him to just start cleaning Bastian's cum off of his chest. He pulls out when he moves lower, getting a slight hiss out of Bastian, looks up to see Bastian looking straight into his eyes.

"Look at you, so eager, aren't you?" Bastian breathes out heavily. "Not even recovered yet but you're so hungry you don't even care," he adds, and Jake feels the heat on his cheeks. "Don't stop, then, if you're so needy, make sure I'm all cleaned up," Bastian says, spreading his legs to make his meaning ubiquitous.

Jake keeps moving down, then, collecting every drop he can find on Bastian's stomach before taking Bastian's softening cock into his hand to lick that clean, too, smirking when he earns a shudder from Bastian. That done, he presses his hands on Bastian's thighs to give himself better access and keenly starts licking his ass, eating himself out of him. He can't help but to moan through it all, every pore of his body so satisfied to have been good enough to earn praise from Bastian. He wants nothing but to keep pleasing him. So he prods, he laps, he takes pride in making sure that nothing is left for Bastian to clean once Jake is done. And when he is, he gets pulled up by his hair, up Bastian's body, until their lips are crushed together and Bastian lets his actions speak of how proud he is of his boy.

Chapter Seventeen

*J*ake throws his keys carelessly on the bench by Bastian's front door. Well, his front door, if he's honest. Theirs. He's been here for long enough that he should probably stop thinking of this place as Bastian's place, of the neighborhood as Bastian's neighborhood, of their bed as Bastian's bed. At the same time, he conflates; he has come to be seldom able to differentiate himself from Bastian, because his own body and mind also feel like Bastian's, so really, it's not his fault he'll always think about the apartment as Bastian's apartment.

He toes off his shoes and arranges them carefully by the door; he likes the order, it's a satisfying contrast next to the however many pairs haphazardly kicked around from when Bastian comes home, because Bastian's brain never slows down enough to take the time to arrange his shoes neatly. He's got a million things to do. Jake hopes he's one of them.

He's got reason to believe he might be. Bastian sent him to run errands, said he had to work on stuff while Jake would be out. But Bastian, in an effort to ensure that Jake wouldn't forget about him (or so does he rationalize, as if Jake ever could), well. He sent him out with a little extra. He'd taken a few minutes out of his day to work Jake up enough to give him one of the plugs he'd bought for him, and he does that when he wants Jake to be ready for him when he's ready for Jake, so. Jake felt it with every step while he was out, and to say he's eager to be home would be an understatement. So he wastes no time putting away his purchases and heads to the living room where he can hear Bastian shuffling around.

He stops dead in his tracks when he takes in the nature of Bastian's "work." The coffee table, usually throning in the middle of the place, is pushed flat against the wall, by the window. The couch is pushed back too, and whereas they usually can walk behind it, they can no longer. Even the reading chair and the lamp and the TV desk have been moved to create space, and Jake can't help but to notice that the only available wall space that isn't made inaccessible by various pieces of furniture is the bare area by the bookshelf, where Bastian, forever ago it seems, pushed him and gave him his first real orders, where they first played with each other. Needless to say that space means something, a lot, to Jake. He hopes it holds meaning for Bastian, too.

Without even a glance to Jake's immobile figure in the doorway, Bastian speaks up while he arranges the furniture around. "Back so soon, aren't you fast? Wait for me against the wall, cielo, I'm almost ready," he says nonchalantly.

Jake frowns, but complies nonetheless. He strides across the room, taking in his unusual surroundings, a thousand and one scenarios and memories unfolding through his mind, things they have done by that wall, things they haven't. He automatically crosses his wrists behind himself when he rests his back on the cold surface, just the way he's used to, just the way he knows Bastian likes.

"The other way around. Face the wall, pretty thing. I don't want you to look around more than you already did. Forehead to the wall." Bastian's voice is strict.

There's no reason for Jake not to listen. He feels his heart speed at the accusation that he looked around too much, but there was nothing much to look at, nothing specific, was there? Plus, he didn't know that he wasn't allowed, so he can't be punished for a rule he didn't know he was breaking, can he? He turns around nonetheless, keeps his wrists crossed behind his back. He rests his forehead to the unforgiving surface and closes his eyes. He tries not to guess what Bastian is doing on the sole account of the sounds he makes out behind him, but everything becomes quiet suddenly – did Bastian leave? Is he simply immobile and looking at him? Jake has nothing to go on, and he feels very exposed, with nothing to defend himself, at Bastian's mercy despite the fact that realistically, they haven't even really started anything yet.

After what feels like an eternity in regards to the whirlwind of thoughts in his skull, Jake hears movement again, approaching steps. So he'd been left alone. He feels a shiver down his spine, from antic- ipation, and the thrill of having no idea what's coming. He knows Bastian, knows that he went to get something, but he has no way of knowing what.

What comes first is the grip of Bastian's fingers in his hair, so tight, tangling in his curls, and dragging up from his scalp, forcing a soft yelp past Jake's lips in surprise. He can't escape, what with the wall in front of him and the death grip on his curls keeping him forcefully in place. Next comes the warmth of Bastian's body, slam- ming into him, pressing tight behind him, trapping Jake's arms between them and forcing him flat against the wall. Skin on skin – Bastian is shirtless against his arms. He's radiating heat in waves. Jake gets Bastian's free hand snaking under his shirt to grab his hip hard enough to leave a vivid hand print. He's utterly unable to move. His breathing is ragged already from Bastian's roughness. He whimpers when Bastian starts rotating his hips behind Jake, grinding up against his helpless body, and Jake pants. He's already feeling the rush of blood to the pits of his stomach, arousal and adrenaline coursing through his veins. His head might be confused, but his body knows exactly how to respond to Bastian's forceful actions. Every movement of Bastian's body is shifting the plug he's wearing infinitesimally.

Bastian's hands don't stay immobile for long, however. He's soon pulling back to grab Jake's crossed wrists, and without warning, bends his elbows, yanks his hands up his back; Jake is helpless, in this position, Bastian's grip is tight and he has no upper-body strength to defend himself, not like this. He tries to take a deep breath before his train of thoughts gets interrupted by Bastian's rough voice.

"Your muscles are so tense, handsome. You must be so desperate, having to go out knowing I want you open and waiting for me to be done working, aren't you?" Bastian drawls against his neck. Jake lets out a sound halfway between moaning and whining.

Bastian pushes his torso flat against Jake's back, solid, strong, and traps Jake's arms between their bodies. He snakes around Jake's waist, going straight for the button of his jeans, wasting no time in unbuttoning them and pushing them down Jake's legs. Jake is trying not to focus on the brief but welcome feeling of friction against his crotch when his pants are dragged down.

"Where did your resistance go, cielito? Have you given up already? I don't even need my hands to hold you down. And here I was, looking at those guns you have, under the impression that you were supposed to be strong..." Bastian breathes, dragging his short nails up the backs of Jake's thighs.

He's clearly trying to get Jake to react. It's just, it takes him a little while to get his body to cooperate when Bastian's getting all rough with him. He's all slowed down, it's not his fault.

"You're so into this, you haven't even considered using your muscles, have you?"

Jake lets out a soft grunt, and he tries to retrieve his arms, but Bastian's body is a barrier he can't quite get past. The only thing he manages is to make himself a little frustrated due to his helplessness in this position.

Then, as suddenly as Bastian had pressed in close behind him, his warmth is gone, save from both his hands grabbing at his wrists and pulling them back down in a vice grip. "Come on, show me what you've got," Bastian says dryly, tugging him back forcefully from the wall.

Jake first staggers back, not expecting this behavior from Bastian and not entirely sure where he's trying to take him, and he tries to put up a fight to regain control of his arms. When he can't squirm out of Bastian's grip, he twists his entire body – and lays eyes on, oh, leather. Across Bastian's chest. Over a shoulder, under the other, and a steel buckle that looks very solid and kind of intimidating. His mouth goes dry.

Bastian uses the break in Jake's train of thought to slam him back into the wall and press a forearm to his clavicles, pinning him in place. He presses in and up, his face millimeters away from Jake's. When Jake tries to close the distance, Bastian pulls back, attuned to him as he is. "Fight back," he instructs.

So Jake does. He's got his hands back, he's got all the free space in the living room – he doesn't care that he's probably walking right into Bastian's plan. But he grabs both hips, and he has leverage from the wall behind his back to shove Bastian off of him. He's got leverage to push him and get the upper hand, and while Bastian is having fun and not letting Jake have his way easily, it's not long before the scrabble of hands turns into Jake's fingers wrapping themselves around the leather strap on Bastian's chest, a leg slotted between Bastian's, and one hooking just behind his calf, so that when Bastian tries to move away, he does nothing but make himself trip backwards on Jake's heel.

They end up on the floor in a loud thud, Jake holding himself up with his hands on Bastian's chest. They're ruffled, a little out of breath, and whereas he feels a little silly in nothing but a t-shirt and fitting underwear that is getting increasingly tighter, he can't help but look the body beneath his up and down. It must be one of those things he didn't know he needed until he saw it, but. Bastian in a leather harness, in black pants that fit him like a glove, trapped under Jake's weight and obviously getting a rouse out of Jake on purpose even though he knows Jake's stronger than him, well. Jake isn't out of breath solely because of the physical exertion caused by their bouts of wrestling.

Jake reciprocates, feeling increasingly desperate, and incredibly aroused. He feels Bastian's fingers dance on his skin and skirt up his shirt, dragging the fabric with him. His intent is clear, so Jake lifts his arms to help him undress him, and momentarily forgets that he should be on his guard; Bastian catches him in the net he's cast, then, and uses Jake's distraction without missing a beat to flip them around viciously, landing Jake brutally on his back and settling between Jake's open knees. The thin fabric of Jake's boxers isn't much to shield his obvious arousal from the friction of their rough-housing and he can't help bucking up into Bastian. When he tries to get his hands on Bastian's warm skin, he gets caught back and his wrists end up violently pinned against the floor. Bastian isn't playing fair at all and Jake's brain is conflicted between fighting him and protesting or letting Bastian win and giving himself to him. Both options have too many benefits to rationally pick.

"Oh, no, cielo. These aren't your rules and you won't get what you want, not today," Bastian says with venom on his tongue, sending a shiver straight down Jake's spine. He's maybe a little too into being manhandled. And denied. It's fucking hot.

Chapter Eighteen

*B*astian manages to pull Jake's hands back to his stomach, and traps them both with one hand; he leans over and Jake is trapped under his weight, and he can't do anything but look while Bastian reaches over to the nearest table within reach to retrieve – Jake blinks hard – the bondage belt they'd gotten at the store, what now feels like eons ago. Fighting Bastian is becoming harder and it has left the forefront of his brain, so when Bastian quickly wraps it around his wrists, Jake doesn't think of struggling. He could probably squirm out of it, it's not expertly tied and it's not like the belt really could be used as cuffs. But the intent is clearly there, so whereas that might not be enough to send Jake flying out of his skin, it's enough to make him want more. He relaxes into the feeling, until Bastian gets up on his knees to remove his own belt from the loops in his jeans. He pulls Jake's hands to get his shoulders off the floor, and it's not comfortable but Jake holds position when Bastian orders him to stay, just long enough to slide his belt under Jake's shoulder blades. He pushes Jake back down and Jake closes his eyes when Bastian closes the buckle around him, trapping his elbows tight by his sides. Jake has a fleeting thought for the fact that they kind of match each other now, what with the leather bands going across both of their chests. He kind of really likes the thought.

He's taken out of his clouded thoughts when Bastian frees his wrists and pulls Jake up by the belt, and Jake has to follow his lead. Bastian repeats the same steps, sliding the bondage belt he'd gotten from Jake down to the small of his back, and Jake lets him when he secures the strap tightly around him, trapping his wrists firmly on either sides of his hips. Jake can't move. He doesn't want to. Bastian gets off of him and Jake can't tear his eyes away from his body, he just looks so ridiculously good and he's not sure why Bastian has waited so long to show him this outfit. Jake figures they can talk about it later. Bastian goes off to the desk he's pushed aside and Jake can't make out what he gets from his position on the floor, and he's unable to do more than undignified wiggling so he doesn't try, but he's putting something in his back pocket so Jake can only imagine he'll know sooner rather than later. When Bastian comes back, it's with a ravenous stare down Jake's whole body, a quiet "You're so pretty when I tie you up," and the muted thud of Bastian's knees on the wooden panels by Jake's feet.

Bastian takes his time, starts with picking up one of Jake's legs to press kisses on his ankle, up his calf, bite marks on the inside of his thigh, and all Jake can do is watch and whimper. His hips twitch when Bastian's teeth sink into a particularly tender muscle, but either to press in the bite or away from it, Jake can't tell. He's not sure that it matters. When Bastian makes it all the way to his underwear, he grabs the fabric tightly between his teeth, slides his hands up under Jake's ass and drags the garment off of Jake, who maybe has never felt this vulnerable and this wanted before. It's intoxicating. His head hits the floor with a muted thump.

The respite doesn't last long, though. Jake hears what sounds like a bottle cap and smells solvents just long enough to snap his eyes open before something cold touches his chest. He looks down to see Bastian's face consumed with intent and a hunger that wasn't there seconds prior. He sees the distinct pale grey plastic of a permanent marker and the straight lines that Bastian is drawing on him, without being able to make out what it is, but it sends a rush down his spine, to be marked by Bastian in this way. He's transfixed on the look in Bastian's eyes, until his left hand has etched across the whole of Jake's pecs, from one side to the next.

"So that you don't forget, handsome," Bastian says simply, and Jake cranes his neck as best he can.

Four large letters, traced a few times over, are inking his chest. M I N E, in bold, black script, and Bastian's free hand reaches to take a nipple tightly, to pinch and to twist and to make Jake arch up into the touch.

"Can't have you forgetting who you belong to, can we?" Bastian asks rhetorically while he pulls. It's not like Jake can find the words to answer, so he just gasps at the pressure on his sensitive flesh instead. "And who would that be, pretty thing?" Bastian says, eyes burning into Jake's.

"You. Yours, Bastian, I'm yours," Jake replies, and he feels the warmth spreading through him, the need coursing through his veins and the arousal of knowing he's right coiling deep inside him.

He's having a hard time keeping still. Especially with Bastian writing more on his stomach, filling up the spaces not covered by the belts, spelling out PRETTY THING and BASTIAN'S TOY and GOOD BOY.

BITE ME on his thighs.

A simple BASTIAN'S curling right around his cock and he chases the touch he's not getting. Bastian's dexterous. He doesn't give in. He doesn't touch Jake.

"Bastian, Bastian please," Jake whispers, although he couldn't tell what he's begging for. He just needs.

"Shhh, handsome, you look so good like this," Bastian says, wide eyed and rough voiced.

Time seems to stand still then, because Bastian moves on to his collarbones and Jake can't see what he's doing. He can't see how he's being marked and it's driving him a little mad. Bastian bends down to lick a stripe up his neck, making Jake shudder beneath him.

"If anyone sees you right now, they'll know what to do, cielo," he whispers against his ear. "You're mine to play with, you're my toy and you've got instructions on your skin and I'll take what I need and I'll use you to my satisfaction and you'll be happy with that, won't you?"

Jake's brows furrow, and he's nodding desperately, biting his lip. He's not sure what it says about him that he always gets so deep inside the spaces that Bastian creates inside his head, without even any proper touch, but all he knows is that he's willing to do a lot to please him and if that includes being covered in the ink that Bastian puts on him, then so fucking be it.

"I think I'll follow my instructions, cielo, what do you think?" Bastian says, but before Jake can really wonder what he means, he pulls away and his hands close around Jake's exposed neck. Jake's eyes, though he must make a conscious effort to keep them open, strain to hold Bastian's gaze. "It says choke here on your throat, my love," Bastian continues and Jake has to close his eyes at that. His blood is pounding, he can feel the veins pulsing under Bastian's fingers but not being able to send the circulation past the pressure around his neck. Jake is strangely calm, even when his lungs start burning and he can tell that his face is turning a deep shade of crimson. He would normally care, but he doesn't want to waste energy thinking about anything other than the feeling of Bastian's belts around his body and Bastian's hands on his neck.

When Bastian lets go, Jake gasps loudly, by reflex. The red spike in his lungs had been trying to get him to care about the lack of oxygen, but the weight of Bastian straddling him and the pressure of his fingers around his airways were much more interesting to him. Bastian bends down, his face hovering a mere inch from Jake's, just to see him lose the ability to train his irises on Bastian's with the loss of his ability to breathe.

"Don't stop looking at me, Jacob, I want to see you," Bastian whispers, voice so full of lust. "I want to see the blue of your eyes to compare with the blue of your lips," he says.

The visceral need to please Bastian is battling with the heaviness in his eyelids, but he tries, he tries, he tries. He wants. And the noises he makes are more desperate every time, because past the panting and the gasping for air, Jake also lets out a few moans. A few pleads for Bastian, although he couldn't voice what he's asking for. He feels so much, he feels more at peace than ever, he feels as strung out as the string of a bow when it's being pulled back, as free as the arrow that's about to take flight, and his skin feels prickling with electricity, he's alive. He's so alive.

He barely feels it when Bastian leans down, presses closer to Jake's skin, instead of speaking up to make Jake realize he's back inside his head, to drag the tip of his tongue on Jake's bottom lip. His eyes snap open when Bastian takes hold of it between his teeth and bites down sharp, he makes a strangled noise, because Bastian's hands are tight around him – he's only been releasing the pressure periodically to let Jake's lungs refill with clean oxygen. The second he relaxes his vice grip, though, Jake can feel a tear threatening to spill out of the far corner of his eye, and a soft "Oh, please," escapes his mouth.

Bastian finally kisses him, while he's being choked one last time. Jake can hardly reciprocate when Bastian is holding him like this. When he pulls back, Jake can't follow, because Bastian has taken hold of the belts holding Jake tightly. He's moving off of his straddling position, and the contrast of the cold air next to the warmth of Bastian's thighs is enough to have him erupt in goosebumps. Bastian kneels next to him and yanks at the belts, solid and real around Jake's arms, and shoves his body roughly about until Jake's chest is flat against the floor. He moans when his cock gets trapped between himself and the cold floor, it's not great but it's something and Jake is far enough gone inside his head that he will take anything. He feels Bastian's short fingernails dig into the soft flesh of his ass and pushes back into it, stills when he feels the cold tip of the marker on his skin.

A word on each cheek. Something on the small of his back. Jake can't see, and he can't even try twisting, but he wants to know, he needs to know, so despite the calm in his brain he thrashes a little in his bonds until Bastian's hand connects, hard, with his ass. The reverberated sound stuns him and he whimpers.

"Oh sorry, did that come as a surprise? Not my fault, cielo, your ass says SPANK HERE," Bastian explains nonchalantly, as if that explained everything, as if he hadn't written that himself.

Jake doesn't bother replying. He rests his forehead on the cold floor and pushes his ass up as best he can, tries to make himself inviting. It seems only logical, now, that losing his wrestling match with Bastian would be followed with this consequence, and if Bastian's game plan is to give Jake's ass a thorough beating, Jake is undeniably here for it. Bastian rubs what must show as a vivid handprint on his skin, if Jake knows himself at all. The force of the blow and the sting that he felt are definitely indicative of a beautifully delimited rush of blood to the surface of his skin.

"What do you want, handsome?" Bastian asks. Jake groans.

He doesn't know how to answer that because so many options are rushing to the forefront of his brain and answering that makes Jake feel like he has to make a choice. Jake doesn't like making choices. Jake likes giving up all of his options and offering all of the choices like jewels on a velvet cushion lined with golden tassels. He doesn't want to have to pick which gem he prefers. So he gulps for an answer, he pants shorts puffs of warm air.

"Come on, cielo. Tell me what you want," Bastian says this time, more impatient. His fingers are digging deep into the muscle of Jake's ass.

Jake thinks of Bastian's hands on him. Or Bastian's implements. Being spanked, or being flogged, he thinks of how much he loves the way Bastian looks at him when his skin is a color palette of his making, every cell of his body vibrating with a bottomless hunger. He thinks of how much he hates when Bastian spends hours stringing his body along, continuously edging him but preventing him from the release he so desperately needs. He hates that he will always welcome Bastian taking over his body until he's besides himself with want and need and despair. He hates that he loves it so much. His cock twitches at the thought of being so helpless in Bastian's hands. He thinks of being at Bastian's mercy, Bastian penetrating him, making him feel so good, he thinks of the incredible white noise that fills his every neuron when Bastian uses his body like just some other object with which to pleasure himself, he thinks of Bastian ever so slowly prepping Jake's body for a thorough fucking, he thinks of the opposite when Bastian barely prepares him for the stretch, how the dull ache mutates to pleasure gradually until he's wanton with arousal. He thinks of the multiplicity of ways he's catalogued of Bastian being unbearably mean to him, Bastian ignoring him, Bastian making him wait, Bastian over stimulating him, Bastian pleasuring himself and not letting Jake touch, or taste, Bastian making him cry because he likes the brightness of Jake's irises when he does, Bastian humiliating him when Jake is so eager to be used because all he wants is to make Bastian feel good, because if Bastian feels good Jake will too.

And through all of that, no word makes it past Jake's lips, no whine turns to syllables, to words, to phrases. To choices. Jake wants it all at once.

"I've got patience, Jacob. I can stay here all day waiting for you to tell me. I know what you want, I know what you need, but I can't give it to you if you can't ask for it, gorgeous."

"I, Bastian – I want to feel you, please?" Jake croaks out.

"How are you not feeling this?" Bastian retorts, fingertips turning into short nails dragging on his sensitive skin.

Jake huffs. This isn't fair, Bastian asked and he answered, Bastian knows he isn't good with words. He takes a few deep breaths, willing the words to come out from where they're trapped on his tongue. I want you inside me, that's only five words, it's easy. Should be easy. Subject-verb-object. Or maybe the opposite, I as the object to Bastian's subjectivities. Who knows.

It isn't easy.

He breathes in. Out. Bastian is still kneading, keeping Jake from forming coherent sentences. Then stills, and somehow that doesn't help.

Until Bastian's fingertips drag inwards, to his cleft. To the plug he's still wearing. And Jake is strung out enough that the barest of movements send fireworks through his spine.

Jake lets out a shaky breath when Bastian takes hold of the base of his plug and starts shifting it, rotating it inside him, rubbing ever so deliciously against his prostate with every twist, the breaths turn to quiet moans. He pushes back into the contact.

Bastian chuckles. Pushes Jake's hips back down, gentle but firm. "Such a good boy, aren't you? But I'm still waiting for an answer, why didn't you say this is what you wanted?"

Jake still his hips, blushes. He did, he tried. It's not his fault words are so heavy. Bastian doesn't move until he's immobile, until every muscle in his body is on hold. Until Jake can get his breathing evened out.

"There it is, you're so good for me. Stay still, pretty thing, good things come to those who wait."

Bastian pulls on the base, almost enough to remove it, but every time it catches on Jake's tight rim, just before Jake can relax and let it get past, the pressure is gone and the plug goes right back in. The torment is exquisite, and Jake doesn't care that the floor is cold and hard and unforgiving under his face and his torso, he can't keep still for this. Bastian never has enough of teasing him. It's not long before he starts wanting more. He wants so much more. He wants everything.

"Why so tight?" Bastian teases. "God, look at you. I stretched you earlier, Jacob, was I not good enough for you?"

Jake makes an indignant noise. That was hours ago, it could have been decades ago if you asked him, he'd gone out and come back, of course he isn't as pliant as he was! He had to wait before he could even dream of putting his underwear on before he left, thinking as he'd been that Bastian was about to take him apart, not send him out, he was very much in a predicament and wouldn't have been responsible if a wet spot had appeared on the front of his trousers. So he waited until he was down enough to act normally, to walk decently without his cock filling out at an embarrassing rate in a store aisle. At checkout. On the way back home, waiting at the stoplight, crossing the street.

"Bastian, please, please," Jake begs. This early on. He can't remember how to speak in any way other than pleading.

"What do you want, handsome?" Bastian asks, and Jake isn't about to lose the stimulation again.

"Y-your hand – I want your fingers, please Bastian," his voice dripping with need. "I want you inside me," he lets out breathily, finally letting the thought out in the open, out for Bastian to see for himself.

Jake doesn't expect the hand that slips up his body, curls around his shoulder and his throat and his chin, and past his lips, into the warm and wet heat of his mouth. He sucks on the intruding digits almost instantly, before he realizes that Bastian is playing him better than he could any instrument. This isn't what he meant, come on, Bastian, god, but now Jake can't speak to rectify. What would he even say, no, no, not my mouth, fuck me? Jake's never refused Bastian's fingers in his mouth. He knows full well that if it took this much work to get I want you inside me past his lips, all requests in the fuck me register might take light years.

Bastian is resting most of his weight on Jake, his free hand still pushing and pulling and twisting and shifting the plug inside him, so Jake moans loudly around the solid weight of Bastian's fingers. That he can't help. Then Bastian pulls back, not without dragging Jake's spit all over his chin and down the side of his neck. He grabs a more solid hold on the plug, and steadily, steadily he pulls it out, until Jake gives and arches his back and the plug pops out of him. The feeling, god, the stretch is so intense because Jake's worn it for hours but the stem is so small that he isn't accustomed to the size of the bulb anymore, and god he would be lying if he said it didn't feel wonderful. Without a break, though, he feels Bastian's fingers replace the solid weight of the steel. Slick, dexterous, skilled fingers who know exactly just how to take him apart. He makes a contented noise. He doesn't care to know when Bastian got the lube without Jake noticing because Bastian's fingers feel so fucking good inside him that Jake could cry. Bastian could keep him like this for the rest of forever and he'd thank him, probably. He's unwinding Jake with every push and pull and if it were possible for bones to go liquid, Jake would have melted into a puddle by now. Jake's maybe never felt this pliant, what with the belts so snugly fit around his body and Bastian just, slowly, slowly, so slowly exploring inside him like he doesn't know Jake's body like the back of his hand already.

"Look at you, honeybee, all tied up and eager, is this what you wanted?" Bastian asks.

Jake can't formulate words, he's lost his tongue and his vocal chords aren't cooperating, but he rolls his hips against Bastian just to encourage him to keep moving. This is so goddamn good.

"I wonder, Jacob," Bastian starts nonchalantly, like he's not knuckle deep into Jake, like he's not rubbing just that much against his prostate with every drag, like he's not causing Jake to create a dripping mess on the hardwood panels. "How much do you think you can take, if I do this nice and slow? How many fingers do you think I can get inside you before you beg? I wonder what you'll beg for. More or mercy, my pretty little toy, what do you think?"

"More," Jake says, a whisper that is as much an answer as it is a plead. You know I'll always beg for more, he thinks. Doesn't say that.

Bastian pulls out, Jake almost wails, until he feels a cool line of lube being painted down his cleft, until Bastian comes back – still with two fingers, but smearing it around, stretching Jake slowly, scissoring his fingers and spreading Jake open on every way out. Bastian is working so slowly, he's so thorough to prepare Jake and stretch him open just right, Jake can't help arching his body to give Bastian a better angle.

"You're opening up so nicely for me, handsome, look at you," Bastian praises him. "Just because you can't say what you want doesn't mean you don't want it, does it?"

When he pulls out, this time, Bastian does so completely, but when he comes back with three fingers, he lets out an obscene moan, as if he was the one on the receiving end, and Jake feels the warmth that it sends spreading through his entire torso. Hearing Bastian vocalize the pleasure he's getting from fingering Jake open is something Jake never knew he needed, and it sends white hot need through his spine and straight down to his neglected cock. It's a wire straight through him and he's never needed to hear anything as much as he needs that sound from Bastian again. He hears the distinctive sound of a zipper being pulled down.

"If I can fit this much in with so little effort imagine what I'll get in you by the time I'm done."

Jake's feels the warm and solid weight of a torso flush against his back. When he feels a wonderful pressure against his prostate, Jake's breathing hitches, he doesn't want to focus on air if he can focus on how fucking good those fingers feel inside him. "Ah, ah, no, cielo, breathe for me."

That shouldn't have been so hard to obey.

The stimulation stops until Jake's lungs start functioning again, save for a free hand lightly running up and down his ribcage. When Jake gains minute control over his body again, or at least enough to listen to the orders, the rhythm of the fingers inside his ass starts matching the patterns of expansion of his chest. Out when he inhales. In when he exhales. Not putting sufficient care into his breathing means not getting pleasure. This is a whole new aspect of breath play Jake had never considered. It's an excruciatingly effective way of controlling his body.

"Good boy, you're doing so well, darling," a hushed whisper into his ear.

They're quiet for a moment, just long enough for Jake to start feeling desperate, save for the sounds making it out of his throat. He knows he's making a mess on the floor, he can feel it, his helpless squirming is spreading the wetness leaking from his cock all over the varnished wood, all over his stomach. He's slowly rocking, chasing the touch he wants and fucking himself on the fingers milking and stretching him, beautiful and long and agile fingers that are so attuned to his pleasure, they fill him up so well.

The noises are spilling from him freely now, and he knows he's ramping up steadily to a toe-numbing orgasm. Quick, breathless "ah, ah, ah" sounds rolling on his tongue until they're past his lips. With the right flick and pressure, he lets out deeper, wanton moans, dripping with pure lust. When a harder thrust feels particularly good, Jake almost whines, he keens, high pitched at the back of his throat. He starts thrusting back on the pushes, needing so much more than what he's getting. He's got three fingers stretching him open, slick and strong fingers, rubbing against his prostate so well, Jake doesn't care that his knees, his shoulders and his face are starting to protest at his prostrated position on the floor, skin directly against the unforgiving wood. He feels the higher belt by his elbows being yanked back as he does, and now he's getting shoved down onto the three digits penetrating him, he's getting so thoroughly fucked, he's so lost in his pleasure, he is flying away, nothing matters outside of this moment. He's rocking back as much as he can, riding those fingers. He can't get enough.

"Oh, oh, please," he begs with a shaking voice.

"Please what, handsome?"

"Please, Sir, oh please," Jake replies, choking back a sob, every syllable in time with the rhythm of the fingers stroking his prostate so fucking good.

There's a slight hitch in the movement while the warm body behind Jake bends down to rest flush against him and he gets teeth sinking into the flesh of his shoulder. A muffled moan. "Oh, well when you ask so nicely, don't worry handsome I'll take care of you." The low rumble of exertion and arousal in his voice are filling Jake's head with white noise.

The few neurons that aren't drowning in the waves of pleasure crashing against all the right parts of Jake's brain are chanting more, more, more in unison. He distantly remembers Bastian wondering out loud how much Jake's ass could take, and as much as Jake just wants to cum – and he does, oh god does he want to cum and do so now –, he also wants to be good and be patient and wait and find out just how many fingers can fit inside him. Besides, it's not like he'd been told he could cum, but oh god, he hopes he can, because he needs to so fucking bad, but his brain counters every wish for an orgasm with "Sir hasn't given you permission," or "be patient, handsome," in his voice. So as much as there's less and less free space in his brain for Jake to think of anything that isn't how fucking great his body will feel when he lets his orgasm wash over him, Jake knows he isn't allowed, so he focuses as best he can on rocking back and fucking himself thoroughly on Bastian's fingers.

After what feels like hours, Jake feels Bastian slowing down a little, but he can't seem to find his voice to ask why, Bastian, to ask what's going on. Bastian is pulling back from him and Jake lets out a choked sob, he's not ready for him to stop, he's so not ready to have to go on without his Sir pleasuring him, without having had the chance to release, so all he can do is to let a keening moan past his lips and hope that Bastian hears the pleas.

"Shh, cielo, don't worry, I'm far from being done with you," Bastian says, his voice so low and rough, the voice that affects Jake the most. Can't be by chance – he's got to be using it on purpose to keep his boy on edge. "Remember what I said I was going to do to you? Do you remember that, Jacob? I said I'd see how much I can fit inside you, so be a good boy for me and you'll get what you want if I decide that you deserve it."

With that, Jake feels warm fingertips teasing at his rim again. When he goes in, though. Oh fuck, oh, fuck. Jake can feel both palms resting on his ass cheeks, spreading them open. Angled in a way that Bastian's fingers are pointing inwards, teasing his cleft, circling him. He can feel two of Bastian's fingers back inside him, one from each hand, before they're joined by a third, and, and, a fourth? And they're working wonders, he's feeling so good, and Bastian's goal is clear, he's working relentlessly to make sure Jake is stretched and open and Jake's never felt this much on display. He's got Bastian entirely focused on him, and that's a lot, Bastian's hyper focus could be hard to handle if his boy didn't want and need him so much. And Christ, he's being effectively pulled open, and if Jake can trust the sensations that his body is relaying to his brain, the only way this can work is if Bastian is using a few fingers from both hands to work him open, and that image on its own is worth more than Jake ever thought he deserved. He's stopped caring about the mess he's making a long time ago, he can't care about that when he's got both of Bastian's hands prying him open.

Bastian keeps working on him like this for what feels like light years, stretching and pulling and relaxing his rim, and Jake feels like he's about to explode, but he's also never wanted for something to last more than this. His skin is starting to protest, the floor isn't exactly comfortable, but relocating is the last thing he wants. He can barely register what Bastian is doing to him anymore, and he's stopped trying to keep track of his movements.

When Bastian slows down, and pulls out, both hands, Jake breaks. "Oh, no, please don't stop, please Bastian, don't," he pleads.

"Please don't stop? You're a greedy boy, now, aren't you…" Bastian says, and he sounds just a little distracted by Jake's body, in the best way. "You're so open right now, so hot and slick for me, begging for my hand, isn't that right?"

Jake nods as best he can. He can feel more lube, he's feeling so wet for Bastian, and that's sending tingles down his spine because he doesn't know what Bastian could possibly have left in store for him. He almost cries out when one hand is back, two, maybe three fingers inside him again, and Bastian starts rhythmically stroking the sweetest of spots, causing Jake to dissolve in pleas that are oh so close to begging for the release he doesn't know if he will be granted.

"Is this what you want, Jacob? I can't hear you," Bastian teases, setting up a new speed that might make Jake lose his mind at last, but the overstimulation feels so good, he'd be a fool to want it to stop even though he's leaking everywhere underneath himself. "What do you want, handsome?"

"This, Bastian, please keep going, I'm so close," he pants hard against the hardwood.

Bastian, after that, doesn't speak. He pushes inside Jake, though, and the last bit of extra lube he added finally makes sense, because Jake unmistakably feels the rough edge of Bastian's knuckles stretching the sensitive and overworked ring of muscle of his entrance. He's too stunned to think properly. He's too shocked to even sob; the only sound coming out of them, when Jake realizes what's happening, are the staggered gasp from the air catching in Jake's throat, and a low, breathy moan from Bastian.

Bastian moves and the world starts spinning again. The waves and the strong gusts of wind and Jake's flying away, with only Bastian to keep him grounded and make sure he's never going to be lost to the ocean. Everything is moving again, the universe is tumbling down, and Bastian, Bastian, Bastian, perfect and warm and solid and his beautiful hand inside Jake, and the thumb that isn't in him just rubbing so good at the seam that goes across his perineum, and the stretch is so divine, his fingers know just how to make Jake fall apart, every time, there exists no instrument in this world that Bastian knows better than that of Jake's body.

Jake whispers. Please, Bastian, quiet inside his head. He wants to let go of the tension and the need and he's so desperate. "Bastian," soft, spoken amongst the storm inside him, threatening to crush his bones and break his resolve any moment now.

"I haven't even told you if you could seek your release, have I? Well I don't think you really have a choice. With the mess you've made I bet you are so close. Be a good boy and give in, Jacob," Bastian instructs, just as calmly, the contrast with how Jake is feeling so obvious, so strong. He hears faint, slick sounds, Bastian's free hand moving on himself.

Jake has been riding this high, this pressure for so long, he's been so mindless with pleasure that he doesn't know anymore, he can't tell when and where his orgasm starts and stops, all he knows is that he's maybe never felt this good before, and he wants to remember this moment forever. The climax is so intense, he can't make heads or tails about what's happening to him, he's never felt anything this wholly and intimately before, and maybe never will again, but that's okay, because he's here now and he's with Bastian and he can't move, couldn't even if he wanted to, with the bands around his body and the warmth of Bastian's body right there, so close. Jake's lost in his mind and he's hypnotized by the endless lightning bolts connecting throughout his entire being.

He barely takes notice, when Bastian stimulates him slowly through the endorphin rush, when he slows down, dead slow, and eventually stops. Eventually slides out. A whimper, maybe his. The storm is quieting, it's continuing elsewhere, leaving nothing but calm in her wake. He barely realizes when his hips are pulled upwards, back a little. Jake is on his knees, but he doesn't care that he's awkward and not very comfortable on his face and shoulders; Bastian wants him, and he wants him like this. Bastian's slick fingers are between his thighs, spreading the wetness around. When they're replaced by the heavy warmth of his erection, fucking the space between his legs, occasionally dragging against the over sensitized skin of his softening cock, Jake starts pleading, for Bastian's release this time. He wants to be as good for Bastian as he is for Jake; he needs to reciprocate, to give himself up for Bastian, so that hopefully Bastian feels a fraction of how good Jake feels right now. So he tries to meet him halfway on every thrust, he listens for when he moves in a particularly good way that makes Bastian's moans almost carnal, so that he can provide him with that pleasure over and over. Bastian's hands spasm on Jake's hips, and when he gets close, he falls flush against Jake's back, and Jake tries to spur him on. "Please, Bastian, I want to make you feel good, please let it go, please cum, I want it, please let me feel you, I want to feel it," Jake begs, frantically working to find Bastian's release as hard as he would his own.

When Bastian spills, it's with his teeth in Jake's shoulder, his breath hot against his skin, his fingernails fixed in Jake's hips, and the warmth of his release, Jake can feel, only adding to the mess before Jake's body. It makes him shiver with the pride of having provided Bastian with what he needed from him. Having let Bastian take what he wanted from Jake. There is maybe no better feeling in Jake's universe, and for long minutes, all they can hear are the pants coming out of both of them, after Bastian has tugged Jake to the side and they're both laying on the floor, recuperating. Jake has Bastian's arm as a pillow and everything is right in the world.

Eventually, though, the spirits are cooling down; their heart rates, both working overtime, are starting to settle, and so are their breaths. Jake feels Bastian's free hand scourging about for the buckles of the belts that were still holding him captive, and as much as Jake doesn't really want them off, he's starting to be a little bit chilly. He doesn't want to move, but he knows anywhere but the floor would be more comfortable, in the long run. Warmer. Softer. But he's got Bastian's lips at the top of his spine and his arms around him so he doesn't want to care about a cold floor or the mess sticking to his skin.

"Let's clean you up, cielo, what do you think?" Bastian asks, disturbing the quiet surrounding them. "I'll take care of you. I'll need you to get up, though, I'm not strong enough to carry you to the shower," he adds, running his hand up and down Jake's newly freed arm. "Can you do that for me, handsome?"

Jake can, he will, he just. He needs another moment or two. He's having a hard time getting his body to respond to him. Everything feels so heavy, every limb too weighted, every muscle too tired. His veins might as well be filled with lead. That's just the effect Bastian has on him. He needs a few more minutes to get his body moving, getting up, flexing. Bastian leads him to the shower, and Jake could do it on his own, he can walk, still, but. The little attentions are always appreciated. Bastian takes the time to wipe his body off before they get under the stream. It's domestic. Jake loves it. The feeling of all the steamy hot drops on his skin is wonderful and time just stands stills for them. Jake's thankful for the fact that Bastian is scrubbing as softly as he can where the ink stained his skin. Probably wants it to stay as much as Jake needs the reminders.

Jake's still in a bit of a daze afterwards, when Bastian finds him a nice shirt of the softest blend of cotton, some lounge shorts he can wear in the late August heat of New York City. They don't go far, not out, really; Bastian makes him some tea and leads him to the stoop, the nice porch by their front door that gives on the quiet street on which they live. They can hear the birds in the heavy air, Jake thinks it must rain soon; but for now all is still peaceful and the weather feels like a hug from Mother Nature. He holds onto his mug and leans against Bastian's shoulder.

Bastian rubs his back while the tea steeps and cools enough for Jake to drink it. "Thank you, cielo. For this," Bastian says, breaking their comfortable silence.

Jake looks up at him, eyebrows raised in question. He thinks he might always wonder why, might always feel like he should be the one thanking Bastian, not the other way around.

"You always make me so proud." A kiss to his forehead; Bastian continues. "There's so many ways I can push you and you let me try all of them." He's quiet for a second, a few heartbeats. "And I mean… I think you'll agree with me that taking my time to stretch you open and push that limit might have been one of the hottest things you've let me do to you, gorgeous," he adds, pretending like they aren't outside, like people might not hear them. Or maybe he doesn't care.

Jake clears his throat, the way he knows Bastian likes. "I, um. Yeah. That was..." He can feel himself blush. "That was great. That was really great," he says softly, half out of always being shy about the things he enjoys, half because the setting gives him a reason to keep his voice low.

He's maybe a little too thankful for knowing he can't or won't get aroused again this soon, not in his secondary state, because, well. The vivid reminiscence that flashes in his brain is definitely making him feel some type of way.

"You said something," Bastian says after that. "It made me very happy," he adds.

Jake's eyebrows frown just a tad. He doesn't know where Bastian is trying to go with this.

"When you begged me for more."

It's very rapid, after that, the way the Jake's brain processes the information and tries to scan his memories to find – and it finds – he feels his conscience stutter when he remembers. His eyes widen.

"I, Bastian –" the words are hard to get out of his mouth. "I called you Sir. I called you... Sir. Didn't I? Oh my god, I did, I called you –" he says, quickly, then shuts up. Hopefully he can blame the afternoon sun for the blood rushing to his face. He gulps. "Oh god, Bastian. I'm sorry. I didn't," he starts, but he doesn't know what he didn't. He meant it, that he did. He knew it, somewhere. He liked it. There's no denying how much he liked it, perhaps needed it, if his brain supplied it without a way for Jake to stop running his mouth.

"Jacob," Bastian says, and Jake's brain stops so that he can look at him. "It was a good surprise, cielo. You let it slip, didn't you? I don't mind, I liked it. A lot. It made me feel incredibly special." Bastian pauses for a second, and Jake doesn't know what to say to that, so he doesn't say anything. "It's okay if you didn't necessarily mean to say that, I don't have expectations. But I really... My beautiful boy was so entranced that he begged me in the most reverent way. I'd be lying if I said it didn't affect me."

The absolute fondness, the joy in Bastian's voice, the pride – Jake could feed off on that alone for the rest of his life. He wants it, all the time, until he finds out if there is ever a point where he doesn't starve for more of it. He doubts he'd ever get enough of the delight that colors Bastian's tone when Jake does something he likes.

He feels Bastian's fingertips, warmer than the air, somehow, tilt his head up and towards him. He feels his lips, soft but demanding, against his own. The soft scratch of his beard, that's starting to grow again after he last shaved it. The palm splayed on his neck. He responds automatically, out of habit maybe, but he can't be blamed when he maybe loves nothing more than the intimate moments he shares when they kiss.

They only let go, abruptly, when the sound of shattering glass reaches their ears and Jake realizes, foolishly, that he'd completely forgotten about the tea that Bastian had made for him. The tea that is now trickling down the stoop stairs, amongst the few fallen leaves and the sharp pieces of white porcelain from the teacup he's just shattered on the crimson brick. Jake stills in shock, but Bastian captures his mouth again after pulling Jake's face back to his own.

They pull away when Bastian rests his forehead against Jake's. Without being unnecessarily heavy, the air between them feels thick, with promise and possibility, with euphoria and electricity.

"Have you thought about that for long? Why today?" Bastian asks, with a bluntness so characteristic.

"I haven't, not that I'm aware," and Jake realizes the truth of it as he speaks it. "I don't know why today. I think it just... happened, and it felt right, so it worked." He's quiet for a moment, the gears in his brain working. Part of him wants to know... it's hard to admit, it's big, even to himself, but he wants to know if he can say it again, when the time is right. He needs to know but his throat isn't letting him ask.

"Was it what we were doing? Was it the position? The location?" Jake can tell that Bastian is looking for more, maybe so that he can recreate that moment, or maybe he just wants to get a little further inside Jake's head. "Did something I did make you want to address me with it?"

"No, Bastian, I..." he tries. "I don't know where it came from, but I – can I – can I use it again? When the time is right? Please, can it be a reoccurring thing? How did it make you feel?" Jake's words are fighting for a space and he's trying to prevent them from all coming out at once.

He realizes he'd looked away when Bastian's fingertips softly turn his head so that he can look at him.

"Yeah. Yes, mi cielo, you can," Bastian responds fondly. "Have you used that honorific with anybody else?" He inquires. "Not a bad thing – I'm just curious."

"No, god no," Jake replies, almost horrified at the thought of giving this title – Bastian's title – to somebody else. At the thought that he'd use something anything but free of baggage for Bastian, at the thought of calling him what had previously belonged to somebody else. "I wouldn't... I wouldn't do that to you," he says softly, and kisses Bastian of his own volition this time.

"I'm honored," Bastian pants when they part. "I'll do my best to make sure I deserve you calling me that, handsome, every day if I can. I'll live up to your expectations. I'm proud of you, and I'm proud that you feel safe enough to retreat far enough into your head when you're with me. Proud doesn't even begin to cover it, but it's all I got, so you'll have to forgive me for not having better words for you. I'm proud to have the permission to call you mine, my good boy – isn't that what you are – and I'm proud to be yours," he concludes. They breathe. "Your Sir," Bastian adds after a few seconds of quiet.

Jake thinks this might be all they ever need. The space to allow each other in, to let each other dive into the other's ribcage and crack it open and replace the marrow with stardust and the bones with vines, they each have planted a garden deep into each other's core where they can watch everything grow from inside their reciprocal wells. He can't wait to see the flower bloom from Bastian's lungs and the roots take deep into his heart so that wisdom always has a place to call home.

And if Jake's feet never touch the ground again, if he's forever destined to fly, to soar ever so higher, and to keep his head in the clouds that Bastian has placed around him, well.

That's enough. It's so much more than enough. It's everything he never knew he needed.

Chapter Nineteen

"*D*on't stay out too late, then, cielo. Say hi for me," Bastian's voice comes crackling through the receiver.

"Yes, Sir, I will," Jake replies, flustered as he is by the conversation they've just had.

He's at the theatre, they're done early, and Karla had come knocking on his dressing room door, asking if he wanted to join her for coffee. To catch up. It's been a while since Jake's gone out to anyone from the company. So he's called Bastian to let him know, to ask him really, whether that'd be fine, or if he already had made plans for Jake when he'd come home. Bastian had said yes, of course, but not before he made sure to make Jake blush, even over the phone, because Bastian likes playing Jake like his favorite keyboard and Jake is incredibly sensitive to the touches of Bastian's playful dominance. He'd asked about the previous night, about how he felt some twenty hours after almost having been fisted. Bastian must have known that Jake had spent the whole day thinking of him (and his hand inside him) every time he took a step, or moved on his seat, or relocated in any way, really, because Bastian's passage left some twinges of sweet soreness behind. It's not that Jake doesn't usually spend the day with Bastian on his mind one way or another, it's just… he's had to focus hard on not getting surreptitiously aroused during the day, because he's taken right back to how he felt in Bastian's belts on the floor, or when he'd seen him walk into the room in his harness, and really, it would take harder-than-iron will to pretend to be unaffected by it all. Jake's will to purposefully not think of Bastian is soft at best.

So naturally, as soon as Bastian heard Jake's voice through his phone, he'd asked Jake how he felt, how his ass felt, how sore he was, and he left Jake blushing and momentarily silent on the other end of the call. He gave him a sly order and Jake, in his typical Bastian headspace, had replied with the honorific he was starting to give Bastian in his head, and Bastian had called him his good boy before he ended the call. All this couldn't have taken more than a minute or two, but to hell if Jake isn't affected. He flips his phone off and turned to Karla, who'd been there the whole time.

"Good to go?" She asks.

"Good to go," he replies with a smile in her direction while turning around, welcoming the excuse to look away and grab his bag. He resolutely avoids his reflection in the mirror.

"Really formal with your boyfriend huh?" Karla asks when they make their way to the stage door.

"What? He's not — we aren't—," Jake stammers, because Karla doesn't know he's with Bastian, does she?

The second he looks at her, though, a single glance is enough for him to know how wrong he is about her innocence.

"You don't have to hide around me, Jake," she responds, her voice so kind as always. "You seem to have forgotten that I know him, too, not just you. And while he usually is subtle around here, he's not exactly good at hiding the things he's excited about, when he's excited about them. And he's been excited about you since… the day I introduced you two. So it isn't really a big deal for anyone who doesn't know you, they just know Bastian's got someone in his life for the first time in a while, which is good. I simply happen to know who the mystery guy is," she finishes with a fond smile in his direction. "Not to mention the extra makeup you've been subtly applying, must be one passionate affair," she adds with a wink that makes Jake blush to the roots of his hair. "He doesn't do anything in half measures, I'm sure that also applies in his private life, doesn't it? I guess that isn't too surprising."

"I hadn't realized we were so.... obvious," Jake says quietly. He might have to talk to Bastian about this, he isn't entirely sure how he feels about the fact that people know he's dating someone, that plus the fact that he comes to the Lewinsky after his own show all the time, people can probably put two and two together, which means there are risks for him.

"'Sir. That, however, is surprising to me. I've never known Bastian to be one for such formal address, that must have been some joke, yeah?" She probes with a mock salute gesture and a quick laugh, "yes, Sir!"

When Jake fails to respond and trails behind her, she slows down in her tracks and looks back to see him skittishly avoiding her gaze.

"Or... not a joke?" she tries to salvage.

Jake shakes his head, still refusing to meet her eye. "Not a joke, no," he says quietly.

Jake's never been a man of many words, so when he fails to reply, she tries to get some type of explanation out of him. "Not that it's any of my business, don't feel like you have to share... but would this have anything to do with the bruises you've been covering up?"

"Are they that visible?"

"Not to someone who doesn't know what they're looking for, no." So it's her turn to be cryptic.

"And what is that supposed to mean, Karla?" Jake asks, a bit defensive despite feeling that he should owe her the trust. She's always been a good friend and colleague to him.

"What, a girl can't have an active fantasy life? I've read enough, and experienced my fair share of pretty, sought-after bruising. I may have never had marks like yours but I figured they were somewhat sex-related. Some type of badges of honor, if you will, or am I completely wrong?"

"No, I... can't say you're wrong," Jake replies, relief flooding through his system. At least she is open-minded enough that she can understand the type of relationship he and Bastian have, and that is never a given, so if anything, he's thankful to have her in her life. Maybe he doesn't have to be as wary of everyone as he constantly is. "So, are my makeup skills decent? It's really hard to see what I'm doing sometimes and I constantly have to hope that none of it is coming off with my pants for that scene on the platform," he asks, trying to lighten the tension he was momentarily feeling.

"Nah, you're good, seriously. No one can see that unless they're in the wings and know what they're looking for, which is making me realize that I sound just a little bit stalkerish," she says with a laugh while she pushes the door to a coffee shop that seems a bit removed from the bustle of Times Square and Hell's Kitchen. Somehow she knows how to put him to ease, even when they're casually the fact that she's been looking at concealed bruises all over his ass while he performs on stage.

They chat for a bit, enough for Jake to notice that the sun is shifting, and he's realizing that summer is indeed coming to an end and that fall is at their door. Jake learns that while Karla may never have had the type of all-consuming relationship he has with Bastian, this constant, kind of 24/7 dynamic they have developed, she isn't a stranger to the concept and it feels incredibly freeing to be able to discuss his life without fear for retribution.

"Is that also why you call him 'Sir,' then?" Karla asks eventually, bringing that on the table again, and Jake can't help the warmth spreading through his body at the thought that he's going home to Bastian, soon, to be with him, to be his.

"Yeah, it just… works. You know?" He tries to say, and she nods slightly. "It makes me feel lighter all day, just to know that someone is caring for me in a way that just saying 'my boyfriend' doesn't really explain. It's more than that. I think. Or it's more than what I had with my ex, that's for sure, so they definitely can't be compared or talked about as if they were equivalent. They couldn't be more different. But yeah it happened kind of accidentally and I didn't really noticed that I'd called him that until after when he brought it up and asked me about it, and then I just got really flustered because I realized that I let that slip," Jake says, not quite hesitant if he is to be judged by the debit of his speech.

She smirks, an understanding smile over the rim of her coffee cup. Jake hasn't felt this weightless outside of his own private bubble and hideaway life in a long time.

Epilogue

*I*t's been a day, Bastian has been unable to stop thinking about how mouth-watering Jake looked the night before, bound to himself, face first on the hardwood panels, and eager and aroused and desperate and so good he took the most part of Bastian's hand inside him. That's an image he shouldn't have been dwelling on for as many hours as he did, but his mind always has at least four different tracks and one of them has been completely taken over by that delicious thought. And now Jake isn't coming home just yet, which is fine. Or rather, it would be fine, if it weren't for Bastian feeling this strong a hunger for him, but he's been fizzing with anticipation and running scenarios through his mind all day while waiting for Jake to come back, and now he has to wait more, so he can't reasonably be blamed if he's almost primal by the time his boy comes through the front door.

There's also a part of him that's been imagining Jake's reaction and body language when he called. Bastian will never turn down such a perfect opportunity to get Jake frazzled, regardless of how casual or long-distance the conversation. So when Jake's voice crackled through the receiver, Bastian couldn't help but make sure he would be reminiscing their evening together. Setting traps for

Jake to fall in like flies in honey. "How is your ass feeling from last night? I hope your body can still feel me, even though I'm not with you right now. Can't have you forgetting," he'd said, and he could just picture the deep blush settling high on Jake's cheeks when he had failed to respond. But Bastian wouldn't be satisfied with that, Jake ought to know; so he'd pressed in, "I can't hear you, Jacob," full-name, until Jake cleared his throat and replied with a shaky "I'm fine, I'm… uh, a little sore, thank you," which was simply delightful to hear.

He had followed up with a simple "Don't stay out too late, then, cielo. Say hi for me," and Jake, ever-so-sweet, had breathed out a soft "Yes, Sir, I will." Reinforcing the good habit, Bastian had been sure to let Jake know how he appreciated the honorifics.

By the time Bastian hears the key turn inside the lock, he's made the bed properly, and set a pair of soft leather cuffs and a pair of clamps nicely in the middle of it. It's unnecessary, really, but he likes going the extra mile, he likes to show off, and he especially likes the way Jake stops in his tracks and stutters halfway through his sentence when he lays eyes on the restraints. Bastian trails behind him.

"Had to keep my hands busy while you were gone, wouldn't you agree?" Bastian asks, entirely rhetorical.

He's leaning against the door frame, waiting to see Jake's reactions. A slight shiver up his spine, in anticipation most likely; his shoulders drop, the tension already leaving, and his breathing, while slow, gets a bit heavier, a bit louder.

"What's… what's the plan?" Jake asks quietly.

"First, I want you to answer something for me." He pauses to let Jake turn around and face him. "You've called me 'Sir' again on the phone earlier."

"I did."

"Is that a thing, then?" Bastian pushes. He wants to know whether they're taking this to another level, if they're entering another dimension in their dynamics.

Jake can't meet his eye, which Bastian codes as an admission, it's as good as one when he knows Jake as well as he does. A faint blush is creeping up Jake's neck, below the soft skin. His knees are unsteady. He clears his throat.

"Do you want me to call you 'Sir'?" He asks, his voice so very small. He still refuses to meet Bastian's gaze; his is fixated somewhere around his collar bones but will not stray any higher.

"Do you want to call me 'Sir'?" Bastian replies, rebounds with a question, because as much as he does want that from Jake, this is the type of development and growth that Jake needs to do on his own, and not because he thinks that Bastian wants him to. Bastian can't clear that path for him, regardless of how much he wishes he could. He owes it to Jake to trust that he's given him all the tools he needs to get through to the clearing that awaits him.

Jake nods, shyly at first, but the weight of the confession seems to lift off of his shoulders.

His entire body seems freer for Bastian, it's like flicking a switch, so the second Jake finds it within himself to finally look up and into Bastian's eyes, Bastian strides across the short distance to reach him. He needs the physical connection to enhance what they already have. He needs to ensure that Jake knows just how loved and cared for he is in this very moment. He brings a hand to hold Jake's neck, better to feel his pulse and how it stutters when Bastian leans in, and then doesn't quite kiss him. Jake's hands softly land on his hips, and when their lips finally meet, Bastian can feel the solid fingertips holding onto him tighter. It's a slow kiss, but they both need it to anchor this moment down and engrave it in their respective memory palaces. It's languid, and it's hot, and all of the free space in Bastian's brain is taken up by Jake. Jake's lips, Jake's mouth, Jake's fingers on his waist, Jake calling him 'Sir' and the word rolling off his tongue so naturally, so effortlessly, so organically. His boy, his boy, his boy. There may always be a hunger inside Bastian's being for him, that much is true – but this, this is all encompassing, it's consuming, it's a low heat that is inherently inescapable in comparison with the rapidly burning fire that he feels most of the time. It's the sun on his skin during a heat wave, the feeling that doesn't leave when the moon rises as a promise that tomorrow will be even warmer. It's the steam rising off of his skin in a too-hot shower. It's going to bed and waking up with Jake clinging to him like his life depends on it, and maybe it does, maybe Bastian's depends on Jake, it's the feeling of home under the covers when they're overheating but neither would dream of lifting the duvet because what's under there is theirs and theirs only. So he kisses Jake, and it's not that he's forgotten about his plans to ravish him, to have him bound and writhing, but that all can wait another minute or ten because Bastian is busy soaking up as much of Jake's energy as he can.

He stops, eventually, because he has to. He holds Jake's face with both hands, rests his forehead against Jake's. Breathes him in. They're quiet for a minute, until Jake breaks the silence, to Bastian's surprise considering Jake's affinity with the quiet.

"So can I? May I call you that? Will you be my Sir, Bastian, please?" Jake asks, his voice soft but firm, more confident than he usually is, his piercing blue eyes looking at Bastian with all the hope in the world.

"Yes. Yes, of course you may handsome," Bastian says, and he knows his hunger, temporarily cast aside, is coming back, perhaps stronger than before.

He kisses Jake again, fiercely, he is sweet yet ravenous. The hand he previously had rested on the side of Jake's neck moves back to tangle in the curls at the nape of his skull. His free hand comes up to hold Jake's throat, the tip of his thumb pressing into Jake's jaw, and he presses his whole body forward, into Jake, moving him backwards until Jake is on the bed with Bastian on top of him.

Bastian feels Jake's hands gripping him tightly, pressing their hips together. He breaks the kiss just long enough to pull Jake's shirt over his head. He has every intention of worshipping every freckle he can find on Jake's skin, every nerve ending, every sweet imperfection. He lets his lips pursue a trail down the tendons of Jake's neck, every now and then leaving indents from his teeth, sometimes reddening the skin, periodically sucking deep bruises that will bloom purple by the time Bastian is done with him. He spends what must, to Jake, feel like forever playing with his nipples, because Jake is so good he will take next to anything Bastian decides to give him without complaints. So he rubs feather light touches to the sensitive skin, he pinches, he digs his teeth and fingernails in, to see what gets Jake writhing most desperately. He sits on Jake's hips and pulls on them, to see how far back he will be able to let the clamps bite down. He urges Jake to make eye contact because he knows that that costs him, and if he focuses on keeping his eyes on Bastian's he will pay less mind to the pain in his nipples, and Bastian will be able to get deeper inside Jake's head, and faster.

He doesn't use the clamps until Jake has stopped writhing. He waits until his breathing slows, until the only movements from the body underneath his are the Adam's apple bobbing up and down and Jake's chest heaving to a slow and steady rhythm. Methodically, he rolls the buds between thumb and forefinger, to get them pebbled hard, and he pulls again to make sure to set the minute devices far back into the soft flesh so that Jake will feel the pinch for hours after the clamps are back in their designated box. It's a set of clovers, now, not the nice alligator clamps Bastian had used on him that last time. Bastian wants the sweet, sweet sound of Jake gasping when the clamps bite down, and then holding his breath by reflex when the pain doesn't go away, as if the lack of movement from his rib cage would make it easier on him. As if.

When Jake is all spaced out, Bastian continues his path down Jake's body. Light scratches down his ribcage to get deep red lines standing out vividly against his skin. Slow bites on his stomach for faint bruises that might show tomorrow. Bastian settles on his knees between Jake's legs to finish undressing him and to see for himself if his body is as interested as his head, and what a thrill it sends down his spine to see a little wet spot on his boy's underwear from nothing but playing with sensations and painting pretty pictures on his body. Bastian collects the clear fluid that's nearly dripping from Jake's cock and, when he sees Jake open his eyes at the feeling, leans above him and smears his fingertip messily across Jake's bottom lip. He elicits a deep moan and can't help but leaning back down against Jake to kiss him hungrily.

He relocates to straddle one of Jake's strong thighs, scrambles for the cuffs without looking, without daring to break the kiss, and maybe if someone asked Bastian would tell them it was for Jake's sake, but he knows he would be lying; he can't reasonably get his mouth off of Jake's when he's tasting his arousal on his tongue. He only parts when he's got a hold on the leather and it's physically necessary for him to let go of Jake's lips in order to get the cuffs fastened around his wrists. He moves to reach up above Jake's head, with the intention of ordering him to keep his wrists to the mattress. He's interrupted by a deep moan from underneath himself.

A moan that might have been the loudest, the most wanton this evening.

Because when he decided to lean up, Jake simultaneously thought it was time to arch up into Bastian, which resulted in Bastian's knee accidentally crashing into Jake's crotch – but before Bastian can even process and attempt to apologize, the pained gasp he would've expected comes from Jake as one of pleasure, and the reflexive look to Jake's face to ensure that he is okay tells him that Jake is so much more than okay. It all happened at once, within the span of a single second, and Bastian isn't sure that Jake is aware that this all was accidental.

He pushes the cuffed wrists into the mattress above Jake's head.

"Stay."

A single-word order, clear enough, predictable enough that Jake won't get taken out of his head for it. Won't open his eyes. Yet. Which is good, because now, Bastian is heavily interested in the proceedings, somehow more than he already was.

He wants to explore. He wants to know more.

So, slowly, he brings a hand to Jake's erect cock that's resting against his belly. He drags his short, sharp fingernails against the sensitive skin he finds there. He gets from Jake a slow roll of his hips that doesn't seem entirely on purpose, an exposed throat. When Bastian's fingers curl around Jake's balls, to touch, to squeeze, to tug and to pull, Jake visibly melts into the mattress, a long drop of precum pools to his belly, and isn't that an interesting reaction. Jake's got Bastian hyper-focused. It's good. And Bastian wants to pry further, so he does, and he lets go of his hold to better be able to slap, not too hard, at his balls, then presses down on them.

Jake opens his eyes at that, bright blue eyes overcome with lust, and looks down to himself before making eye contact with Bastian. He's met with an interested grin and the rise of an eyebrow.

"So that's a reaction I wasn't expecting. Have we discovered a new type of pain you enjoy, handsome?" Bastian says, voice as playful as it is fond.

Jake doesn't seem to know what to reply to that. Bastian can tell he's visibly fighting between his need to keep obeying his order, to keep his arms above his head, and the discernable urge to hide his face behind them. He's squirming beneath Bastian, and that's also something new. Jake gets shy about liking the things he likes, he sometimes gets slightly ashamed after a scene when he's let Bastian push him to the brink, but he doesn't quite get embarrassed the way he manifestly is now.

"Your words, Jacob. Use your words. What's this?" Bastian asks, as much in reference to Jake's unexpectedly shy behavior, and to his evident enjoyment of Bastian giving him his fix of pain.

It's several more seconds of Bastian watching Jake's throat work, of waiting for the words to spill, before Jake can speak them out loud. "It isn't... um... new," he stutters, flustered to the point of attempting to twist away from Bastian, despite the fact that Bastian is sitting on his thigh, despite being unable to resign to moving his arms.

Bastian doesn't interrupt this time. He waits for Jake to look at him again, his sweet and blooming masochist of a boyfriend who's got everything to learn and everything to grow into, because he knows he can spur Jake on with a simple equivocal look. He gets it, eventually, with some effort.

Jake still won't look him in the eye for more than a fraction of a second. "Sometimes, when I, uh... when I touch myself, I... pull on them? Or hold them a little too tight?" He tries, and he's so tentative all Bastian wants to do is scoop him up, because that isn't worth Jake beating himself over. That's Bastian's job. And that's exactly the kind of information Bastian wants to get about what goes on inside Jake's head.

"How long have you known this for?" Bastian asks. He wants to know more about how Jake's grown into himself. He wants it all.

And the fact that Jake manages to be all shy and embarrassed about something as healthy as masturbation makes Bastian want to ravish him, but that will have to wait until the conversation is over. Bastian has a task to accomplish first.

"Uh, awhile?" Jake replies. When Bastian brings a hand to stroke his neck, he continues. "I was having a really awful day once and was trying to… distract myself, but I couldn't get comfortable and nothing was working. And I accidentally tugged on them too hard, but it, it felt… really good," he says and while he blushes furiously at the admission.

Bastian can't help but think about how wonderful a sight that would be – a flustered, slightly sweaty Jake, on his back, with a hand stroking his cock and the other pulling on his testicles until he makes his own breath catch in his throat, or until he's a squirming, whimpering mess, until he's leaking all over himself like he is now, just because he would rather wait and make his orgasm more powerful rather than go the quick and easy route. Maybe he sometimes takes a break to pinch his nipples, too, or to tug and stretch them, give himself something to focus on other than his arousal. It might be fun to make Jake demonstrate, one day, so that Bastian can see first-hand Jake's favorite ways to pleasure himself, or even just to give him a show. He knows that Jake would do it for him, because it's an opportunity for him to please Bastian and be good for him and there is nothing he likes more than the praise he gets from his Sir for doing as he's told.

Bastian has a fleeting thought of wonder for how lucky he got to find Jake, before that sentiment is swallowed by an ardent need to use this newfound knowledge and ruin him. He removes his hand from Jake's neck. Wraps slender fingers around Jake's balls, and tugs.

"Anything else I should know before I start my own exploration?" He says, voice suddenly dark, while holding Jake's gaze and increasing the tension until Jake whimpers for him.

Jake shakes his head. Doesn't break eye contact, not this time, not even when Bastian's free hand reaches up to pull at the chain linking the clamps, not even when his gaze unfocuses slightly. He's trying, so hard, to be good for Bastian, and Bastian loves him for it.

Bastian brings the chain up, pulls it tight until he reaches Jake's mouth, makes him bite down on it. "Don't let go," he says simply. The decision has a dual purpose, the pull adding tension to Jake's nipples, the angle twisting them, and Jake is doing it to himself, which is a powerful move, a sure fire way to send him flying while keeping him grounded. And it frees Bastian's hands, which he needs to honor the information he's just uncovered. Jake's natural state when Bastian is playing with his body is arching and baring his neck, which will simply translate to the muted burn of the increased pressure on his nipples. It's very good, and Bastian is very eager to see how much Jake will be pulling.

Bastian lets go of looking into Jake's eyes so that he can scan his body with a stare that matches the ravenous hunger he feels for Jake deep in his stomach. His hyper focus must show on his features, because Jake moans when he sees Bastian's need sketched across his face, and his abs tense from the strength of his desire. His cock jumps slightly, and he hasn't stopped dripping on himself, a clear line of fluid connecting the head of his cock to the small puddle forming on his stomach. Bastian loves how wet Jake gets before they even start properly playing, he's barely even touched him, yet Jake is so sensitive, so incredibly reactive to everything Bastian might do, no matter how subtle.

"Give me your hands."

Bastian gets a muffled "What?" from behind the chain. Jake's breathing is a little erratic, and that sends a jolt down Bastian's spine.

"Give me your hands, handsome, don't make me repeat."

It's not quite that Bastian is done playing. It's just that he's eager and impatient and he wants to spend hours stretching Jake thin and if he wants to do that, well, he better start soon.

He takes Jake's wrists as soon as Jake brings his arms down, Jake and his big blue eyes, looking at him all confused, even though he should know to follow Bastian's lead by now. That's always better for him. Bastian always knows what's best for him. So Bastian unclasps the connector joining the cuffs, then manhandles Jake's legs until his knees are tight against his own chest – all the better if he's pressing them hard against Jake's nipples, even more so if they're rubbing against the sensitized tips. He takes hold of the connector again and refastens the cuffs together, in such a way that Jake has no choice but to hold his own thighs tightly against his torso.

Bastian's got unrestricted access to his boy, like this. This is good. This is maybe perfect. He grins and lets a dark laugh escape his chest. He leaves the bed just long enough to gather everything he needs to get his plan to completion. He uses the opportunity to unbutton the shirt he's wearing, take his pants off. It's not the perfect strategic move, but he knows Jake won't mind, and he's no über-menschen. Jeans were getting slightly… inconveniently tight.

Bastian gets back on the bed. Sits on his haunches, perfectly positioned below Jake. On a whim, without warning, he bends down. Trails the tip of his tongue to the base of Jake's cock. Takes a tiny thin bit of skin from his balls and worries it between his teeth, just to feel Jake tense up and shiver, just to hear his moans and whimpers. Continues his descent south and circles the tight ring of muscle at Jake's entrance with his tongue, to get it wet, maybe to scare Jake that he might fuck him but for spit. And the sounds that he gets out of Jake, when he probes in with his tongue, the sounds of metal clunking when he pulls on the cuffs, the unabashed moan that starts deep in his chest, the slight stutter of his breath when he realizes he can't shudder without pulling on the chain, stretching his nipples as far as they'll go, the keening when Jake realizes the predicament where Bastian left him, all of these sweet details Bastian is saving about Jake, part gets stored for later and part go straight to feed his own overwhelming lust and heavy arousal.

Getting this wonderful balance of pleasured and pained noises out of Jake from having his tongue inside him — and consequently having Jake rock his hips and pull on his chain — is giving Bastian too many ideas. He doesn't have enough body parts to enact them all at once, and that's a shame, really. He brings his unoccupied hands to the backs of Jake's thighs, so vulnerably exposed as they are, and scratches them. Lightly at first. Before he turns harsh. He keeps going like this, until his fingertips feel numb, until Jake's shaking and his skin is warm, until his own jaw aches from pushing his tongue inside Jake as deeply as he can. Only once he's debated with himself as to whether to keep rimming Jake despite the ache, because Jake is rightfully being taken apart and the relentless moans he's producing are music to Bastian's ears, only once his muscles win out and he's forced to pull out does he stop. He hates that he has to, because he loves nothing more than to wind his Jacob up and shatter him to better be able to put him back together in the aftermath.

So he stops, but not without biting the soft, sensitive skin over Jake's testicles again. He sits back up, and can't help but swatting lightly at the reddened backs of Jake's thighs, over all the vivid scratches he left. He loves seeing Jake's cock twitch and pulse between his legs; his pretty boy is so worked up already, and Bastian hasn't even touched him properly yet. The touching can wait, Bastian decides, after a short round of spanks, until Jake is moaning his name and his title and begging him for more.

Jake is so pretty when he begs. Even more so when he can't enunciate properly.

Bastian indulges him, eventually. He wraps agile fingers around Jake's length, weighing his arousal in his hand, tilting it up so that he can reach the wet tip of his cock with his tongue. He might be trying to convince himself that sporadically touching and pleasuring Jake is an active and thought out part of his game plan, but he knows he'd be manipulating the truth. If he's honest, he really just felt an intense need to taste him before he continued. Jake tastes stupidly good.

Once he feels like he's done a good enough job of collecting the fluids that Jake is producing, he reaches for lube and pours a small amount on Jake's seam, watching it drip down his perineum. He spreads it around when it reaches Jake's sensitive rim, he's drawing tight patterns with his fingertips against the muscles. He has a hand on Jake's ass cheek, pulling the skin taut. He takes his sweet time, loving how Jake is getting increasingly vocal and squirming and desperate before Bastian even penetrates him. Drawing out the anticipation between the pull of the bow string and the release that sends the arrow soaring. Making him work for it.

Bastian drags his fingernails until he reaches Jake's balls, because now that he knows that Jake likes that type of pain, that it turns him on, that it satisfies him more, he's going to be sure to take advantage of it. He rubs his scrotum, spreading the leftover lube around. He makes a tight circle with his fingers around Jake, starts pulling slowly but relentlessly, stretching the thin skin until his testicles are tight and shiny in the palm of Bastian's hand, all the while pushing two fingers inside Jake, and stroking up to play with his prostate. He wants Jake over stimulated enough to have trouble deciding what to focus on, the pain or the pleasure, if those are even distinguishable at all for his sweet boy at this point.

"Is this what you like? Is this what you wanted, pretty boy?" Bastian asks.

Without waiting for Jake's answer, Bastian brings up his free thumb, uses it to rub patterns over Jake's perineum in time with the movements of his fingers inside him. Bastian loves the sounds he's pulling out of Jake like this, the breathless moans and the quiet, muffled Bastians. He loves seeing Jake let himself go, loves seeing how all of Jake's barriers disappear, how he lets Bastian do with his body as he wishes. Feeling the way Jake opens up so nicely under his care, how he's having an increasingly easier time letting Bastian stretch him, feeling how eager Jake is to be good for him makes it ever harder for Bastian to ignore his own growing arousal, the ache he's starting to feel. He doesn't think he will ever get used to the thrill he feels when Jake entrusts him with so much of himself.

It doesn't take much longer for Bastian to release the tension of his pull on Jake's balls in order to reach up, past Jake's neglected cock, to unclasp the cuffs. Almost immediately, Jake's hands fall to his sides. Bastian pulls out of him, holds Jake's thighs in place just long enough to get up and off the mattress, then lets them fall – might as well give Jake's muscles a bit of a break before what he still has in store for him. He's facing a bit of a situation with the fact that he is somehow still wearing clothes, and he can't fuck Jake without remedying that; so he does the second his feet hit the floor.

He doesn't get back on the mattress right away. He walks up to be level with Jake's headfirst.

"Open up," he says, simply, his voice hard.

He doesn't give Jake much of a chance to process the order, not blissed out as he is. Bastian bends down, pulls the chain from the clamps out of Jake's mouth. He grabs fistfuls of his hair, and tugs Jake's head closer to the edge of the bed, yanking his whole upper body with it so that he can avail himself in Jake's warm, welcoming mouth, getting the edge off himself and planning on using Jake to get himself wet enough to fuck him. Bastian holds Jake's head tightly in place, locks eyes with him, and rocks his hips, shallowly at first, not deep enough to hit the back of Jake's throat or to make him gag. But Bastian's never been known for showing restraint, especially not when a task needs accomplishing, so he quickly gets sloppy. He loves seeing how Jake's lips redden and quickly become as shiny with spit as the cock sliding between them. Jake's eagerness to be used, even when his eyes start watering, even when his cheeks get flushed because Bastian isn't careful not to go too deep or stay sheathed for too long, that might be Bastian's favorite type of abandon to witness. He's aware of Jake's own hips twitching, of the way Jake's cock jumps a little and drips some more every time his eyes stay closed longer than a blink and he'd give so much to be able to read Jake's mind in those moments, to know exactly how he thinks of them, how he constructs himself as a toy for Bastian's use, how his own physical needs come second because it's easier for him to take care of Bastian than it is to let Bastian take care of him.

Bastian eventually removes a hand from Jake's hair, relocates to his throat for no better reason but to feel it work to accommodate him, his Adam's apple bob up and down whenever Jake has the time and liberty to swallow. He doesn't choke him, not quite, or at least not with his hand – it's not exactly necessary anyways. It's not like Jake has much control over his breathing with the way Bastian's fucking his mouth. And the only thing that Bastian loves more than the pleasure he's getting from Jake like this is the fact that he can see on his face and in his eyes how much he's also getting out of Bastian's proceedings.

When Bastian feels as satisfied from Jake's mouth as he is dissatisfied from not being in the process of properly fucking him, he lets go of Jake's head, he pulls out in a swift motion that leaves Jake gasping for more and a thick trail of spit connecting Jake's tongue to Bastian's erect, bobbing cock. It's the opposite of careful and collected; Bastian is sloppy, Jake is disheveled, his eyelashes are spiked with wet and his hair is properly unkempt, he is a beautiful tableau of blood blooming into a blush under his skin, sweat pearling at the surface, lips flushed and swollen and shiny, arousal seeping through every pore of his being. He might love receiving this more than Bastian loves giving it to him, and that's an image in itself.

Bastian grabs a discarded pillow and shoves it under Jake's hips, the better to fuck him senselessly this way, the better the angle, the better the access to all of his boy's taut and shivering body.

"Look at me, handsome," Bastian says when he rubs the head of his cock around Jake's sensitive rim, collecting the lube he'd spread out earlier. "Do you want this? Will you let me fuck you, huh, will you be good and let me make myself feel good with your body, cielo? Will you?" Bastian asks, the slight tremble in his voice traitor to how enthralled he is with Jake, how lucky he feels to have him so wanton and desperate for him. Jake nods, but Bastian wants more. "I can't hear you, pretty thing," he says, carefully positioned just right to be able to push into Jake upon his answer.

"Please, Bastian, please, please, please," Jake begs, for the first time able to enunciate properly without the chain held tightly between his teeth. He's so pretty when he begs.

Bastian pushes in, a sure, steady movement that has them both moaning so wantonly. Jake's legs, out of instinct for it does not seem deliberate, come to cage Bastian between strong thighs, pulling him into Jake's body until Bastian can go no further. Bastian holds himself with a hand on Jake's sternum, and brings the free hand he's got to Jake's face, the better to smother him with it. The clamps are set tightly in Jake's chest, he knows they won't budge, so grabs the chain and pushes it back into Jake's mouth, he pushes fingers in with it to hear how prettily Jake can beg around him. He wants to hear Jake try to plead while he swivels his hips, fucking himself as best he can on Bastian, and it's so hot to watch Bastian doesn't know what to do with himself. He takes an ostentatious moment to look, only look and feel and witness, passively, how keen and earnest and eager Jake is, and it isn't clear who Jake is most trying to please, himself or Bastian.

The muffled sounds coming out of Jake, the movements of his tongue under Bastian's fingers, the feeling of the saliva coating his digits and Jake's lips and his chin, Jake's solid thighs around his waist. The insanely warm, inescapable, fucking aphrodisiac feeling of Jake clenching rhythmically and steadily around him, in time with the rotations of his hips. Bastian can't – won't, doesn't want to – rein in his own uninhibited moans and whispers and cries of pleasure.

He swiftly removes his hand from Jake's face, causing Jake, in his frazzled glory, to look at him, unfocused pleading gaze meeting Bastian's hard one. Bastian wipes his hand on Jake's skin. He pulls and twists at the clamps to witness Jake's breath hitching and his eyes fluttering, struggling to stay open. Jake loses the fight then, when Bastian lightly but purposefully lays light swats to his cock, watching it bob, watching the line of precum dripping from Jake's slit swaying with the momentum. He starts fucking into Jake, then, meeting him halfway and steadily swatting and slapping just enough to make Jake's eyes roll back into his head. Bastian wants this moment to last forever.

"Look at yourself, handsome, you're enjoying this so much, aren't you? You're so hot when you let me hurt you, does this feel good, Jacob?" Bastian pants in time with the swift and steady back and forth of his hips, in time with the clear and soft sounds of skin hitting skin every time his hand comes in contact with Jake's flushed cock.

Jake has managed to hold himself up a little, his disconnected cuffs affording him some freedom of movement. He's got his lip caught between his teeth, the enamel digging in so forcefully that his lip, usually so plump and so pink, is taut, turning white. His face his flushed, his neck showing veins where Bastian can track the force of his heartbeat, the tendons straining. He's looking down at his heaving chest, pearly and damp with sweat, his nipples hard and angry and dark and held tight, likely causing him welcomed pain, his stomach messy and wet with the precum that's been leaking out of him for so long, especially so in volume with Bastian relentlessly fucking straight into his prostate.

"Just look at yourself, you're being so good, so eager, you're so desperate, you're so turned on, you love this," Bastian breathes out hotly. "Stay with me, cielo, don't get carried away, not today," Bastian instructs. This is an important moment for him, for them, he wants them both as present as can be, as aware and focused as their distracted brains will allow.

He couldn't tell how long he's fucking Jake for, it feels simultaneously like he's just started but also that anything prior to this doesn't matter, his life might well have started with Jake, for all it is worth now. Seeing the beautiful picture before him, Jake debauched and still glorious, always glorious in his candor and eagerness to please, so vibrant with energy despite how exhausted this thriving must have him feel, his spit on Bastian's fingers and the glistening wet all over Jake's own stomach, the perfect, tight, wet warmth of his body surrounding Bastian's every nerve ending, all of it is pushing Bastian right to the brink. The cliff is right before him, he can feel its edge and its depth and the ridges connecting the top where he's standing to the deep seas where he will crash. And oh, won't that be the most wondrous of crashes, it will be marvelous and delightful and it might kill them both but how much of a detail is that if they get to take the fall together.

When Bastian cums, it's buried deep inside Jake and he stops thrusting just long enough to empty himself in him. He's stopped flicking at Jake's cock, he doesn't have enough control over his body to keep doing that when the waves of pleasure rippling through his body are shaking him to his core, but he's wrapped his fingers around Jake and he's holding on tightly. He knows, for having been in his position often enough, that Jake can feel every pulse, every twitch inside him. When Bastian can open his eyes and breathe again, he looks at Jake, this poor, beautiful thing, looking so on edge and so close but also, so content, so fulfilled and peaceful. He's not sure how Jake manages all that at once.

He pulls out, slowly, fights the urge of laying down next to Jake. There are so many things that Bastian could do next, there are so many paths and he's not sold on which one he'll follow. He could just lie there, tease Jake into oblivion, never touching him satisfactorily until Jake begs for mercy. He could talk him down from this high and not let him cum today, even though he's been so good for him as always, even though he would, by all accounts, absolutely deserve it. He could keep stimulating him while telling him he's not allowed to release, just to see how long Jake can rein in his own needs and put Bastian's wants first, and Bastian would ensure that what he's doing inevitably would lead Jake to an orgasm, and then he'd stay close and comfort him and care for him through how much that would affect Jake. Mindfucking his boy is always a fun time and, while intense for both of them, allows them to get ever closer, allows trust to build and build between them, if done right. Bastian knows how to navigate Jake's boundaries, the soft ones and the hard ones, knows how to push against them and expand them but never break them. He owes Jake that much.

He settles for sitting back on his haunches, still between Jake's legs. Now that he can think somewhat clearly again, he wants all the access he can have, and he's going to need both hands to carry his plan through.

He makes eye contact with Jake, holding his gaze while he removes the chain from Jake's mouth, then takes two fingers to Jake's stomach, to collect the small pool of fluids that has accumulated there. Bastian doesn't break his gaze when he wipes his digits off on Jake's lip. He likes to make his mouth glisten in the low light. Jake doesn't need to be told to lick himself clean, so Bastian repeats until the mess on Jake's stomach is somewhat manageable. His boy gets so wet.

Once relatively cleaned up, Bastian takes his hand to Jake's rim, teases the familiarly sensitive muscle. He's gentle when he gathers some lube around Jake's cleft, he's careful not to be rough when he penetrates him. He goes straight to Jake's prostate, so slow, so careful, but he knows just how to massage it to get Jake's brows furrowed and his lungs filling and emptying erratically.

"There's the face," Bastian comments, when Jake's eyes lose their focus, their grip on reality. Bastian rubs slow but steady circles inside Jake. "Is this the kind of sensations you were looking for, handsome? You like when I fuck you but you like it better when my hands are being mean to you, don't you," he continues, voice low and seductive while Jake nods.

Bastian is in no rush, not anymore. He's got all the time in the world to unravel Jake. So take his time he does.

"What do you love about this, handsome?" Bastian asks, not wanting to ask a more specific question because he wants Jake unfiltered. "Tell me, pretty thing," he adds when his question only gets him as far as Jake's throat working, Adam's apple bobbing but no sounds being produced.

"You– your hands, Bastian," he says, a shiver running up his spine. "You feel so good," he adds, unable to stay still with Bastian inside him like this. He throws his head to the side, tries to hide his face. "You always know, exactly, what to do, and how, and you," he adds, breath hitching and voice unsteady. "You looked so good, Bastian, earlier when you were inside me," and Bastian won't bring up the fact that he technically still is, he knows what Jake means, "and you hurt me, and you held me, and the pain," and Jake is visibly affected by the fact that he's being made to focus on his own wants and needs. "And now I – Bastian, will I, will you please let me cum?" Jake asks, so frazzled, visibly working so hard not to let himself be consumed with an orgasm he doesn't know if he's earned even though Bastian is invariably bringing him there.

"Why should I?"

Bastian earns a sob.

"Please, please, Bastian, I'm so close, I need to, I – I was good, I made you feel good, I tried to make you feel good, please, make me cum or, or, hurt me," and Jake is shaking by the end of his plea, with the force of his need and because Bastian isn't giving him a chance to breathe at all, not with how oversensitive his prostate must be by now.

Bastian is driving relentlessly into him, milking him, stroking the sweet spot he knows so well, winding Jake higher and higher. His right hand, still free, still resting on his thigh, goes to take Jake's balls hostage, he pulls them just a bit, not enough to really hurt but enough that Jake will feel the tightness and enough that it'll make coming just that much harder.

"Go on, then, my pretty boy," he says while he pulls, while he fingers Jake with clear intent.

Jake's back strains off the bed with the effort he must be making to finally shift from caging his need in to being able to release all the tension he's harboring, and with the hurdle that Bastian puts in place for him by preventing his testicles to tighten and pull up how they would need. Bastian lets go when, out of obvious despair, Jake hits the mattress beneath him, because he's so on edge but unable to grasp the orgasm that is otherwise so within reach. When Bastian releases his death grip, Jake's body seizes up, his moan of ecstasy gets caught in his throat. The second Jake starts coming, Bastian pulls his fingers out, stops touching his cock altogether, and reaches up to rip the clamps off of Jake's oversensitive nipples, just to see how his brain will short out, how he won't know how to process what should have been the climax of his pleasure but is now almost agonizing from the lack of stimulation through it and the excruciating flash of pain Bastian just gave him by ripping the clamps off him.

The quiet, voiceless scream that gets caught in Jake's throat before it can be heard, while he so obviously fails to process how something that should have been so pleasurable became so mindlessly painful, the look on his face when his brain short-circuits, those are images that will fill Bastian's dreams, the daydreams and the slumber ones, for a long time to come.